"HOLD, ASSASSIN!"

Jordan gestured mystically, and blue-white flames flared up about his hands. The mercenary took one look and started backing quickly away. Jordan adopted his most impressive High Warlock stance. The trick was to keep the audience looking at you rather than at your hands. He ran his hands through a quick series of mystical gestures, using the movements to hide his palming of another flare pellet from his sleeve, and threw the pellet at the mercenary. It cracked open as it hit the man's chest, and the liquid in the pellet burst into flames. The fire took a savage hold upon the mercenary's clothes. He screamed shrilly and dropped his sword, and Jordan stepped forward and ran the man through.

Roderick looked at the dead man and then at Jordan. "Don't believe in fighting fair, do you?" he asked.

"I believe in winning," said Jordan.

BLOOD AND HONOR

by

Simon R. Green

A ROC BOOK

ROC
Published by the Penguin Group
Penguin Books USA Inc., 375 Hudson Street,
New York, New York 10014, U.S.A.
Penguin Books Ltd, 27 Wrights Lane,
London W8 5TZ, England
Penguin Books Australia Ltd, Ringwood,
Victoria, Australia
Penguin Books Canada Ltd, 10 Alcorn Avenue,
Toronto, Ontario, Canada M4V 3B2
Penguin Books (N.Z.) Ltd, 182–190 Wairau Road,
Auckland 10, New Zealand

Penguin Books Ltd, Registered Offices:
Harmondsworth, Middlesex, England

First published by Onyx, an imprint of New American Library,
a division of Penguin Books USA Inc.

First Printing, May, 1993
10 9 8 7 6 5 4 3 2 1

 REGISTERED TRADEMARK—MARCA REGISTRADA

PRINTED IN THE UNITED STATES OF AMERICA

CHAPTER 1

Hidden Faces

The demon appeared from nowhere in a puff of evil-smelling smoke. The warped and twisted trees of the Darkwood loomed protectively over the crouching figure. The High Warlock stood tall and proud before the demon, his jet black cloak swirling ominously about him in the evening breeze. The stage lights gleamed brightly from the cloak's silver embroidery of stars and moons and sigils. The warlock gestured imperiously, and a sword suddenly appeared in his right hand. Gaudily colored lights shrieked and flashed around the crouching demon, and the warlock stepped back a pace. The sword was no longer in his hand. He drew himself up to his full, imposing height, and raised his arms in the stance of summoning. He chanted a spell in a deep, ringing voice. The audience watched breathlessly, and then gasped in awe as blue-white flames flared around the warlock's upraised hands. The flames danced and crackled noisily on the gusting wind, but the warlock's hands remained unburned. His voice rose to a commanding roar, and then the demon burst into flames as the warlock gestured sharply with a flame-wrapped hand. The twisted creature burned fiercely, and the audience cheered. The High Warlock turned and smiled coldly at them, and they fell silent before his unwavering gaze.

"And thus did the demons of the Darkwood fall before me, in the darkest hour of the Forest Kingdom. In that faraway land, I stood shoulder to shoulder with the noble King John, and his heroic sons Harald and Rupert, and the forces of darkness could not stand against us." The High Warlock lowered his hands to his sides, and the blue-white flames sputtered and went out. "The long night ended, the demon hordes were thrown down and destroyed, and the Forest Kingdom was saved. That was the way it had to be, for is it not written that evil cannot prevail against good, and that the darkness shall always give way to the light?"

He clapped his hands sharply, and the stage lights flared brilliantly for a moment, pushing back the shadows of the falling evening. The lights dimmed again, and the warlock folded his arms across his chest. His black cloak folded about him like great membranous wings. His gaunt face was harsh and forbidding, and his cold gray eyes stared unwaveringly out over the hushed audience. "And that, my friends, is the true history of the great and wondrous High Warlock, and his part in the destruction of the Darkwood. A tale of adventure and intrigue, honor and treachery, and the inevitable triumph of good over evil. My honored friends . . . the performance is at an end."

He bowed once, and then gestured imperiously with his left hand. Smoke billowed up around him from nowhere, and then drifted away to reveal the actor standing alone in the middle of the crude wooden stage, dressed once again in his simple everyday clothes. He stepped forward and bowed deeply, and the audience beat their hands together until they ached. The Great Jordan smiled and bowed graciously, but all too quickly his audience began to drift away, and only a few of them paused to drop a coin in his offerings bowl.

Jordan waited until the last of his audience had left, and then he sat down on the edge of his stage and began wiping the makeup off his face with a piece of dirty rag. Without the carefully placed shadings and highlights, his face looked younger and softer, and nowhere near as forbidding. His shoulders slumped wearily as the tiredness of the day caught up with him, and the air of mystery and command that had surrounded him on stage vanished like the illusion it was. The sword he'd used in his act poked him unmer-

cifully in the ribs, and he pulled it out of the concealed
sheath under his clothing. Seen up close, it was battered and nicked and not at all impressive. It was just
a sword that had seen too much service in its time.
Jordan yawned and stretched, and then shivered suddenly. Nights were falling earlier as the summer gave
way to autumn, and the rising wind had a cold edge.
He glanced across at the smoldering demon, but the
roughly carved prop had pretty much burned itself
out. He'd have to do some more work on the demon.
It still looked all right from a distance, but the spring
that threw it out from behind the concealing piece of
scenery must be getting rusty. This was the third time
in a week that its timing had been off. Any later and
the damned fireworks would have gone off first. Jordan sighed. The spring wasn't the only thing whose
timing was off. He was getting too old for one-night
stands in backwater towns. At twenty-seven he was
hardly an old man, but he just didn't have the stamina
anymore to put up with an endless round of poor
food, hard travel, and never enough sleep.

He got to his feet, strapped the sword to his side,
and walked unhurriedly over to the offerings bowl.
For a moment he allowed himself to hope, but when
he looked it was even worse than he'd expected. The
dozen or so small copper coins barely covered the
bottom of the bowl. Jordan emptied the coins into his
purse, and glumly hefted the trifling weight in his
hand. Bannerwick was only a small mill town deep in
the desolate North country, but he'd still looked for
better takings than this. If things didn't improve soon,
he'd have to go back to cardsharping and picking
pockets to make ends meet. He hadn't seen takings
this bad since he first started out on the stage as a
juvenile. Maybe he was losing his touch. Or maybe
his material was getting old; the Demon War had
ended seven years ago. Jordan shook his head, and
tied his purse securely onto his belt. It wasn't him,
and it wasn't his act; if truth be told, it was simply
that times were hard in the kingdom of Redhart.

Money was scarce, and strolling players had become a luxury beyond the purses of most.

It wasn't just Redhart, of course. Jordan had spent most of his professional life in Hillsdown. He'd known good times there. Not once had he ever thought he might one day be forced to leave the country of his birth by poor takings. He'd appeared three times before the duke himself, and known the company of great men and their ladies. They'd been the first to name him the Great Jordan. He'd traveled widely, even to the Court of the Forest Kingdom itself, though that was some time before the Demon War. He hadn't been back since. The demons had been defeated, but not nearly as simply and easily as he made it sound in his performance as the High Warlock. The war had devastated the forest, and much of the countries that bordered it. The land was slowly recovering, but there were those who said it would take a generation and more before trade fully recovered. In the meantime, Hillsdown and Redhart and the Forest Kingdom struggled to keep their heads above water, and had little time or money to spare for the great players who had once touched the hearts of all who'd heard them.

Jordan frowned as he tried to work out if he had enough money to buy provisions and to get drunk, and if not, which of the two was the most important. The mental arithmetic took a depressingly short time, and he scowled unhappily. It would have to be provisions. Bannerwick stood alone and isolated in the middle of Redhart's moorland, and it was a good two or three days' traveling to the next town. He could always pick up a few grouse along the way, but the local margrave's men took a very dim view of poaching. When all was said and done, it might prove rather tricky trying to do his act with only the one hand . . . No, it would have to be the provisions. Jordan looked about him at the squat little houses clustered around the narrow main street of Bannerwick. How had he come to this?

The stone and timber houses huddled side by side as much for comfort as support. The rough and dirty walls were all much the same to look at, like so many defeated faces. Smoke curled wearily from the narrow chimney pots, and the bitter wind tugged at the tiled roofs as it came gusting in off the moors. The last light of evening was already fading away, and the main street was deserted. Country people awoke with the first light, worked while it lasted, and went to their beds when darkness fell. It was only Jordan's show that had kept them up this late. He supposed he should be flattered. They hadn't been a bad audience, all told. They'd laughed and cheered in the right places, and even gasped in awe as his conjuring produced the illusion of magic powers. Jordan smiled slightly. He'd always believed in giving value for money. Of course, there had been a time, and not that long ago, when he'd been able to include real sorcery in his act, but that time was past. Hiring sorcerers was always expensive, and of the few spells that remained to him, most were slowly wearing out.

Still, there was no denying he'd been in excellent form tonight. The times might be hard, but he was still the Great Jordan, and the High Warlock was one of his best roles. He'd always prided himself on his choice of roles. He'd played all the best parts in his time: everyone from the fabled King Eduard, who loved the deadly Night Witch, to the heroic starlight Duke of Hillsdown, to the sad and tragic sheep minder, Old Molly Metcalf. The Great Jordan was nothing if not versatile. He'd played before lords and ladies, townspeople and villagers, and once even for a scar-faced man who claimed to be a prince in exile. Though he never actually said where he'd been exiled from. Jordan smiled, remembering. In those days, his bowl had known the heavy clunk of gold and silver and even precious jewels. His ears had rung to roars of joy and admiration from packed theaters, and tearful pleas for just one more encore. But those days were over. The times had changed, and other names had risen to prominence as his had faded, and now he had to take his offerings where he could find them.

The Great Jordan, showing his act to a few gawking

peasants for a handful of coppers. There was no justice in the world. Or at least, none a man could learn to live with.

He got slowly to his feet and shook his head. It was getting too cold to sit around brooding. He threw a blanket over the smoldering demon prop to douse the last of the flames, and then set about transferring his props and scenery into the back of his small caravan. He gathered up his stage lights and counted them carefully twice, just to make sure none of them had disappeared with some unprincipled member of his audience. He stacked the lanterns and lamps in their proper places, and then went back for his stage. It was supposed to break easily into sections, but Jordan had to struggle with each square until he was red in the face and short of breath. He scowled as he slid the last section onto the floor of his caravan. He was going to have to do more work on the stage before it would come apart properly, and he hated working with wood. No matter how careful he was, he always ended up with splinters in his fingers. His scowl deepened as he laced up the caravan's back flaps. He shouldn't have to do scut work like this. He was an actor, not a carpenter.

Jordan smiled sourly. That was his past talking. Stars might not have to do scut work, but actors did. If they wanted to eat regularly. And if nothing else, exercise did help to build a healthy appetite. He set off down the main street, looking for a tavern. Late as it was by country standards, the town inn would still be open. Such inns always were. *I don't care if the specialty of the house is broiled demon in a toadstool sauce, I'm still going to eat it and ask for seconds,* he thought determinedly. Halfway down the narrow street, his nose detected the smell of hot cooking, and he followed it eagerly to a squat grimy building that looked no different from any of the others, save for a roughly painted sign hanging over the door: *The Seven Stars.* Jordan tried the door. It was locked. He banged impatiently on the stained wood with his fist. After a long moment he heard footsteps approaching, and eventually a panel slid open in the door. A dark-bearded face studied Jordan suspiciously.

"Ah, good evening, innkeeper," said Jordan pleasantly. "I find myself in need of a room and refreshment for the night, and I hope to satisfy that need at your splendid establishment. I fear my funds are somewhat depleted at the moment, but no doubt I can provide payment by entertaining your good customers with my songs and stories. How say you?"

The bearded face glowered at him, and then sniffed loudly. "We don't take theatricals."

Jordan dropped his aristocratic actor-manager voice, and tried his all-friends-together-in-adversity voice. "Listen, innkeep, I know I'm a bit short of the ready at the moment, but surely we can come to some sort of arrangement? It's going to be bitter cold tonight, friend."

The innkeeper sniffed again. "We don't take theatricals. Hop it." And the portal in the door slammed shut.

Jordan lost his temper completely. He kicked the door and hammered on it with his fist. "Open this door, you son of a bitch, or I'll use my magic to make you even uglier than you already are! I'll give you fleas, and boils, and warts, and piles! I'll give you warts on your piles! I'll shrink your manhood to an acorn, and turn your nose inside out! Now open this bloody door!"

He heard a window's shutters open above him, and looked up. He just had time to throw himself to one side, and the slops from the emptied chamber pot just missed him. The shutters slammed together, and the evening grew quiet again. Jordan slowly picked himself up off the filthy street, and brushed the worst of the mud from his clothes. Ungrateful peasants. Didn't know a class actor when they saw one. He started back down the street toward his caravan. It looked like he'd be sleeping with his props again, and that damned demon was starting to smell something fierce.

As he passed a narrow opening between two houses, Jordan thought he heard someone moving surrepti-

tiously, deep in the gloom of the alley. He slowed to
a halt just past the opening, and scratched thoughtfully at his ribs, letting his hand drift casually down
to the sword at his side. Surely it was obvious to anyone with half the brains they were born with that this
particular actor had nothing worth the effort of taking
it, but it was best to be wary. A starving man would
murder for a crust of bread. Jordan's hand idly caressed the pommel of his sword, and he eased his
weight onto his left foot so he could get at the throwing knife hidden in that boot if he had to. And if all
else failed, there were always the flare pellets he kept
concealed in his sleeves. They might not be quite as
effective as they appeared onstage, but they were dra-
matic enough to give most footpads pause. He swallowed dryly, and wished his hands would stop shaking.
He was never any good in a crisis, particularly if there
was a chance of violence. He let his gaze sweep casually over the dark alleyway, and then stiffened as his
hearing brought him the rasp of boots on packed
earth, and something that might have been the quiet
grating of steel sliding from a scabbard. Jordan whipped
his sword from its sheath, and backed away. Something stirred in the darkness.

"Easy, my dear sir," said a calm, cultured voice.
"We mean you no harm. We only want to talk to
you."

Jordan thought seriously about making a run for it.
Whenever anyone started talking that politely, either
they were intent on telling him something he didn't
really want to know, or they wanted to sell him something. On the other hand, from the sound of it there
had to be more than just the one man hidden in the
alley darkness, and he wasn't that fast a runner at the
best of times. Maybe he could bluff them . . . He held
his head erect, took on the warrior's stance he used
when playing the ancient hero Sir Bors of Lyons-
march, and glared into the gloom of the alley.

"Honest men do their talking in the light," he said
harshly. "Not skulking in back alleys. Besides, I'm
rather particular about who I talk to."

"I think you'll talk with us, Jordan," said the polite voice. "We're here to offer you an acting role—a role beyond your wildest dreams and ambitions."

Jordan was still trying to come up with an answer to that when the three men stepped out of the alley mouth and into the fading light. Jordan backed away a step, but calmed down a little when they made no move to pursue him. He quickly resumed his warrior's stance, hoping they hadn't noticed the lapse, and looked the three men over carefully from behind the haughtiest expression he could manage. The man in the middle was clearly a noble of some kind, for all his rough peasant's cloak and hood. His skin was pale and unweathered, and his hands were slender and delicate. Presumably this was the owner of the cultured voice. Jordan nodded to him warily, and the man bowed formally in return. He raised one hand and pushed back the hood of his cloak, revealing a hawk-like, unyielding face dominated by steady dark eyes and a grim, humorless smile. His black hair was brushed flat and heavily pomaded, giving his pale skin a dull, unhealthy look. He was tall, at least six foot two, probably in his early forties, and looked to be fashionably slim under his cloak. He wore a sword at his side, and Jordan had no doubt at all that this man would know how to use it. Even standing still and at rest, there was an air of barely contained menace about him that was unmistakable.

"Well?" growled Jordan roughly, trying to gain the advantage before his knees started knocking. "Are we going to stand here staring at each other all night, or are you going to introduce yourself?"

"I beg your pardon, Jordan," said the noble smoothly. "I am Count Roderik Crichton, adviser to King Malcolm of Redhart. These are my associates: the trader Robert Argent, and Sir Gawaine of Tower Rouge."

Jordan nodded to them all impartially, and then sheathed his sword as an act of bravado. It seemed increasingly important to him that they shouldn't think they had him at a disadvantage. According to the count's graceful gestures, the man to his left was Robert Argent. He was short and sturdy, and wore a merchant's clothes. His stomach bulged out on either side of a wide leather belt. His peasant's cloak hung around him in drooping folds, as though it had been meant for a much taller man. His face was broad and ruddy, with the broken-veined cheeks of the heavy drinker. His eyes were a pale blue, and strangely dull and lifeless. His hair was straw yellow, cropped close to the skull. He looked to be in his late thirties, but the empty eyes made him seem much older. He wore a sword on his hip, but from the shiny newness of the scabbard, Jordan doubted the sword had seen much use. His eyes lingered on the man for a moment, though he wasn't sure why. There was just something about Argent, something . . . cold.

Sir Gawaine stood to Count Roderik's right, leaning casually against the wall. He was chewing on a cold leg of chicken, and not being too careful about where the grease went. Jordan's stomach rumbled loudly, and he gave the knight his best brooding scowl to compensate. Gawaine looked at him briefly, and then gave his full attention back to the chicken leg. Sir Gawaine of Tower Rouge . . . Jordan had a feeling he knew the name from somewhere, but he couldn't place it. Maybe he was a minor hero from the Demon War . . . He was tall and muscular, and though he had to be in his late fifties, his chest and shoulders were still impressively broad. Chain mail glinted under the peasant cloak, and Jordan caught a glimpse of a heavy-bladed hand ax at the man's side. His hair was iron gray and cut in a style that hadn't been fashionable for at least ten years. His face was lined and weathered, and when he looked at Jordan his eyes were dark and cynical. His scarred hands looked disturbingly powerful, and for all his apparent casualness he was no more at ease than Jordan. Everything about Gawaine shouted to the observant eye that this knight was a trained warrior, and experienced in his craft. Jordan decided immediately that if these three men turned out to be villains after all, he'd better go for

Sir Gawaine first. And he'd better be bloody quick, because he wouldn't get a second chance.

"You mentioned an acting role," said Jordan to Count Roderik.

"The greatest role you'll ever play," said Roderik.

"What's the money like?" asked Jordan.

"Ten thousand ducats," said Robert Argent. His voice was flat and unemotional, and his cold gaze fixed unwaveringly on the actor.

Jordan kept his face calm with an effort. Ten thousand ducats was more than he'd ever earned in a year, even at the peak of his career. And that was a long way behind him. Ten thousand ducats . . . there had to be a catch.

"Assuming, for the sake of argument, that I'm interested in this job," he said carefully, "what kind of role would I be playing?"

"Nothing too difficult," said Roderik. "A prince— the middle of three sons. There's a great deal of background information you'll have to learn by heart, but an actor of your reputation shouldn't have any trouble with that. After all, you are the Great Jordan." He paused, and frowned slightly. "Is Jordan your real name, or would you prefer I used another, offstage?"

The actor shrugged. "Call me Jordan. It's a good name, and I earned it."

"I was most impressed with your performance this evening," said Roderik. "Did you write the material yourself?"

"Of course," said Jordan. "A strolling player has to be able to adapt his story to suit the level of his audience. Sometimes they want wit and eloquence, sometimes they want conjuring and fireworks. It varies. Did you like my High Warlock? I created the character after extensive research, and I flatter myself I caught the essence of the man."

"Nothing like him," said Sir Gawaine. His voice was harsh, with bitter undertones. He looked at the ragged chicken leg in his hand, and threw it casually over his shoulder. Jordan's stomach rumbled again, and he glared angrily at the knight.

"Is that so, Sir Gawaine? Perhaps you'd care to tell me what he was really like?"

"He chased women and drank too much," said Gawaine.

"He was a great sorcerer!" said Jordan hotly. "Everybody said so! He saved the Forest Kingdom from the demon prince! All right, there were a few rumors about him, but there are always rumors. And besides . . . it makes for a better show my way."

Sir Gawaine shrugged, and looked away.

"If we could return to the subject at hand," said Roderik icily, glancing angrily at the knight. "You haven't yet said if you'll accept the role, sir actor."

"I'll take it," said Jordan. "I've nothing better to do, for the moment." For ten thousand ducats he'd have played the back end of a mummer's horse, complete with sound effects, but he wasn't going to tell them that. Maybe he could hit them for an advance . . . He looked at Count Roderik. "Well, my lord, shall we get down to business? What exactly is this role, and when do I start?"

"You start now," said Argent. "We want you to return with us to Castle Midnight, and impersonate Prince Viktor of Redhart."

Jordan's heart sank, and for a moment he wasn't sure whether to scream or faint. "You have got to be joking! Forget it! I'm not getting involved in any conspiracy to commit treason. I once saw a man hanged, drawn, and quartered. It took him two hours to die, and he only stopped screaming when his voice gave out."

"There's no question of anything treasonable," said Roderik soothingly. "Prince Viktor knows all about this substitution, and has agreed to it."

Jordan looked suspiciously at the three men before him. They all looked very serious. Sir Gawaine had even pushed himself away from the wall to stand upright. Jordan noticed uneasily that the knight's right hand was now out of sight under his cloak, resting just where the hand ax had been. Jordan turned his attention back to Count Roderik, mainly because it was less disturbing looking at him than it was at Sir Gawaine. He gave the count his best intimidating scowl, and tucked his thumbs into his sword belt to stop his hands shaking. "If the prince knows about this, then what . . . oh, I get it. You want me to act as a decoy—a double to draw out an assassin! The deal is off. I'm an actor, not an archery target."

"My dear fellow," said Count Roderik, his voice practically dripping sincerity, "I assure you we wouldn't waste someone of your undoubted talents on a simple decoy's job. Allow me to explain the situation. Prince Viktor is required by law and tradition to undergo a series of rituals shortly, at Castle Midnight. Unfortunately, he is indisposed at present with a rather troublesome illness, and is unable to perform the rituals. But if he doesn't appear, he'll lose his inheritance. So, we need someone who can act enough like the prince to take his place in public and perform the rituals. It's as simple as that."

"Ah," said Jordan. "I see." He didn't believe for one moment that Roderik was telling him the whole truth, but for the time being, he might as well act as though he did. After all, if he'd learned anything as an actor, it was that the aristocracy hadn't a clue as to the real value of money. You could charge them extortionate amounts for performances, not to mention expenses, and they didn't even blink. If he played his cards right and watched his back, ten thousand ducats could be just the beginning . . .

"Assuming I was interested in this job," he said carefully, "there are some obvious difficulties. What about appearance, for example? How similar are the prince and I in looks? There's a limit to what I can do with makeup."

"That won't be a problem," said Roderik. "I have a small talent for sorcery. A simple glamour spell, and you'll become an exact double of the prince. Much more important is your being able to convince Viktor's friends and family that you are who you seem. For that, we need an actor of your considerable talent. Our agents have been traveling throughout the land, searching for someone suitable, and you can imagine how delighted we were when word came back to us that you might be available. To be honest, we hadn't even heard you were in Redhart . . ."

Jordan shrugged airily. "Every career has its ups and downs. If you'd have asked me this at the same time last year, I'd have had to turn you down. The pressure of work was just too great. But, luckily for you, at the moment I'm at liberty to give you my full attention."

"This time last year," said Robert Argent, "you were in a debtors' prison in Hillsdown. You haven't appeared in a major theater in almost three years. You're just another strolling player, Jordan, and if you don't want this job, we can find a dozen just like you to take your place."

Jordan gave him a hard look. "There is no one like me," he said flatly. "I'm the Great Jordan. And if I hear one more word out of you that I don't like, Argent, I'll double my fee." He deliberately turned his back on Argent, and looked thoughtfully at Count Roderik. "This glamour spell that's going to make me look like Viktor; can it be removed easily when the job's finished?"

"Of course," said Roderik. "But now, my dear fellow, we are in something of a hurry. It will take us at least a week's hard traveling to reach Castle Midnight, and the rituals are due to begin shortly after that. I'm afraid we must insist on knowing your answer now."

Ten thousand ducats . . . maybe more . . . a chance to start over again . . . a role that could be a real challenge . . . There's got to be a catch, but I don't give a damn.

"I'm your man," said Jordan. "We can leave as soon as I've brought fresh provisions."

"We already have everything you'll need," said Argent. "Roderik, start the spell. We've wasted enough time in this filthy hole."

"Wait just a minute," said Jordan quickly. "You want to cast the glamour spell right here and now? Where everyone can see us?"

"No one will see us in this light," said Roderik. "The spell is quick and quite painless, I assure you. There's nothing at all to worry about."

Jordan looked suspiciously at Roderik. *There's nothing to worry about* was the kind of thing the traveling dentist said as he knelt on your chest and poked his pliers into your mouth. But he couldn't argue. He'd agreed to take on the role, and the spell was a necessary part of it. He'd just thought he'd get a bit more warning . . .

Roderik took Jordan's silence for assent, and raised his left hand. He frowned, and muttered something under his breath. Jordan strained his ears to try and catch the quiet words, but the few he caught were in a language he didn't recognize. They sounded harsh and grating and somehow . . . disturbing, and Jordan suddenly wondered if perhaps he'd made a mistake after all. Count Roderik fell silent, and made a sharp, twisting motion with his left hand. Jordan gasped, startled, as his skin suddenly began to itch and creep. His face twitched convulsively. He started to lift his hands to his face, and found he couldn't. His whole body had locked solidly in place. He couldn't even blink his eyes. He struggled furiously, to no avail, and then his anger gave way to panic as the first changes began. His bones creaked and groaned. His flesh shuddered, rising and falling like a series of ripples on the surface of a pond. He tried to move or run or scream, and couldn't. His panic rose another notch when he found his breathing was becoming increasingly shallow. Sweat poured off him. His vertebrae popped one after the other as his back stretched, giving him an extra two inches in height. His fingers tingled painfully as his hands grew long and slender. New cords of muscle crawled along his chest and arms and back. His legs grew thick and sturdy. His face trembled as his features lost definition and then grew firm again in a new shape. And as suddenly as it had begun, the paralysis was gone, and his flesh grew still again.

Jordan swayed on his feet, and Sir Gawaine was

quickly there at his side. Jordan clung to the knight's
arm as his head slowly cleared, and his harsh breathing gradually returned to normal. He finally straightened up, and let go of Gawaine's arm. He gave
Gawaine a quick, grateful nod, and then stared in
something like horror at his hands. He lifted them up
before his face and looked at them, turning them back
and forth before him. They weren't his hands. The
length, shape, and shade were wrong. But the fingers
flexed obediently at his command, and he could feel
the cool of the evening moving over them. He lowered
his hands and looked down at his body. His clothes
no longer fit him. He was taller now, and his arms
and legs were longer. His shirt was tightly stretched
across his new chest and shoulders, and his belt hung
loosely about his flatter stomach. Jordan felt a brief
surge of vertigo as his mind refused to accept the new
body it found itself in, and then the feeling died away
as he brought it under control. Jordan was used to
being different people at different times. He was an
actor. He looked at Count Roderik, who bowed
formally.

"Your Highness. Would you like to see a mirror?"

Jordan nodded dumbly. Argent produced a small
hand mirror from a pocket in his cloak, and handed
it to Jordan.

The face in the glass was traditionally handsome, in
a dark, saturnine way. The jet black hair was thick
and wavy, and showed off the firm bony planes of the
face. The eyes were a surprisingly mild brown, but the
mouth was flat and uncompromising. Someone had
broken the nose a long time ago, and it hadn't been
set quite right. The owner of the face looked to be in
his midtwenties, but there was something about the
eyes and mouth that made him look older.

Yes . . . thought Jordan finally. *I can do something
with this face. This . . . Prince Viktor.*

He handed the mirror back to Argent, who replaced
it carefully in his pocket. Jordan scowled at Count
Roderik, and let his new right hand drop to the sword
at his side.

"When you said a glamour spell, Roderik, I thought you meant some kind of illusion." The new voice sounded a little deeper than he was used to, but not enough to throw him.

Roderik smiled at Jordan, and shook his head. "Illusions are too easily seen through—especially at Castle Midnight. This spell is fixed, until such time as it is specifically reversed. Physically, you are now an exact duplicate of Prince Viktor of Redhart."

Jordan looked at Argent and Sir Gawaine. "Well, what do you think? Will I pass?"

Argent nodded stiffly. "No one will be able to tell the difference. You even sound like him."

"The voice is right," said Sir Gawaine, "but you'll have to learn Viktor's way of speaking. The prince has been away from court for almost four years, and we can use that to explain away some differences in behavior, but you'll have to study his background every chance you get. You screw up on this, and we're all dead."

Jordan looked quickly at Roderik. "I thought you said we had Prince Viktor's permission for this little masquerade?"

"We do," said Roderik. He shot an angry glance at Gawaine. The knight ignored him. Roderik looked seriously at Jordan, and the actor tensed up inside. He knew that look. It was that particular mixture of sincerity and hesitation that meant he was about to be told something necessary but unpleasant.

"The situation at Castle Midnight is rather complicated at present," said Roderik. "King Malcolm died four weeks ago, some say by poison. His daughter, the Lady Gabrielle, found him dead in his chambers. It's not clear yet which of his three sons will succeed him, so it's vital that no one finds out that Viktor is ill, and . . . vulnerable. Once he's well again, he'll take over the necessary rituals and public appearances, but until then you'll take his place. It's really quite straightforward. However, should you be exposed as an impostor at any time, Viktor's brothers will undoubtedly have you killed. Princes tend to be very sensitive about the use of doubles."

"I can imagine," said Jordan. "Look, are you sure you can get me away safely afterward?"

"We'll take care of everything," said Roderik reassuringly. "You don't have to worry about anything but your performance."

Jordan nodded slowly. "So, King Malcolm is dead. All those campaigns he led, all those battles he fought in, and he finally dies in his own castle, poisoned. A dirty way to die. How long before the news gets out?"

"So far, the Regent's been able to keep a lid on things," said Roderik. "No one outside the castle knows anything yet. It has to be that way. If the news gets out before the succession is decided, there'll be panic in the land. There might even be civil war, and none of us wants that."

"If Malcolm was poisoned," said Jordan slowly, "who did it?"

"There are several suspects," said Argent. "Not least Viktor's two brothers, Lewis and Dominic. But there's no proof against anyone, so far."

"I doubt there'll ever be any real proof," said Gawaine. "It was a very professional job. The autopsy couldn't find a trace of poison."

Jordan frowned. He was getting too much information at once to be able to make sense of it. He decided to concentrate on the only details that mattered: those directly affecting the prince he had to play. He sighed silently. He hated politics, and Court politics in particular. Intrigues made his head hurt. He supposed he just didn't think deviously enough. He thought hard about what he'd been told so far, and a question occurred to him.

"Gawaine, you said Prince Viktor had been away from Court for four years. Where's he been all that time?"

"The king sent him into internal exile," said Roderik, before Gawaine could answer. "A minor border city, called Kahalimar. Like his brothers, Viktor was never known for his self-control, and eventually he

went a little too far. It was thought a few years in the
back lands might help to cool his blood."

"I see," said Jordan. "So I'm playing a villain, am
I?"

"Viktor's not that bad," said Gawaine quickly.
"He's headstrong, and too easily led for his own good,
but at heart he's a true prince. I've sworn to defend
him with my life."

Jordan made a mental note to talk to Roderik and
Gawaine separately; their views on Viktor seemed to
differ quite a bit, and that might be important. A new
thought struck him, and he gave Roderik a hard look.

"You still haven't said why you chose me for this
job. All right, I'm an excellent actor, one of the best,
but there are others almost as good as me. And most
of them are much better known these days than I am."

"That was part of the problem," said Roderik. "If
one of your more illustrious colleagues were to suddenly disappear, it would be bound to be noticed.
Questions would be asked. However, in your case . . .
well—you understand, I'm sure. And there was one
other reason why we particularly wanted you."

"Oh yes?" said Jordan. "And what might that be?"

"You're a conjurer, as well as an actor."

Jordan looked at him blankly for a moment, and
then nodded slowly. "Of course, the royal Blood . . ."

The kings of Redhart were magic users, and had
been for generations. Every member of the royal line
inherited the ability to manipulate one of the four
elements: earth, air, fire, and water. The spreading
Bloodlines were jealously guarded and nurtured down
the centuries, as it was discovered that the purer the
Blood, the more powerful would be the resulting
magic. For a while, the royal line became dangerously
interbred, producing monsters and mules more often
than normal children. These days there were strict
laws and traditions to protect the magic-carrying
Bloodlines, and the elemental powers only remained
truly powerful in the carefully monitored royal line.

"Prince Viktor has the fire magic," said Roderik.
"Whoever was to take his place had to be able to

counterfeit this magic convincingly. You're a conjurer, Jordan; a few flames on demand shouldn't prove too difficult for you."

Jordan frowned unhappily. "They'll see through it. They're bound to. My tricks are good, but they're still only tricks and illusions."

Roderik smiled, and shook his head reassuringly. "No one will suspect anything. They'll see only what they expect to see."

Jordan looked at him for a moment, and then shrugged. "You've obviously put a lot of thought into this, so I suppose you must know what you're doing."

"Then may I suggest, Your Highness, that we get a bloody move on," said Sir Gawaine. "We're pressed for time."

Jordan nodded, and went to get his horse. Roderik sent Sir Gawaine with him, just to keep him company. They walked in silence. Jordan didn't know what to say to the knight, and Gawaine seemed content to leave it that way. They walked quickly through the darkening evening, their steps echoing dully back from the stone walls on either side of them. The houses were silent, and no lights showed past the closed shutters, but Jordan had no doubt he and Gawaine were still being watched. People in small towns didn't miss much, if they could help it. Jordan sneaked a few sidelong glances at Gawaine. He wasn't sure yet what to make of the knight. The man was obviously competent, not to mention dangerous, but there was a bitter, brooding quality to Sir Gawaine that intrigued Jordan. If he was going to get answers from anybody in the conspiracy about what was really going on, Gawaine looked to be the best bet. It might pay to cultivate the knight . . .

Jordan found his horse still waiting patiently beside the parked caravan at the edge of the town. He wasn't surprised. He didn't even hobble his horse these days; he didn't have to. Smokey was well trained, and too lazy to go anywhere she didn't absolutely have to. There was a time Jordan had worried someone might steal her, but of late the ominous runes and curses he'd painted on the sides of his caravan kept everyone at a respectable distance. After the Demon War, even footpads and outlaws had discovered a new respect for the supernatural. Jordan looked proudly at the runes he'd painted. He hadn't a clue what they meant, but they looked great. He glanced at Gawaine, who was studying the grazing horse. His gaze suggested that he was used to companions who rode a better class of animal. Jordan had to agree that Smokey wasn't exactly pedigree stock. She was mostly brown, with white patches, and reputedly even older than she looked. On a bad day, it was all she could do to break into a canter. But she pulled the heavy caravan for hours on end without complaint, once he got her moving, and she accepted resignedly the occasional hungry days that were a part of every strolling player's life. Though having Smokey around meant he could keep the strolling part to a minimum. He reached into his pocket and brought out the half carrot he'd saved from his last meal. Smokey picked it daintily off his palm and crunched it up while staring vacantly into the distance. *Ungrateful animal*, thought Jordan, but smiled anyway. He and Smokey were used to each other's little ways. He made to harness her up to the caravan, but Gawaine stopped him with a raised hand.

"You needn't bother with the caravan. You won't be needing it."

"What do you mean, I won't need it? How else am I supposed to carry all my stuff? There's my stage, the costumes, the props . . ."

"We'll supply everything you need to be Prince Viktor. Everything else gets left here. No arguments, Jordan. We know what we're doing. You can't afford to be found with anything that might give away who you really are."

Jordan scowled unhappily. "What about Smokey? I won't leave her behind. She's a good horse, in her way."

Gawaine looked at the horse, sniffed, and then looked away again. "We can always say your usual mount went lame. Now then, if you'll look in the back of your caravan, you'll find a parcel containing a set of Prince Viktor's clothes. Get changed, and don't take too long about it. I want to put a few miles between us and this town while there's still some light left."

Jordan looked at him for a long moment. "You put these clothes in my caravan before you'd even talked to me? You must have been pretty damned confident I'd agree to this."

"Roderik wanted you," said Gawaine. "And he usually gets what he wants."

Jordan had several quick answers to that one, but decided it might be politic to keep them to himself for the time being. He started to unlace the back flaps of his caravan, and glanced irritably at Gawaine. "You don't need to hang around, you know. I'm quite capable of getting dressed on my own."

"Think of me as your bodyguard," said Gawaine. "Anyone who wants to kill you has to get past me first."

"A gray-haired bodyguard," said Jordan. "Just what I always wanted. You're not fooling anyone, Gawaine. You're just here to make sure I don't change my mind and run out on you. Right?"

"Of course," said Gawaine calmly. "We can't have you running around the countryside wearing Prince Viktor's face, can we? That could prove very unfortunate."

"Yeah, your little conspiracy would sink without a trace, wouldn't it?"

Gawaine grinned and shook his head. "I was thinking more of how unfortunate it would be for you, Jordan. Because if you were dumb enough to run out on us, I'd track you down and kill you. Don't let the gray hair fool you, lad. I may not be as fast as I once was, but I'm twice as mean when I'm annoyed. And don't make the mistake of thinking you're irreplaceable. We can always find another actor, if we have to."

"Not like me," said Jordan flatly. "I'm the best."

Gawaine glanced briefly at the small shabby caravan, with its peeling paint and mismatched wheels. "Sure you are, Jordan. You've just come down in the world, like me. Now hurry up and get changed, and forget any ideas about running. I've sworn to protect Viktor from any and all dangers, and that includes small-time actors with delusions of grandeur."

Jordan's hand dropped to the sword at his side, but before his fingers could even touch the hilt, Gawaine had drawn his ax and stepped forward to set its edge against the actor's throat. Jordan started to back away, and the ax followed him. Its edge cut a little deeper, and Jordan stood very still and fought down an urge to swallow. He breathed very shallowly, and felt a thin trickle of blood run down his throat.

"Understand me, actor," said Gawaine softly. "I swore an oath upon my life and upon my honor to protect Prince Viktor. I stood at his side when his father banished him, and I followed him into internal exile for four long years. If I even think you're going to be a problem, I'll cut you into pieces. Remember that, actor."

He stepped back a pace, lowered his ax, and sheathed it at his side again. Jordan put a hand unsteadily to his throat, and his fingers came away bloody. His hackles rose, and a cold breeze caressed the back of his neck. His legs were shaking slightly, as much from shock as fear. He'd seen his share of violence in his travels, and even been in a few sword fights himself when there was no other way out, but never in his life had he ever seen anyone move as quickly as Sir Gawaine.

What the hell have I got myself into this time?

He pulled out a handkerchief, cleaned the blood off his fingers, and then pressed the cloth to his throat. He was pleased that at least his hands weren't shaking. He tried concentrating on the ten thousand ducats, but the thought didn't comfort him as much as it once had. He turned his back on Gawaine, and climbed up into his caravan. He pulled the leather flaps shut behind him, and then sat down on his unmade bed and thought hard.

There was no doubt in his mind that Gawaine had
meant every word he'd said. If he tried to back out
now, the knight would kill him. On the other hand,
there was obviously a great deal about this conspiracy
he wasn't being told. For example, what the hell had
Viktor done to get himself sent into internal exile?
Jordan took the handkerchief away from his throat,
and looked sourly at the bloodstained cloth. Maybe
he could sneak up on the knight while he was sleeping
. . . But there was still the ten thousand ducats to
consider. As long as there was a chance of getting his
hands on that kind of money, he wasn't sure he
wanted to back out. He put the handkerchief back in
his pocket, and looked around the crowded interior
of his caravan. The rough-wooden walls weren't even
varnished, let alone painted, and the floor had disappeared under a confused mess of props and costumes.
When he'd been at the top of his career, he'd had
dressing rooms that were bigger than this. He looked
at the package Roderik had left for him on his bunk,
and sighed quietly. He'd go along with the others, for
now. It wasn't as if he had a choice.

The clothes turned out to be elegant, richly colored
and a perfect fit. Well tailored, too. Presumably
they'd been made especially for the prince he now
resembled. Jordan fumbled a little at the unfamiliar
hooks and fastenings, and stopped every now and
again just to admire a particularly fine piece of attire,
but finally he was ready. He strutted back and forth
in the narrow space, sweeping his cloak around him,
and wished he had a full-length mirror. He wore his
own shirt underneath the long waistcoat, even though
he had to leave half the buttons undone. He needed
the hidden pockets sown into its sleeves to carry the
flare pellets and smoke bombs he used to counterfeit
his magic. He stuffed the pockets as full as he could.
He didn't know how long it would be before he'd have
a chance to make any more.

He strapped his own sword on his hip. Roderik had
provided a blade of far superior quality and workman-
ship, but Jordan preferred to stick with the sword he

was used to. And just to be on the safe side, he slipped a throwing knife into the top of his knee-length boot. He'd always been good with a throwing knife. Better safe than sorry, as his dad always said. That left only one item to put on, and Jordan stared at it for a long moment. The chain mail vest stared blankly back at him. Given the circumstances, the vest was a sensible precaution, but he was still reluctant to put it on, as though by acknowledging the danger, he somehow made it real. He shook his head, took off the cloak, and put on the chain mail vest. It was lighter than it looked, but he could still feel its solid weight tugging at him every time he moved. He pulled on the heavy burgundy cloak again, hiding the vest from sight, but it didn't help. Jordan looked around his caravan one last time, and then pushed past the leather flaps and jumped down onto the ground.

Sir Gawaine was still waiting for him. Jordan stood haughtily before him, and took up his best aristocratic stance. Gawaine bowed formally to him.

"If you're quite ready, Your Highness, we should rejoin the others."

Jordan nodded stiffly. A chill wind was blowing from the north, and he pulled his cloak around him. "I trust we won't be traveling far tonight, Gawaine. It's going to be bitter cold on the road once the sun goes down."

"I think the sooner we leave Bannerwick behind us, the better, sire," said Gawaine. "We aren't the only ones who have agents out in the kingdom."

Jordan nodded reluctantly. He turned to his horse and found Gawaine had her already saddled and waiting. He swung up onto Smokey's back without saying anything. Gawaine reached up and took hold of the bridle, and led horse and rider back down the deserted main street to where the others were waiting. Their horses were fine Thoroughbreds, beside which Smokey in her battered trappings looked very much the poor relation. Jordan patted her neck and muttered a few comforting words as Gawaine moved away to mount his horse. They all looked at each other in

silence for a moment, and then Robert Argent started
off and the others followed him. The quick hoofbeats
sounded loud and distinct on the quiet as the small
party left Bannerwick behind them and headed out
into the falling dusk.

The evening was still and silent as they made their
way out onto the moor. The sun was sinking below
the horizon in a mass of bloodstained clouds. Sir Gawaine lit a lantern and hung it from his saddle horn,
so that the small party moved in its own pool of amber
light. A cold wind gusted across the open moorland,
ruffling the tall heather with a heavy hand. It rose and
fell like the slow swell of a purple sea. The thick
smoky scent of the heather made a pleasant contrast
to the open-sewered stench of the mill town, and Jordan began to relax a little. He'd always liked traveling
by night, and the lonely moors held no horrors for
him. Bandits and wolves tended to prefer the forests,
and he was too old to believe in ghosts. Besides, away
from the stage he liked his solitude. It gave him time
to think, to be himself rather than one of the many
masks he wore for other people, on and off stage. The
moors had their own stark beauty, for those with eyes
to see it, and yet for once their open grandeur had no
power to soothe his soul.

It was all very well playing brave warriors and noble
heroes on the stage, but he was well aware that out
in the real world he had none of the qualities necessary to bring off such a role. He was an actor, not a
fighter, and he was perfectly happy to leave it that
way. In his experience, heroes tended to lead short
and very dangerous lives, and usually came to a nasty
end. Standing up to be counted just made you an
easier target to hit. And yet here he was, heading into
an arena more perilous than any battlefield: a Court
torn by intrigue. Jordan decided he wasn't going to
think about it anymore, for the time being. It just
made his stomach ache. He glanced surreptitiously at
Sir Gawaine, riding close beside him. He wasn't sure

whether the knight's presence made him feel more secure or more threatened.

"Roderik," said Jordan finally, as much to break the silence as anything, "tell me about Prince Viktor. Just an outline to begin with, to give me a feel for the part. And I'll need to know about his brothers as well."

"Of course," said Count Roderik. As he spoke, his voice remained casual and unhurried, but he never once looked at Jordan. "You are the middle of three sons. Prince Lewis is the eldest. He inherited earth magic by his Blood. There isn't much call for earth magic inside a castle, so he's spent most of his life training to be a warrior. He favors the sword, and is very good with it. In many ways he was King Malcolm's favorite, but of late he and your father had grown distant. He has a vile temper, and won't be crossed on anything. His private life is a scandal. In his position, he could have practically any woman for the asking, but instead he prefers to intimidate and take by force young ladies from the lesser nobility. Any who dare complain are dismissed from Court, and their families are disgraced. Few are prepared to make an enemy of the man who may one day be their king. He's known to have strangled one girl when she declared she was pregnant by him. It was never proved, of course, but everybody knows."

"Sounds a pleasant chap," said Jordan. "What does he do for a hobby, poison wells?"

"Don't underestimate his support," said Roderik sharply. "He's quite popular among the guards and men-at-arms, due to his undoubted martial prowess. They tend not to hear the rumors about his other exploits. And as the eldest son, and your father's acknowledged favorite, he's always commanded quite a large following at Court."

"Could he have killed King Malcolm?" said Jordan, frowning.

"It's possible, I suppose. If your father had threatened to disinherit him because of his behavior, I can see Lewis striking back at him in a rage. But poison

. . . no, that's not Lewis's style. Now then, your younger brother is Prince Dominic. He inherited water magic by his Blood, but he's never made much use of it in public. He's the quiet, thoughtful one of the family, and has an unhealthy interest in sorcery. He's had many teachers, and is rumored to be something of an adept, though again he's shown little sign of this in public. Dominic has always been a very private person. He is also somewhat . . . strange."

Sir Gawaine laughed shortly. "That's one way of putting it."

"How would you put it?" said Jordan.

"He's barking mad," said Gawaine flatly. "And dangerous with it."

"Like his brother Lewis, Dominic also has a following at Court," said Roderik, continuing calmly on as though Gawaine hadn't spoken. "Dominic is married to the Lady Elizabeth, a very ambitious woman. She helped to build Dominic's following through a series of well-thought-out political deals. Many of us believe Dominic and Elizabeth to be the prime suspects in your father's murder, though it must be said that so far no proof has been found to lay against their door."

"How do I feel about my brothers?" said Jordan thoughtfully. "Are we close?"

"Hardly. In Redhart, inheritance of the throne is rather a complicated matter. In most countries the crown goes to the eldest son, and any other sons get nothing. But here the king chooses which of his sons he considers to be most fit, and that son inherits the crown. This is a throwback to the days of inbreeding, when many eldest sons simply weren't . . . suitable. The dangers of that time are mostly past now, but the law and custom remain. However, if your father had made a choice, it remains unknown. The will has vanished without a trace. Since Lewis is no longer the favored son, all three of you now have an equally valid claim to the throne.

"Neither you nor Dominic care much for Lewis. He is arrogant and brash, and has always used his position as favorite to lord it over both of you. He in turn

despises Dominic as a weakling, for spending most of
his time as a scholar rather than a warrior, and considers you a fool for letting your emotions get the better
of you. You detest Dominic, not least because of his
choice of wife. The Lady Elizabeth was once . . . close
to you, until Dominic won her away."

"Tricky," said Jordan. "Do I have any friends at
Court?"

"Not really," said Roderik. "Most of your followers
were sent with you into internal exile, and for the
most part they've chosen to remain there until the
succession is decided. But Dominic and Lewis are also
finding themselves more isolated than usual, for the
same reason. No one wants to be remembered as having backed the losing side . . ."

Jordan rode for a while in silence, sorting out the
new information as best he could. It was fine, as far
as it went, but it wasn't what he needed. If he was
going to pass off this impersonation successfully, he
was going to have to know not just the facts of Prince
Viktor's background, but also the secrets and motivations that underlay those facts. And interesting though
Viktor's family background was, there was still a great
deal he wasn't being told.

"Viktor's been in internal exile for four years," he
said finally. "What exactly did he do that warranted
such extreme punishment? I mean, you've already told
me that Lewis once strangled a young woman of the
nobility and got away with it."

Argent and Roderik looked at each other. Sir Gawaine stared at the road ahead. Finally Roderik sighed
and looked at Jordan.

"Forgive me, Jordan, of course you need to know.
It's just not something we normally talk about. In fact,
we seem to have spent most of the last four years
using every bit of influence we had to keep the truth
of what really happened from ever coming out. Prince
Viktor . . . has always been one for the ladies. However, unlike Lewis, Viktor was normally sensible
enough to limit his wandering eye to the servant
classes. Such assignations may be deplorable, but

they're of no real importance. But, as I said earlier, Prince Viktor somehow became involved with the Lady Elizabeth, at a time when she was officially betrothed to Prince Dominic. How they kept it a secret for so long in a Court noted for its love of gossip is beyond me, but of course it couldn't last, and eventually Dominic found out. And that was when the tempers really began to fly. The Lady Elizabeth is a charming, beautiful young woman from an impeccable family background. Unfortunately, she is also a cold, calculating bitch. She delighted in playing the two brothers off against each other, possibly to determine which would make the better husband, but more likely just because she enjoyed it. Viktor and Dominic were on the point of a formal duel when the king finally discovered what was going on, and stepped in to put an end to it. He called all the parties before him in a private session, and apparently demanded that the Lady Elizabeth make her choice there and then. She chose Dominic.

"For a time, nothing happened. Viktor shut himself in his quarters and refused to speak to anyone, even Gawaine. We were all very worried about him. Viktor had never been one for brooding: when he was angry he spoke his mind, and let the sparks fall where they would. His continued silence was . . . disturbing. Meanwhile, Dominic and Elizabeth made the preparations for their marriage. The invitations went out, presents began to arrive, everything seemed perfectly normal. What happened next isn't entirely clear. The full facts were only ever discussed with the king, behind closed doors, and Viktor still won't talk about it. What is clear is that Viktor tried to murder Dominic. He almost succeeded. From all accounts, the king was frantic when he found out. A formal duel was one thing; that at least was honorable, if not strictly proper. But murder . . . to attempt to strike down one's own brother by stealth and treachery, to steal his fiancée . . .

"King Malcolm couldn't put Viktor on trial. If he had, the whole story would inevitably have come out, and the royal family would have been brought into disrepute. Malcolm was always very conscious of the family honor. But if he couldn't try Viktor, he couldn't let him go unpunished either. And he certainly couldn't have Dominic and Viktor living under the same roof any longer. Indefinite internal exile was the compromise he came up with, and it worked well enough."

"I was right the first time," said Jordan. "I am playing the villain."

"Viktor was betrayed by a woman who said she loved him," said Sir Gawaine. "And save your sympathy for Dominic until you've met him. There were demons in the Darkwood that had more humanity in them than Prince Dominic."

Jordan shook his head tiredly. Just when he thought he was getting the hang of the characters of his new role, they kept changing.

"All right," he said slowly. "That's his family, and his ex-love. Anyone else I need to know about?"

"The Lady Heather Tawney," said Gawaine. "Viktor's present love."

"What's she like?"

"A very forceful lady," said Roderik, quickly.

"Forceful," said Gawaine. "That's one way of putting it, I suppose."

"Viktor met her in Kahalimar," said Roderik. "She comes from an old, though fairly minor, noble family, and she's linked her star very firmly to Viktor's. She was one of the very few people who followed Viktor back to Court. The two of them are practically inseparable, and there's no doubt Viktor sees her as his main support in these troubled times."

"In other words," said Gawaine, "don't upset her. If she were to turn against us, Viktor would throw us to the wolves without a second thought. Heather's agreed to the impersonation; we couldn't do it without her cooperation. But watch your arse, Jordan. Her loyalties are strictly to Viktor himself."

"Great," said Jordan. "Just great. Isn't there anybody in this conspiracy I can trust?"

Sir Gawaine chuckled loudly. "Not a damned one, Jordan. Now you're starting to think like a prince."

Jordan decided not to ask any more questions for a while. The answers were getting too depressing. The four men rode in silence in the gathering darkness, each lost in his own thoughts. The stars came out, and the bent moon cast its light over the open moors. Jordan huddled inside his cloak, and looked gloomily about him. The moors were starting to get on his nerves. The hoofbeats of the four horses seemed eerily loud, echoing on and on in the quiet. Jordan scowled uneasily, and wondered what the hell he'd ever seen in the moors. They were a desolate place when all was said and done. Only the desperate and the outlawed lived there, and never for long. There were hidden bogs and marshes, and no place to shelter from the bitter cold nights. More than anywhere else in Redhart, the moors were untouched by man and his civilization. They looked just as they had before man came to Redhart, and would still be there after man had gone. The moors had no need of man, nor any love for him.

"Don't look around," said Sir Gawaine quietly, "but we're no longer alone."

Jordan sat stiffly in his saddle, jolted out of his melancholy. The other three glanced casually about them, barely moving their heads.

"Bandits?" said Argent.

"Unlikely," said Roderik. "I had my people check this whole area out before we came in. There are a few footpads and liers in wait, but no armed gangs. There aren't enough steady pickings here to support them."

"They could be agents working for the other princes," said Argent.

"It's possible, I suppose," said Roderik. "But what would they be doing in a backwater place like this? No one but us knew about Jordan. How many are there out there, Gawaine?"

"Five, maybe six," said the knight calmly. "They're

laying low in the heather up ahead. They're pretty good. I almost missed them."

"What are we going to do?" said Jordan hoarsely.

Gawaine chuckled quietly, and let his hand fall to the ax at his side.

"No one knew we were coming here," said Roderik. "I'd stake my life on it."

"You did," said Gawaine. "Now it looks like someone's planning on calling in the bet. One of our people must be a traitor."

"That's not possible," said Argent. "Everyone was carefully chosen . . ."

"Don't be naive," said Gawaine. "There's always someone who can be bought, or broken. We'd better look into it when we get back to Castle Midnight."

"Assuming we ever get there," said Jordan. "Whoever those people are out there in the heather, they outnumber us six to four, remember?"

"They may have the numbers," said Roderik, "but we have Sir Gawaine."

Gawaine smiled nastily. Jordan tried hard to feel reassured.

They rode on down the beaten path. The heather stirred ominously as the wind moaned briefly. Jordan searched the surrounding shadows as best he could without being too obvious about it, but couldn't see anything. He wondered if he could take advantage of an ambush to turn his horse around and race back to town. If by some chance Roderik's people survived, he could always emerge later when all the fighting was over, and swear blind his horse had run away with him. It only took him a moment's thought to see the plan wouldn't work. Firstly, the others would never believe it, and secondly, Smokey was too damned lazy to run anywhere. Jordan swallowed hard, and loosened his sword in its scabbard. When it came to violence, Jordan always believed in seeing the other person's point of view. If that failed, he tended to favor kicking the other guy in the nuts and running away quickly. It wasn't so much that he was afraid of violence, though he was, it was just that Jordan had

too good an imagination. He found it far too easy to
visualize all the terrible things that could go wrong,
and just what it would feel like to have your head
ripped clean off your shoulders. He swallowed hard
and wished he was somewhere else. Anywhere else.
He eased his boots out of his stirrups so that he could
jump free of his horse if he had to, and flexed his
arms surreptitiously to check that the flare pellets and
smoke bombs in his sleeves were within easy reach if
he needed them.

A dark figure suddenly leapt out of the heather before Gawaine's horse, and grabbed for his bridle. The
horse reared up on its hind legs, and Gawaine tumbled
backward out of the saddle. He landed on the packed
earth of the trail with a heavy thud, and rolled away
into the heather. The dark figure went rushing after
him. Moonlight shone brightly on his upraised sword.
Jordan and the others reined their horses to a sudden
halt as more dark figures rose up out of the heather
on either side of the trail.

Jordan glared wildly about him. He counted six figures, including the one that had gone after Gawaine,
and they all looked to be armed. In the dark, they
looked more like demons than men. Jordan reached
into the hidden pocket in his left sleeve, and pulled
out one of the small wax pellets. He nicked the wax
coating with his thumbnail, and threw the pellet onto
the ground between him and the nearest of the advancing figures. The pellet split open on impact, and
the liquid within burst into flames as it was exposed
to the air. Flames roared up in the middle of the trail,
lighting the scene in vivid shades of crimson and gold.
For a moment, the ambushers stopped dead in their
tracks, stunned by the unexpected heat and light. The
dancing flames reflected brightly from their chain mail
and blank shields. *Mercenaries*, thought Jordan sickly.
We're up against professional bloody killers. He groped
frantically for another flare pellet.

There was a horrid scream from out in the heather,
and then Sir Gawaine stood up, his ax dripping blood.
There was no sign of his attacker. "Well-done, Prince

Viktor," he called loudly. "But we won't need any more of your fire magic. My friends and I will take care of this trash."

He laughed unpleasantly, and Jordan shivered. There was something harsh and awful in that laugh: an open delight in murder and human butchery. Sir Gawaine hefted his great ax once, and started forward. The mercenaries snapped out of their daze, and two of them went to meet him. The others moved cautiously forward, giving the flames in the middle of the path plenty of room as they passed. Roderik drew his sword and dismounted, all in a single supple movement, and Argent swung quickly down to join him. They moved confidently forward to meet the mercenaries. The fighting had already begun by the time Jordan got down from his horse.

Gawaine stood his ground, grinning nastily, as the two mercenaries closed in on him. They had to wade through the tall heather to reach him, and he didn't miss the way it slowed them down. He chose his moment carefully, and then launched himself forward, his ax a silver blur in the moonlight as it swept out to punch deep into the first mercenary's ribs. The heavy steel blade buried itself in his side with a harsh, chunking sound, and the impact threw the mercenary to the ground. Sir Gawaine yanked the ax free, and blood and splintered bone flew on the air. The second mercenary's sword swept out in a long arc, reaching for Gawaine's throat. The knight ducked under the blow at the last moment, and his ax whistled through the air toward his attacker's legs. The mercenary jumped backward, and the ax just missed. Gawaine recovered his balance and moved forward, swinging his ax lazily before him. The mercenary backed away, peering warily at him over his shield. Gawaine feinted to the left and then threw himself forward as the mercenary hesitated, undecided. The ax rose and fell, sweeping past the shield to smash through the mercenary's collarbone and bury itself in his chest. The two men fell to the ground in a heap, but only Gawaine got to his feet again. Blood soaked his chain mail, none of it his.

There was a weak thrashing sound behind him, and Gawaine spun around as the first mercenary lurched to his feet, favoring his smashed ribs but still clinging to his sword. Blood ran from his mouth and nose, and he showed his teeth in a bloody grin. Gawaine watched him warily. When a man knows he's dying, he becomes a much more dangerous opponent. He'll try anything, take any risk. He knows he's got nothing to lose. The mercenary rushed forward, and his sword cut viciously at Gawaine's belly. The knight met the blow with the flat of his ax, and the shock ripped the sword from the mercenary's weakened grasp. He watched his sword fly through the air, and Gawaine's ax leapt up to sink into his throat. He fell limply to the ground, and lay still. Gawaine pulled his ax free with a sickening tearing sound.

Count Roderik cut down the first mercenary to reach him with practiced ease, his sword a shining blur in the uneven light. He turned quickly to meet the second mercenary, his face a cold and calculating mask. He moved confidently forward, and steel clashed on steel as the mercenary parried his attack without flinching. He took most of the blows on his blank shield, content to let Roderik tire himself, and then launched his own attack. The two men stamped back and forth on the narrow trail, sparks flying in the gloom when their swords met.

Roderik gritted his teeth against a growing ache in his sword arm. It had been too many years since he'd used a sword for anything but sport or exercise. That was the trouble with a good reputation as a swordsman: after a while it became practically impossible to find anyone foolish enough to duel with you, even just to first blood. Roderik pressed his opponent hard, and the mercenary backed cautiously away, leaving no opening. Roderik scowled. It was taking too long. Old instincts and skills were slowly returning to him, but already his breath was coming fast and hurried, while the mercenary wasn't even breathing hard. Roderik felt an almost forgotten chill run through him as he realized the man before him might just be a better swordsman than he.

The fifth and last mercenary slipped past the struggling figures and made for his main target, the prince. The merchant could wait; he wasn't going to be a problem. Prince Viktor, on the other hand, was looking more dangerous by the minute. He had to be taken care of quickly, before he could call up any more magical fire. Besides, there was a bonus for the man who killed the prince. The mercenary grinned. For a hundred ducat bonus, he'd wipe out a whole royal family. And then he pulled up short, startled, as Robert Argent blocked his way with a drawn sword. The mercenary looked at him, and his grin widened. One short, tubby merchant with a brand-new sword shouldn't be much of a problem. The mercenary glanced briefly at Prince Viktor, just in case he was about to launch any more magic, but he was apparently busy fumbling with his sleeves and muttering to himself. Argent lashed out clumsily with his sword, and the mercenary parried it easily. He quickly took over the attack, and forced Argent back step by step, the merchant defending himself more by strength and determination than skill. In a matter of seconds, the mercenary knocked Argent's sword out of his hand, and drew back his blade for the killing thrust.

"Hold, assassin!" roared Jordan, in his most commanding voice. He gestured mystically, and blue-white flames flared up about his hands. The mercenary took one look, and started backing quickly away. Jordan adopted his most impressive High Warlock stance. The trick was to keep the audience looking at you, rather than the hands. That way they wouldn't notice how quickly the flames started to die down. He ran his hands through a quick series of mystical gestures, using the movements to hide his palming of another flare pellet from his sleeve, and threw the pellet at the mercenary. It cracked open as it hit his chest, and the liquid in the pellet burst into flames. The fire took a savage hold on the mercenary's clothes, and leapt up around his face. He screamed shrilly, and dropped his sword to beat at the flames with his hands. Jordan stepped forward, and ran the man through with his sword. The mercenary fell to the ground, and lay still. The flames burned fiercely on the unmoving body.

Jordan looked quickly about him. The flames licking around his hands were already beginning to gutter. Argent gave him a quick nod to show he was all right. Gawaine was just finishing off his last opponent, but Roderik was being beaten slowly back by his. Jordan blew out the flames on his hands, and moved stealthily in behind the mercenary. It only took a moment to remove his cloak and sweep it over the mercenary's head, blinding him. He grabbed frantically at the heavy material, and Roderik ran him through. Jordan pulled his cloak away as the mercenary collapsed, and put it on again. Roderik looked at the dead man, and then at Jordan, and raised an eyebrow.

"Don't believe in fighting fair, do you?"

"I believe in winning," said Jordan, settling his cloak comfortably about him.

"A very sensible attitude," said Sir Gawaine, stepping over a dead body as he came forward to join them. He looked sternly at Argent, who was still groping in the shadows at the side of the trail, trying to find the sword he'd dropped. "If you're going to stay with us, Argent, I'd better teach you how to fight. Or at least how to hang onto your sword."

"If you were doing your job properly, I wouldn't need to know how," said Argent, finally straightening up with his sword in his hand. "You're supposed to be our bodyguard, remember?"

"We all fight when we have to," said Roderik quickly. "Now, may I suggest we all get the hell out of here? Those mercenaries knew where to find us; for all we know there could be more of them on their way right now. Damn it, Gawaine, I would have sworn nobody knew we were coming here." He frowned unhappily at the mercenary he'd just killed. "It's a pity we couldn't take one of them alive to answer questions."

"Sorry," said Gawaine. "I'll try to remember next time."

He strode away to round up the scattered horses. Jordan noticed with pride that of all the party's mounts, only Smokey had stayed put. In fact, when he thought about it, Jordan was actually quite proud of himself, too. He'd helped to take on six fully armed mercenaries, had killed two himself, and had come out of it without a scratch. Not bad going . . . The rising wind brought him the smell of burned pork from the mercenary he'd killed, and the reality of the situation suddenly caught up with him. He felt faintly sick, and his hands began to shake. He'd only been on this job a few hours, and already people were trying to kill him. Next time, there might be a hell of a lot more of them . . . He stepped forward to confront Roderik, and fixed him with an icy glare.

"When I took on this impersonation, nothing was said about having to face bands of armed mercenaries. I'm an actor: a strolling player. I've damn ill skill with a sword, and no real interest in acquiring any. If I'd wanted a life of danger and excitement, I'd have joined the tax collectors. In short, either you give me one hell of a good reason to stay, or I'm for the nearest horizon and you can find some other half-wit to play Prince Viktor."

Roderik nodded slowly. "I see. And what would you consider a good reason to stay?"

Got him, thought Jordan gleefully. *All I have to do is name a price they can't possibly meet, and I'm free!*

"Fifty thousand ducats," he said flatly. "Take it or leave it."

"Very well," said Count Roderik. "Fifty thousand ducats it is."

Jordan swallowed dryly. "That's a good reason to stay," he said finally.

"There's really no need to worry," said Roderik as Gawaine came back with the horses. "A week from now, we'll be back at Castle Midnight. Our people can protect you there."

"A lot can happen in a week," said Jordan darkly.

He thought for a moment. "What's Castle Midnight like? Will I be safe there?"

"Depends what you mean by safe," said Gawaine. "Castle Midnight isn't exactly your average castle."

"How do you mean?" said Jordan.

"You must have heard some of the stories," said Roderik.

"Well, yes," said Jordan. "But they're just stories. Aren't they?"

"Are you going to tell him," asked Gawaine, "or shall I?"

"Castle Midnight is very old," said Argent, "and a place of power. Within its walls, what is Real and Unreal is sometimes largely a matter of opinion."

"Great," said Jordan, shaking his head. "Just what this job needed. More complications."

CHAPTER 2

Bloody Bones

Castle Midnight stands alone: a lowering, brooding hulk of black basalt stone, set atop Brimstone Hill. The castle is unspeakably old, but its walls are still as thick and sturdy as they ever were. No ivy clings to the smooth stones, and all the many years have left no trace on the grim walls to mark their passing. The tall dark towers look out over the surrounding land through narrow, watchful embrasures, sometimes lit with strangely colored fires. The castle did not always belong to the kings of Redhart; they took it by force of arms and sorcery some seven hundred years ago. But it is theirs now, and they gave it the name by which it has been known and feared for centuries: Castle Midnight.

Within the towering black walls, the Real and the Unreal exist side by side, drawing strength from each other. Midnight is, after all, the hour that divides day from night, light from dark, the waking from the sleeping. It is that fleeting moment when the reality of what is and the possibility of what may be lie in balance . . . and sometimes in harmony. Those who rule in Castle Midnight draw their power from the juxtaposition of Real and Unreal, but all who live there know the balance is at best precarious and easily disturbed. And should things ever get out of control, one way or the other, there is no power in or out of this world that could put things back together again.

Castle Midnight stands alone, unique and awful, ominous and powerful. Its shadow falls across all of Redhart. It has seen wonders and terrors beyond counting in its time, and known the passing of kings.

King Malcolm is four weeks dead, and the throne stands empty. Within the black walls, the Unreal stirs and grows strong.

The Monk stood motionless before Prince Lewis, his cowled head bowed as though in thought. His long, flowing robe was the pale gray of dirty cobwebs. Its hem brushed against the floor, and the billowing sleeves were linked together in front of him. Prince Lewis studied the bowed head warily. It wasn't natural for anyone to stand that still for so long. He wondered if he ought to say something, but decided against it. The Monk didn't like to be disturbed when he was working. Lewis shifted his weight from one foot to the other, and scowled uncertainly. The Monk was his most powerful ally, and his only real hope against Dominic's sorcery, but Lewis wasn't blind to the risks involved in such an alliance. For some hidden reason of his own, the Monk followed Lewis's requests as though they were orders, but the prince knew beyond any shadow of doubt that all his secular power and elemental magic wouldn't be enough to save him if the Monk ever turned against him. The Monk was acknowledged by all as the most powerful sorcerer in Castle Midnight.

There were also those who whispered that the Monk wasn't Real.

Lewis decided, not for the first time, that he wasn't going to think about that. He turned his back on the Monk, and walked away to stand under his oak tree. He found its shade soothing. He looked aimlessly around his apartment, but there was nothing he could see that needed his attention. Everything was as it should be. The apartment had started out as just another stone-walled chamber deep in the castle, but over the years Lewis had adapted it to suit his needs and whims. The earth magic he'd inherited by his Blood gave him power over everything that lived or grew in the earth. It wasn't a very useful attribute inside the castle, but Lewis liked to exercise his magic, so he brought the outdoors inside. The floor of his apartment was covered with a layer of earth, from which grew a thick carpet of neatly trimmed grass. Its rich scent perfumed the air. A huge oak tree filled one corner of the room, its branches pressed flat against the high ceiling. It had no real roots, but Lewis's magic kept it alive. From time to time, Lewis would grow flowers or vegetables in his apartment, just to prove that he could, but of late he hadn't been in the mood. Since his father's death, he'd had more important things on his mind. Killing Dominic and Viktor wasn't going to be easy.

Lewis leaned back against the wide trunk of his oak tree, and glared at the still figure of the Monk. He hated to be kept waiting. No one but the Monk would have dared to make him wait. Lewis pushed himself away from his tree, and walked over to look at himself in the full-length mirror on his wardrobe door. His scowl slowly gave way to a satisfied smile. Every now and again, Lewis liked to check that he was still looking good. Not that he ever doubted it, but he found the confirmation soothing. He nodded approvingly to his reflection, who nodded politely back. Lewis was a tall, imposing man in his late twenties, with a harsh bony face and thinning brown hair. His chest and shoulders were muscular, and his waistline hadn't varied by so much as an inch in almost twelve years. His superbly tailored clothes were cut in the latest fashion, but dyed in the only colors he ever wore: earth brown and forest green. Even his cloak was a pleasant russet brown. He carried a sword at his hip, and though the scabbard was ornately decorated with gold and silver curlicues, the sword within was standard military issue. Lewis was a master swordsman, and ready to prove it to anyone at the drop of an insult. People talking to Lewis tended to be very careful about how they chose their words.

The Monk's cowled head rose suddenly, and Lewis felt a familiar chill run through him as he saw the open cowl held nothing but an unfathomable darkness. The Monk's robe might hold a human shape, but if there was a body inside the robe, no one had ever seen it.

Lewis kept his face calm as he strode over to rejoin the Monk, and held his head a little higher. He was a prince of Redhart, soon to be its king, and he stood in awe of no man.

"Well?" he said coldly. "Have you located them?"

"Yes, Your Highness," said the Monk. "They're out on the moors, by Barrowmeer. Count Roderik's spells of concealment misled me for a while, but I have them now."

The Monk's voice was distant and echoing, as though it came not from just inside his cowl, but rather from some unimaginable distance further in. The words were clear, if quiet, and the tone was polite enough, even courteous, but there was no animation in the voice: no emotion or humanity.

Lewis nodded curtly. "All right, you've found Roderik's party, but is Viktor with them?"

"See for yourself, Your Highness." The Monk's sleeves parted, revealing no hands at the gray cuffs, and only darkness within. The right sleeve gestured gracefully, and the air before Prince Lewis shimmered and then cleared to show a vision of Barrowmeer. Lewis fought to keep his expression calm and unimpressed. It was like looking through a window that wasn't there, save that the scene was utterly silent. Lewis watched closely as the four men on horseback reined in their horses and looked out across the open moor. His gaze settled on one familiar face, and he nodded grimly.

"Viktor. I knew he wasn't in the castle anymore."

The Monk gestured lightly, and Prince Viktor's face filled the view.

"Are you sure that is him, Your Highness? All my magic indicates that Prince Viktor has not left Castle Midnight."

"Of course that's him! Do you think I don't know my own brother when I see him?" Lewis scowled angrily. "I should have had him killed when he was still safely in exile."

"He was no threat then, Your Highness. He had no allies of any worth, save for Sir Gawaine."

"Well he's got allies now," snapped Lewis. "I don't know what they've been out looking for, but it must have been bloody important for them to leave the castle at this time. Maybe they've found a clue as to where the crown and seal are hidden . . . And if they get to them before we do . . ."

"They won't, Your Highness," said the Monk. "If you allow me to deal with them. You've seen for yourself that assassins are not the answer. The mercenaries you sent were no match for Gawaine and Roderik. But if I were to use my arts . . ."

"Do it," said Lewis, staring unblinkingly at Viktor's face in the vision. "Do it now."

The sun had been up an hour, and the rain had finally stopped. It had been raining all night, and Jordan had begun to wonder if it would ever end. The early morning felt sharp and fresh after the storm, and the rich scents of earth and grass and heather lay heavily on the air. A few birds were calling to each other out in the heather, and Jordan glared in their general direction. Roderik had kept the party moving all through the night without a break, despite the storm, and as far as Jordan was concerned, the rest of the world had no business sounding so cheerful when he felt so lousy. He sighed heavily, and swung down out of his saddle. Roderik didn't know it, but he was lucky to be alive. Because if he hadn't called this halt, Jordan would undoubtedly have killed him. He stamped back and forth beside his horse, working out the cramps in his legs and trying to coax some warmth back into his chilled bones. *Ah well,* he thought resignedly, *it could be worse, I suppose. It could still be raining.*

Roderik and Argent set about hobbling the horses, while Gawaine gathered fuel for a fire. Infuriatingly, none of them seemed particularly bothered by the long ride. Jordan scowled, and kicked at the muddy trail with the toe of his boot. It was going to be a rotten day, he could tell. He knew he ought really to be doing something to help the others, but he couldn't seem to summon up the energy. He hated missing his sleep. Finally he moved over to help Roderik remove the saddles and gear from the horses, on the grounds that it looked like the least work he could get away with. Besides, if he didn't do something soon, they'd probably make him dig the latrines. Roderik nodded shortly to him, but he didn't seem particularly appreciative of his help.

"Nice morning," said Jordan, just to be polite.

"Indeed," said Roderik, not looking up from the bridle he was checking.

"Do we have much farther to go before we reach Castle Midnight?"

"Quite a way."

"Have you been this way before?"

Roderik gave him a hard look. "Be a good chap, and stop bothering me, Jordan. I've got work to do. Why don't you go for a little walk, or something?"

It was the long-suffering patience in Roderik's voice that annoyed Jordan the most. It was the kind of voice a harried adult used with an overactive child. Still, never let it be said that the Great Jordan was one to push himself in where he wasn't wanted. He turned away, and then stopped as he saw Robert Argent coming toward him. He smiled at the merchant determinedly. He was going to have some friendly conversation this morning if it killed him. After a whole night's traveling in the cold and the rain, he felt he was owed a little friendly conversation.

"Good morning, Robert," he said brightly. "Looks like it's going to be a nice day."

"Shut up and go away," said Argent.

"I beg your . . ."

"Shut up. Go and find something useful to do. If you can do anything useful, actor."

Jordan spun on his heel and walked away, fuming. Argent would pay for that. No one talked to the Great Jordan like that and got away with it. Maybe he could hide a snake in the man's bedding . . . or his britches . . .

Roderick watched Jordan stalk off, and glanced at Argent. "I think you've upset him."

"Good," said Argent. "He gets on my nerves. Always strutting around like a damned peacock. Actors should know their place."

"Give him his due," said Roderik. "He was rather famous, in his day."

"Theatricals," sniffed Argent. "Never knew one that was worth the breath it took to damn him. Gypsies, tramps, and thieves, the lot of them. Never done an honest day's work in their lives."

"Be that as it may," said Roderik, diplomatically, "the fact is that we need him, Robert, and most of all we need his willing cooperation. Try not to upset him, for the time being at least. I get the feeling he could do something really creative in the way of sulking if he put his mind to it."

Argent sniffed again, but said nothing. Roderik looked at him, started to say something, hesitated, and then started again.

"Robert, how long have we known each other?"

"Twenty-odd years. Something like that." Argent smiled slightly. "Most of it seemed to make sense, at the time. Why?"

"Because the only time you get this touchy is when something's troubling you. We've been involved in quite a few schemes over the years. Some came off, some didn't. There's no reason to get yourself worked up, Robert; it's just another scheme, that's all."

"I know, Rod. Just another scheme."

"Then why are you so tense?"

"I am not tense!"

"You want to shout that again, Robert? I don't think they caught all of that at Castle Midnight."

"I'm fine," said Argent, more quietly. "There's nothing wrong with me."

"Bull. I've seen men on their way to the headsman's ax who looked more relaxed than you do. You're not really worried about the actor, are you? He'll do his job, and do it well. He's already so like Viktor it frightens me."

"I'm not worried about the actor," said Argent. "I can't stand the man, but he seems competent enough."

"Then what is it? What's the problem?"

"Nothing! I'm fine! Now go away and leave me be, Rod. I'm tired, and I'm wet, and I think I'm starting a cold. I'm really not in the mood for conversation."

He turned away from Roderik, and began brushing his horse down with great energy and concentration. Roderik sighed, and decided he'd try again later. He knew from long experience that when Argent decided he wasn't going to talk, a team of wild horses couldn't drag one word past his lips.

Jordan was busy helping Gawaine get a fire started. The early morning was still bitterly cold, despite the bright sunshine. Unfortunately, like everything else in the moor, the heather was soaking wet, and so far it had stubbornly resisted all the knight's efforts to set it alight with flint and steel. Jordan watched silently for a while, and then crouched down beside Gawaine. He palmed a fire pellet from his sleeve, cracked the coating deftly with his fingernail, and then dropped the pellet into the piled heather with a quick mystical gesture. The heather immediately burst into flames, and thick smoke curled up as the fire took hold. Jordan and Gawaine straightened up, and held out their hands to the leaping flames. Gawaine looked sideways at Jordan.

"That was very impressive. Mind telling me how you did it?"

Jordan smiled. "Professional secret, I'm afraid. The quickness of the hand deceives the eye, and all that. It's really quite simple, when you know how."

Gawaine nodded. "It seems Count Roderik was right in choosing you. If that wasn't fire magic, it's the nearest thing I've seen to it outside Castle Midnight."

Jordan bit his lip, and looked seriously at Gawaine. The knight seemed in a companionable enough mood, and there were a few questions Jordan very much wanted answered . . . "Tell me about Castle Midnight, Gawaine. Some of the stories I've heard about it have been . . . pretty damned strange. Are there really ghosts and monsters walking through the corridors at all hours of the day and night? Is there really a dungeon that eats people? Is it true that anyone can work magic in the castle, just as long as they've spent the night there?"

"Yes and no," said Gawaine, smiling slightly. "There are all sorts of stories about Castle Midnight, but most of them have got rather confused in the retelling. Magic, elemental magic, that is, is very common at the castle, but that's only because so many of the aristocracy have some ties to the royal Bloodline. In fact, status among the castle's High Society is largely determined by the power of your magic, as that demonstrates the relative purity of your Blood. As for ghosts and monsters . . . that's a little more complicated. You have to understand that what is Real and Unreal can easily become rather confused at the castle. It's always been that way. Some say there's High Magic built into the ancient walls. Others claim there's Wild Magic in the hill the castle rests on. No one knows the whole truth. But for as long as anyone can remember, there have always been ghosts in Castle Midnight, day and night. They're mostly harmless, as long as you don't upset them, and after a while you get used to them. They're only people who have become lost in time. Who wandered from the path and cannot find their way back."

"And the monsters?" said Jordan, hesitantly.

"There are a few monsters, every now and again. Our steward takes care of them, as and when necessary. I suppose I'd better tell you about her. Catriona Taggert is the third of her line to serve as steward to the castle. Good-looking girl, and tough with it. She has no Blood, but like all her family she's very proficient at the High Magic. She and Viktor don't get on. I think he disapproves of anyone outside the aristocracy wielding so much power. Anyway, it's the steward's job to keep an eye on the Unreal, and make sure it doesn't get out of hand. In normal times, there isn't much for her to do.

"You see, the combination of Real and Unreal in one place generates a hell of a lot of mystical power: a power the king can draw on through the ancient

Stone set under his throne. The power amplifies the king's elemental magic enormously, and at the same time enables him to keep the Real and the Unreal in balance. This, of course, ensures that the power keeps on flowing, which means . . . and so on, and so on. However, at times like these, when there's no king on the throne, things can get pretty hairy at Castle Midnight. Without the king to maintain the balance, the Unreal starts trying to break loose and run free. All kinds of insanity take shape and form, and come to life. Ghosts and monsters are only the half of it. And this, of course, is where the steward really comes into her own. Her job is to hold things together as best she can with her sorcery, until a new king takes the throne, and restores the balance."

"You make it sound as though the Unreal is . . . alive," said Jordan slowly.

Gawaine shrugged. "No one knows for sure what the Unreal is. Ask ten different people, and they'll give you ten different answers. You'll see for yourself when we get to the castle." .

"Wait a minute," said Jordan. "I think I'm missing something here. If there's that much power just waiting to be grabbed, why haven't Lewis or Dominic simply declared themselves king, and taken the throne by force? From what I've heard about those two, it ought to be the first thing they'd think of."

"As I keep pointing out, inheritance isn't quite that simple at Castle Midnight," said Count Roderik.

Jordan looked around sharply. Roderik and Argent stepped forward and warmed their hands at the fire. Jordan wondered if he ought to say something cutting, given their earlier slights, but decided against it. For better or worse, he had to learn to work with these people. And they were, after all, the ones who were paying him. *Fifty thousand ducats,* he thought grimly. *And I'm earning every bloody penny of it.* He realized Roderik was still talking, and paid attention to him.

"In order to inherit the kingship," said Roderik patiently, "the claimant has to produce both the king's crown and his seal of office, and present them to the

Stone in the correct ceremony. The Stone then grants the king power over the Unreal. Without that power, no king can rule in Redhart."

"Don't tell me," said Jordan. "The crown and the seal have both gone missing, right?"

"I said you were starting to think like a prince," said Gawaine. "Viktor and his two brothers have been turning the castle upside down since Malcolm died, but there's no trace anywhere of crown or seal."

"Wait a minute," said Jordan, frowning thoughtfully. "If Lewis or Dominic had killed King Malcolm, that would mean they'd have to have the crown and seal. Since they obviously haven't got them, that proves Lewis and Dominic couldn't have been the murderers! I mean, they wouldn't have been stupid enough to kill the king without being sure where the crown and seal were first. Would they?"

"The best laid plans can go adrift," said Roderik. "Or perhaps there was a third party involved that we don't know about . . . There's a great deal concerning the king's death that remains unclear. What is clear is that if it becomes known at Court that Prince Viktor is ill, and therefore vulnerable, he'll lose all hope of support. That's why we need you, Jordan. We need you to be the prince in public, so that our people can carry on the search behind the scenes."

The four of them stood silently around the fire for a while, each man considering the complications of the situation, and his own part in it. Gawaine roused himself first, and set about preparing a frugal breakfast. Argent went to make sure each of the horses had a nose bag. Roderik pulled a folded map from one of his panniers, and busied himself plotting the quickest route back to Castle Midnight. Once again, Jordan found himself rather left out of things, and decided to go for a little walk to see what there was to see. Besides, the exercise might warm him up. He blew on his hands and wished, not for the first time, that he hadn't bet his gloves on that last roll of the dice two towns back. He never had been lucky with dice; unless they were his own.

The open moor stretched away in all directions, colored gray and purple by the hard-wearing heather that flourished where little else would. The only disturbance in the even landscape was a smooth oblong mound that rose a good ten feet above the moor, lying not far from the rough trail. Jordan walked slowly through the heather toward it. Despite the patchy heather that covered the mound from crown to foot, he could still tell the shape was too regular for it to be a natural phenomenon. More likely it was a barrow of some kind: a burial mound for some ancient chieftain.

When he was a child, Jordan's mother had told him never to go near a barrow, because that was where the faerie kind lived, and if they tempted him through the secret door in the heart of the barrow, he'd never be seen again. When he was a little older, he sat and listened wide-eyed to the old ballad of Silbury Hill, which told of a king in golden armor who lay sleeping under a barrow with his great sword in his hand, waiting to be called forth to do battle with the final evil at the end of time. When he reached a man's age, Jordan decided that all the stories and ballads were nothing more than myths and legends, and barrows were just graves and mounds of earth. He still had a fondness for the old stories, and often incorporated them into his act, but he knew there was no truth in them. Or so he'd believed. Until now.

Approaching the great mound of earth was like knocking on the door of a haunted house. There was something about the barrow: a disturbing sense of *presence,* of something evil waiting and watching . . . Jordan stopped halfway to the mound, and stared at it for a long moment. He shivered suddenly, and pulled his cloak about him. The chill of the early morning air grew sharper, and a gusting wind tousled his hair. The temperature dropped sharply, and Jordan was startled to see his breath suddenly steaming on the air before him. The light began to fade away. Jordan looked up at the sky. Dark clouds were rolling overhead, cutting off the sun. The wind began to blow steadily, carrying a bitter cold that sliced through Jordan like a knife, despite his thick cloak. He moved quickly back to join the others, who were chattering agitatedly together.

"What is it?" demanded Jordan. "What the hell's happening? The sky was clear ten minutes ago. Storm clouds can't gather that quickly. It's not natural!"

"Damn right it isn't," growled Gawaine. He drew his ax, and hefted it lightly. "Stay close, Your Highness. We're under attack."

Jordan looked up at the sky again. The dark clouds stretched across the sky, and thunder rolled menacingly close at hand.

"Is this what you meant by elemental magic?" he asked Roderik.

Roderik shook his head quickly, still staring at the darkening sky. "No, Jordan, you'd need more than air or water magic to build a storm like this. This has got to be High Magic."

"All right, it's High Magic. What do we do about it?"

"I don't know!" said Roderik. "Give me time to think! Gawaine . . . stand ready with your ax."

"His ax?" said Jordan incredulously. "What's he going to do with that; climb on my shoulders and start carving chunks out of the clouds?"

"Keep the noise down, Your Highness," said Gawaine calmly. "This isn't just an ax. The High Warlock made it for me a long time ago."

He hefted the heavy weapon easily in his hand, and for the first time Jordan noticed a series of spidery runes traced across the steel blade. They seemed almost to glow and shimmer in the reduced light. Jordan looked back at the sky. Dark clouds boiled above them, seething with energy. The light had gone out of the day, and the moor was gray as twilight. Thunder crashed suddenly, a deafening roar that shook the air. Jordan staggered back a step, and clapped his hands to his ears. Rain hammered down. The heather bowed under its concentrated pressure. Jordan was soaked to the skin in moments. He looked frantically about him for some kind of shelter, but there wasn't any. The horses were rearing and neighing shrilly, despite everything Argent could do to soothe them, spooked by the sudden storm.

Lighting flared across the sky, and cracked down to strike the ground barely a dozen yards away from the group. The ground shook violently, and where the bolt had hit, the heather burst into flames. The pouring rain put them out again before they could spread. Thunder roared again, even closer and louder than before. It seemed to echo on in Jordan's bones, even after the sound was gone. Lightning struck again, closer this time, and the impact sent all of them flying to the ground. Jordan burrowed down into the heather, knowing even as he did that it wasn't going to be enough to hide him. Roderik called for them all to stay close together, but his voice was all but lost in the roar of the storm. Jordan looked up, and then buried his head in his arms as the lightning struck again. The earth shuddered beneath him, and he could feel the heat of burning heather not far away. The lightning was drawing steadily closer.

Gawaine surged to his feet in the pause after the lightning struck, and held his ax above his head. Jordan watched incredulously, half convinced the knight meant to sacrifice his life to save the others. The lightning flared again: a jagged arc of light that stretched from the clouds to the ax's head in a fraction of a second. The steel blade glowed fiercely as the lightning hit it, but Gawaine barely flinched. And then the lightning was gone, and Gawaine still stood there, unharmed. Jordan brushed the rain out of his eyes with the back of his hand, and watched disbelievingly as lightning flared again and again, blinking on and off in quick succession, drawn to the glowing ax head like moths to a candle. Gawaine stood firm, holding the ax above him, his head turned away and his eyes squeezed shut. Slowly, gradually, the lightning strikes grew farther apart, and the thunder lost its roar. The wind died away to nothing, and the rain lost its sting.

Roderik clambered to his feet, and raised his hands

above his head. The rain spattered on his upturned
face as his brow furrowed in concentration. A breeze
blew from his hands, building quickly into a roaring
gale. Gawaine staggered as he felt its first touch, then
realized what was happening and threw himself to the
ground. Jordan did the same. The heather was pressed
flat by the howling wind. Jordan dug his fingers into
the muddy ground to try and anchor himself. Roderik
stood tall and proud, unmoved by the tempest he had
summoned into being. The rain began to die away,
and a gap appeared in the dark storm clouds. A shaft
of morning light fell onto Roderik like a spotlight.
More breaks appeared in the clouds as the wind broke
them apart and moved them on. The rain gradually
stopped, and was replaced by the returning sunshine.

Roderik lowered his hands, and as quickly as that,
the gale died away to a wind, and then to a breeze,
and then was gone. For a while there was only an
echoing silence, and then one by one the birds began
calling to each other in the heather. The storm had
passed, leaving nothing behind to mark its fury save
a few patches of blackened and smoldering heather.
Gawaine got to his feet, nodded briefly to Roderik,
and sheathed his ax. He moved away to calm the terrified horses, while Jordan and Argent got up and went
to join Roderik, who was rubbing tiredly at his
temples.

"Are you all right, Rod?" said Argent anxiously. "I
never knew you had so much Blood."

Roderik gave him a quick, reassuring smile. "I'm
fine, thanks. Just a little out of practice. It's been a
long time since I dared use my air magic in public."

"Why's that?" asked Jordan. "I thought you said
strong elemental magic was a mark of status in High
Society?"

Roderik smiled sourly. "It also makes you a target
for intrigues and assassinations. The fewer people who
remembered I was Malcolm's cousin, the safer I was."

He swayed suddenly on his feet as a wave of tiredness caught up with him, and Argent quickly took his
arm and helped him sit down. From the way Argent

fussed over Roderik, it was clear the two of them were old and close friends, and Jordan decided his presence was something of an intrusion. For want of anything better to do, he walked over to help Gawaine with the horses. The hobbles had kept them from bolting, but their nerves were shattered. Their eyes were rolling wildly, showing the whites, and it was some time before the horses would let anyone get close enough to begin calming them. Gawaine and Jordan stuck at it, talking slowly and smoothly, and gradually the horses began to respond. Normally, Jordan wouldn't have had the patience, but as it was, he welcomed the chance to do a little quiet thinking. Roderik had said the sudden storm had been caused by High Magic, which suggested two things. Firstly, there was definitely a traitor among Roderik's people. The mercenaries finding them might have been just an unlucky break, but the storm had been planned and delivered right to them. And secondly, it was now clear that Prince Viktor had some very powerful enemies. Elemental magic might be fairly common at Castle Midnight, but High Magic was a different matter. High Magic meant a first-class sorcerer, and there weren't many of those left in the world these days.

"Who do you think was responsible for the storm?" he asked Gawaine finally.

The knight frowned, and took his time about answering. "High Magic, rather than Blood magic. That narrows the field, but there are still too many suspects for my liking. Any number of people could have good reason to want to stop us reaching Castle Midnight. Sorry I can't be more specific, but the castle's lousy with magic users of one kind or another. Still, look on the bright side."

Jordan looked at him suspiciously. "What bright side?"

"Since they're trying this hard to kill us, they must be convinced that you're really Prince Viktor. Our scheme is working."

"Terrific," said Jordan. "Wonderful. I notice none

of these powerful enemies were mentioned when Roderik first offered me the role."

Gawaine chuckled, and moved away from the quietened horses to look out over the open moor. Jordan went after him, shaking his head disgustedly. *I should have asked for a hundred thousand ducats, when I had the chance* . . . He came to a halt beside Gawaine, and the two men stood in silence together. The moor seemed quiet and peaceful after the storm's passing.

"Did the High Warlock really give you that ax?" said Jordan finally.

"It was a long time ago," said Gawaine. He didn't look around, but as he spoke his eyes were far away, watching yesterday once more. "I was a captain of the guards, fighting for the Forest Kingdom in its Border War with Hillsdown. It was a messy little war, and no good came of it. But, I was in the right place at the right time, so I ended up a hero. King John knighted me, and the warlock made me this ax. It's a good ax. Its edge never dulls, and I haven't found anything yet that can even mark the metal. More importantly, the blade cancels out all offensive magic in my vicinity. All in all, it's some ax. Which is probably why I've stayed alive so long at Castle Midnight."

Jordan looked at Gawaine thoughtfully. The Border War had come to its inconclusive end some thirty-six years ago. If Gawaine had been a captain then, that would put him in his late fifties now. At least. For a man that age, he was in extraordinarily good shape. He was also extraordinarily modest. Kings don't knight commoners for simple acts of bravery; whatever Gawaine did, it would have had to have been very impressive. And yet there had been something in Gawaine's voice all the time he'd been speaking: a quiet edge of bitterness . . . For no good reason he could name, except perhaps his actor's instinct for truth and fallacy, Jordan suddenly felt he could trust this man.

"Tell me the truth," he said quietly. "What exactly have I let myself in for, Gawaine? Can I trust these people I'm working for?"

Gawaine said nothing for a long time, staring out over the moor. "You're being paid a great deal of money," he said finally. "Do your job well, and keep your eyes and ears open, and you'll walk away from this a rich man. That's all you need to know."

Jordan waited awhile, but the knight had nothing more to say. Jordan sucked at his lower lip thoughtfully. It wasn't difficult for him to read the tension and frustration in Gawaine's stance. The knight wasn't necessarily lying to him, but there was certainly a great deal he wasn't prepared to say straight out.

"You swore an oath to protect King Viktor," he said suddenly. "You even followed him into exile from the Court, and followed him back to Castle Midnight when most of his other supporters wouldn't. Now you're risking your life to help put him on the throne. What's he really like, Gawaine? Roderik's been giving me Viktor's life history till it's coming out my ears, including everything he's said and done from the cradle onward, and everyone he's ever known, but I need more than that. What kind of man is Viktor?"

Gawaine looked at Jordan for the first time. His gaze was steady, but tired. "Viktor . . . is the best of a bad bunch. Lewis is vile, Dominic is insane, and Viktor has been badly used. His brothers plotted against him, the woman he loved betrayed him, and he's spent most of his life trying to be something he was never suited to be. You keep calling him a villain, but he isn't. He's done . . . deplorable things, yes, but only because in some matters he is too weak and easily led. As the son of a minor lord or baron, with lesser responsibilities and burdens, he might have done quite well. But he never had the strength of character or purpose to be a successful prince of Redhart. He lacks the pragmatic, ruthless nature that such a position demands. Of all the three princes, Viktor is undoubtably the most human. He's made fewer enemies than anyone else at Court, but then he's also achieved the least. He's brave enough, when he has to be, and I've taught him everything I know about the sword and the ax. He's killed seven men in duels, and I've never once known him to back down from a quarrel."

Jordan shook his head. "Weak, easily led, lacking strength of character . . . and this is the man you want to make king?"

Gawaine shrugged. "The way things are, he'll either be king or he'll be dead, and all his followers with him. And as king, he should be . . . better advised."

Jordan looked at him narrowly. "You're being very careful with your words, Gawaine, but you're still not telling me what I need to know. Do you like him, Gawaine?"

"I'm his friend, I suppose. He listens to me sometimes. He has a good side, a noble side; I try to encourage it, when I can. I swore to his father that I would protect Viktor as best I could, for the rest of my life."

"Why?" said Jordan. "What made you swear such an oath to King Malcolm?"

Gawaine looked at him steadily. "You ask too many questions, actor."

"Yeah, I know. One of these days it'll get me into trouble." Jordan grinned at him easily. "Just doing my job, Gawaine. If you're uncomfortable, we'll change the subject. What do you know about that barrow over there? Are there any local legends about it?"

Gawaine studied Jordan for a disturbingly long moment. There was a cold calculation in his eyes, and Jordan carefully kept his smile open and disarming. Gawaine finally turned away to look at the barrow, and Jordan breathed a silent sigh of relief. For whatever reason, it was clear the knight wasn't prepared to talk about his oath, or the reasons behind it. It was also clear to Jordan that if he'd tried to press the point, Gawaine would almost certainly have knocked him down. He casually moved a step farther away from Gawaine, and turned his attention to the great mound of earth that marked the barrow.

"Barrowmeer," said Gawaine slowly. "It's very old. Some histories claim it was here even before Castle Midnight was built on Brimstone Hill. Barrowmeer got its name from the time there was a great lake here. That's long gone now, together with quite a few other landmarks; wiped out during a sorcerers' war in the time of the Shadow." His left hand made an instinctive warding sign against evil. "The barrow is a grave, of course, but it's no ordinary grave. That mound of earth you're looking at was built to hold something evil. Originally there was a ring of standing stones around the barrow, to keep the sleeper quiet. But one by one they disappeared over the centuries. Stone for building has always been scarce in this part of the world. Now there's just the barrow itself left to hold Bloody Bones."

"Who the hell's Bloody Bones?" said Jordan. "He sounds like a pirate in a bad mummer's play."

Gawaine looked at Jordan, and the smile faded quickly from the actor's lips. Gawaine nodded sternly. "Believe me, Jordan, there's nothing funny about Bloody Bones. Not if half the stories I've heard are true. Bloody Bones is one of the old creatures, the Transient Beings. They say he was here long before the coming of man, stalking across the moors in search of prey, leaving a trail of bloody footprints behind him. He had no need for meat, but he lived on blood. When he walked the moors, the sun hid behind the clouds and the air was full of the stench of the grave. No one knows who finally put him down and bound him in the earth, but he's lain in that barrow for God knows how many centuries—held there by spells and wards older than Redhart itself, and he's still not dead."

"You're very well-informed on the subject," said Jordan. He tried to make his voice light and cheerful, but couldn't.

"I collect old stories," said Gawaine. "A hobby of mine. I had hoped we'd not be coming this way. This is a bad place, even now."

"I shouldn't worry about it," said Jordan. "In my experience, there hasn't been a historian yet who wouldn't change or exaggerate the facts to make a better story."

Thunder rumbled, not far away. Jordan flinched,

and looked up at the sky, expecting to see the dark clouds reforming, but the sky was clear and open. The heavy rumbling sound came again, louder and closer, and Jordan felt the ground stir uneasily beneath his feet. For the first time, he realized that what he was hearing was the sound of earth rending and tearing apart, and he looked instinctively at the barrow. His breath caught in his throat as the huge earth mound shook itself apart. Loose earth ran down the sides of the mound like water, carrying with it clumps of displaced grass and heather. A jagged crack ran along the top of the barrow, widening and lengthening as Jordan watched. Something pale and indistinct appeared in the gap, and clawed at the open air. It took Jordan several moments to realize he was looking at a huge bony hand. Another hand appeared out of the widening crack, and the two hands sank into the crumbling earth and forced the gap open. The air grew cold and the moor grew silent, and Bloody Bones emerged from his grave.

He stood nine feet tall, and the light shone clearly between his bare bones. He was a huge, ill-formed skeleton, held together by ancient and awful magics that had no place in the rational world. Blood ran from his grinning jaws in a steady stream, and fell down to splash on his chest bone and ribs. The bones were browned and yellowed with age, and smeared with mud and grass from his grave, but still the main color was the horribly vivid red of freshly running blood. It dripped from his fingertips and oozed out from under his feet. It ran down his leg bones, and welled ceaselessly from his empty eye sockets.

Bloody Bones.

Jordan found he had his sword in his hand, though he didn't remember drawing it. He couldn't for the life of him think what good it was going to be against something like Bloody Bones, but he clutched the hilt tightly anyway. The familiar weight of the sword was a comfort, if nothing else. The wind suddenly changed direction, bringing him the stench of blood and carrion that hung around the skeleton like a rotting shroud.

Jordan's stomach heaved, and he backed away involuntarily. Behind him, the horses were screaming in
terror. Jordan realized he was whimpering himself and
clamped his mouth shut, clenching his teeth together
until his jaw ached. He wanted very badly to turn and
run, and keep on running until he found his way back
into the safe and rational world again, but deep down
he knew that wherever he hid, the creature would
come and find him. He swallowed hard and stood his
ground, and realized for the first time that Roderik
and Argent had joined him, swords at the ready. Gawaine stood at his other side, holding his ax. His face
was pale, but very calm. Jordan felt strangely light-
headed. The sight of Bloody Bones disturbed him
deeply on some fundamental level. A skeleton
couldn't move without muscles and tendons to move
the bones, but Bloody Bones stood tall and awful
above his violated grave like some horrid vision from
a child's nightmare, held together by foul magics and
his own undying hatred. The blind head turned slowly
to stare at Jordan, and he somehow knew the skeleton
could see him, despite the empty eye sockets.

"What happened?" he said sickly. "How did that
thing escape from its barrow after so long?"

"Someone must have undone the warding spells,"
said Roderik tightly. "The same sorcerer who raised
the thunderstorm."

"He must be getting desperate," said Gawaine.
"Raising Bloody Bones is one thing, but putting him
back in the ground afterward . . . Even the High Warlock might have some trouble doing that."

"That's as maybe," said Argent. "In the meantime,
what the hell are we going to do? Can we fight it?"

"I don't think we've much choice," said Gawaine.
"After all those years in the ground, he's probably
very thirsty by now."

"Of course," said Roderik. "He drinks blood,
doesn't he . . ."

"If he drinks blood, that makes him a vampire,"
said Jordan. "I played one, once. Can't we drive a
stake through his heart?"

"He hasn't got a heart!" snapped Roderik. "And he's not a vampire; he's much more dangerous than that."

"Scatter!" yelled Gawaine.

Jordan's heart missed a beat as the nine-foot-tall skeleton lurched forward impossibly quickly. Argent and Roderik backed hurriedly away to the right, while Gawaine dived to the left. Jordan stood frozen where he was, unable to move, as Bloody Bones swayed toward him. The huge creature looked more dreamlike and nightmarish than ever. A massive bony hand reached down, the twig-like fingers flexing before his face, and then Gawaine slammed into Jordan's side, and the two men fell sprawling to the ground. Jordan hit the packed earth of the trail hard, driving the air from his lungs, and the struggle to get his breath back cleared his head in a matter of seconds. He forced himself doggedly to his knees, and saw that Gawaine was already on his feet and swinging his ax. The runes on the blade were glowing with a scintillating white fire. Bloody Bones grinned down at Gawaine, his fingers twitching eagerly. Drops of blood flicked from the bone fingertips in a steady stream. Gawaine's ax whistled toward the nearest bony hand, but the skeleton drew it quickly back at the last moment. Gawaine lurched forward, momentarily off balance, and Bloody Bones's right foot shot out and slammed into his gut. Gawaine crashed backward into the heather and lay still.

Roderik raised his hands above his head, and a wind began to blow. Sweat ran down his straining face as he used the last of his strength to fuel his magic. The wind hummed and whistled as it whipped through the skeleton's empty rib cage, but he stood his ground easily, unmoved. Argent crawled through the heather on his hands and knees, trying to sneak around and behind the skeleton while he was distracted. Jordan saw what he was doing, and decided he'd better add to the distraction. He lurched to his feet, palmed a flare pellet from his sleeve, and nicked the wax coating with his fingernail. He threw the pellet into the heather between the skeleton's feet, and it burst into flames as the pellet broke open. The fire spread slowly through the damp heather, and flames leapt up around the skeleton's leg bones.

Bloody Bones tilted back his grinning skull, and screamed. The deafening sound was shrill and piercing, and went on long past the point where a natural voice would have had to stop for breath. *How can it scream?* thought Jordan crazily. *The bloody thing hasn't got any lungs* . . . He felt a chill of horror run through him as he realized the flames weren't really hurting the skeleton. The blood on the bones blackened and smoked in the heat, but the bones themselves were untouched.

Argent rose to his feet behind the skeleton, holding his sword awkwardly out before him. He braced himself, and then cut savagely at the creature's spine. The blade bit into the vertebrae and stuck. The skeleton lurched forward a step under the impact, and looked back to see who had dared attack him. His body twisted all the way around so that his skull was facing Argent, in a move made possible only by his complete lack of flesh. Argent tried to pull his sword free, but the trapped blade wouldn't budge. A bony hand lashed out and closed around Argent's throat. Bloody Bones picked him up and dangled him in midair before his grinning skull. The sword fell harmlessly from his spine. Argent clawed at the bony fingers, but couldn't budge them an inch. Blood ran down his neck as they slowly tightened their hold. Roderik abandoned his air magic and charged forward, sword in hand. Bloody Bones lifted Argent effortlessly above his head and threw him far out into the heather. Jordan winced as the sound of Argent hitting the ground came to him with a harsh, hopeless clarity.

He realized suddenly that Gawaine was back at his side again. The knight favored his left ribs, and his face was beaded with sweat, but he was still clinging grimly to his ax. Roderik was darting back and forth before the skeleton, trying for a blow at the creature's spine, but unable to stand his ground long enough.

Bloody Bones's long-fingered hands swept through the air in vicious arcs, missing Roderik by less and less each time.

"Smoke," said Gawaine hoarsely to Jordan. "I saw you use smoke in your act. Can you do it here?"

"Sure," said Jordan, "but how's that going to help? If the fire doesn't bother him . . ."

"Just do it!" rasped Gawaine. "And stand ready to help me. Argent had the right idea, rest his soul. We've got to cut this bastard down to size. Wait till I've worked my way behind him, and then give me all the smoke you can."

Jordan nodded, and Gawaine disappeared into the heather. Jordan tried to follow his movements, but quickly lost track of him. Gawaine was good. He palmed one of the smoke pellets hidden in his right sleeve, and hefted it uncertainly. He stared at the huge skeleton, and for a moment his breath caught in his throat. It was just so damned big . . . Blood dripped steadily from the discolored bones, and soaked into the ground where the creature stood. The flames between its legs had already gone out. The skeleton's carrion stench was growing steadily stronger. Jordan glanced briefly at the horses, but knew there was no point in trying for one of them. They were all too spooked to be ridable; and besides, Bloody Bones would never let him reach them. Much as he wanted to run, Jordan knew he had no choice but to stand his ground and fight.

And when all was said and done, he couldn't let Gawaine down. He was hard-pressed to come up with one good reason why not, but somehow he just couldn't stomach the thought. He sniffed disgustedly. A few days as a prince, and already he was acting like a hero. A hero . . . maybe he was sickening for something.

He watched Roderik sway back and forth before Bloody Bones. His movements were growing slower and more awkward as his tiredness caught up with him. The skeleton was just playing with him now, and they both knew it. Jordan decided he daren't wait any

longer. If Gawaine wasn't in place by now, he'd just
have to take his chances. Roderik had already run out
of luck. Jordan shouted an insult at Bloody Bones to
draw the thing's attention, and drew back his hand to
throw the smoke bomb. His heart lurched as the skeleton slapped Roderik aside with a single blow, and
headed straight for him with outstretched hands. Jordan took one look at the huge skull with its bloody
grin, and threw the smoke bomb onto the ground between him and the advancing skeleton. A dark oily
smoke boiled up from the heather, quickly spreading
to form an impenetrable foul-smelling cloud. The skeleton swayed to a halt, and batted at the smoke with
his blood-dripping hands. Jordan decided that if the
skeleton even looked like taking another step toward
him, he was going to turn and run like crazy until his
lungs gave out. And then from out of the smoke there
came the flat chopping sound of steel slicing through
bone, and Bloody Bones screamed and fell helplessly
forward.

The ground shook as his great weight hit the earth.
The remnants of Roderik's winds rose for a moment,
partially dispersing the smoke, and Jordan swallowed
hard as he saw the skeleton had fallen so that its huge
grinning skull was now only a few feet away from him.
The skeleton already had his hands under him, and
was levering himself up out of the heather. Jordan
started forward, sword held out before him, not sure
what he was going to do, but determined to do something. The skeleton had made him afraid, and it
seemed to Jordan that this had been happening to
him too often just lately. He'd had a bellyful of being
frightened, and just this once he was going to do
something about it. Maybe he could whittle the bloody
thing to pieces. And then the smoke cleared some
more, and Jordan grinned fiercely as he saw the jagged stump that ended Bloody Bones's right leg just
below the knee. Gawaine loomed out of the smoke,
brandishing his glowing ax.

"Get the head!" he roared at Jordan. "Hold it still
while I go for the neck! And watch out for the teeth!"

Jordan sheathed his sword and leapt forward to grab the huge skull with both arms, hugging it to his chest. The grinning jaws snapped viciously, grating on his chin mail vest. Blood poured down Jordan's chest and stomach, none of it his. The stench was almost overpowering. *What the hell am I doing?* he thought crazily. *I could get killed doing this. Stupid bloody hero . . .* The skeleton reared upward, lifting his head clear of the heather, and dragging Jordan off the ground and up into the air. Jordan hung on tenaciously, and the great head began to sag under his weight. And then Gawaine was there at his side, and the glowing ax swept down. It sheared clean through the neck bone, and Jordan fell back into the heather, still clutching the huge skull to his chest. He lay on his back, gasping for breath, and watched dazedly as the headless skeleton took two uncertain steps and then collapsed to lie still among the heather. He realized he was still holding the skull, and threw it away from him with a sudden feeling of revulsion. It rolled to a halt, and then rocked back and forth for a while, grinning at nothing.

Jordan watched it until he was sure it was no longer bleeding, and then he rose painfully to his feet. His chain mail was slick with the skeleton's blood, and he made a few halfhearted attempts to brush it away with his sleeves before giving it up as a bad job. He grinned stupidly at Gawaine, feeling light-headed and rather shaky about the legs. He was alive. He was alive! He took one deep breath after another, savoring them. Gawaine moved cautiously forward to stare down at the grinning skull. He stirred it with his boot, and the lower jawbone fell away from the skull. Gawaine looked at Jordan, and nodded curtly.

"That was well-done, actor. For a moment there, I thought you might just turn and run."

"Never crossed my mind," said Jordan blandly. "After you've faced Hillsdown audiences seven days a week and twice on Saturdays, there isn't much in this world that can frighten you."

Roderik came over to join them, limping slightly but otherwise apparently unharmed.

"Are you badly hurt?" he asked Gawaine. "That was a nasty blow you took."

Gawaine smiled and shook his head. "Just a few cuts and bruises. I've been hurt worse in training sessions."

"I'm fine, too," said Jordan. "Just in case you were worried."

Roderik looked at him calmly. "I was never worried about you for a moment, Jordan. Actors always land on their feet. Did either of you see what happened to Robert?"

"There can't be much doubt," said Gawaine, sheathing his ax. "That creature must have thrown him a good thirty feet. Probably broke every bone in his body."

"Not quite," said Argent. "It just feels that way."

They all looked around to see Argent making his way through the heather toward them. He paused beside the headless skeleton, and kicked it once. Roderik moved quickly over to offer him a supporting arm, but Argent just smiled and waved it away.

"I'm all right, Rod. I was lucky; the heather broke my fall. I got the wind knocked out of me, and I'm carrying some bruises I'll be feeling for a while, but on the whole, I seem to have come out of it pretty much intact."

Roderik laughed, and shook his head. "I should have known you were too devious to die that easily, old friend. You know, it's a pity we can't tell anyone about this. Destroying Bloody Bones would make us all heroes: maybe even legends. They'd write ballads about us."

Jordan frowned. The thought had occurred to him. "Why can't we tell anyone?"

"Because officially Your Highness has never left Castle Midnight, and neither have we," said Gawaine.

"Oh. Yes." Jordan sniffed, and looked unhappily at the heap of blood-spattered bones lying among the heather. "What are we going to do with the body?"

"We'll drop it back in the barrow, and seal it up again as best we can," said Roderik. "Only I think we'll take the skull with us until we find a nice deep river, and then we'll get rid of it there. Just to be on the safe side."

"Never mind, lad," said Gawaine to Jordan. "Maybe you could write it up as a play."

"Nobody would ever believe it," said Argent.

"When I'm on stage, people believe whatever I want them to," said Jordan, grinning. "Isn't that why you chose me?"

Prince Lewis scowled at the silent scene before him. He couldn't tell what they were saying, but it was obvious they were congratulating themselves on their victory. Viktor had done surprisingly well. All the intelligence reports on him suggested he'd grown harder and tougher during his years in exile, but even so . . . And that smoke had been a new trick. Viktor must have been working on his magic, refining it. Lewis turned his back on the vision, and it faded away.

"I apologize for my failure, Your Highness," said the Monk, in his cold, distant voice.

"I don't want apologies, I want results!" Lewis glared at the Monk. "And what the hell did you think you were doing, raising Bloody Bones? If you hadn't been able to put him back in his grave, he'd have been a bigger menace to us than Viktor ever could be!"

"It was a calculated risk," said the Monk. "There was never any danger to us. I was in control of the situation."

"Sure you were," said Lewis. "That's why Bloody Bones is now nothing more than a pile of old bones, and our enemies are still on their way here."

"Gawaine's ax was an unknown factor," said the Monk calmly. "I can only deal with known factors."

Lewis glared at him, and then shook his head slowly. "All right; what else can you do to stop them from getting here?"

"Not a great deal, Your Highness. My magic has

its limits. I'll need to rest for a while before I can use my power again."

"But they'll be here in a matter of days! And you saw how good they were. That bloody Gawaine and his ax . . . and Viktor and his fire magic . . ."

"You do have other allies, Your Highness," said the Monk. "Allies you can call on when Prince Viktor and his party arrive at Castle Midnight. There is, for example, Ironheart."

Lewis looked at the tall suit of armor standing in one corner of his room. "Yes," he said finally. "There's always him."

CHAPTER 3

Real and Unreal

Jordan got his first sight of Castle Midnight on the evening of the fifth day after leaving Bannerwick. His whole body ached after so long in the saddle, but even so his first glimpse of the castle was enough to drive the pain right out of his mind. The great brooding shape of Brimstone Hill could be seen for miles away, the castle squatting at its top like a skull on a burial mound. Jordan studied it obsessively through the darkening twilight. Open fields lay stretched out around the hill, neat and even within their low stone boundary walls. The single straight road that led to the castle was wide, even, and well maintained. All in all, everything seemed pleasant, ordinary, and civilized, and yet Jordan felt increasingly uneasy. It was the castle, of course; as out of place in the peaceful countryside as a toad in a rose garden. It stood stark and forbidding against the blood-streaked evening sky, and unhealthy lights burned in its narrow windows like so many watching eyes.

Not for the first time, Jordan got the feeling that he was well out of his depth and sinking fast. He was an actor, not a double, and what little experience he'd had with Court intrigues had left him with a steadfast determination to avoid them like the plague whenever humanly possible. He had little talent for treachery and double-dealing, and trying to keep track of who was really working for who gave him a headache. He wasn't even particularly happy about working as a double. Roderik and Argent had been very thorough in filling him in on the background details, and Gawaine had grudgingly offered a few anecdotes that helped to reveal the prince's character, but when all was said and done, Jordan was an actor and used to a script, stage, and props. He could ad-lib when he had to, as could any actor worth his salt, but if truth be told, Jordan hadn't varied his act much in almost four years. He hadn't needed to. Now he had to take on a new character, in a strange setting, with no script and an audience who would probably have him executed if he didn't do an extremely convincing job.

Fifty thousand ducats didn't seem nearly as much as it once had.

Brimstone Hill drew steadily nearer as Count Roderik led his party along the deserted road. Both he and Argent had become grim and silent, and the suppressed tension in their body language hadn't done a thing for Jordan's nerves. He steered his horse in beside Sir Gawaine's. The knight nodded to him absently, but said nothing, his gaze fixed on Castle Midnight.

"Glad to be home again, Gawaine?" said Jordan finally.

"The castle isn't my home, Your Highness; it's just a place where I happen to be living. But yes, I am glad to be back. We'll all be safer once we're inside the castle walls. Not that our enemies will give up on us, but their attacks will have to be more subtle, and therefore less effective."

"Speaking of my two brothers," said Jordan, "just how are we going to get into the castle without being spotted by their agents? As far as everyone else is concerned, we're not supposed to have left the castle."

"It's all been arranged, Your Highness. The head of castle security is one of us. A group of men who looked sufficiently like us from a distance set out for a little hunting earlier today. They'll disappear into the countryside, and we take their place. Simple, but effective."

"Wait a minute. How did they know we'd be here today? Any number of things could have happened to hold us up."

"Count Roderik and the head of security have an

understanding," said Gawaine. "Don't ask me to explain. It's to do with sorcery, and I've never had much interest in that."

Jordan decided to let that pass without comment. "Any last words of advice, Gawaine? Once we've ridden through the main gates, I'm on."

"You're doing fine, Your Highness. Just remember that you are a prince of the Realm, and act accordingly. Treat everyone like dirt, expect the best of everything and look scandalized if you don't get it. When in doubt, be offensive and obnoxious. Everyone will expect you to be in a foul temper after an unsuccessful day's hunting, so they'll all make allowances. Lots of them."

"I am not playing a villain, I am not playing a villain . . ."

"I beg your pardon?"

"Nothing."

Jordan's stomach churned with first-night nerves as the horses toiled steadily up Brimstone Hill toward the castle. He didn't even have the usual comfort of being able to lose himself in running through his lines. In the end he fell back on his last resort, and ran through a series of breathing exercises while concentrating very hard on the surrounding scenery. The hill itself looked surprisingly ordinary, being nothing more than a huge grass-covered mound. For a moment it reminded him uncomfortably of Bloody Bones's barrow, but he refused to let his mind dwell on that. He looked up at the castle, and his mouth went dry. The stark black walls towered above him, bare and unadorned. Guards watched silently from the battlements, but no flags or pennants flew from the narrow towers. There was something subtly disquieting about the shape of the castle, a sense of wrongness in its angles and dimensions that grated on Jordan's nerves, made even more nightmarish by its very elusiveness. His horse tossed her head uneasily, and Jordan realized he was holding the reins so tightly that his hands were aching. He looked away from the castle, and made himself concentrate on the breathing exercises.

Slowly, he began to relax a little. He was the Great
Jordan, and this was just another acting engagement.
He could do it. He just didn't want to. All too soon
the party reached the main gates, and the horses
waited impatiently as the huge iron portcullis inched
into the air amid a squealing of chains and counter-
weights. Finally it was up, and Roderik urged his
horse forward. Jordan swallowed hard, and followed
him.

The courtyard was brightly lit with flaring torches,
and grooms and servants came hurrying forward to
help the party dismount. Jordan started to swing down
out of his saddle, and then quickly settled back again
as he saw the others hadn't moved yet. He waited
patiently while the servants produced wooden blocks
and placed them beside the four horses. Gawaine
swung out of his saddle and stepped down onto the
block, and then onto the courtyard cobbles. Jordan
raised a mental eyebrow, and then followed suit. A
dismounting block; he'd fallen into the lap of luxury
here. He stretched slowly, glad to be out of the saddle
at last. He hadn't done so much riding in years, and
now he knew why. He massaged his tired back with
both hands, and wished he felt unself-conscious
enough to do the same to his aching thighs. He sighed
heavily, and looked around him. His gaze fell on the
dismounting block, and he frowned slightly. The others should have warned him about that. Ignorance of
such everyday details was just the kind of thing that
could show up an impostor. Of course, the others
hadn't warned him simply because it was so much a
part of their lives that they took it for granted. Jordan
scowled unhappily. What else was there he hadn't
been told about?

The grooms took the horses away, and the servants
closed in around the newcomers, proffering damp tow-
els with which to clean the dust of travel from their
face and hands. Jordan used his gratefully, and when
he was finished, he looked around for the servant
who'd given it to him. The man had already vanished
back into the bustling crowd of servants. Without hesi-

tating, Jordan screwed the towel into a ball and tossed it over his shoulder without bothering to check if there was anybody there to catch it. *I'm a prince, damn it. Princes don't care. They don't have to.*

He glanced unobtrusively around the courtyard, getting the feel of the place. There were far more torches and lanterns than he'd have thought necessary, but the courtyard was still a cheerless place, even with all the light. There were too many shadows, and the black stone gave the courtyard a brooding, claustrophobic atmosphere. The cobbled yard seemed to swallow up every sound, producing an eerie, dreamlike hush. *This isn't home*, Gawaine had said. *It's just a place where I happen to be living.* A door opened to Jordan's right, and he looked around quickly as a middle-aged, plainly clad man entered the courtyard, flanked by two armed guards. Jordan's hand started to move toward his sword belt, and he stopped it with an effort. He couldn't afford to be seen looking worried. He held his head arrogantly high, and waited for them to come to him.

The new arrival was slightly below average height, with a solid stocky frame and heavily muscled arms. At first glance, his face seemed open and even amiable, but the green eyes were wary and watchful, and did nothing to mirror his professionally vague smile. His hair was a vivid red, brushed back from a sharp widow's peak, and Jordan realized with something like shock that this obviously hard, competent man dyed his hair. He made a mental note to remember that; it might be important to understanding the man. He came to a halt just before Jordan, and bowed formally. The two guards nodded stiffly.

"Welcome home, Your Highness," said the man graciously. "I trust you had an enjoyable day's hunting."

"Bloody awful," said Jordan shortly. "Didn't see a damn thing worth chasing." *Who the hell is this? Somebody better give me a clue quickly, before I say the wrong thing.*

"How are things at Court, Brion?" said Roderik,

moving forward to stand beside Jordan. "Anything important happened since we left this morning?"

"Not so far, my lord. Now if Your Highness will permit, I would like to accompany you to your chambers. There are security matters I need to discuss with you in private."

Brion. Brion DeGrange, head of castle security. He's one of us.

Jordan nodded quickly to DeGrange. He'd never been any good at recognizing people from a description. "Of course," he said curtly. "Will you accompany us, Roderik?"

"As you wish, sire."

"With your permission, I will leave you now, sire," said Argent, bowing formally. "I have business matters that must be attended to."

"And I've got work to do," said Gawaine. "With your permission, Highness . . ."

"Yes, yes," said Jordan testily, waving his hand at them in dismissal. He glared at DeGrange. "Well, get a move on. I've got better things to do than stand around all day in a drafty courtyard."

DeGrange bowed deeply, and led the way into the castle interior. Jordan wondered if he'd imagined the glint of anger he'd seen in the man's eyes just before he bowed. The two guards fell in on either side of Jordan as he left the courtyard. He did his best to pretend they weren't there. He hated to admit it, but with Gawaine gone, he felt decidedly more vulnerable.

DeGrange led him through a series of wide passageways and intersecting corridors, filled with bustling people who immediately stopped what they were doing to fall back and bow deeply as Jordan approached. At first, Jordan found this rather pleasant and not a little gratifying, but it soon became boring and finally irritating. The endless bowing was getting on his nerves. It was like walking through an endless supply of headwaiters. He enjoyed the adulation he'd received as an actor because he felt he'd earned it by his art, but these people were bowing to him because they had to, not because they felt he was worthy of it.

Jordan decided he didn't care for that at all. Receiving acclaim you hadn't earned was like drinking wine with no alcohol in it. It didn't thrill. Finally he just ignored them all and didn't acknowledge anybody. He kept an eye out for ghosts and monsters and other traces of the Unreal, but so far Castle Midnight seemed much like all the other castles he'd visited: dark, crowded, and drafty.

The corridors became steadily narrower as they made their way deeper into the castle, and Jordan began to find the endless black stone walls both depressing and disturbing. It never seemed light enough, despite the many lamps and torches set in every conceivable niche. Echoes lingered on that fraction too long, and shadows caught at the corner of his eye with hints of unnatural shapes. He tried to tell himself it was all in his imagination, but he couldn't make himself believe it. He glanced surreptitiously at De-Grange, Roderik, and the guards to see if they shared his mood, but they seemed unaffected. Presumably they were used to it. And then they came to a simple stone chamber, and the oppressive atmosphere was suddenly gone.

Jordan stopped dead in his tracks, and the others stopped with him. Jordan sighed, and stood up a little straighter. He stretched, and flexed his muscles. He hadn't realized what a weight he was carrying until it was gone. He felt calm and relaxed, and at peace with himself and the world. It was an unfamiliar feeling for him, and he stood there breathing deeply for a while, savoring it. He looked about him curiously, studying the chamber. The walls were the same black stone as everywhere else, but here the color was flat and lifeless. Two torches burned in iron wall brackets, and their light filled the chamber with a warm comfortable glow. A plain wooden crucifix hung on one wall, with a garland of fresh flowers beneath it. There was a row of simple wooden seats, but no other furniture or fittings.

"What is this place?" asked Jordan softly.

"This is a sanctuary, Your Highness," said Roderik, in a voice that was at once polite and a subtle warning.

"Of course," said Jordan. "A sanctuary."

He nodded to DeGrange to carry on, and they left the chamber behind them. The moment they passed through the doorway, the feeling of peace and restfulness was gone. Jordan said nothing, but decided he'd have quite a few questions to put to Roderik once they were safely out of the public eye. He didn't dare ask anything in front of the guards; Viktor would have known what a sanctuary was.

Finally, long after Jordan had lost all track of where he was in the castle, they came to a large, ornately carved and decorated door. DeGrange opened it, and then stepped back and gestured for Jordan to enter first. He did so, trying to put across with his upraised nose that he'd never expected anything else. The room before him was wonderfully spacious and luxuriously appointed. Thick carpets covered the floor, and brightly colored tapestries livened up the gleaming white walls. More than a dozen doors led off into adjoining rooms. Elegant and expensive furniture stood casually about, drawing attention to itself, though it seemed to have been assembled with little feeling or taste. Some of the pieces clashed so ostentatiously in style and period that Jordan felt like wincing. Having briefly been a nouveau riche during his more successful days, Jordan was a terrible snob where taste was concerned. He waited impatiently while the two guards busied themselves lighting candles under DeGrange's direction, and the moment they were finished, he gestured for them to leave with a quick jerk of his head. They did so, after bowing politely, and Jordan was finally left alone with Count Roderik and Brion DeGrange.

The moment the door had shut behind the two guards, Roderik sank limply into the nearest chair and fanned himself with his hand.

"So far, so good. What do you think of your quarters, Your Highness?"

"Very nice," said Jordan. "Very . . . opulent."

"Yes," said Roderik, smiling, "Viktor's never been known for his taste. And if you think this is bad, wait till you see the bedroom. Brion, dear fellow, allow me to introduce you to the Great Jordan."

Jordan grinned at DeGrange, and stuck out his hand. Degrange put his hands on his hips and studied Jordan coolly. "You made a good choice, Roderik. The likeness is exact, even down to his voice and the way he walks. He'll have to work on the arrogance, of course, but that should come easily enough to an actor. Does he understand what his job here entails?"

"Yes. He's been thoroughly briefed."

"I've no doubt he's word perfect on Viktor's background, but does he understand what we all stand to lose if he fouls up?"

"I'm sure he does, Brion."

"I wouldn't bet on it. I know his sort. He may style himself the Great Jordan, but deep down he's just like any other actor; idle, shiftless, and unreliable."

"If you don't stop talking about him as if he wasn't here," said Jordan calmly, "he is going to punch you right in the throat."

DeGrange looked at him. "You forget your place, actor," he said softly. "You're a hired man, nothing more. We own you, body and soul. Out there in public I may have to bow and scrape to you, but here in private you'll call me sir, and like it. Because if you don't, I'm going to hurt you. I know a lot about hurting people. I'm very good at it. Now get down on your knees where you belong, actor, and call me sir."

"Blow it out your ear," said Jordan.

DeGrange's hand dropped to the sword at his side. Jordan stepped forward and kicked him smartly, just below the knee. DeGrange grunted in surprise at the sudden blinding pain, and fell awkwardly to the floor as his leg collapsed under him. Jordan palmed one of his flare pellets and crushed it in his hand. Blue-white flames leapt up around his clenched fist without consuming it. Jordan leaned forward and stretched out his blazing hand toward DeGrange. The security man froze where he was. Beads of sweat formed on his face as Jordan stopped his hand only inches away from DeGrange's face.

"You will treat me with respect at all times," said Jordan quietly, "both in public and in private. I can't afford to have you give the game away by reacting wrongly to me at any point. You're not a good enough actor to cover it up. Now get up, and address me properly."

He didn't threaten the man; he didn't have to. He stepped back a few paces, and blew out the flames on his hand. His skin was tingling faintly, but as always he'd taken no harm from the heat. The protection spell he'd bought all those years ago was still good. It ought to be; it had cost enough. DeGrange got slowly to his feet, still favoring his bruised leg, and Jordan watched him carefully. He'd been bluffing, but he was fairly sure DeGrange didn't know that. He'd believe Jordan's implied threat because his own threat had been real. Jordan preferred to avoid violence whenever possible, but if he was to get any respect here, he was going to have to act the hard man or they'd walk right over him.

DeGrange nodded briefly to Jordan, and then looked at Roderik. "He'll do. When his hand burst into flames like that, I thought for one horrible moment that I'd got it wrong, and he really was Prince Viktor."

"As far as you're concerned, he is," said Roderik coldly. "He's quite right; we have to be consistent in our attitudes toward him, or we're bound to make a mistake at some crucial moment. Now apologize to him."

"Apologize to him? That jumped-up actor?"

"He is your prince," said Roderik. He locked eyes with DeGrange, and the security man's face went pale. "Do as you're told, Brion. Apologize to him."

DeGrange's jaw clenched, and the muscles in his face jumped spasmodically. His hands curled into shaking fists at his sides. And slowly, remorselessly, he turned and bowed stiffly to Jordan. "I apologize for my disrespectful words and actions, Your Highness."

"Then we'll say no more of it," said Jordan graciously. He cocked an eyebrow at Roderik. "Something happened there. You forced him to do that somehow."

"Oh yes," said Roderik easily. "It wasn't difficult. DeGrange was once a widely respected and even more widely feared outlaw. He commanded one of the largest bands of cutthroats and bandits Redhart has ever known. They were finally hunted down and tracked to their lair some five years ago. Most of them were slain, but Brion was taken alive. Rather than waste the man's obvious abilities, King Malcolm had Brion put under a geas: a controlling spell. Brion is compelled to function as head of castle security, and to do a good job of it. Originally he was answerable only to Malcolm, but with his death that control has passed to me."

"That was convenient" said Jordan.

"I arranged it that way," said Roderik. "A simple rider, attached to the original spell. So small and insignificant, you'd never know it was there, unless you were looking for it. Malcolm never knew, of course, and Brion was prevented from volunteering the information. And you needn't worry about someone else taking control away from me; I changed the spell so that no more riders are possible. Malcolm never did know much about High Magic, and how it worked. You can trust Brion implicitly, Jordan. He can no more betray us than he can grow wings and fly. Every now and again he tries to assert his independence, but all it takes is a few words from me to bring him back to heel. Isn't that right, Brion?"

"Yes, my lord," said DeGrange.

Jordan scowled at them both. He'd heard about the geas spell, but he'd never seen one in use before. Now that he had, he didn't like it at all. The geas seemed like nothing more than a particularly nasty form of slavery. A man in chains can at least dream of escaping someday, but what hope has a man got when his mind and soul are in chains? *Roderik, you'd better hope and pray your spell never breaks down*, Jordan thought coldly, *because if DeGrange ever gets loose, he'll make your death last a hell of a long time.*

"Now then, Brion," said Roderik pleasantly, "tell us what's been happening in our absence. How is Prince Viktor?"

"There's been no real change in his condition," said DeGrange. "He's still weak and feverish, though he remains lucid—for the most part. Neither the surgeons nor the magicians can figure out what's wrong with him."

"When do I get to see Prince Viktor?" said Jordan suddenly. "I'm going to have to meet him, and soon, if this impersonation is to work. So far, all I've had are your descriptions of what you think he's like. I need to see the real thing for myself."

"He'll be here any minute," said Roderik. "Sir Gawaine has gone to fetch him. Brion, what have Lewis and Dominic been up to?"

"Our spies have been keeping a close watch on them in public," said DeGrange, "but in private they're both protected by strong magical shields, just as we are. Their people are still tearing the castle apart searching for the missing crown and seal, but so far they've had no more luck than our agents. Lewis has been spending a lot of time with the Monk and Ironheart. Dominic and the Lady Elizabeth have been campaigning openly at Court, trying to drum up support among the nobles."

"Have they had much success?" asked Roderik, frowning.

"Quite a bit," said DeGrange. "The Court's never cared much for Lewis. Princes are supposed to have a taste for dueling, but he takes it too far. And he's always been too devious for his own good. These days, nobody trusts Lewis further than they can throw him, particularly since he became allied with the Monk."

"I keep hearing that name," said Jordan. "He's a sorcerer, right?"

"We think so," said Roderik. "It's probably best if you meet him for yourself and make up your own mind. The Monk is a rather . . . disturbing person.

Carry on, Brion. How does the Court feel about Viktor?"

"Prince Viktor lost most of his support when he was sent into internal exile," said DeGrange. "And since his illness, he's been unable to get about and rebuild his influence. There's been a lot of gossip about his absence from Court of late, but nothing we can't handle. However, all this leaves Dominic in a very strong position. With the Lady Elizabeth's help, he's been building his power base practically unopposed."

"Wait just a minute," said Jordan. "According to Sir Gawaine, Dominic is insane."

"I wouldn't argue with that," said DeGrange, "but the current attitude at Court seems to be that the Lady Elizabeth is sane and tough enough for both of them. And while Dominic is a little . . . strange on some subjects, his mind appears to be perfectly clear and lucid when it comes to political matters."

The main door swung suddenly open, and the three of them looked around sharply. Roderik took one look at the hooded figure in the doorway, and got to his feet and bowed. DeGrange bowed, too, and Jordan suddenly realized who the figure must be. The newcomer moved slowly forward into the room, supported on the one side by Sir Gawaine and on the other by a beautiful young woman. One of the guards outside pulled the door shut behind them. The hooded man raised a shaking hand and pushed back his robe's cowl to reveal Prince Viktor's face. Jordan stared at him. It was the same face he'd first seen in Roderik's mirror, back in Bannerwick. It had the same sardonic features, the same crooked nose, and the same jet black hair. But this man wore the face differently. There was a weak petulance in the mouth and eyes, and deep frown lines clustered together between the scowling eyebrows. His skin was very pale, and slick with a sheen of fresh sweat. The woman at his side helped him into the nearest chair, and Jordan seized the chance to study her.

She was tall for a woman, about five foot nine or ten, with a tight boyish figure that was still openly sensual. She couldn't have been more than nineteen or twenty, and was brimming over with life and energy. She had a long mane of light brown hair that fell almost to her belt, pulled back from a sharply etched, intelligent face. She was beautiful and graceful, but Jordan felt a sudden chill when she looked up suddenly and their eyes met. He saw ambition written clearly in her face, together with a ruthless determination. In that moment, Jordan knew her mind as though he'd known her for years, and in a way he had. She had the look of every hard-edged leading lady he'd ever worked with: the kind of woman who always made sure no one else in the cast sang better than she did. When she broke the gaze and looked away, he felt almost relieved. There was an unwavering strength that burned in her like a bright flame, implicit in every move she made—even in the soft, soothing murmurs she was bestowing on Prince Viktor. Jordan didn't need to be told who she was. She had to be the Lady Heather Tawney, the latest love in Viktor's life. Prince Viktor finally got himself settled comfortably, and looked hard at Jordan.

"Come closer," he said finally. His voice was surprisingly strong and resonant, despite his illness. "Let me look at you. It's a strange thing to see your own face on another man's body."

Jordan moved forward obediently and stood before the prince's chair, letting Viktor and Heather look him over. Their eyes weighed and measured him as impersonally as a butcher judging a side of beef.

"Say something," said the prince.

"I am happy to meet Your Highness," said Jordan smoothly. "I hope I meet with your approval."

Viktor frowned. "He looks all right, but his voice is too high. I don't sound like that."

"Hush, Viktor dear, his voice is perfect," said the Lady Heather. "He sounds just like you, honestly."

Viktor shrugged, but said nothing more. Jordan looked to Roderick for a cue, but the count avoided his eyes. Jordan looked back at the prince. There was no doubt that the man's illness was eating away at him inside. He didn't look to have lost much weight, but his feebleness was apparent in every shaky movement.

The Lady Heather patted Viktor comfortingly on the arm, and glared at Roderik and DeGrange. "It's been weeks since Viktor first fell ill, and you still haven't found out what's causing it! How much longer is it going to take?"

"We're doing everything we can," said DeGrange calmly. "Our magicians are adamant there's no trace of any sorcerous attack; not even anything as vague as a curse. The new quarters we've moved him to are a closely guarded secret, and are warded against every kind of magic. He couldn't be any safer if he was in a sanctuary. In fact, right now Prince Viktor is probably the most securely guarded person in Castle Midnight—and that includes the Regent. His food is prepared freshly every day, under Robert Argent's supervision. Up until he left with Count Roderik, Argent even went so far as to taste the prince's food first, in his presence. Since Argent is still well and hale, I think we can rule out poison. I don't see what else security can do, my Lady Heather. As far as any of us can tell, Prince Viktor has simply contracted a rather nasty illness, and that is the province of the castle surgeons, not security."

"The surgeons are doing everything they can, Heather," said Roderik. "We all are. It's only a matter of time . . ."

Heather sniffed disparagingly, but said nothing more. Viktor roused himself, and fixed Roderik with his fever-bright eyes.

"Gawaine tells me we're no nearer finding the crown and the seal. Are you sure you've checked all the places I suggested?"

"Yes, Your Highness," said Roderik. "There's still no sign of them. But then again, there's nothing to suggest your brothers are any closer to finding them either."

Viktor stirred irritably in his chair. "They've got to be here somewhere. I thought I knew all Dad's secret hiding places . . . but then, anything I'd know, Lewis and Dominic would know . . ."

"Wait a minute," said Jordan excitedly, "I've just had an idea! Castle Midnight is lousy with ghosts, right? So why don't we just call up King Malcolm's ghost and ask him where he hid the crown and seal?"

Everyone in the room looked at him with varying degrees of exasperation.

"Don't you think we would already have done it, if it was at all possible?" said Roderik cuttingly. "All members of the royal line are protected by spells from their birth, precisely to make sure that their rest won't be disturbed once they've died. There's nothing like everyday contact with ghosts to make you very determined never to become one."

Viktor snorted angrily, and everyone turned their attention back to him. He was still scowling, and rubbing his hands slowly together, as though they were bothered by a vague ache. "Everything's getting out of hand, and I'm helpless to do anything about it. Ah well, just means we'll have to work harder, that's all. Roderik, they tell me Dominic's been busy at Court. Him and his tame bitch, Elizabeth. He's making too many friends. We can't allow that. You, actor!"

"Yes, Your Highness?"

"Do you think you're up to appearing as me at Court?"

"I'm ready, Your Highness. What do you want me to do?"

"Sway some of those fools at Court over to our side. Be calm and charming and persuasive. Promise them anything, for now. Roderik, dig up all the dirt you can on Dominic, and see that it reaches the right ears. If you can't find anything nasty enough, invent something. We haven't time to be fussy. Lewis has magic on his side, with Ironheart and the Monk. Dominic has Elizabeth's cunning, which is no less competent for all its deviousness. And both Lewis and Dominic have a great many guards and men-at-arms under their command. I have one company of guards, a little sorcery, and damn all support at Court. All of

which means we have to work twice as hard and twice
as dirty, just to stay in the race." He cocked a sardonic eye at Jordan. "You look surprised, actor. My
body may be ill, but I assure you that my mind is still
sound. Gawaine!"

"Yes, sire."

"Talk to the unattached guards and men-at-arms.
Sound out how many might be willing to fight for us,
and how many more might be swayed by promises of
loot or patronage. When you've done that, start thinking of ways to get at my dear brothers. I've no doubt
their protection is as good as mine, if not better, but
there's always the chance they've left some small
opening we can take advantage of. I won't feel secure
until Lewis and Dominic are dead and safely buried
in their graves."

"You'd kill your own brothers?" said Jordan slowly.

Viktor looked at him tiredly. "My God, you're actually shocked. Listen, fool, either Lewis or Dominic is
almost certainly responsible for the death of our father. He and I may have had our disagreements, but
I was still fond of the old man, and I will avenge his
murder. No matter what the cost. Besides, Dominic
is barking mad and always has been. And Lewis . . .
I think I'd prefer it if he was mad. It might make
some of his excesses easier to stomach. I've no love
for my brothers, actor. I knew them too well. The
world will be a better place for their passing." Viktor
suddenly stopped and smiled crookedly. "And anyway, they stand between me and the throne. I've
waited a long time for this chance, and I won't be
stopped now—not by anything or anyone. I will sit
upon the throne of Redhart if I have to see all the
corridors of this castle soaked in blood to do it!" He
broke off suddenly, racked by a long coughing fit.
Heather spoke to him softly and comfortingly, and
dabbed the sweat from his forehead with a handkerchief. Viktor finally got himself under control again
and sank back in his chair, his eyes closed. When he
spoke again, his voice was quiet and very tired. "Roderik, Gawaine, get me the crown and the seal. I've

had enough excuses, I want results. Get them—I don't
care how. Spend as much as you need to, kill as many
as you have to. Heather, I'm tired. Get me out of
here. I'm tired . . ."

"Of course, darling. You lean on Gawaine and me,
and we'll get you back to your new quarters."

Between them, she and Gawaine got Viktor to his
feet again, and Heather pulled the cowl forward so
that it hid his features. They left the room in silence,
and the door closed quietly behind them. Jordan
looked at Roderik.

"So that's Prince Viktor."

"Yes. What did you think of him?"

"He's certainly . . . determined. Is he really being
poisoned?"

"No," said DeGrange flatly. "The food comes from
Argent's personal supplies. He's even tasted it himself, in Viktor's presence. The prince is flinching at
shadows."

"And now, if you'll excuse us for a moment," said
Roderik, "Brion and I need to discuss Viktor's instructions, so we'll leave you to settle into your new
quarters. We won't be gone long, and the guards will
stay outside your door to see that you're not disturbed. If you need anything, there's a bellpull by the
fireplace. Someone will come when you call."

"Fine by me," said Jordan. "I think I'll do a little
exploring. I've never seen a room with so many doors.
If I'm not back in an hour, send a pack of hounds in
to look for me."

Roderik smiled politely. DeGrange just looked at
Jordan. After a moment they bowed formally, and
left. The lock made a hard, final sound as the key was
turned from the other side. Jordan shook his head
slowly. It was times like this that made him wish he'd
taken up a career in carpentry, like his mother
wanted.

Robert Argent sat alone in his study, leafing
through the letters and business papers that had accu-
mulated in his absence. He'd been doing it for some

time, but he wasn't getting anywhere. He realized he'd just read the same paragraph for the third time, and it still hadn't sunk in. He dropped the letter onto his desk, and rubbed tiredly at his eyes. He knew he ought to be concentrating; the letter was important, they all were, but none of it seemed to matter much anymore. The man who sweated his guts out over every deal, who squeezed each bargain till it screamed to get the last drop of credit: that was a different Robert Argent. That man lived only in the past now. Argent missed him.

He sat back in his chair and looked around him. It was a medium-sized, simply appointed study; modest but comfortable. The carpet had been a gift from his late wife, and the portraits on the walls had been painted by his daughter-in-law. They were quite good, some of them. With the money he was making these days, he could easily afford living quarters that were much more ostentatious, but he'd never seen the point. He was a man of simple tastes, and always had been. It might have been different if he'd married again, but somehow he'd never got around to it. He could have married again: among the merchant community, political marriages were even more popular than among the aristocracy, but he no longer believed in arranged marriages. He believed in love and romance, though there'd been precious little of either in his life.

When he'd been younger, he'd pictured many possible futures for himself, but this hadn't been one of them. Argent smiled slightly, remembering his early days with Rod, more than twenty years ago, when his friend had been plain Rod Crichton, instead of Count Roderik. They'd had some times together, the two of them . . . One night in Hub City, they'd been thrown out of fourteen inns in less than three hours; a record that still stood. Argent sighed, and looked listlessly at the wine bottle on his desk, still unopened. He'd always liked his wine, but of late he'd lost even that.

When Rod had first come to him with his lunatic scheme of finding a double for the prince, it had seemed like old times all over again. The two of them together, against an uncaring world. And, of course, a chance to rebuild his fortunes after the failure of their last great scheme. But the deal had gone sour, right from the beginning. Not his fault this time, or even Rod's; it had just turned out that the world had grown stronger and nastier than he remembered, while he had grown old and soft.

Robert Argent stared unseeingly at the wall before him; a man with too much past, and no future at all.

Jordan wandered around the huge room, looking for somewhere to settle. The room seemed uncomfortably large and echoing now that he'd been left alone in it. He trailed his fingertips across the furniture, trying to get the feel of the place. Something about the furnishings and fittings just didn't add up. The look of the room was a total mess: a hopeless mixture of styles. It was as though every item had been chosen to impress the viewer with its appearance and value, but without caring about the overall picture they presented. The room was more like a showroom than a place where someone actually lived. Jordan shrugged. Maybe that was how Viktor saw it . . .

Jordan crossed over to the nearest window, and pulled back one of the drapes to look out. Night had fallen, and the stars were out. He could faintly hear a wind blowing outside, though the thick glass reduced the sound to the barest murmur. The night looked cold and forbidding, and Jordan shuddered briefly as he let the drape fall back and turned away from the window. So far, Castle Midnight was proving as gloomy and uncomfortable as he'd thought it would. He hadn't come across an architect yet who could design a castle that was fit to live in. All in all, Jordan was beginning to feel thoroughly depressed. He hadn't seen a single happy face or cheerful sight since he entered this great hulking pile of black stone.

And then his ears pricked up as he heard something moving, not far away. He glared quickly around, but he couldn't see anything. It could always be a mouse

or a rat . . . but it hadn't been that sort of sound.
He listened carefully, but the sound wasn't repeated.
Jordan shrugged uncomfortably. An old castle like this
was bound to make the odd settling noise from time
to time. He spotted a drinks cabinet set against the
opposite wall, and moved determinedly toward it. He
felt very strongly that after the day he'd had, he was
owed a drink or two. Or several. He pulled open the
rococo cabinet doors, and then stared nonplussed at
the row of cut-glass decanters before him. They had
all been fashioned into the shapes of strange fantasti-
cal creatures, such as unicorns, wyverns, or cocka-
trices. The shapes were grotesque and distorted, and,
more importantly, there were no labels to describe
the contents. Jordan smiled briefly. Of course there
weren't any labels; Viktor would know what his own
decanters held. And the shapes might be a bit queer,
but then Viktor's taste in furniture wasn't that hot
either.

Jordan picked up the nearest decanter, and hefted
it in his hand. The cut glass was a solid weight, and
hideously expensive. He let his mind play idly with a
few schemes for making off with the decanters, as a
sort of insurance in case things went wrong later, and
then reluctantly discarded the notion. He stood to
make fifty thousand ducats out of this impersonation,
and he wasn't about to risk that for a few cut-glass
decanters. He pulled out the heavy stopper, and gripping the decanter tightly to make sure he wouldn't
drop it, he sniffed cautiously at the dark purple wine
inside. It smelled strong and acidic, not to mention
malevolent, so he replaced the stopper. The next decanter he tried held plum brandy, and Jordan passed
on that as well. He'd tried the sickly stuff once, and
the hangover lasted four days. The third decanter held
a good malt whiskey, and Jordan was just about to
pour himself a very large glass when he heard the
sound of sudden movement again. It sounded louder,
and closer.

Jordan whirled around, sword in hand, and put his
back against the drinks cabinet. The room lay open

and apparently harmless before him. All the doors were still shut, and no one could have got past the guards outside without his hearing. Jordan remembered some of the things Gawaine had told him about ghosts and monsters, the Real and the Unreal, and a slow chill ran through him. He checked the distance between him and the main door, swallowed hard, and wondered if the guards would hear him if he screamed for help. He took a hold of himself and shook his head angrily. So far he hadn't seen anything that looked even remotely threatening, and a right twit he'd look if he summoned the guards and then had to admit it was only his imagination . . .

He realized he was still holding the decanter in his left hand, and put it back in the drinks cabinet. He looked cautiously around him. The room was very quiet. Jordan moved slowly forward, holding his sword out before him. The nearest door lay to his right. If he remembered Roderik's gesture correctly, that was the bedchamber. What better place for an assassin to be hiding . . . Jordan padded quietly over to the door, and pressed his ear against the wood. He thought he heard a few quiet, furtive sounds on the other side of the door, but he couldn't be certain. He took a firm hold on the doorknob with his left hand, and turned it slowly. He waited until he was sure the catch had disengaged, and then eased the door open an inch. He let go of the doorknob very carefully, and wiped his sweaty palm on his trouser leg. He still couldn't hear anything. His breathing was getting faster, and his legs were just a little shaky. He began to wonder if the assassin was standing on the other side of the door, listening to him, waiting for him to make the wrong move. Jordan decided he wasn't going to think about that. He also decided he'd better do something fast, before what little was left of his nerve disappeared completely. He took a firm grip on his sword hilt, kicked the door wide open, and stormed into the bedchamber.

The large dog by the bed looked up, startled by Jordan's sudden entrance. It started to back away, and then stopped and wagged its tail hopefully. Jordan looked quickly around the bedroom, but there was no one else there. He put his sword away and shook his head, grinning. All that fuss over a pet dog . . . he was getting paranoid. He walked slowly toward the dog, holding out his hand and making quiet encouraging noises. The dog looked at him for a moment with its head cocked slightly to one side, and then bounded forward to greet him, its tail wagging furiously.

Jordan sat on the edge of the bed and petted the dog happily. It pushed against his legs and showed every sign of intending to stay there for some time. Jordan told the dog it was a good boy, and it looked up at him, grinning in agreement. It was a good-looking dog, obviously pedigree, and apparently quite happy, though it was rather hard to tell with a bloodhound. The face wasn't really equipped to register happiness. And it had the saddest eyes Jordan had ever seen. The dog was obviously well trained as well as friendly, in that it hadn't tried to jump up on him the moment it met him, and Jordan's estimate of Viktor went up a little. Anyone who kept a fine animal like this as a pet couldn't be all bad. He just wished someone had mentioned it was there . . . He grinned down at the bloodhound, and it put its head into his lap for him to scratch behind his ears.

Jordan looked about him, taking in his bedchamber. He hadn't seen anything this luxurious since he'd sung for his supper in a top rank brothel in Hub City. There was no denying it was comfortable, very comfortable, but it was also gauche, gaudy, and almost terminally sensuous. His boots practically disappeared into the thick pile carpet, and the bed was so soft it was like sitting on a cloud. In fact, he'd sunk so deeply into it, he wasn't sure if he could get up again without help. As usual, the fittings and furnishings clashed loudly, but Jordan was growing inured to that. His gaze fell on the huge blocky wardrobe that covered most of one wall, and a thought occurred to him. Sooner or later he was going to be meeting the important people at Court, and when he did he'd better not be wearing his present attire. After several days on the road, his clothes smelled strongly of sweat, dust, and a few other things he didn't even want to think about. He was surprised flowers hadn't wilted in their vases when he walked past them. He stretched slowly, feeling his back muscles grate against each other. Presumably there was a bathroom somewhere in this suite, but he'd look for it later, when he had the time, and when he was fairly sure he wouldn't be interrupted. Roderik or the others could be back any time, and he hated being interrupted in the bath. Right now, he'd settle for a change of clothes.

Jordan pushed the dog gently to one side, and struggled up off the bed. The wardrobe's doors slid smoothly back on their runners, and Jordan stared in amazement at more clothes than he'd ever seen in one place in his life. He'd worked in theaters that had smaller wardrobe stocks than this. There were robes and outfits for every conceivable occasion, and a few so outrageous they had to be either strictly traditional, or left over from some best-forgotten masquerade. Jordan stripped off his travel-stained clothes, and tossed them casually in the direction of the bed. He kept his shirt, even though it was no longer really a good fit for his new body. He'd have to adapt some of Viktor's shirts when he had the chance, but for now the hidden pockets in the sleeves, with their flare pellets and smoke bombs, were an advantage he didn't intend to give up. He chose an outfit pretty much at random, and dressed quickly. The clothes felt almost sinfully comfortable, and fitted perfectly. Jordan struck a pose in front of the wardrobe's full-length mirror, and sighed wistfully. It had been a long time since he could afford clothes like these. The rich scarlet color really suited him, particularly when set off by the billowing burgundy cloak.

There was a loud crash from the other room as the main door swung open, and Jordan frowned as he heard Roderik calling anxiously for him. Surely something couldn't have gone wrong already? He hurried out into the main room, and found Roderik and Gawaine waiting for him. Jordan's heart sank as he took in their worried expressions.

"What is it?" he asked quickly. "What's happened?"

"The Regent has summoned all three princes to attend a special audience at Court," said Roderik. "The last time he did that, it was to inform them of their father's sudden death. I hate to think what he might have to say this time."

"Does he know about us?" said Jordan. "About me?"

"I don't see how," said Gawaine. "But that doesn't mean much where the Regent's concerned. The man has an uncanny knack for discovering things that everyone else had thought were safely hidden. It wouldn't matter so much if he wasn't so damned honest. Beats me how he's survived at Court all these years."

Jordan worried his lower lip between his teeth and thought furiously. If he remembered his briefing correctly, with the king's death it was traditional for a Regent, chosen in advance by the king, to rule over the day-to-day problems of the kingdom, until a new king was declared. The Regent at this time was one Count William Howerd, first cousin to King Malcolm. A fair man, but a hard man, had been Roderik's summing up. And too honest for everyone's good, Gawaine had added.

"How soon does he want to see me?" said Jordan. "And where's DeGrange and Argent? Shouldn't they be in on this?"

"DeGrange is busy checking into whether there really is a traitor among our people," said Gawaine. "He'll join us when he can."

"I've sent word to Robert," said Roderik, "but we can't wait for him. The Regent wants to see you immediately. Lewis and Dominic are probably already on their way to Court by now. We must leave at once, Your Highness. It would look very bad if you were to arrive late."

Jordan nodded, and let them usher him out of the

main door and into the corridor. The two guards followed along as an honor escort. It was only then that Jordan remembered he'd left the dog behind in the bedroom. *Ah well,* he thought, *I could hardly have taken it into Court with me. I just hope it doesn't crap on the carpet while I'm gone.* He glanced at Sir Gawaine, striding hurriedly along beside him.

"What do you think of the new clothes? Is it a suitable outfit for meeting the Regent?"

"It'll do," said Gawaine. "You've worn worse, in the past."

Jordan scowled. "You're a great help. Look, what if the Regent really has found out about us? What can we do?"

"I don't know about you," said Gawaine, "but if things do turn nasty, I personally will head for the nearest window, crash right through it without pausing, and keep on running until I reach a different country. Somehow I don't think the Regent will see the funny side of all this."

"Terrific," said Jordan.

He thought hard as they hurried down yet another corridor. Of all the confusing details in his new role, the missing will interested him the most. Whoever took it must have either wanted to know who the king had named as his successor, or believed the will held a clue as to the whereabouts of the crown and the seal. But it seemed clear that neither Lewis nor Dominic had the crown and seal: if they had, they'd have made themselves king by now. Jordan didn't like the way his thoughts were heading. If the princes didn't have the will, then who did? Could there be some other, separate party at work?

Jordan looked up, startled, as his party came to a halt before the huge double doors that led into the Great Hall. Two servants swung open the doors, and stood rigidly to attention as the herald announced the arrival of Prince Viktor and his party to the assembled Court. The packed hall fell silent as Jordan, Roderik, and Gawaine stood a moment in the great doorway, taking in the scene, and then a slow ripple moved through the Court as the men bowed and the women curtsied. For a moment, Jordan wanted to look behind him to see who was there, and then he realized they were paying homage to him, Prince Viktor of Redhart. He nodded curtly in response, and the courtiers relaxed a little. Jordan strode unhurriedly forward into the hall, and Roderik and Gawaine moved with him. The two guards fell back a few paces, to give them the illusion of privacy. The courtiers chatted quietly on unimportant matters, but Jordan noticed that their eyes never moved far from him or his party. He stopped and looked boredly around him, doing his best to project an air of total indifference. Roderik leaned close to murmur in his ear.

"Lewis and Dominic don't seem to have arrived yet. That's ominous. Given their head start, they should have been here long before us. I'm going back to find DeGrange, and see what's happening. Gawaine will look after you. For the moment, don't take any risks. Just scowl at everyone and say nothing. They'll accept that as normal behavior, particularly after a bad day's hunting. I'll be back with you as soon as I can."

He bowed formally to Jordan, and left unhurriedly. Only another actor would have spotted the telltale stiffness of tension in Roderik's back and shoulders. Jordan looked casually about him, keeping his face carefully calm and neutral. This wasn't the first Court he'd ever visited, but it was the largest hall he'd ever seen. It had to be easily two hundred feet long, and half again as wide, and was packed from wall to wall with brightly costumed courtiers. With their vivid colors and never-ending gossiping, they reminded Jordan of so many chattering parrots.

At the far end of the hall, stood a roughly carved marble throne, set atop a raised marble dais. Beneath the throne, clearly visible between the squat legs, was a roughly hewn block of weather-beaten stone. Jordan studied it thoughtfully. Presumably this was the Stone to which the crown and the seal had to be presented: the Stone that was the heart and focus of Castle Midnight's magic. It didn't look like much, but then nei-

ther did the throne. Its surface was cracked and pitted,
and the bas-relief carvings were crude and functional.
Even with the thick cushion on the seat, the throne
looked very uncomfortable to actually sit on. It looked
strangely out of place in the ostentatious elegance of
the Great Hall. Jordan let his gaze drift casually over
the wood-paneled walls. It wouldn't do for him to be
caught gawking like a tourist. But there was no denying that the woodwork was very impressive. Each
panel of lightly stained beech wood held fantastic and
intricate carvings of the people and animals of Redhart,
at work and at play. The detail was incredible. Jordan
wished he had a sketch pad with him. He studied the
richly wax-polished floor and the wonderfully carved
and painted domed ceiling, and felt a sudden desire
to turn and run from the hall. How could he ever
hope to fool people who spent their days in glorious
surroundings like this, taking its beauty for granted?
Surely they must have recognized him immediately for
the crude common impostor he was, and were only
waiting for the right moment to cry out on him?

Something of this must have shown in his face, for
Sir Gawaine was suddenly at his elbow, leaning forward solicitously.

"Are you all right, sire? You look a trifle pale."

"I'm fine," said Jordan quickly. "Fine. I could use
a drink, though."

The knight bowed. "I will fetch you one immediately, sire."

He moved off toward a buffet table set to one side.
Jordan felt a sudden urge to call Gawaine back rather
than be left on his own in the midst of strangers, but
his pride wouldn't let him. He was the Great Jordan,
damn it. He was the actor and they were the audience:
he was in control. They only saw what he wanted them
to see. The hall was certainly impressive, but he'd
seen better. At the peak of his career he'd performed
at Forest Castle, and Duke Alric's Palace in Hillsdown. Three nights at each, and not once had he
failed to get a standing ovation. He could handle these
people. What had Roderik said: speak to no one and

scowl at everyone. Easy. He caught the eye of the nearest courtier, and let his features fall into his most intimidating glare. He used it mostly when walking through strange market towns and bazaars, when he wasn't too sure of the local mood. It was his *I am poor but incredibly violent so there is absolutely no point in trying to rob me* look. Jordan had put a lot of work into that glare, and was quietly proud of it. It never failed to have an effect. On a good day he could get people parting to either side of him like waves. The glare seemed to be going down well at Court, too. The courtiers around him apparently felt a sudden need to be somewhere else, and the man Jordan had chosen as the direct target for his glare had gone distinctly pale. Gawaine returned with a glass of wine, and Jordan gulped at it thirstily.

"Ease up on the glare a little," murmured Gawaine. "We don't want to scare them too much—we still want some of them as our allies. And remember, you're supposed to be recovering from a chill. You're looking a bit too strong at the moment."

"Understood," said Jordan quietly. "Just as a matter of interest, why am I getting such strong reactions? That guy there looks scared to death. All right, it's a good glare, but not that good."

"On a previous occasion, shortly before you went into exile, one of the courtiers was foolish enough to ridicule your choice of clothing. You gave him a chance to apologize, and when he refused you called up your fire magic and fried the man where he stood."

Jordan looked at Gawaine, but there was nothing in the knight's face to suggest that he was exaggerating.

"What happened?"

"The man died, sire. Eventually."

"I gathered that. I meant, what happened to the prince?"

"Nothing."

"Nothing? He wasn't punished, or disciplined?"

"Of course not, sire. There wasn't even a trial. You are a prince of the Realm. And you did give him a chance to apologize."

Jordan thought about that. He didn't like the taste of it at all. In his time, Jordan had played all kinds of aristocrats, from lords to barons to dukes to kings, and every single one of them had followed the old ways of duty and honor. It wasn't enough to have noble blood: a ruler had to show noble behavior to justify his exalted position. A noble could only rule with the consent of his subjects: the alternative was a land permanently wracked by civil wars. That was the tale he always told, the tale he'd told so often he had finally come to believe it himself. Jordan suddenly felt very tired. The truths he was finding at Castle Midnight kept hitting him like hammer blows. Perhaps the more so because deep down he'd always known them.

He knew about King Malcolm. Most people did. The king had fancied himself a general, and had sent his troops into battle after battle to test his own theories of warfare. At first he took on the bandits and outlaws in his own land, and then, as his confidence grew, he moved against his neighboring countries in a series of border campaigns intended to spread the boundaries of Redhart. With his elemental magic to aid him, he won more battles than he lost, but still the campaigns cost him more in revenue and men than his newly conquered lands could replace. And so it went. King Malcolm had not been a cruel man, as kings went, but it could not be said he was greatly loved by his people for all his victories. His sons appeared to be cast from the same mold: only worse. *Dominic is mad, and Lewis is vile . . .* and now it seemed Viktor was no better. It came as no real surprise. Jordan had seen a dangerous weakness in the prince's face, for all his brave words, added to a petulance that changed all too easily into arrogance and viciousness.

I will sit upon the throne of Redhart if I have to see all the corridors of this castle awash in blood to do it . . .

Jordan sighed inwardly. His dreams and illusions had never really been any more than that. His audiences might have believed in the heroic nobles he had portrayed for them, but he never had. Not deep down, where it counted. The aristocracy held its power and position by force of arms and magic, nothing more. Anything else was just a dream . . .

Jordan drank the last of the wine Gawaine had brought him. It was too sweet for his taste, but he was thirsty and it was something to do. He felt restive without any planned moves or actions to fall back on. He strolled casually forward, headed nowhere in particular, and the courtiers fell unobtrusively back before him. Gawaine moved silently at his side. It didn't have to be just a dream, Jordan suddenly realized. He was a prince now, and could act as a prince should. But if he did, he'd be acting out of character, and could be revealed as an impostor. Besides, there was Count Roderik to consider. Viktor might think he was in charge, but it was clear to Jordan that Roderik was the real brains and power in this conspiracy. It wouldn't surprise Jordan to discover that Roderik was using Viktor, rather than the other way around.

Jordan looked around for another drink. He was damned if he was going to get through this sober.

Brion DeGrange sat in his study, nursing a glass of wine and staring at it bitterly. There was a time he'd been a real drinking man, but not anymore. The geas wouldn't let him do anything to himself that might interfere with his duties as head of security. The bastard spell wouldn't let him get drunk, no matter how much he needed to. One glass of wine an evening, sometimes two. A mug of beer with his dinner. And that was it. He couldn't get drunk, he couldn't run away, and he couldn't even kill himself, let alone the men who'd done this to him. DeGrange scowled at his half-empty glass. He might have been an outlaw, but at least he usually granted his enemies the kindness of a quick death. And he'd never kept slaves.

One day, he would have his revenge. One day.

Until then, he worked hard as head of castle security. Partly because the geas demanded it, but mainly because it wasn't in his nature to do sloppy work. If

he did something, his pride demanded that he do it
well. He'd never been able to settle for being second
best. Even if that meant killing the man in front of
him. DeGrange grinned wolfishly. That was what had
got him outlawed, all those years ago, and he'd never
regretted it. The bastard shouldn't have got in his way.
He winced as a familiar headache began, pounding
dully in his temples. The geas was warning him. If he
persisted in dwelling on his past as an outlaw and the
things he'd done, the headache would grow worse,
until the pain drove him screaming into unconscious-
ness. He'd learned the hard way that there was no
profit in trying to fight the geas.

He concentrated on calm, neutral thoughts, with the
bitter ease of long practice. When all was said and
done, security at Castle Midnight was never less than
interesting. On a good day he could lose himself in
his work and go for hours on end without remembering he was a slave. The pain in his temples slowly
began to subside, and DeGrange sighed heavily. He
drank his wine, hardly noticing the taste. He was getting maudlin again. It was the approaching autumn
that did it. He'd always loved riding through the forests in the fall, the changing leaves hanging around
the trees like bronzed tatters . . . he missed the forests. He hadn't been able to set foot outside Castle
Midnight in seven years.

He looked about him, taking in the bare walls of
his study. It wasn't a large room, but it was warm,
comfortable, and private. He'd lived in much worse,
in his time. He called it his study, but actually it was
his bedroom and living room as well. No sense in
wasting precious space on a slave, after all. It wasn't
as if he was going to object. The room would have
been too small for two people, but there was only
DeGrange. There had been a woman once, who'd
warmed his heart and given him a reason for living,
but the king's men had cut her down when they
stormed his camp. If she'd lived, she would have been
twenty-nine this year. DeGrange hadn't found anyone

else after her. The geas saw to that. A close personal attachment might interfere with his duties.

DeGrange shook his head slowly, tears burning unshed in his eyes, gripped again by a familiar feeling of utter frustration. He was trapped, he couldn't escape, and he couldn't even strike out at his jailers. DeGrange threw his glass aside, and his hands clenched into fists. He struck out at the tabletop before him, slamming his fists against the unyielding wood over and over again. When he finally stopped, his hands were bruised and bloody and the warning headache throbbed fiercely in his temples. He hated himself for his weakness, but he hated Count Roderik more, and finally that hatred gave him the strength to regain his calm again. One day the geas might relax its grip on him, if only for a moment, or Roderik might make some foolish mistake. When that chance came, DeGrange was determined not to miss it.

There was a peremptory knock at his door. DeGrange quickly thrust his bloody hands out of sight under the table. The door swung open, and Count Roderik walked in without waiting to be asked. The door was never locked: DeGrange wasn't allowed a key.

"What can I do for you, my lord?" said DeGrange. His voice was carefully calm and polite.

"The Regent's summoned Lewis, Dominic, and Viktor to a special audience at Court," said Roderik. "Why didn't you warn me about this?"

"It's the first I've heard about it, my lord." DeGrange frowned. "I should have heard something . . . Either this was a very sudden decision, or he's discovered that I'm your man first, and his second."

"Lewis and Dominic weren't at Court when the actor and I got there." Roderik paced back and forth in the small room. "They should have got there first. What's keeping them?"

"I can venture an educated guess," said DeGrange calmly. He loved to see Roderik getting rattled. "Lewis and Dominic's private troops have been jockeying for position in the castle for days. If the Regent's troops weren't there to enforce the peace, there'd have been open fighting in the corridors by now. Presumably Lewis and Dominic are waiting till the last possible moment to leave their own areas, while their troops make sure it's safe for them to walk to Court."

"Yes. That makes sense." Roderik stopped pacing, and looked steadily at DeGrange. "What do you make of the Great Jordan, now you've had time to think about him?"

"He's arrogant and conceited, like all actors, but that's not exactly a handicap to impersonating a prince. He's untrustworthy, of course—he has no real reason not to be. I've no doubt he'd betray us in a moment if anyone put any pressure on him. But he seems competent enough. Have you left him alone at Court?"

"Of course not; Gawaine's with him."

"That should help to keep him safe from assassins, but if the actor's to deal successfully with the courtiers, he's going to need some more subtle help. Perhaps the Lady Heather . . ."

"Good idea. I'll go and see her now. What would I do without you, Brion?"

Roderik smiled at him pleasantly, and turned to leave. DeGrange sat very still. Blood dripped slowly from his clenched fists. The door had just started to close behind Roderik when DeGrange surged to his feet and snatched for the sword at his side. The pain hit him before his hand could even close around the hilt, and he collapsed back onto his chair, moaning and clutching at his head. He glared dully at the closed door as the pain died slowly away. Roderik hadn't even noticed. DeGrange sat slumped in his chair, and his agonized breathing slowly settled.

One day, he promised himself. *One day . . .*

Jordan was getting impatient. He'd been waiting in the Great Hall for almost half an hour, and there was still no sign of the Regent, or Lewis, or Dominic. The Court was buzzing with conversation, but he didn't dare join in. He didn't know enough yet to be sure of not saying the wrong thing. Gawaine stood at his side, calm and unmoving. Jordan had noticed that everyone else at Court tended to give Gawaine plenty of room. He didn't seem to be much liked at Court, but he was certainly respected. There was a stir among the nearby courtiers, and Jordan looked around in time to see Prince Lewis's entrance.

His men came in first: a dozen guards in full chain mail, with drawn swords. They all had the hard, untrusting faces and professional wariness of the trained bodyguard. They took their time assuring themselves there was nothing immediately threatening in the Great Hall, then they fell back to either side of the doors as Lewis walked in. He wore his usual brown and green, but a quiet murmur swept through the Court as they saw the chain mail vest he was also wearing. For a prince to wear armor at Court was an open insult to the Regent. Lewis was saying very clearly that he no longer trusted the Regent to protect his life or his interests at Court. The courtiers bowed and curtsied, and Lewis acknowledged them with a vague wave of his hand. The guards watched the courtiers carefully. Jordan studied Lewis as openly as he could without staring. He'd been told about Lewis till he could have recited the man's life history in his sleep, but Jordan was a great believer in first impressions. Lewis looked normal enough, even handsome in his way, but there was a strained, intense look to the man that grated subtly on Jordan's nerves. It was as though Lewis was on a tight leash that he might slip at any moment, and run loose, out of all control. Jordan also didn't like the sleek musculature of Lewis's chest and arms that spoke of the trained swordsman, or the way Lewis's eyes lingered on some of the fairer ladies at Court.

Jordan turned his attention to the two companions that had followed Lewis into the hall: Ironheart and the Monk. Ironheart was a tall knight in full battle armor, a strange enough sight at Court, but if he was strange, the Monk was downright unnerving. Just looking at the Monk, Jordan felt a cold shiver run through him, as though someone had just walked over his grave. There was something almost arrogant in the impenetrable darkness that filled the Monk's cowl, in the blatant admission of his own supernatural nature. Jordan wasn't sure whether there really was a body inside the robe or not. The arms were folded across the chest so that the cuffs were hidden, and the end of the Monk's robe brushed against the floor. It could be nothing more than a simple illusion—the Monk was, after all, supposed to be a sorcerer. Jordan remembered the sudden thunderstorm at Barrowmeer, and Bloody Bones rising from his grave. If the Monk had been behind that, he could be more dangerous than Lewis and Dominic put together. Jordan looked hard at the Monk. There was something . . . *wrong* about him. And then Jordan swallowed dryly as he finally saw that the Monk, of all the people at Court, didn't cast a shadow.

Jordan decided he'd rather look at Ironheart for a while. The knight stood motionless, a step behind Lewis, wearing full plate armor and a blocky steel helm with the visor lowered. There was no insignia or device on his armor to give a clue as to his identity. It was a knight's armor, but that didn't prove anything. In fact, if he was really a knight of the Realm, why wasn't he called Sir Ironheart? In his own way, the armored knight was as mysterious and anonymous as the Monk. And like the Monk, no one at Castle Midnight seemed too sure of where he'd come from originally. The two of them had simply appeared at Lewis's side one day, and they'd been there ever since.

It was hard to tell which of the two was feared most. Ironheart was Lewis's pet murderer. Under Lewis's direction, he'd challenged seventeen men to duels and killed them all with the great double-edged broadsword he carried slung on his back. Before Ironheart came along, Lewis had been content to do his own killing, but with the crown so nearly in his grasp of late, Lewis had grown cautious. Jordan studied Ironheart carefully. The armor was old and battered, and looked like it hadn't been polished in years, but it was still clearly in good working order. The bone hilt of the broadsword peered over his left shoulder like a watchful eye. Jordan stared at the helm's closed visor, and frowned thoughtfully. The man must be boiling hot inside all that armor, but still had made no move to take off his helm, or even to raise the visor. In fact, he seemed perfectly at ease.

"I'm starting to get the feeling I may have joined the wrong side," said Jordan quietly to Gawaine. "We're supposed to take on those two? A monk who isn't there and an armored killing machine? I think we're seriously outclassed here, Gawaine. All right, we beat Bloody Bones, but you know and I know that was only because we got lucky. A few conjuring tricks and a magic ax aren't going to be enough this time. I mean, we don't even have a real sorcerer on our side! I wish I was drunk. I wish I was very drunk. Maybe then my knees would stop shaking."

"Will you get a hold of yourself!" Gawaine's voice was no less sharp for being quiet. "We knew about Ironheart and the Monk when we started this. They're impressive, but not unbeatable. No one's unbeatable. Now brace yourself, Lewis is coming over."

Jordan quickly adopted his bland, untroubled face; the one he used when dealing with angry creditors. It was a very calm and relaxed face, with more than a little *I know something you don't* about it. It worked very well, as often as not. Jordan breathed deeply and carefully, bringing himself under control. Show time. Nothing to worry about. Viktor was just another character. He ran quickly through what little he'd been told about Viktor and Lewis. They disliked each other, but they both hated Dominic. *Dominic is insane, and Lewis is vile* . . . Jordan smiled easily as Lewis came to a halt before him. Lewis bowed formally. Ironheart and the Monk stayed back a way, politely out of earshot but within easy call. They didn't bow to Jordan, so he ostentatiously ignored them. He nodded briefly to Lewis.

"Well, Viktor, it's good to see you up and about again," said Lewis. His voice was warm and hearty. The smile was fairly convincing, but it didn't even touch the cold eyes. "I had heard you were quite ill."

"I was," said Jordan. "I got over it." He would have liked to leave it there rather than risk his characterization at such an early stage, but he could see Lewis was waiting for more. Going by its sudden silence, so was the Court. Jordan cleared his throat, and then wished he hadn't. It made him sound nervous and insecure. "It was just a chill, Lewis; nothing more. I probably caught it on my travels."

"Nasty things, chills," said Lewis. "They can get serious. People have been known to die of them, if they don't take care."

Oh subtle, Lewis, thought Jordan. *Really subtle.*

"That's true," he said calmly. "All kinds of people. You never know who's going to catch one next, do you?"

"I take precautions," said Lewis.

"So do I," said Jordan. "Lots of them."

"You certainly sound better. But appearances can be so misleading."

"Don't bet on it, Lewis. I feel strong enough to take on the whole damned world."

Lewis looked at him thoughtfully, and Jordan suddenly wondered if he'd walked into a trap. Lewis was the duelist in the family, after all. Jordan thought quickly back on what he'd said, but there didn't seem to be anything Lewis could take as an insult. Had he appeared too confident, perhaps? Viktor had looked to be rather a weak sort, but Gawaine had said he never backed down to anyone. Jordan shrugged mentally. What the hell, everyone knew Viktor had been away for four years. Exile can change a man.

"I'm glad to hear you've got your strength back," said Lewis finally. "You're going to need it. I imagine things are going to be rather hectic around here for a while."

"Looks that way," said Jordan. "Do you know why the Regent wants to see us?"

"Haven't a clue, but I doubt it's anything good. Have you seen Dominic?"

"Not recently."

"I understand he and Elizabeth have gone into politics. They're doing rather well, I believe. But then, they always were a splendid team."

"Yes," said Jordan. "I always knew Elizabeth would go far, one way or another."

Lewis looked at him. "You've mellowed, Viktor. Your time in exile must have agreed with you."

Jordan smiled. "I learned a great many things while I was away from Court, Lewis. You'd be surprised." He glanced at the Monk and Ironheart, still keeping a respectful distance. "I see your taste in friends hasn't improved."

"They have their uses. And they are very loyal."

"Oh, I'm sure they are, Lewis. But have you ever stopped to ask yourself why? All loyalty has its price. You should know that."

Lewis started to say something, and then stopped. He looked at Jordan thoughtfully, then nodded politely, and moved away. Ironheart and the Monk went with him. Jordan watched them go, and felt a little of the tension drain out of him. He was only too aware that the encounter could have ended nastily, in any number of unpleasant ways. He looked at the dozen armed guards surrounding Lewis, and felt an immediate desire to start checking for exits he could get to in a hurry. He took a deep breath to calm himself, and let it out slowly.

"Well, Gawaine," he said quietly, "how am I doing?"

"Very well, Your Highness," murmured the knight. "I'm impressed. If you'll pardon a little advice, you are coming on a bit strong, but that's not necessarily a bad thing. No one's been quite sure how to react to you after your long absence, and a little show of strength now might help to keep the flies off."

"That crack Lewis made about Dominic and Elizabeth; should I have been more upset? I mean, I know how important Elizabeth was to me, but I've got

Heather now. Though come to think of it, where is Heather? Shouldn't she be here with me?"

"She'll be joining us shortly, sire, I've no doubt. As for Elizabeth and Dominic; you've waited four years for a chance to make them pay. I think you can wait a little longer, to be sure of getting them. You've had a lot of time to learn patience."

The main doors swung open again, and the Court fell silent as the herald announced the arrival of Prince Dominic and the Lady Elizabeth. Jordan studied them both interestedly as they stood a moment in the doorway, acknowledging the bows and curtsies of the Court. Dominic was tall and slender, with a dour ascetic face, and pale straw-colored hair that fell lifelessly to his shoulders, held back from his face by a gleaming silver circlet. His outfit was a blue so dark as to be almost black, making his pale skin seem even paler. Jordan had seen corpses that looked healthier than Prince Dominic. He looked pretty much as Jordan had expected him to, given the various descriptions he'd had, but even so Jordan was unprepared for the cold air of menace that hung about Dominic like a shroud. And there was something disturbing about the pale blue eyes. It took Jordan a few moments to realize that Dominic didn't blink often enough.

The Lady Elizabeth stood close by Dominic, her arm linked possessively through his. She was easily as tall as Dominic, and had a voluptuous figure that was almost too full. Jordan knew her type. Only strict diets and ruthless self-control kept her figure from exploding into fat. Her hair was a thick tangled mane of raven's black that tumbled unconfined to her bare powdered shoulders. Her dress of aquamarine blue had been cunningly tailored to make the most of her spectacular figure. Her face . . . Jordan wasn't sure how he felt about her face. Elizabeth was certainly beautiful, no doubt of that, but the lips were a shade too full, the cheeks a trifle too broad, and her flawless skin owed a little too much to the makeup box. Probably no one but an actor would have noticed these

things, but to Jordan they made all the difference.
Working in the theater you meet more beautiful
women than not, and you soon learn to see the true
nature beneath the pretty face. Elizabeth was undeni-
ably gorgeous, but it only took Jordan a few moments
to decide that he wouldn't touch her with a barge
pole. There was a subtle streak of cruelty in the twist
of her smile, and in her narrowed eyes; a catlike delight in seeing her prey suffer before she destroyed it.
Her dark eyes fell on Jordan, and she caught his ap-
praisal. She smiled mockingly at him, and murmured
something to Dominic. He turned slowly to stare at
Jordan with his cold unwavering gaze. Jordan inclined
his head slightly. Dominic walked unhurriedly toward
him, with Elizabeth at his side. The courtiers fell
quickly back to make way for them, and a breathless
hush filled the Court. Gawaine stirred at Jordan's
side. Jordan held himself as conspicuously relaxed as
possible. It was important that he didn't seem at all
nervous or intimidated. The Court was watching too
closely. Dominic and Elizabeth finally stopped short
a few paces away from him, and Dominic bowed very
briefly. Elizabeth didn't curtsy.

"Welcome home, brother," said Dominic. His voice
was surprisingly deep and resonant, but it was still as
cold as his eyes. "My apologies for not meeting you
before, but I've been rather busy just lately. You must
be glad to be home again, though I think I should
warn you that many things have changed in your
absence."

"Oh sure," said Jordan amiably. "But then, some
things never change, do they? I hear you and Elizabeth have gone into politics."

"Dominic has many friends at Court these days,"
said Elizabeth. "Powerful and influential friends, who
expect him to do great things in the future. They're
all being very supportive."

"Yes, I imagine they are," said Jordan to Dominic,
ostentatiously ignoring Elizabeth. "But as I was just
saying to Lewis, all loyalty has its price. Even simple
friendship often has a price these days. Personally,

I've never cared much for friendships that have been bought and paid for. They tend to be so . . . impermanent."

Dominic said nothing, but Elizabeth flushed angrily at being ignored. "Then again, dear Viktor," she said tartly, "some friendships aren't worth buying, are they? Because some people don't have any future worth the mentioning. You'd do well to watch your step, Viktor. There's a new order at Castle Midnight, and you're not a part of it, and never will be."

"Talks a lot, doesn't she?" said Jordan to Dominic. "She even mutters in her sleep, from what I remember."

Elizabeth stood very still, two bright spots of color burning on her cheeks. Dominic frowned slightly.

"I never liked you, Viktor," he said finally, his voice calm and even distant. "I'll weep no tears at your funeral. If you're wise, you'll leave Castle Midnight while you have the chance. If you don't, I can't be responsible for your safety."

"I can look after myself," said Jordan. "And if anyone's stupid enough to try anything against me, their friends will be carrying what's left of them home in a bucket. You're a pain in the arse, Dominic. That's all you ever were, and it's all you'll ever be. Still, I shouldn't be too hard on you, I suppose; you did do me one great favor. You took that arrogant loud-mouthed bitch off my hands. I don't know how you stand it, myself. If I were you, I'd invest in some earplugs and a gag."

"You bastard!"

Elizabeth raised her hand to strike Jordan across the face. He quickly palmed one of his flare pellets, and crushed it in his hand. Flames leapt up around his fist as he held it up before him. Elizabeth dropped her hand and fell back a pace. Dominic didn't move. The Court was utterly silent, the only sound the crackling of the blue-white flames as they leapt and danced around Jordan's fist.

"Never raise a hand to me," said Jordan softly. "Not you, or anyone else."

Dominic looked at him impassively. "You're a dead man, Viktor."

"Blow it out your ear, Dominic."

Dominic turned and walked unhurriedly away, followed after a moment's hesitation by Elizabeth. Not far away, Lewis stood watching silently, flanked by Ironheart and the Monk. Jordan blew out the flames and lowered his hand, and the Court's chatter slowly resumed, if a trifle subdued.

"You're pushing it, Your Highness," said Gawaine quietly. "What would you have done if Dominic had challenged you to a duel, and raised his magic? Your conjuring tricks wouldn't have lasted five seconds against his water magic."

"It was a risk," Jordan admitted, "but I was pretty sure he wouldn't start anything. Not in front of the Court. There'd be too many witnesses if he lost. From everything you've told me, Prince Viktor's fire magic is very impressive. If Dominic was confident enough of his magic to fight a duel with me, he'd have done it by now, or even years ago, when the two of us first quarreled over Elizabeth. He didn't. Mind you, Viktor didn't either, which suggests that back then he wasn't sure. My using fire was a calculated bluff, and it seems to have paid off. You're right, though: I am pushing it. I don't have any other choice. I've got to come on as strong and confident as I can, or there'll be challenges and assassins crawling out of the woodwork. In the meantime, I need you to back me up. Keep your hand near that ax of yours, and glare at anyone who gets too close."

"Yes, Your Highness."

Gawaine said nothing more, but Jordan got the impression he was pleased. Jordan felt a little more relaxed, now that he was finally getting a feel for the part he was playing. His problem was that he'd been basing his characterization on secondhand views and a brief meeting with a man who was clearly very ill. By playing the role as he felt it should be played, he was doing much better. So far. What happened next would depend on what the Regent had to say when he finally deigned to show up. Jordan felt very definitely that he needed more advice on that. Where the hell were Roderik and DeGrange? Even Argent's unsmiling face would have been something of a relief. The main doors swung open and Jordan looked around eagerly, but it was only the Lady Heather. He quickly hid his disappointment as the herald announced her, and smiled widely at Heather. She gave him a smile that would have melted the heart of a lesser man, and hurried over to join him. He kissed her outstretched hand, and she fluttered her eyelashes at him.

"Don't overdo it," muttered Gawaine.

"Don't fuss," said Heather, not taking her eyes off Jordan. She took his arm and looked around her. "Roderik thought you might need a little help and support. He can't be here himself: he's staying with Viktor to keep him company. Viktor insisted. He doesn't like being left on his own. The poor dear hates being ill. I see Lewis and that creepy Dominic are here. Have you met them yet?"

"We've had a few words," said Jordan, casually. "I think I've got them both nicely rattled, and just a little bit off balance."

"So I should hope, actor."

Jordan took her hand in his and squeezed it hard. "I'm Viktor, Heather. In public, I'm *always* Viktor. Got it?"

"You're hurting me!"

"Got it!"

"Yes, yes, I've got it. Now let go of my hand before the fingers start dropping off." Jordan let go, and Heather shot him a puzzled glare as she massaged her aching hand. "You didn't have to be so rough about it, darling. A simple reminder would have been enough."

"Just remember that a slipup at the wrong moment could get us all killed." Jordan glared at the closed main doors. "Have you seen DeGrange anywhere? Or Argent?"

"No. Have you said anything to Elizabeth yet? How did she take it? Did she suspect anything?"

"I had a few words with her, and put her in her place. She didn't take to that at all."

"Good," said Heather firmly. "She can be a rotten cow, that one. I've never known such airs and graces. And you should hear how she treats her servants. No, as soon as Viktor is safely on the throne, the Lady Elizabeth is going to have a nasty and very fatal accident."

Jordan looked at her sharply, but said nothing for the moment. He was still trying to make up his mind about Heather. She talked like a lovesick teenager, but her eyes were the hardest and most determined he'd ever seen. There was a sugarcoated ruthlessness to her that appalled him. She certainly didn't make his job any easier. On the one hand he had to appear to be in love with her, while on the other there was no getting away from the fact that she made his flesh crawl.

"Look at the Monk," said Heather, clinging tightly to his arm. "Isn't he the creepiest thing you've ever seen? Honestly, darling, I don't think Lewis should be allowed to have him. He's obviously Unreal. The only reason the steward hasn't had a go at him is because Lewis has taken him under his personal protection." She turned imperially to Gawaine. "Get me a drink, Gawaine, there's a dear. My throat is absolutely parched."

Gawaine looked at Jordan, who nodded and held out his own empty glass for a refill. The knight said nothing, but his eyes spoke volumes. He turned away, and headed for the buffet table. Jordan had to grin. Gawaine obviously wasn't happy about being used as a waiter.

"Thank goodness he's gone," said Heather. "I need to talk to you, *Viktor.*"

"Go ahead," said Jordan. "But keep your voice down. If you can."

"I don't like you either," said Heather, "but that's not important. What is important is your doing the best job you can, for Viktor's sake. This is his big chance, his one and only chance to be king, and I won't stand for anyone or anything getting in his way. Viktor will be king, whatever it costs. Is that clear?"

"Very clear," said Jordan. "I wonder what it is about Viktor that attracts such *positive* women—first Elizabeth, and now you . . ."

"Flattery will get you nowhere," said Heather primly. "The point is, you're being paid a great deal of money, *Viktor,* and I intend to see to it that we get our money's worth."

"You'll get it," said Jordan. "But my chances of pulling this off successfully would be a great deal better if you could fill me in on as much background detail as possible. Not on Viktor. I've had his life history drilled into me until I could recite it backward in my sleep. I need to know about his fellow conspirators: what moves them and what binds them to Viktor. Your motivations seem fairly clear, but how about Gawaine, for example. I don't doubt his loyalty, but sometimes I get the impression he doesn't like Viktor at all."

"You could be right," said Heather. "Gawaine's a funny sort. He came to Redhart about fourteen years ago. He was quite famous then, in a small way. I take it you know about the Border War and the High Warlock's ax? Of course you do. Everyone does. It's one of those stories men like to tell around the fire late at night, so they can feel all brave and honorable without actually having to do anything themselves. There was even a song about Tower Rouge once, though it's been out of fashion for some time."

"Of course!" Jordan shook his head slowly, kicking himself for not having made the connection before. "The Ballad of Tower Rouge . . ."

It wasn't one of the great ballads, but in its time it had been very popular, and had been a standard in most minstrels' repertories. During the Border War between Hillsdown and the Forest Kingdom, the fighting had bogged down temporarily around a long narrow valley called Hob's Gateway. It wasn't much of a

valley, being mostly bare rock and scree, but strategi-
cally it was vitally important. Whoever controlled the
valley controlled that whole section of the border.
And the key to controlling the valley was Tower
Rouge. There were seven of the towers, scattered
along the boundaries of the Forest Kingdom. They'd
been built by the first generation of Forest kings, long
centuries ago, to cover weak spots in the kingdom's
defenses. Unfortunately, Tower Rouge had become
cut off from the Forest army, and only a small group
of five Rangers remained to man the tower. Hillsdown
sent three full companies of guards to take Tower
Rouge. The seige lasted five days. When Forest reinforcements finally arrived, they found two hundred
and forty-seven dead guards, and two surviving Rangers: the Hellstrom brothers, Vivian and Gawaine.
They'd held the Tower. King John had knighted them
both, on the spot.

"I always thought the song was overrated, myself,"
said Heather. "All those verses about flashing swords,
and blood soaking the ground like dew . . . when
you've heard one battle song, you've heard them all.
Anyway, Sir Gawaine came to Castle Midnight with
his wife, the Lady Emma."

"He's married?"

"Very. They're an inseparable couple, most of the
time. In fact, Emma's been a real pain in the neck all
the time Gawaine was off looking for you. You'd have
thought her husband had died, or run off with another
woman, rather than just left her on her own for a few
weeks. Anyway, when Gawaine first came here, he
had a private audience with King Malcolm, and they
talked together for hours. Nobody knows to this day
what they talked about, but finally they came out together, and the king announced that Sir Gawaine was
now a subject of Redhart, and a member in high
standing of the royal Court. Well, my dear, everyone
was very excited about that. Sir Gawaine was a famous figure even outside of the Forest Kingdom, and
having him at our Court was a real coup. But what
really made people prick up their ears and pay atten-

tion was that Gawaine had been appointed the special duty of looking after Prince Viktor. This was long before Viktor took up with Elizabeth, of course, but even then it was clear he needed someone to look after him and keep him out of trouble. Dear Viktor's always been too impulsive for his own good. But for a man like Gawaine to agree to act as his guardian . . . It was a mystery then and it's a mystery now why he agreed to do it."

Jordan frowned. "And nobody knows what Gawaine wanted to see the king about in the first place?"

"No one has ever got a word out of him or Emma or the king. So it must have been something pretty important, mustn't it?"

"All right," said Jordan. "That's muddied the water nicely. See if you can be a little more helpful about Count Roderik."

"I don't trust him," said Heather. "But then, nobody does. He was supposed to be in line for the Regency, a few years back, but there was a big scandal about his intrigues with the grain merchant Robert Argent, and the king refused to have anything to do with him after that. No one was ever able to actually prove anything against him, but everybody knew. He was ostracized at Court for simply ages. I mean, it was bad enough for him to be cheating over the grain prices, but to be caught at it . . . If it hadn't been for his Blood and position, he'd have been a laughing stock. As it was, he was left very much to himself. People had been looking for a good excuse for years. Everyone expects a little intrigue at Court: it adds spice to what would otherwise be very boring occasions, but Roderik's obsessed with intrigue for its own sake. He's never happier than when he's making plans to stab someone in the back, or throw them to the wolves."

Jordan raised an eyebrow. "And this is the man Viktor trusts to run his conspiracy for him?"

"For the moment, his interests and Viktor's are the same. And he is very good at conspiracies. He's had a lot of practice."

"All right, tell me about Argent. He's a grain merchant, and he's had dealings with Roderik in the past, at least one of which went spectacularly wrong. What's his connection with this conspiracy? What does he hope to get out of it?"

Heather looked at him pityingly. "God, you're dense sometimes. Dealing with Roderik the last time pretty much wiped Argent out. This is his chance to rebuild his fortunes. With a sympathetic king on the throne, all kinds of juicy contracts could come his way."

Jordan smiled slightly. "You're right, that was an obvious one."

"Besides," said Heather, "Roderik and Argent have been friends for years. He's one of the few people Roderik knows he can trust. And vice versa, of course."

"All right, one last name, Heather. Tell me about Brion DeGrange."

Heather frowned unhappily. "He's been head of castle security for seven years now, and as far as I know he's done a very good job. It's not easy keeping things under control in a castle like this at the best of times, and when the Unreal starts playing up, it can be a nightmare. Even with the steward to deal with the worst cases of the Unreal, there's still a lot of general chaos seeping out of the woodwork. This Court loves its intrigues, but it's hard to keep secrets in a castle where the walls literally do have ears on occasion, and ghosts walk through locked doors whenever they feel like it. So any man who can do a good job of security under conditions like that has to be respected. And yet . . . I don't know anyone who feels comfortable around DeGrange. I mean, he was an evil bastard in his day, one of the worst outlaws Redhart's ever known, and he only does a good job here because the geas says he has to. And now Roderik says control of the geas has passed to him. I don't think I like that. If Roderik can mess about with the geas and get away with it, so could anyone else who knew how. And we wouldn't know till it was too late."

"It would need someone with power," said Jordan thoughtfully. "The Monk, perhaps?"

"Or Dominic," said Heather. "He may be crazy, but he's been studying sorcery for years. He doesn't use it much in public, but everyone knows he's got the power."

"Great," said Jordan. "Just great."

"Anything else you'd like to ask me?"

"No, thanks. I think I'm confused enough for one day. Though I would like to know why the High Warlock made that ax for Gawaine . . ."

"Simple enough, Your Highness," said Gawaine, behind him. "He was my father, and he was proud of me."

He handed Jordan his glass of wine, and gave another to the Lady Heather. He then took up his position at Jordan's side again, staring resolutely straight ahead of him. Jordan looked at him speechlessly. In all his research on the High Warlock, he'd never found any mention of the warlock having a son, let alone two as famous as the Hellstrom brothers. There was a scandal of some kind here, he could tell, but it was obvious from Gawaine's rigid face and stance that he wasn't prepared to discuss the matter any further. Pity. But if he was that sensitive about it, why say anything in the first place? Jordan sighed quietly to himself. That was all he needed, another damned mystery.

What was the High Warlock really like? he'd asked Gawaine.

He was a drunk who chased women, said Gawaine, coldly.

Jordan was still chewing on that when he noticed that the Court's mutter of voices had suddenly stopped again. He looked quickly around, and saw courtiers falling respectfully back as a black-cloaked figure made his way slowly across the hall toward him. Jordan let his hand fall casually to his sword belt, and then realized that the man's attention was directed toward Sir Gawaine rather than him. Heather gripped his arm tightly, her face flushed with excitement and anticipation.

"That's Dark John Sutton," she murmured breathly. "Sword for hire. He works for Dominic, mostly. I've seen him in action a few times—he's very good with a sword. This should be fun."

Jordan checked again how far it was to the main doors. He'd heard of Dark John Sutton. Forty-seven kills to his credit, all of them with the sword. His past was pretty much a mystery, and it seemed he liked it that way. He had no politics, no scruples, and no friends. He killed for money, and he was expensive. And he'd never once failed to carry out his commission. Jordan glanced quickly at Gawaine. The knight had seen Sutton approaching, and was studying him coolly. Jordan looked back at Sutton. The man's gaze was still fixed on Gawaine, and he was smiling slightly. Jordan thought furiously. This was all his fault. He'd insulted Dominic, so Dominic had sent his pet assassin to take on Gawaine. The question was, how close a contest was it? Gawaine was one hell of a fighter, and his ax gave him an edge, but Sutton was a professional killer and maybe thirty years younger. But when all was said and done, Jordan knew he couldn't interfere. Firstly, he doubted Gawaine would let him, and secondly, the code duello was sacred in Redhart. If Gawaine backed down from a challenge, the Court would lose all respect for him. Jordan scowled fiercely. He couldn't just stand by and watch Gawaine get cut down. There had to be a way out of this. There had to be . . .

Dark John Sutton came to a halt a few yards short of Sir Gawaine. He was average height and average build, and his clothes were quiet and nondescript. His face was surprisingly bland, with little trace of strength or character in it, but his eyes were dark and steady. The sword at his side hung in a battered leather scabbard that had seen a great deal of use down the years. He could have been just another man-at-arms or mercenary, but there was an air of cold confidence about him that was subtly unnerving. His movements were calm, controlled, and very graceful. He nodded to Gawaine, ignoring Jordan and Heather.

"So you're Gawaine. Old man with a magic ax and a noble reputation. I could insult you, call you names, but what's the point. We both know why I'm here. We don't need an excuse to fight—it was bound to happen, sooner or later."

"It doesn't have to happen," said Gawaine. "You could turn and walk away."

"So could you."

"No. I don't do that."

"Neither do I," said Sutton. He smiled suddenly. "Besides, I've already taken half the money in advance."

"Don't do this," said Gawaine. "I don't want to have to kill you."

Sutton chuckled softly. "Confident, old man. I like that." He drew his sword. The brief rasp of steel on leather was very loud in the quiet. "Let's make a start, shall we? It's bad manners to keep our audience waiting."

Gawaine drew his ax. "Don't do this, John. You can still return the money."

Sutton shook his head sadly. "Can this really be the great Gawaine Hellstrom? The hero of Tower Rouge? What's the matter, old man, does your blood run a little more thin these days? Don't worry—I'll make it quick. And you needn't worry about that nice little wife of yours. I'll send her after you, as soon as I've got a free moment."

"You shouldn't have said that," said Gawaine. "Now you've made it personal."

Sutton grinned. "It's more fun that way. Make room."

He didn't raise his voice, but the courtiers around them fell back to form a wide circle. Heather tugged urgently at Jordan's arm, and he reluctantly allowed her to pull him away from Gawaine to join the edge of the crowd. The courtiers watched eagerly as Sutton and Gawaine took up their stances opposite each other.

Where the hell's the Regent? thought Jordan angrily. *If he was here, he could stop this.*

Except this was a duel, and therefore sacrosanct, above and beyond the law. The Regent couldn't stop it now. Nobody could. The two men began to slowly circle each other.

Don't let him get you angry, Jordan said silently to Gawaine. *He wants you to get mad at him and wear yourself out pressing the attack. Keep your cool, and make him do most of the work.*

Sutton's sword swept out suddenly in a vicious blow at Gawaine's throat. The knight parried the blow easily with the flat of his ax and then had to guard himself again as Sutton cut at him a second time without pausing. The two men stamped and shuffled back and forth, feinting and thrusting and parrying, feeling out each other's strengths and weaknesses, and watching all the time for that momentary gap in the defense that would allow a killing stroke. The clash of steel on steel echoed loudly in the silent Court, underlined by the scuffing of boots on the polished floor and the quiet grunting of effort from the two men. Sutton thrust lithely at Gawaine's gut. The knight slapped the blow aside, and then swept his ax back in a sideways cut that sliced through Sutton's jerkin and left behind a thick red line of blood to mark its passing. Sutton grinned coldly, and his blade flashed out in a cut Gawaine couldn't quite parry in time. The tip of the blade scored a razor-thin line just above Gawaine's left eyebrow. Blood ran down past his eye, but he didn't waste time trying to brush it away. The two men fought on, neither yielding an inch.

Jordan began to wonder what he would do if Gawaine lost. He felt disloyal even thinking about it, but he had to be realistic. Gawaine was holding his own for the moment, but he was a great deal older than his opponent, and he just didn't have the stamina to maintain his attack for much longer. Tower Rouge was a long time ago. Sooner or later he'd start to slow down, and then Dark John Sutton would kill him. Sutton was the best. Everyone knew that.

Even as he thought that, the two men locked their weapons together and struggled face-to-face. Gawaine was already gasping for breath after his exertions, and Sutton smiled as he slowly began to force Gawaine's arm back against him. The knight struggled to hold his ground against the increasing pressure, his arms trembling with effort, but inch by inch Sutton's greater strength won out. And then Gawaine spat directly into Sutton's face. Sutton jerked back, startled, and in that moment when he was off balance, Gawaine brought his knee up sharply into Sutton's groin. The duelist's face screwed up with pain, and shocked tears ran down his cheeks as he fought for breath. He tried to lash out at Gawaine, but his sword arm wouldn't respond quickly enough. Gawaine ducked easily inside the blow and slammed his ax into Sutton's side. The ax head buried itself between Sutton's ribs, and the impact drove the duelist to one knee. Gawaine jerked the ax free, and it came loose with an ugly sucking sound. Blood flew on the air. Sutton tried to lift his sword, and couldn't. Gawaine raised his ax. Sutton tried to say something, and then Gawaine brought the ax swinging down, again and again and again. For a few moments the Court was full of the sound of butchery, of steel cleaving meat. Gawaine finally stepped back, and looked at the still and bloody figure on the floor before them.

"You shouldn't have threatened my Emma," he said softly. He looked around at the herald. "Clean this mess up."

The herald nodded quickly, and gestured to two nearby servants. The Court slowly resumed its buzz of conversation, its voice respectfully hushed, at least at first. Gawaine wiped his ax clean with a piece of rag, and then sheathed it again. He moved back to rejoin Jordan and Heather. His sleeves were covered in blood, little of it his own. Heather smiled broadly at him, and leaned forward to kiss him quickly on the cheek. Jordan nodded to him respectfully.

"That was . . . very impressive, Gawaine."

"It wasn't difficult, sire. He was a duelist, and I'm a soldier. He never stood a chance."

The servants wrapped up Sutton's body in his own cloak, and carried him away. Jordan looked around to see how Dominic was taking the death of his pet assassin, but for the moment he was lost in the crowd. The Court was just starting to get back to normal when the main doors suddenly slammed open, and the herald drew himself up to his full height and announced in ringing tones the arrival of His Excellency the Regent, Count William Howerd, and his wife, the Lady Gabrielle.

Everyone bowed or curtsied, including the three princes. The Regent and his wife ignored everybody, and strode majestically through the crowd toward the raised dais at the back of the hall. The crowd opened up before them, making a wide passage for them to walk through. They finally reached the dais and stopped before it to bow and curtsy to the empty throne. Then they slowly climbed the marble steps, and took up positions standing on either side of the throne. The Regent and his wife stood looking out over the packed Court, their faces calm and impassive. Jordan studied them both carefully.

Count William looked more like a king than any of the three princes. He was tall and powerfully built, with wide shoulders and a fashionably slim waist. His stance was firm and noble, and there was an unselfconscious dignity in his every movement. He wore his dark formal robes with grace and quiet style. He was traditionally handsome, with short dark hair and a neatly trimmed beard. He had the relaxed confident air that adorned so many aristocratic portraits in country houses, and yet there was warmth in his eyes and a slightly self-mocking smile on his lips. *He'd make a great romantic lead*, thought Jordan. *If he didn't look so bloody perfect, I might even like him.* Unfortunately, in the game he was playing, the Regent was one of his most powerful opponents.

His wife, the Lady Gabrielle, was a famous beauty. She was tall and slender, with a graceful willowy body.

She wore a long flowing gown of creamy white, with frothy lace cuffs. Her long tawny hair hung in carefully arranged curls around a heart-shaped, almost childlike face. Her eyes were gray and very large, adding to her helpless-little-girl look. Jordan wasn't fooled for a moment. He'd seen that look on too many girls in the chorus: girls who spent all their spare time trying to get out of the chorus and into speaking roles. Usually via somebody's bed. There was a calm, self-satisfied arrogance in Gabrielle's face, when looked at dispassionately. She obviously gloried in being the Regent's wife, and having all the Court bow and scrape to her. It wasn't really surprising. She'd never known anything like it before, even though she was King Malcolm's daughter.

Under Redhart law, only the king's sons could inherit the throne, even though the daughters had just as much Blood and elemental magic as the sons. This had often been a sore point down the centuries, even to the point of civil war on one occasion, but still the law and tradition held. There had only ever been kings ruling Redhart; never once a queen. The ladies of the royal line were just . . . breeding stock. They had much standing in Court, but no political power. In theory, anyway. In practice, it tended to depend on who they were married to. As the Regent's wife, Gabrielle wielded more power through her husband than she'd ever dreamed of as the king's daughter. Jordan looked at her thoughtfully, and wondered what would happen when she had to give it up.

"My lords and ladies, and honored guests," said Count William, his deep, measured voice rolling majestically on the silence, "I thank you for your patience. I have grave news that cannot be withheld from you any longer. As you know, since King Malcolm's sudden and tragic death, there has been no trace of his will, his crown, or his seal of office. Despite extensive searches of Castle Midnight, by all the parties concerned, they still remain lost to us. And without them, Redhart can have no king.

"My friends, Redhart must have a king. The Unreal

is growing stronger. Creatures that were once securely
contained now stalk the corridors openly. The gargoyles on the battlements are growing restive, and the
dead no longer rest in peace. Plants bleed, and statues
weep. There are voices in the earth, and a wall has
learned to scream. The steward is doing her best to
cope, but there is a limit to what she can do on her
own. Her authority over the Unreal stems from the
Stone, and without a king on the throne, its power is
weakened. I have summoned the steward here. Let
her tell you what is happening in Castle Midnight."

He gestured to the herald, and the servants opened
the main doors. The steward hurried in, followed by
her apprentice. The herald glanced at them nervously,
and then bellowed across the silent Court, "Catriona
Taggert, and her apprentice, Damon Cord!"

Once again the whole Court bowed and curtsied,
this time including the Regent and his wife. Taggert
stopped just inside the doors and nodded briefly in
reply, clearly impatient to begin speaking. She was
short, only an inch or so over five foot, and delicately
formed. She looked almost frail at first glance, but
there was a strength and determination in her raw-
boned face that appealed greatly to Jordan. She was
in her late twenties, good-looking in a brisk, undemanding way, and she wore her short chestnut hair in
a style that was more functional than attractive. Her
stance was firm and uncompromising, and she looked
extremely competent. The steward was supposed to
have extensive knowledge of the High Magic, and Jordan, for one, didn't doubt it for a moment. There was
something about her eyes . . .

There was also something about Damon Cord, the
steward's apprentice. He was a tall gangling man who
looked as though he had dressed in a hurry in the
dark. His clothes looked as though they might once
have been best-quality tailoring, but now they were
torn, ragged, and filthy almost beyond belief. He was
also the biggest and most muscular man Jordan had
ever seen. Old scars formed a bizarre tracery on his
bare arms, and somewhere in the past someone had

made a determined effort to cut Cord's face in half. The resulting scar stretched from forehead to chin, just missing the left eye, crossing the nose, and nicking the right corner of the mouth, giving him a permanent half smile. He looked grim, brooding, and not a little crazy. He also looked decidedly dangerous, if anyone was ever dumb enough to upset him. A low murmur ran through the courtiers as they assessed the new arrivals.

"All right, everyone shut up and listen," said the steward. "We don't have much time. There's been a major outbreak of the Unreal. I don't know what brought it on, but over the last two hours my staff and I have been run ragged all over the castle, just trying to hold things together. First, the good news. As far as we can tell, no one's died yet. That's it. Now the bad news. The Old Library is gone. When you open the door, there's nothing there but cobwebs. They look like they go on forever. We sent one man in on a rope. He got a hundred yards from the door and still couldn't find a wall in any direction. He also thought there was something in the cobwebs with him, watching. We've nailed the door shut for the time being. I'll try and get the Old Library back when I've got the time, but I'm not promising anything. And stay away from the Musician's Gallery over the East Ballroom. There's a new ghost there, and it looks like a bad one. It's got teeth you wouldn't believe. The gargoyles are running loose on the roof, but I've got some of my people up there taking care of it.

"All in all, we were just about holding our own, until I did a routine scan of the castle, and discovered there was a pattern to the outbreaks. All the incidents were carefully timed to mislead me into missing one major outbreak. Sometime during the past two hours, the Unreal broke through right here, in the Great Hall."

There was utter silence when she stopped talking. Jordan glanced unobtrusively around him. On every side there were pale, frightened faces and wide, staring eyes. The Court was terrified. Jordan badly

wanted to ask Gawaine or Heather what the hell the
steward was talking about, but he didn't dare draw
attention to himself with a display of ignorance.

The Regent stepped forward a pace. "You're the
steward, Catriona. Do what you have to."

The courtiers stirred uncertainly, and looked warily
about them. In ones and twos, and then in groups,
they started to edge away from each other. Jordan
quickly became aware that even Gawaine and Heather
were doing it, in what seemed to be an unconscious
reaction. He let his hand rest casually on the sword
at his side. Something was about to happen: something awful. He could feel it on the air: a tense atmosphere that was thickening from anticipation into
certainty. The Steward looked slowly around her, her
dark eyes cold and watchful.

"Nobody is to interfere, whatever happens. I don't
need distractions."

She glared about her, and the courtiers nodded
dumbly. Catriona Taggert smiled grimly, and spoke a
Word of Power.

Jordan staggered back a step as reality shuddered
around him, torn and sundered by the force of the
steward's sorcery. Something roared in the hall like
captive thunder, and the world changed. Jordan shook
his head dazedly as for a moment two different views
of the Court fought for dominance in his mind, and
then the illusions were blown away like leaves on the
wind, and reality became clear again.

The courtiers screamed and fell back from the dead
man in their midst. He had looked like just another
courtier before, hidden by an Unreal glamour, but
now it stood exposed as a grinning, rotting corpse.
Flies swarmed about it, their buzzing unnaturally loud.
Its flesh was blackened and torn, revealing discolored
bones and frayed strands of decaying muscle. Witch
light burned in its empty eye sockets. As the lich realized it stood revealed for what it was, it howled with
rage and struck out viciously at the nearest courtier.
The man died instantly as the lich's bony fist buried
itself in the side of his skull. It ripped its fist free in

a flurry of gore, and whirled around to thrust its clawed hand into another man's face. Blood ran down the man's neck in thick streams, and his screams mixed with the lich's bubbling laughter.

Up above, a gleaming glass chandelier burst apart in a silent explosion. The gleaming crystals shuddered through a dozen ugly colors as they fell, and then suddenly became a hundred and more gore crows that flew off in different directions. They swept back and forth over the courtiers' heads, their beaks and claws drawing blood from those who couldn't dodge fast enough.

Behind the throne's raised dais, a man was melting into the far wall. Already it was hard to tell where his flesh ended and the stone began. He was horribly emaciated, his bones pressing out against the taut skin, but his sunken eyes were alive and aware. He knew what was happening to him.

Damon Cord roared a challenge in a deep, echoing voice and headed for the lich at a run. He reached out with his left hand and pulled a huge steel mace out of thin air. The thick shaft was three feet long, and the great club head was studded with wicked metal spikes. The lich threw away its dying victim and turned to face Cord, hissing in anticipation. It lashed out with a clawed and blood-soaked hand. Cord avoided the blow with almost uncanny ease, and his huge mace rose and fell. The great spiked head slammed down onto the lich's shoulder, and the impact drove the creature to the floor. Its bones broke and shattered under the blow, and it screamed with rage. It tried to get up again, but Cord was already stooping over it. The flies clustered thickly about him and crawled over his face, but he ignored them. He lifted up his mace and then brought it sweeping down in a vicious blow that tore the lich's head from its body. The body convulsed, and grabbed blindly for Cord with its clawed hands. Cord hit it again and again, and finally it lay still as the last of its Unreal life went out of it. Cord growled once, satisfied, and looked around for another enemy. Everyone backed away from him, unnerved by the open savagery in his scarred face.

The steward had deliberately left Cord to fight on his own. They both preferred to work alone. Almost before Cord had started moving toward the lich, she had raised her hands and sent a wave of crackling white balefire seething through the air above the courtiers. The soaring crows screamed like children as the balefire touched them. All over the Court they burst into flames and fell out of the air like so many burning handkerchiefs. Even as the courtiers scattered to avoid the burning birds, the steward was already running down the hall toward the man trapped in the wall. She made a grasping motion with her right hand, and a long slender sword formed itself out of balefire and fitted itself into her clutching hand. At the same time, a glowing silvery shield appeared on her left arm.

Cord glared balefully about him, and his gaze settled on a portly noble to Jordan's left. He smiled slowly, and hefted his mace. Foulness dripped from the metal tines. The noble shook his head, and began to back away.

"No! Please . . . it's a mistake! I'm Real, Real as you! Do I look like one of those things? Just look at me!"

Cord moved steadily toward him. The noble backed away even faster, and the courtiers scattered to give them both plenty of room. The noble glanced behind him, and found he'd run out of room. There was nothing there but a wall. He looked at Cord, and his face suddenly went cold and dead. He grabbed a woman's arm and pulled her to him, holding her before him as a shield. His eyes were empty and lifeless.

"Stay back or I'll kill her."

The voice was distant and horribly distorted. It didn't sound human, though it came from a human throat. The Unreal man pulled a knife from its sleeve and set the edge against the woman's throat. A drop of blood slid slowly down her neck as the sharp edge nicked the skin. She whimpered once, and looked be-

seechingly at Cord. He smiled at her reassuringly, and
then his left arm snapped forward too quickly to follow, and the mace flew from his hand to smash the
noble's shoulder. The knife fell harmlessly to the
floor, and the creature's shattered arm hung limply at
its side. Cord reached into thin air and pulled out a
great two-edged broadsword. It was wide and strong
as a butcher's cleaver, and the edges had been filed
into jagged serrations. Cord sprang forward and
swung the sword at the noble's neck. The creature
dropped its hostage and tried to duck under the blow,
but Cord had timed it too well. The blade sliced clean
through the neck, and the head flew howling through
the air. The body didn't fall. The hostage screamed
once, and fainted. A long split appeared in the noble's
suddenly bare chest, stretching lengthwise and forming
into a mouth that reached from neck to groin, lined
with shining teeth. A long leathery tongue shot out of
the opening and wrapped itself around Cord, pinning
his arms to his sides. His great muscles bulged as he
tried to break free, but the tongue was too strong for
him. It began to contract back into the body mouth,
dragging Cord with it.

Jordan stepped forward and picked up Cord's mace,
which had fallen practically at his feet. He had to use
both hands to lift it, and he grunted in surprise at the
weight. He advanced cautiously on the Unreal noble,
hefting the mace as best he could. He knew the steward had said not to interfere, and given any choice he
would have been happy not to, but he couldn't just
stand by and watch a man die. He moved forward as
quietly as he could, and sneaked up to the thing from
behind. Without a head, the creature shouldn't be
able to see or hear him, but he wasn't taking any
chances he didn't have to. A second mouth appeared
suddenly in the creature's back, lined with chomping
teeth. It knew he was there. Jordan stopped dead in
his tracks and switched the mace awkwardly to his left
hand. He used his other hand to palm a fire pellet
from his sleeve, crushed it, and threw the flaming ball
into the creature's snapping mouth. It slammed shut

on the fire reflexively, and then staggered on its human feet as the flames took hold inside it. The blazing light could be seen clearly through the creature's flesh. Jordan stepped forward and swung the mace double-handed, crushing the thing's other shoulder. It went to its knees under the impact of the blow, and the tongue holding Cord loosened its grip just enough for him to pull himself free. He raised his broadsword and chopped at the writhing body like a woodsman hewing at a stubborn tree trunk. The creature gradually fell apart into twitching pieces that took a long time to die and lie still. Jordan looked away, and saw the severed head grinning up at him. It snarled silently. Jordan smashed the thing with the mace until he was sure it was really dead. He finally looked up, panting, and Cord nodded to him approvingly. Jordan grinned back.

Not all the birds had died from the steward's balefire. A dozen of them dived shrieking toward the Regent, still standing beside the throne. Jordan started toward him to help, and then stopped as the Lady Gabrielle lifted her arm and pointed imperiously at the birds. They fell clumsily out of the air, making harsh croaking sounds. Jordan frowned, confused, and on moving closer saw that the birds were gasping futilely for air. *Of course, Gawaine said she had air magic. She's drawing the air out of their lungs . . .* He looked at Gabrielle with new respect. *Somebody else I'd better not upset.*

The steward skidded to a halt before the man melting into the wall, and her sword of light bit into the stonework beside him. Dark blood spurted from the broken stone. The wall heaved and convulsed around the emaciated body, and then formed into a jagged mouth that spat the body out. The man fell limply to the ground and lay still, moaning faintly. He was little more than skin and bone. The wall had all but sucked him dry. The steward stood over him, her shimmering shield between them and the stone mouth. It grinned at her, and stretched wider and wider until it was the length of the wall. Squat, bulky teeth appeared behind

the thick gross lips. The steward cut at the mouth with
her sword. The stone yielded helplessly to the glowing
balefire, but the blade was too small to do any real
damage to the gigantic mouth. A deep rumbling growl
issued from the stone, and back down the hall Jordan
wondered crazily what the stone mouth would sound
like once it learned to speak. The steward backed
away a step. She made a quick gesture with her hands,
and her sword and shield disappeared. The stone
mouth pursed its lips, and then smiled slowly.

*"We are coming . . . we will be here soon . . . we
are coming . . . we are coming . . ."*

There was nothing human in the voice: only an
awful, purposeful evil that made Jordan want to wince
away from the sound. Many of the courtiers did. The
steward stood her ground, her face drawn and tense,
and spoke a second Word of Power. A blinding light
flared up around the steward, blazing soundlessly as
it fought in vain to consume her, but bound by her
will to do her bidding. She gestured sharply, and the
balefire flew away from her to sink into the wall. The
huge mouth twisted in agony. There was a silent flare
of light too bright to look at, and when everyone's
eyes had cleared, the mouth was gone and the wall
was just a wall again.

The steward knelt down beside the man she'd res-
cued, and felt for a pulse in his neck. After a moment,
she nodded tiredly and stood up again. She gestured
to the nearest servants, and they hurried forward to
take care of the shrunken figure. Jordan looked
closely at the man as he was carried past, and was
relieved to note that the emaciated chest was still rising and falling, if only just. He looked back at the
steward to congratulate her, and then hesitated. She
was clearly unsteady on her feet, and for the first time
Jordan realized just how much her magic had taken
out of her. Her face was pale and drawn, and sweat
trickled down her brow. Her hands were shaking
slightly, but when Damon Cord hurried over to stand
at her side, she brusquely waved away his silent offer
of support.

She looked slowly round the quiet hall, taking in the silent courtiers and what remained of the dead Unreal creatures, and finally she nodded wearily. She turned to the throne on the dais, and bowed to the Regent.

"That's it. I've done all I can here. But things are going to stay unsettled until there's a king on the throne again. My sorcery is strong enough to cope for the moment, but that's all. Tell the people why we're here. We can't put this off any longer."

"Is the hall clear of the Unreal now?" asked the Lady Gabrielle.

The steward looked at the Monk. Lewis stiffened slightly. For a moment Jordan thought the steward was going to say something, but then the moment passed, and she just looked away. "I've done all I can, my lady. Let the Regent say his piece, and then we can all get out of here. I don't know about the rest of you, but I've got work to do."

"Yeah," said Cord. "Lots to be done." He hefted the sword in his hand, and grinned nastily. He opened his hand and the sword suddenly disappeared. Jordan jumped, startled, as the mace in his hand disappeared, too. He flexed his fingers nervously, and fought down an urge to check inside his sleeves in case the mace was hiding there. Heather elbowed him sharply in the ribs as the Regent began speaking, and Jordan quickly paid attention to what was being said.

"My friends," said the Regent, "we live in dangerous times. Without a king on the throne, the whole of Redhart could soon fall prey to the Unreal. But with the will and the crown and the seal missing, we have been unable to declare any of the princes as king. All three brothers have had ample time to find the crown and seal, and they have all failed. We cannot, dare not, wait any longer. It is therefore my unfortunate duty to proclaim the Rite of Transference, as established in precedent. From this moment on, any man with Blood who presents crown and seal to the Stone in the correct ceremony will be declared the next king of Redhart."

For a long time, nobody said anything. The shocked silence just seemed to echo on and on. Jordan looked frantically at Gawaine and Heather for some clue as to how he should be reacting, but they looked just as blank as everyone else. Jordan rummaged quickly through his memory, but couldn't recall anyone saying anything about a Rite of Transference. He looked across at Prince Dominic. The man's face was if anything even paler than before, but his icy calm hadn't wavered in the least. As Jordan watched, the Lady Elizabeth whispered urgently in Dominic's ear. He nodded absently, then turned and left the hall, followed by Elizabeth and several of the courtiers. Jordan looked quickly over at Prince Lewis, but he was already heading for the door, too, followed by Ironheart and the Monk. Jordan slapped Sir Gawaine lightly on the arm.

"If they're going, I'd better go, too," he muttered urgently. "We've got to discuss this, and fast."

Gawaine nodded, and he and the Lady Heather walked beside Jordan as he stalked silently out of the Court. Jordan hoped like hell that Count Roderik, Argent, and DeGrange would be waiting for him in his quarters when he got there. He'd only been in this job a few hours, and already the scenario he'd been given was falling apart. What the hell was the Rite of bloody Transference? Jordan ground his teeth together. This was all he needed. More bloody complications. He'd better get some advice, and quickly. Or come the next morning, there could be a new king on the throne that none of the factions had counted on.

CHAPTER 4

Unexpected Visitors

"That devious bastard! He'll plunge us all into civil war before he's through!"

Count Roderik stalked back and forth in Jordan's suite, waving his hands around as he fumed. Jordan leaned back against the mantelpiece and let him get on with it. Roderik hadn't stopped whining since he arrived, and Jordan was getting more than a little tired of it. After all, Roderik probably wouldn't have been half as angry if he hadn't had to baby-sit Viktor while all the excitement was going on at Court. Jordan looked surreptitiously at the others, to see how they were taking it. Sir Gawaine was standing at parade rest by the closed main door, his face showing a polite interest that wasn't mirrored in his eyes. Robert Argent was sitting slumped in a chair, gnawing at a thumbnail and scowling at nothing in particular. The Lady Heather was sitting on the arm of the chair Prince Viktor was sitting in. They both looked more thoughtful than worried. Viktor looked up irritably as Roderik drew near him.

"Oh do be quiet, Roderik, I'm trying to think. We're all upset, but we haven't the time to indulge in hysterics."

Roderik stopped dead in his tracks and glared at Viktor. "Your Highness, may I point out that you are quite possibly only hours away from losing your throne and your position? To say nothing of your life? As things stand, anyone can just walk up to the Stone with the crown and the seal, and be made king on the spot!"

"Anyone with Blood," said Viktor. "That does limit

the field rather. I agree things are somewhat desperate, but no more so now than they were a few hours ago. If my brothers and I and all our people haven't been able to find the crown and seal in all this time, I don't see how anyone else can hope to. No, our only real fear is that someone already has them hidden, and has been waiting for this chance. Poor fool. Whoever it is, he won't get within ten feet of the Great Hall. DeGrange and his men are already guarding all the approach corridors, ostensibly to keep the peace but actually under my direct orders to kill any pretender who appears. A nice touch, I thought, using DeGrange. It gives the Regent the illusion of security, while ensuring my interests remain covered."

Gawaine stirred unhappily. "I'm afraid it's not that simple, Your Highness. Your brothers' men have also established themselves near the Great Hall, no doubt with similar orders. There have been a few skirmishes already."

"Really?" said Heather. "Who's winning?"

"No one's winning!" snapped Roderik. "We're all losing! While we waste time fighting among ourselves, the Regent is sitting there laughing at us."

"Don't shout at me, Roderik," said Viktor softly. "I have a headache."

Roderik looked at Viktor and seemed to remember where he was and who he was shouting at. He bowed stiffly. "My apologies, sire."

"That's better," said Viktor. "Don't let it happen again, there's a good chap. Now then, I think we'd all benefit from a short break. Heather, hand around my pipes and tobacco. You know where they are. And there are drinks in the cabinet for those who'd like them."

Jordan shot a quick guilty look at the drinks cabinet, and tried to remember if he'd put the whiskey decanter back in the right place. Luckily, nobody seemed interested in a drink or the rack of long clay pipes that Heather passed around. Everyone was too tense to even think of relaxing. Jordan scowled briefly. He could have done with a stiff drink, but he didn't like to ask if nobody else was drinking. They all sat or stood in silence for a while, each of them lost in their own thoughts, and finding little pleasure or hope there.

"I think I'm missing something," said Jordan finally. "You all seem to be implying that the Regent is risking civil war in Redhart for a reason. What reason? What could he hope to gain?"

"It's complicated," said Argent, without looking up. "Basically, King Malcolm made Count William the Regent because William is an honest man. Possibly the most honest and honorable man at Court. Unfortunately, because of his overly strict sense of morality, William has never approved of the present royal line. He certainly doesn't approve of the three princes who stand to inherit Malcolm's throne. By William's lights, none of them are worthy of it. So, by declaring the Rite of Transference, he is hoping a new royal line will emerge to sit on the throne and replace the existing line. That new line would of course be heavily dependent on the Regent when it came to actually running the country . . ."

"Just what is this Rite of Transference?" said Jordan. "I mean, what exactly does it do? And while we're on the subject, why wasn't I told about it before?"

"Because it hasn't been used in three hundred years," growled Roderik. "The last time it was declared, it was used to establish the present royal line, after extensive inbreeding had made the old line worthless. I'd forgotten the damn thing was still on the law books."

Jordan frowned. "All right, so it's legal. But can the Regent back it up? Does he have the troops? And would the Court stand for it? I mean, their interests are tied in with the princes. Aren't they?"

"Not necessarily," said Prince Viktor. He looked increasingly tired and drawn, but his voice was still steady. "The aristocracy is based on Blood, and as things stand, anyone with Blood could use the crown and seal to make themselves king. As far as the Court

is concerned, this is a once-in-a-lifetime chance to as-
cend to the throne. Not that it'll happen that way, of
course."

"Why not?" said Jordan.

Viktor looked at him pityingly. "Because neither I
nor my brothers will stand for it, that's why not. As
you pointed out, in the end it all comes down to force
of arms. The Regent commands the castle guards, but
as princes, we each have our own private troops, more
than enough to take the crown and seal away from
whoever has them."

"You're talking about waging a war in your own
country," said Jordan slowly. "Not just against the
Regent, but against your brothers as well. How many
of your people would die in those wars? Not just your
guards and men-at-arms; how many peasants and
townspeople, how many farmers and merchants, how
many men, women, and children would have to die
to make you king? Hundreds? Thousands?"

"At least," said Viktor. "It isn't important. It is my
right to be king. And it is the duty of all my subjects
to fight and if need be die for their king."

"I'm not sure raising an army would prove all that
easy, Your Highness," said Gawaine quietly. "With so
many questions still unanswered over King Malcolm's
death, nobody trusts anybody anymore. The way
things are, neither you nor your brothers can be as
sure of support as you once could."

"No one can blame me," said Viktor. "I was still
in exile when the old man died."

"Yes, sire, you were," said Gawaine. "But you
could have ordered it done."

There was an awkward pause.

"Look," said Jordan, "it seems to me that we're
worrying too much about things that haven't happened, and might never happen. If we worry about
every little thing that could go wrong, we'll never get
anything done. Let's stick to the things that matter.
For example, how was my performance? Nobody's
said a thing about that yet. Was I convincing? Do I
need to work on the voice more?"

"Trust an actor to care only about his reviews," said Heather.

"You did very well, sire," said Gawaine, smiling slightly. "You were Prince Viktor to the life. And stepping in to help Damon Cord against the Unreal was a good move. It never hurts to be conspicuously brave in front of the right people. It might even draw us some popular support at Court later on."

Viktor sniffed. "That's as may be. In the meantime, we'll let you know if your work's not up to standard, actor." He rubbed tiredly at his forehead, and gestured pettishly at Gawaine. "I've done enough for one evening. My head hurts. I'm going back to my quarters."

"Not yet, Your Highness," said Roderik quickly. "We still have the other glamour spell to do."

Jordan gave Roderik a hard look. "*Another* glamour spell? No one said anything to me about another glamour spell."

"It's just a little something to help you in your performance as Viktor," said Roderik smoothly. "You've done very well so far, considering, but whilst you look and sound very much like Prince Viktor, you still wouldn't convince anyone who knew the prince well. It's not your fault. You haven't had a chance to meet His Highness in person before now, so you haven't been able to acquire all the little mannerisms, phrases of speech and so on, that help to make up his private and public faces. This new glamour spell will graft these things directly onto your memory, much as the first spell gave you Viktor's appearance. That's really all there is to it."

Jordan thought about it. There was something about this new spell that disturbed him very deeply. The first spell had simply altered his outer appearance. That hadn't been so bad, once he got used to it. Actors did it all the time, with costumes, wigs, and makeup. But this new spell would change the way he spoke and moved, perhaps even the way he thought . . . And yet he couldn't say no. They were right. There wasn't time to learn the part by observation; he had to be perfect straightaway. And this was the only way.

"All right," he said steadily. "Let's do it."

Roderik gestured for Jordan to sit down in a chair facing the prince, and he did so. His palms were wet with sweat, and he rubbed them unobtrusively against the chair arms to dry them. The prince was sitting up straight in his chair, despite his obvious tiredness. He didn't even look worried, the smug bastard. The Lady Heather looked at Jordan as if he was some interesting exhibit in a private zoo. *And stuff you too,* thought Jordan, just to keep things impartial. He tried to settle himself more comfortably in his chair, but each position seemed worse than the last. It was all in his mind, he knew that, but it didn't help his nerves at all. He hated to be kept waiting. Robert Argent was watching him closely, and Jordan kept his expression carefully calm. He glanced across at Sir Gawaine, hoping for a little moral support, but the knight had turned his face away, as if he couldn't bear to watch what was about to happen. Jordan began to regulate his breathing, keeping it slow and steady, and set about calming his nerves as he had so often before, standing in the wings of a stage, waiting to go out on the boards and do what he was born to do. His composure slowly came back to him, and his muscles began to relax in ones and twos. He was the Great Jordan. He could handle this. Roderik looked at him and then at the prince. He nodded, satisfied, and then raised his left hand and gestured sharply. Static sparked and snapped on the air before him. He forced out a shout, jerky sentence in a harsh, guttural tongue, and the world disappeared.

Night fell. There was no light, and the darkness was everywhere. Jordan discovered he couldn't hear or feel anything either, and fought down a brief surge of panic. He clenched his hands into fists, but he couldn't feel the chair arms they rested on, or even the pressure of the fingers against each other. The darkness swirled about him in a slow, steady rhythm, and his panic slowly ebbed away. There was nothing disturbing about the dark; in fact, it was almost restful. Like lying in bed at night with your eyes closed. He waited patiently. Something came into the darkness with him, and without knowing how or why, he knew it was Viktor. They drifted closer to each other, and then Jordan tried to scream as a flood of information washed over him in an endless tide.

The garden was full of flowers. Their rich and heady scent filled the air now that the rain had finally stopped. He picked a rose, and the thorn pricked his thumb. The drop of blood it drew was the same color as the rose . . . He rode across the empty moor as twilight fell, his horse plunging beneath him, a good length and more in front of his nearest rival. The cold wind blew tears from his eyes . . . Thick smoky air diffused the lantern light into a dim amber glow in the back-alley tavern. He knew he shouldn't be there on his own, in the worst part of Kahalimar, and he didn't give a damn . . . He had his hands around Dominic's throat, and he was crying as he tried to murder his brother. Elizabeth watched them struggle, and there was nothing in her face but an endless weary contempt.

Past and present rolled into a single kaleidoscopic mosaic that battered at Jordan's mind in overwhelming detail. He swayed and shuddered under the assault, but still clung stubbornly to his own sense of identity. Years of pretending to be people other than himself had given his mind a strength and resilience beyond the norm, and even as Viktor's memories strove to convert him into a duplicate of themselves, Jordan was already fighting back. He had to. His mind, his soul, everything that made him unique was in danger of being supplanted by the other man's memories. He clung fiercely to what was his, and slowly, gradually, the pressure faded. He began to pick and choose among the endless stream of information that flowed to him from Viktor, taking only what he needed. How to move, how to talk, how to seem Viktor without actually being him. And still the memories came and went. Jordan moved among them at his leisure, searching for anything that looked useful

or interesting. He came across something strange, and
Viktor tried to pull back, to hide the memory from
him. Jordan took control easily, and looked closely at
what Viktor hadn't wanted him to see.

*Viktor lay on his back in bed, with Heather snuggled
up against him. He stared up at the ceiling, his eyes
idly following a long wavering crack in the plaster.*

"Viktor . . ." said Heather muzzily.

"Yeah?"

"Do you really think there's going to be a civil war?"

*"Bound to be. Too many factions, and none of them
willing to compromise. Best way, in the long run. I
wouldn't feel safe as long as my brothers or the Regent
were still alive."*

*"I can see that, Viktor. But if there is a civil war,
thousands of people could die."*

*"Probably. It doesn't matter. They're only peasants,
after all. Breed like rabbits. Don't go all squeamish on
me now, Heather. I'm going to need your strength. I
learned my lesson during those long years in exile.
Look out for yourself first, and everyone else second,
if at all. I don't give a damn for the peasants or the
courtiers or anyone else in this stinking country. None
of them lifted a finger to help me when I needed help.
To hell with them all."*

Jordan recoiled in horror. He'd thought he was prepared for almost anything, but the depth of contempt
that Viktor had for his subjects shocked Jordan pro-
foundly. The prince used that moment to pull free.
There was a soundless roar, and a blinding light filled
Jordan's eyes. He lurched forward in his chair, unable
to deal with anything but the returning rush of sensa-
tions. His face twisted as a series of agonizing muscle
cramps hit him. The pains slowly faded away, and he
coughed harshly, his throat dry and raw. His eyes
ached, and he knuckled them as best he could with
his shaking hands. Already much of what he'd learned
was slipping away below the conscious level, but he
clung grimly to what was important. He looked coldly
at Prince Viktor, sitting slumped in his chair. The
prince's face was deathly pale, and he was barely re-

sponding to Heather and Roderik's attempts to wake him up. Jordan shuddered suddenly. He didn't know why he'd been so shocked at what he'd found in Viktor's mind. There was no law that said a king had to love his people. And compared to his brothers, Viktor was almost a saint. Perhaps it was just that Jordan was disappointed in Viktor. He'd hoped for better in the man he was to portray.

I was right the first time, he thought grimly. *I am playing a villain.*

Roderik leaned over him, and asked something about how he was feeling. Jordan gestured vaguely, trying to force words past his numb lips, and then Gawaine was there, pressing a glass of brandy into his hand. Jordan sipped the stuff gratefully, and his scattered thoughts slowly began to settle. He looked up and saw that Roderik and Argent were half leading and half carrying Viktor out of the room. The prince's face was slack and dazed. Roderik and Argent paused just long enough for Heather to pull Viktor's cowl forward so that it hid his face, then they hustled the prince out into the corridor. Heather hurried after them, swearing continuously under her breath. The guards pulled the door shut again, and Jordan was left alone in the room with Sir Gawaine. He held out his empty glass, and Gawaine poured him some more brandy. Jordan indicated for him to keep pouring, and didn't take his glass back till it was full to the brim.

"Have one yourself," he said hoarsely. "How's Viktor?"

"He'll recover," said Gawaine, pouring himself a small measure of brandy, and savoring the bouquet approvingly. "You're looking better, sire."

"I've felt worse. I take it no one expected this strong a reaction to the spell."

"Right." Gawaine frowned. "Sometimes I think Roderik doesn't know half as much about sorcery as he claims. If I'd known the spell would be this dangerous to the prince, I'd never have allowed him to use it. Still, it's done now. Did you learn anything useful?"

"Yes," said Jordan. "I learned a few things."

Gawaine waited a moment, until it became clear the actor wasn't going to say any more. He looked thoughtfully at Jordan, then emptied his glass and placed it carefully on a nearby table. "Seeing as you're well on the road to recovery, sire, I'd better go and see how Viktor's doing. If I were you, I'd get some sleep. Tomorrow is liable to be a very busy day. You'll be quite safe here. This suite is protected by strong magical wards, and the two guards outside will keep anyone from disturbing your rest."

"Before you go," said Jordan, "perhaps you'd answer a question for me."

"If I can, sire."

"Why hasn't Roderik put a geas on me, like he did DeGrange? That way he could be sure of controlling me."

The knight smiled thinly. "I'm sure the idea occurred to him, sire, but a geas would have been far too conspicuous. Any number of people here would have recognized it for what it was. Is there anything else, sire, before I go?"

"Yeah," said Jordan. "What about the dog?"

Gawaine looked at him blankly. "What dog, sire?"

"Viktor's dog," said Jordan irritably. "The one he keeps in his bedroom. What am I supposed to feed it on?"

"I think you must be mistaken," said Gawaine slowly. "Viktor doesn't have a dog. He can't stand the creatures."

"Look for yourself," said Jordan. "It's right there in the bedroom."

Gawaine walked over to the bedroom door and pushed it open. He looked inside, then pulled the door shut again. "There's no dog there now, Your Highness. Perhaps a stray got in here somehow. There are enough of them around the castle. They help keep the rats down. I shouldn't worry about it. Good night, Your Highness. Pleasant dreams."

He bowed formally, and left. One of the guards pulled the door firmly shut behind him. Jordan looked puzzledly at the closed bedroom door, then got up and walked slowly over to it. He was proud to note that his legs were only slightly unsteady. He put his brandy glass down on a garishly ugly little table, and pushed open the bedroom door. The room was empty. Jordan shrugged, and wandered into the bedroom. He sat down on the edge of the bed, and ran his hand caressingly over the luxurious eiderdown. It had been a long hard day, and he had enough things to worry about without brooding over some vanishing dog. He pulled off his boots, and wriggled his grateful toes. The bed felt wonderfully soft and comfortable.

If nothing else, at least while he was at the castle he should be able to get a good night's sleep.

Prince Lewis stood outside his brother Dominic's door and knocked politely. He waited impatiently for a reply, and tugged surreptitiously at the chain mail vest hidden under his jerkin. His guards had sealed off the corridor at both ends, but he still felt uneasy. Ironheart stood motionless in the middle of the corridor, his armor gleaming dully in the torchlight. If anyone did get past the guards, they'd still have to face him. And there was always the Monk. He stood silently at Lewis's side, a gray, baleful presence that was still somehow comforting. If you had to enter the lion's den, the best protection was to take something in with you that was even more dangerous than the lion. Lewis shuffled his feet restlessly, and wondered whether to knock again in case they hadn't heard him. Though he wouldn't admit it to anyone, Lewis was dying to see what Dominic's new quarters were like. No one except Dominic's own people were ever allowed inside, and none of them would talk about it. They couldn't. Dominic had put a geas on them.

Lewis started as the door swung silently open. He quickly regained his composure and stepped forward into the antechamber, carefully keeping both his face and his posture very calm and assured. In dealing with Dominic, it was important to appear confident at all times. He looked around to see who had opened the door for him, but there was no one there. The Monk entered the chamber, and the door slammed shut behind him. Lewis sniffed. More of Dominic's playing at sorcery. Let him keep his little tricks if they amused him; they didn't impress Lewis. He'd seen the Monk do things that would have scared Dominic out of what was left of his mind. Lewis looked casually about him, and frowned. Dominic's antechamber was bare and austere, the only furniture three straight-backed chairs set out on the bare stone floor. The bleak white-washed walls were spotlessly clean, and subtly depressing. This wasn't a room where people lived, it was just a room where people waited, while Dominic decided whether or not to see them. Lewis moved over to the nearest chair, flicked imaginary dust off the seat with his handkerchief, and sat down. The Monk took up a watchful stance beside him.

Lewis looked around sharply as Dominic and Elizabeth came in through a door he would have sworn wasn't there a moment ago. They stood alone by the door, and Lewis stiffened slightly as he realized that Dominic hadn't brought any troops to guard him. Either he didn't see his brother as much of a threat, or he was confident in his own sorcery to protect him. Dominic bowed briefly to Lewis, and he nodded curtly in return. He didn't get up from his chair, but they didn't seem to notice. They sat down on the two remaining chairs, and took their time making themselves comfortable.

"Well," said Lewis finally, "this is very pleasant, isn't it. Must be all of four years since you and I last sat down to talk together, Dominic."

"That's right," said Dominic. "Dear Viktor had just been banished from Court, and you and I were discussing how best to turn that to our advantage. You proposed a partnership, as I recall, but nothing came of it. We didn't trust each other. We knew each other too well, perhaps. Do you feel things have changed since then, Lewis?"

"Probably not. But we do have things to discuss. The Regent has just made a difficult situation suddenly even more difficult with the Rite of Transference. Interfering bastard. I should have had him killed a long time ago. He's always been too honest for our good. We've got to find the crown and seal quickly, Dominic. Since I don't have them, and my spies assure me that you don't have them, it seems to me the odds are very much in favor of Viktor having them. There must be some good reason why he hasn't used them yet, but now that the situation has changed so drastically, he could try for the Stone at any time. We'll have to take the crown and seal from him, and neither of us is strong enough to do that on our own. De-Grange's guards are all over the place, and Viktor's fire magic is as strong as ever. You saw what he did at Court."

"Yes," said Dominic. "It was most impressive. But what makes you so sure Viktor has the crown and seal?"

"Process of elimination," said Lewis smugly. "Outside of the three of us, who is there? A few nobodies who fancy themselves as kings, or kingmakers. My spies have kept a close watch on all of them. On the other hand, something is definitely happening with Viktor and his people. I haven't been able to find out what, they're too well shielded. But whatever it is, it's important. So important they've killed all of my people who even looked as though they might be getting near the truth."

"You're quite right," said Elizabeth. "There is something going on. But they don't have the crown or the seal. They're as baffled as we are."

Lewis looked at her thoughtfully. She was smiling too much, the cold calculating smile of someone who knows something you don't. On the other hand, that wasn't exactly unusual where Elizabeth was concerned.

"Just how sure are you of your information?" he said finally. "Last I heard, your people had been having the same problems as mine. Or have you and Viktor been getting acquainted again, now that he's back?"

"Hardly," said Elizabeth sweetly. "No, my dear Lewis, it's much simpler than that. We have a spy in their inner circle. A traitor. Would you like to meet him?"

Lewis fought to keep his face calm and undisturbed. If Dominic really did have a traitor in Viktor's camp, he had an advantage Lewis couldn't hope to match. How the hell had Dominic managed it? Lewis had tried everything from outrageous bribes to open death threats, without any effect at all. He would have sworn that all of Viktor's people were under a geas, they were so sickeningly loyal. Either that, or they didn't know anything good enough to be worth selling. He realized Dominic and Elizabeth were still looking at him inquiringly. Did he want to see the traitor? They knew damn well he couldn't afford to say no. He nodded stiffly, and got to his feet. Dominic and Elizabeth took their time getting up, and Lewis seethed inwardly. There had to be a catch in this somewhere. They were just baiting him, for the fun of it. If the traitor's identity had any real value, they'd never have mentioned his existence, let alone offer a chance to meet him.

"He's waiting for us in my private chambers," said Dominic calmly. "I thought you might like to take a look at them while you're here. I designed them myself, and I'm rather proud of the way they've come out. This way."

He turned to the inner door, and it swung smoothly open before him. He offered Elizabeth his arm, and the two of them walked unhurriedly through the doorway. Lewis jerked his head at the Monk, and hurried after them, barely able to contain his curiosity. The Monk followed after him, the hem of his long robe brushing noisily against the stone floor. Dominic and Elizabeth stood to one side as Lewis and the Monk entered the main room, and Lewis stumbled to a halt just inside the door, staggered by what he saw.

All of the intervening walls in Dominic's suite had been removed, turning it into one gigantic chamber. Lewis hated to think how many spells Dominic must be maintaining, just to keep the ceiling from collapsing. The outer walls had been painted varying shades of blue and green that shifted subtly as he watched, suggesting the endless tides and swells of the ocean. The air was unpleasantly moist, but the carpeted floor showed no signs of damp or rot. The scattered rugs and hangings were a depressingly bitter shade of green. Lewis supposed they were meant to represent seaweed. They were ugly enough. The delicate fili-greed furniture seemed out of place in the grotesque setting.

Lewis walked slowly forward, drawing strength from the silent figure of the Monk at his side. The glistening wall to his left swirled and heaved constantly, and Lewis suddenly realized he was looking at a vast expanse of water. He thought at first it must be contained behind a wall of strengthened glass, but when he moved over and reached out a hesitant hand to touch it, his fingers slid unimpeded into icy cold water. There was no wall. Only Dominic's sorcery held the water in place. Lewis stirred the surface of the water with his fingers, fascinated by the slow ripples that rolled away from the disturbance, and then something moved deep in the darkness of the water. Lewis watched, openmouthed, as a huge shark, easily thirty feet long, came surging out of the distance toward him, growing larger and larger as he watched. He snatched his hand out of the water and fell back a step. For one horrible moment, he thought the shark was going to burst out of the water after him, but at the last second it turned aside and swam along the length of the wall. Lewis's belly tightened as the shark's flat black eye rolled slowly in its smooth gray head, watching him. It knew he was there. Its teeth were a jagged row in a mouth that had never known a smile, and in its cold dead eye there was all the hunger in the world. The shark flicked its tail suddenly and was gone, gliding back into the immeasurable depths beyond the wall of water.

How far back does the water go? thought Lewis dazedly. *What the hell has Dominic done here?*

"One of my pets," said Dominic behind him, and Lewis jumped in spite of himself.

"Very impressive," he said tightly. "I never knew you were fond of fishing."

Dominic smiled, and Lewis felt something cold move within him. For a moment, Dominic's eyes had looked just like the shark's.

"I promised you an audience with my spy," said Dominic. "And here he is."

A man wrapped in a dark cloak appeared suddenly out of thin air to stand beside Dominic. Lewis jumped again, and flushed hotly. He didn't take kindly to being made the butt of someone else's humor. His hand dropped toward his sword hilt, but stopped a few inches short. He was in Dominic's territory now, and he daren't risk an open attack, even with the Monk at his side. On his own ground, Dominic was too well protected by his sorcery. Not to mention his Blood. Lewis turned his attention to the spy, and his stomach lurched. The man had no face. The eyelids were sealed seamlessly shut, and below the blind eyes there was only a blank expanse of smooth skin, with no trace of mouth or nose. He stood very still, waiting for Dominic's orders.

"This isn't how he usually looks," said Dominic casually, "But I'm not quite ready to trust you with his identity yet. That would require a great deal more commitment on both our parts than I think we're ready to give. But, I assure you, he is one of Viktor's inner circle, trusted by everyone, and privy to all their secrets. Aren't you, my dear traitor?"

"Yes, Prince Dominic." A flat mouth opened in the blank face like a wound. The voice was flat and expressionless, with no trace of character in it to provide clues as to the spy's identity. Lewis frowned.

"No offense, Dominic, but how do I know this . . . person really is who you say he is? He could be anyone."

"No offense taken, dear brother. I've brought him here to tell you things; things only an inner confidant could know. Tell him, traitor."

"Viktor is ill, and has been for some time," said the faceless man. "He is being slowly poisoned, and is growing steadily weaker, despite everything his supporters can do. Of late, he is unable to leave his chambers without help."

"He seemed strong enough this evening, in Court," said Lewis sourly.

"There is a reason for that," said Dominic. "But I don't think I'll share that with you just yet. I have to keep some secrets to myself."

Lewis sniffed. "All right, I'll accept the spy is genuine. I'd heard about Viktor's illness from my own confidential source. But can you trust this spy? Traitors are notoriously unreliable."

"He obeys my every whim," said Dominic flatly. "Traitor, put your hand into the water and leave it there."

The faceless man walked over to the swelling wall and thrust his hand into the water up to the wrist. He stood there unmoving, and Lewis's hackles rose sharply as he realized what was going to happen. Even as the thought crossed his mind, the dark shadow of the shark appeared in the distance. It moved rapidly forward, jaws agape for the tasty morsel of flesh that hung unmoving in the water before it. The faceless man didn't move an inch. At the last moment Dominic gestured sharply, and the traitor pulled his hand out of the water. The shark's jaws snapped together a fraction of a second later, and water splashed down onto the dark green carpet as the shark turned sharply aside. It swam back and forth for a while, and then disappeared back into the depths. The faceless man moved back to stand beside Dominic, who patted him lightly on the arm, as a man might reward a dog that had performed some simple but amusing trick. Lewis's breathing began to return to normal. He didn't give a damn whether the traitor lived or died, but the inhuman control it must have taken for him to just stand there while the shark approached . . . A sudden thought came to Lewis, and he looked sharply at his brother.

"This spy of yours, is he Unreal?"

"Yes and no," said Dominic, smiling. "Really,

Lewis, you can't expect me to tell you all my secrets. Do I ask you about the Monk? All you need to know is that my spy belongs to me, body and soul. He will do anything I require of him. Anything at all. Now then, Lewis, I think we finally come to the crux of your visit. You have come here, not for the first time, to propose an alliance between us against a common enemy. To be honest, I don't see that anything has changed since your last visit. We both want the same thing, and neither of us is likely to step aside for the other."

"Even so," said Lewis, "we still have common cause for the moment. If we can't get to the Stone, we can at least work together to make sure no one else can. There'll be time to worry about each other once we've taken care of the competition."

"I think you overestimate the strength of your position," said Dominic calmly. "To put it bluntly, dear Lewis, you don't have anything I need. My support among the Blood is far greater than yours, my troops are well armed and well trained, and I have my own spy in Viktor's inner circle. You have the Monk, admittedly, but I have my own magic, and frankly I think I trust that more than I'll ever trust the Monk. Particularly after that debacle of his at Barrowmeer. Releasing Bloody Bones from his grave really wasn't a very sensible thing to do, Lewis. I think that's all I have to say to you. You can go now."

Elizabeth smiled sweetly at Lewis, and took Dominic's arm. They started to turn away. Lewis flushed hotly as he realized he'd just been dismissed as casually as any servant.

"You never intended to go into partnership with me, did you, Dominic?"

"No," said Dominic. He stopped and looked back. "If it weren't for the Monk and Ironheart, Lewis, you wouldn't even be in the game any longer. As it is, you're merely a nuisance."

"Then why did you agree to see me?"

"You're a bright boy," said Dominic, turning away. "You'll work it out."

Lewis's hand dropped to his sword hilt, and then he froze as the sound of steel on steel came clearly to him from outside in the corridor. There were angry shouts and more sounds of fighting in the distance. Lewis drew his sword and started for the door. He looked back to curse Dominic, but he and Elizabeth and the faceless man had vanished without trace. Lewis swore briefly, then ran through the door and antechamber and out into the corridor.

The narrow passage was full of struggling men, and the air rang to the clash of swords on armor. A crowd of guards wearing Dominic's livery swarmed around Ironheart, trying to drag him down by sheer force of numbers. More guards lay dead and dying all around him. Ironheart moved slowly but remorselessly through his attackers, his sword still sheathed on his back, perhaps because there wasn't room to use it in the press of bodies, or possibly just because he preferred killing with his hands. His great mailed gauntlets swept back and forth, leaving a bloody trail of dying and crippled men in their wake. Flesh and bone tore and shattered under his inhuman strength, while swords and axes rang harmlessly from his armor. The guards fought like madmen, often scrambling over the bodies of their dead fellows to reach him, but all to no avail. He moved steadily forward, shaking off their clinging arms and slaughtering all those who came within reach of his blood-spattered fists.

Lewis roared a challenge and ran forward, sword at the ready. One of the guards turned to face him, and Lewis's sword flashed out to sink deep into his gut. The guard groaned, and sank to his knees. Lewis tore out his sword in a flurry of gore, and kicked the guard in the face. He laughed breathlessly, and threw himself at the next guard. The smell of blood hung heavily on the air, and Lewis grinned like a wolf as his sword rose and fell.

Ironheart thrust his fist clean through a guard's chest, and the bloody knuckles protruded from the man's back. He died with a look of disbelief still on his face. Another guard ducked under a flailing metal fist, and leaned forward to swing his ax at Ironheart's side. The huge steel blade punched through the armor and buried itself in Ironheart's ribs. As he lurched to a sudden halt, a third guard seized his chance and thrust his sword through one of the eyeholes in Ironheart's helm. The point of the sword jarred to a sudden halt against the back of the helmet. A great cheer went up from the guards, only to die raggedly away as they realized Ironheart wasn't falling. He shook the dead guard free from his hand, and killed both the guards attacking him before they could fall back out of range. He reached up and pulled the sword out of his visor, but left the ax hanging from his side. No blood flowed from either wound. Dominic's guards broke and ran back down the corridor, leaving their dead and wounded behind them.

The last man to go struck out at the Monk in passing, as a final gesture of defiance. The sword didn't even come close. The Monk gestured briefly with an empty sleeve, and the guard burst into flames. He screamed horribly, and careered off down the corridor. The other guards scattered to avoid him. His flesh boiled and ran away like wax from a candle flame. The light from his fire cast strange shadows on the corridor walls as he disappeared into the distance. Lewis wondered idly how far he'd get before the flames finally consumed him. He shrugged, put away his sword, and turned to face Ironheart. The knight pulled the ax free from his side and let it fall to the ground. His armor was battered, dented, and dripping with other men's blood, but there was nothing to suggest that he had taken any hurt at all. Lewis didn't even bother looking at the Monk. He glanced about him, taking in the extent of the carnage, and swore disbelievingly.

Dominic must have really wanted us dead, Lewis thought slowly.

"All right," he said tightly to Ironheart, "report. What's been happening while I was with Dominic?"

"Your brother's men were waiting for us," said Ironheart. "This was a carefully planned ambush, and we walked right into it." The voice from inside the helm was quiet and distinct, but very slightly slurred, as though the knight had some carefully controlled speech impediment. "The guards you set to watch this corridor are dead. They were attacked the moment the antechamber door closed behind you. It seems likely that your brother has arranged further attacks on your men in your absence. I recommend we return to your quarters immediately, and see what can be done to protect your position."

"I agree," said the Monk. "For the moment my magic protects us from sorcerous attacks, but the rest of your people are unprotected."

"I should have known!" Lewis hacked spitefully at the nearest corpse with his sword. "I'll bet this was Elizabeth's idea originally, the rotten little bitch. No wonder she hardly said a word while I was there! She just sat there, smirking at me, knowing that all the time I was talking to Dominic about cooperation and partnerships, my men were being butchered at his command! I'll have their heart's blood for this . . . Monk, I want a full defensive screen over the three of us, and over as many of my people as you can cover."

"That will leave me unable to mount any sorcerous offensives," said the Monk.

"I know!" snapped Lewis. "There's no point in attacking Dominic on his own ground; he's had all the time he needed to set up his own defenses. All we can do now is get the hell out of here, and salvage what we can. Damn them! I'll have Dominic's head for this. And Elizabeth's. I'll stick their heads on the railings outside the main gates and the ravens can eat their eyes! If my magic wasn't just earth magic . . ."

His voice dried up as he came again to his old, familiar frustration. Out on the moors, or in the countryside, his Blood magic made him stronger than either of his brothers, but as long as they remained inside the Castle, Lewis's magic was practically useless. And Viktor and Dominic had always been very careful never to be caught outside the Castle at the same time as Lewis . . . He controlled his anger with difficulty, and thought hard. There had to be something he could do to avenge this outrage . . . but he couldn't think of anything.

He stalked off down the corridor, kicking furiously at the corpses as he went. Ironheart and the Monk followed, a short way behind. Lewis's fury began to settle into a cold, calculating anger. When all was said and done, he had more gold and jewels than Dominic and Viktor put together. He'd always been the thrifty one in the family. Dominic might have cost him some men with this night's treachery, but there were always mercenaries ready to be hired. If he could get word to them in time. Lewis scowled determinedly. The game wasn't over yet. The real game was only just beginning.

Prince Viktor sat listlessly on the edge of his bed, his head bowed forward and his eyes half closed. The Lady Heather unbuttoned his shirt with gentle efficiency, and pulled it back off his arms. His torso was gaunt to the point of emaciation, and the skin was deathly pale. Heather forced herself not to pay it any attention. Viktor knew how ill he looked, but he couldn't bear seeing the knowledge of it in her eyes. She made herself concentrate on the simple business of getting Viktor out of his clothes and into his nightshirt. At first he'd refused to wear one, claiming it was an old man's garment, but as he became weaker, he quickly found the nights too cold without one. Heather did her best to keep up a steam of bright chatter as she undressed him, but she knew he wasn't fooled. He was so feeble now he could hardly help her at all, and it was that simple helplessness that infuriated him the most.

Finally Heather had him ready for bed, and she turned away to the nearby medicine table. Vials and bottles of all shapes and sizes clustered together in an untidy mess, the various liquids, powders, and roots making a dull rainbow of colors. Viktor had tried them all, at one time or another. Heather picked up the latest bottle and gave it a good shake. Viktor growled something under his breath.

"What was that, darling?" said Heather brightly.

"Nothing. Just an idea as to where that muck probably comes from. Are you sure I'm not supposed to rub it on instead of drinking it?"

"You really are a baby when it comes to taking your medicine, Viktor."

"Ah, shut up, or I'll hit you with my rattle."

Heather picked up a teaspoon, uncorked the bottle and poured out a generous dose. "Sooner or later we're bound to find one that helps, my dear, if only by the law of averages. Now are we going to do this the easy way, or am I going to have to hold your nose again?"

Viktor glared at her, but didn't have the energy for any more objections. Heather made herself keep smiling. It tore her heart to see him so down and defenseless. She brought the spoon carefully over to Viktor's mouth, and he gulped the thick chalky stuff down. He swallowed hard, and pulled a face.

"That tastes so vile it must be doing me good. Well, where's my sweetie? A good nurse always has a nice sweetie for afterward, to take the nasty taste away."

Heather leaned forward and kissed him gently on the lips. Viktor smiled at her ruefully.

"Sorry, love. The spirit is willing, but it's not in charge anymore. I'm tired. I'm always tired, these days."

Heather smiled comfortingly, and nodded. She didn't dare say anything for fear her voice would betray her. She carefully recorked the bottle and put it and the spoon back on the table. Then she leaned forward, took firm hold of his legs, and lifted them up onto the bed. He leaned backward, and she helped lower him the rest of the way. She pulled the heavy covers up over him, and his head sank exhaustedly back onto the pillow. Heather let her hand rest on his forehead for a moment. His skin was hot and dry to the touch.

"I never thought I'd die this way," said Viktor quietly. "A battle that went wrong, or a dagger in the back . . . that was something I'd grown used to. I could cope with that. But dying in bed, by inches . . . I'm scared, Heather."

"Don't be, my love. I'm here."

Viktor sighed, and closed his eyes. "I'm tired, Heather. Very tired. I think I'll sleep for a while. Are the guards and wards in place?"

"Yes, darling. Don't you worry about anything; you're perfectly safe here. Rest easy."

She leaned over and kissed him on the cheek, and he murmured something indistinct. She straightened up, and saw that his eyes were already closed and his face was slack. She stood by the bed for a while, watching his shallow breathing, then she turned and tiptoed out of the bedchamber. She shut the door quietly behind her, and sighed wearily. Her shoulders slumped. Being constantly cheerful and encouraging was hard work. She leaned back against the closed door with her eyes shut, gathering her strength. The Lady Emma Hellstrom looked up from her sewing, and smiled at her.

"Heather, my dear, you look tired enough to drop. Come over here and sit with me before you fall down."

Heather opened her eyes and smiled at Emma, and pushed herself away from the door. "He's settled now. I think he'll sleep for a while. I hope so, anyway."

"Still no improvement?"

"Worse, if anything. I've tried him on every medicine the surgeons have come up with, and none of them have made a blind bit of difference. He's so weak now, he can't even walk unaided. Oh Emma, it breaks my heart to see him this way."

The Lady Emma patted Heather comfortingly on the arm as she sat down beside her. "You must be strong, my dear. You have to be strong enough for both of you."

"I know, Emma. You think he's going to die, don't you?"

"Yes, I'm afraid so."

"He's not going to die. I won't let him. I swear, if I ever get my hands on the bastards who've done this to him . . ."

"You still think it's poison?"

"It has to be!"

"I don't see how it can be, Heather. I mean, Argent tastes everything before Viktor even touches it."

"I know, I know." Heather's tiny hands curled into fists, and frustration and anger made her face ugly. "Whoever it is, they've been very clever. When I find out who's responsible, I'll see to it that they die by inches."

"I'll help hold him down," promised Emma. Heather smiled fondly at her.

When they'd first met, Heather had wondered what Sir Gawaine had ever seen in his wife. The Lady Emma was a plump, mousy woman in her early forties. Whatever beauty she might once have had in her youth had faded away into plain, unremarkable features and a more than comfortably padded body. At first, Heather had seen her as just another victim for her wit, someone else to take out the day's frustrations on, but right from the beginning Emma had made a point of answering Heather in kind, and the two women quickly developed a surprisingly strong attachment for each other. As Viktor and Gawaine spent most of their time together, it was hardly surprising that Heather and Emma found themselves often in each other's company, and their early friendship had long since hardened into an unbreakable bond.

"Tell me," said Emma, "have you seen Viktor's double yet? What's he like?"

"Physically, he's so like Viktor it's frightening," said Heather. "He even sounds like him, most of the time. But I don't like him. He's an arrogant sort, like all actors—full of himself and forgetful of his proper place. But he'll do the job well enough. And afterward . . ."

She smiled grimly, and Emma chuckled. "My dear Heather, if you followed through on every one of your dire threats, we'd have to build another cemetery.

You can't kill everyone you don't like, or soon we'd have no one left to talk to."

Heather shook her head. "I'm right this time, Emma, and you know it. The actor has to die. We can't risk his telling anyone about his part in our little conspiracy, can we? It's not as if he was the only one marked for death. Once Viktor is king, he can't allow anyone in a position of power to have undue influence over him. Argent is a tradesman; we can bargain with him. But Roderik . . ." Heather pursed her lips thoughtfully. "He forgets his place too often, the nasty little man. Just because he has some Blood, he thinks he's as good as my Viktor. Sometimes he even seems to think that he's in charge of this conspiracy, and Viktor is only there to follow his orders. We can't have that, can we? No, once my Viktor is safely on the throne, there are going to be quite a few surprised faces at Court . . ."

The two women laughed quietly together, the gentle happy sound at odds with the grim delight in their faces.

Jordan was getting ready for bed when the dog reappeared. He'd just finished drawing back the bedclothes and laying out a tastefully embroidered nightgown, when something cold and wet nudged the back of his leg. He jumped, startled and looked down to see the bloodhound standing at his side, waiting patiently to be noticed. It stared up at him with its perpetually mournful face, and wagged its tail. Jordan took his hand away from his sword, and grinned at the dog. He knelt down beside it, and the bloodhound made a determined effort to lick his whole face spotlessly clean. Jordan laughed, and halfheartedly tried to fend the dog off.

"So you're back again, are you?" he said cheerfully. "Where have you been hiding yourself? Under the bed?"

The dog laid down and rolled over on its back so Jordan could rub its stomach. He did so, and wondered what to do next. He'd never had a dog of his own. He'd had his horse for several years, but the two of them had quickly established a policy of live and let live, and had rarely strayed from it. Jordan supposed he ought to feed the dog, but he wasn't entirely sure what bloodhounds ate, or where in the suite to look for it. And then he frowned, as he remembered Gawaine saying the dog definitely wasn't Viktor's. The prince hated dogs. Having met the prince, Jordan wasn't in the least surprised. The dog had to belong to somebody, though; it was too well groomed to be a stray. Perhaps it had just wandered into his room by mistake, and couldn't get out. He ought to call the guards outside his door and have them remove the dog, but it was a friendly animal, and Jordan felt in need of a little friendly support.

There was a knock at the main door, and Jordan looked up sharply. He wasn't supposed to have any visitors. The guards were under strict orders to turn everyone away until morning. Jordan hesitated, and whoever was outside knocked again. It was a loud, arrogant, demanding knock. Jordan decided he'd better answer it. The caller didn't sound as though he was going to go away, and it might just be important. He looked around for the dog, to get it out of sight, and found it had disappeared again. Clever animal. It wouldn't do for Prince Viktor to be seen being friendly with a dog. It wouldn't be in character. Jordan walked quickly out of the bedroom and over to the main door, and pulled it open. The Regent, Count William Howerd, stood waiting impatiently before him, still dressed in his formal robes. Jordan shot a quick glare at the two guards for not having warned him who it was. They stared determinedly straight ahead, avoiding his eyes. Jordan supposed he couldn't blame them. It was the Regent, after all.

"Well?" said Count William. "Aren't you going to invite me in?"

"Of course, sir Regent," said Jordan quickly. "My rooms are yours."

He stepped back out of the way, and the Regent swept in. He looked around the room distastefully, his gaze implying he'd seen more tastefully furnished slums. Jordan shut the door, and moved hesitantly forward to greet the Regent. He wasn't quite sure what to do for the best. Private audiences with the Regent hadn't been covered in any of his briefings.

"Would you . . . care for a drink, sir Regent?"

"Not at this hour, Viktor."

"Then what can I do for you?" Jordan suddenly decided he was being too polite. He was, after all, a prince of the Realm whose rest had been disturbed. He deliberately turned his back on the Regent, and walked unhurriedly over to the nearest chair. He sank down into it, and draped one leg idly over the arm of the chair. The Regent gave him a hard look. Jordan smiled blandly back.

"I am here to see you on a matter of some importance, Viktor," said the Regent coldly.

"I should hope so, at this hour," said Jordan. "Well, out with it, man. We haven't got all night. What's so important it couldn't wait till morning, when my advisers could be present?"

"You were at the Court this morning," said the Regent slowly. "You were there when I proclaimed the Rite of Transference. No matter what you or your advisers may believe, I assure you, it wasn't a move I made lightly, nor was it intended as a threat to you or your brothers' position. I've never made any secret of my feelings toward you or your family, but I've never allowed my personal feelings to influence my duties as Regent.

"Redhart needs a king. You saw what the steward uncovered at Court; the Unreal is loose in the Castle and growing stronger all the time. Only the king can put a stop to this, by drawing on the Stone; the rest of us are helpless. Viktor, any king is better than none. I'm not blind to the practicalities of the situation. If anyone other than a prince of the line is declared king, a civil war is all but inevitable. People are already choosing sides. They seem to have forgotten the horrors and bloodshed that such wars mean. Hundreds of thousands would die—not just guards and men-at-arms, but ordinary men, women and children, too. Farms would be burned, towns gutted, rivers poisoned. I don't want that. And I'm hoping you don't.''

"I'll do anything I can to avoid a civil war," said Jordan carefully, "but you must understand that I may not have much say in the matter. If my brothers start raising armies, it will be impossible for me to stay neutral. They wouldn't allow it.''

"Yes," said Count William. "I understand." He sighed suddenly, and shook his head. "It's late and I'm tired, so I'll come straight to the point. You always used to be the most reasonable of the princes, so I'm going to appeal to your sense of honor, to your duty to the kingdom. Do you have the crown and the seal?''

Jordan looked at the Regent blankly, while his mind worked furiously. By asking that question, the Regent was openly declaring that he didn't have the crown or the seal, and he had no idea of who did have them. And by that very openness, he was also declaring the weakness of his position, and his need for allies. He was asking Jordan to work with him.

"I don't have the crown or the seal," said Jordan finally. "And as far as I can tell, neither of my brothers have found them either.''

The Regent waited, but Jordan said nothing more. The silence stretched on, pregnant and uncomfortable with hidden meanings, until the Regent nodded reluctantly. "I see. Thank you for being so frank with me. In return, I'll be honest with you. You won't have heard yet, but open fighting has broken out between Lewis and Dominic's troops. My guards are doing their best to restore order, but there's a limit to what they can do. Particularly since they've been spread so thin trying to contain the Unreal. Viktor, it seems to me that you're bound to be drawn into the conflict sooner or later. If I were you, I'd start preparing against magical attacks. Your protective wards here are excellent, but they have their limitations, as I'm sure you're aware. I'll just say one more thing, and then I'll leave. Your time in exile seems to have mellowed you somewhat. I'm glad to see it. But as Regent for the kingdom, I can't stand by and allow civil war to break out in Redhart. I will do everything in my power to support whoever eventually produces the crown and seal. And if that means having to order your brothers' deaths, or yours, I'll do it. For the sake of the kingdom, Viktor; don't stand against me."

He turned suddenly and left, pulling the door quietly shut behind him. Jordan heaved a long sigh of relief. He'd been getting in over his head and he knew it. He was in no position to commit Prince Viktor to anything. He'd better talk to his advisers quickly, and let them decide what to do about the Regent's warnings. He felt better almost immediately, now that he'd shifted the burden onto somebody else. He started for the door, and then stopped suddenly. He couldn't go running to Count Roderik in the middle of the night; he was a prince. It would look very strange, not to mention suspicious. He'd be better off sending one of the guards with a message. Jordan froze suddenly as from behind him came a low, animal growl. He spun around, and saw that the bloodhound was back, and staring fixedly at an empty corner of the room. The dog stood stiff-leggedly, its head stretched out toward the corner, and growled ferociously. Jordan's hackles rose, and a cold hand clutched at his heart. He couldn't see anything in the corner, but when he was a child his grandmother had told him that dogs could often see ghosts where people couldn't. And Castle Midnight was supposed to be full of ghosts . . .

"Easy, boy," he said quietly to the dog. "What is it? What can you see?"

The air before him rippled and grew hazy, and the Monk appeared in the corner. The dog backed quickly away, growling and showing its teeth. Jordan's hand dropped to the sword at his side. He wasn't sure if there was anything inside the Monk's robe that he could hit with a sword, but if the Monk came any closer, he was going to have a damned good try at finding out. He glared at the darkness inside the Monk's cowl.

"I don't recall inviting you in."

"Doors and walls are no barrier to me," said the Monk in his quiet, dusty voice. "I bring greetings from your brother Lewis, and a message."

"All right," said Jordan, "Give me the message, and then get out."

"You waste your breath in threatening me," said the Monk. "You have no authority here, actor."

Jordan's heart stumbled in mid beat, and for a moment he thought he was going to faint. The moment passed, but he could feel his legs trembling uncontrollably. He felt as though he'd suddenly dried in the middle of a big speech, and forgotten all his words. "What do you mean, *actor*?" he said finally, and took a certain amount of pride from the calm evenness of his voice.

"There are no secrets from me in Castle Midnight," said the Monk. "You have Viktor's face and body, but that's all. I've seen the real prince asleep in another room."

"You said you had a message," said Jordan, deliberately not replying to the Monk's accusation. "Get on with it, messenger."

The long gray robe seemed to stir briefly, and Jordan wondered if he was pushing his luck. This was one of the most powerful sorcerers in Castle Midnight, and all he had were the flare pellets up his sleeve and a few spare smoke bombs. Jordan tried hard to think which door was the nearest, in case he needed to make a sudden exit. The Monk's robe grew still again, and Jordan relaxed a little. He still kept his hand near his sword, though.

"I bear this message from your brother Lewis," said the Monk softly. "It's time to choose sides. Those who are not with Lewis are against him. Those who will not kneel to him are his enemies. Lewis will be king of Redhart, and any who dare stand between him and the throne will die."

Jordan waited patiently awhile, and then raised an

eyebrow. "Is that it? Lewis must be getting desperate. Tell him he can take his threats and stuff them where the sun don't shine. And if you ever enter my rooms uninvited again, I'll burn that mangy-looking robe of yours to ashes and then piss on the ashes. Now on your way, or I'll set my dog on you."

He turned his back on the Monk, and ostentatiously studied his appearance in a nearby mirror. There was a deafening silence behind him. His back crawled, and then the Monk laughed. There was no humor in the sound, only an awful patient hatred. Jordan counted to ten slowly, and then turned around. The corner was empty, and the Monk was gone. There was also no sign of the dog. Jordan had a sudden horrid suspicion that the Monk had taken the dog with him as a kind of revenge, but even as he thought it he heard the animal snuffling somewhere nearby. He walked slowly around the room, calling encouragingly, and looking under chairs and behind hanging tapestries. There was no sign of the dog anywhere, and the snuffling sounds had stopped. Jordan came to a halt in the middle of the room and looked around him. *The dog's got to be here somewhere* . . . He knelt down and crawled under one of the tables. There was a suppressed giggle behind him. Jordan straightened up suddenly, and banged his head on the underside of the table. He cursed feelingly, put his hand to his head, and sat down suddenly. The giggles stopped.

"Sorry," said a quiet voice.

Jordan looked around, and found himself face-to-face with a young boy, about seven or eight years old. He was painfully thin, with a narrow pinched face and straight straw-colored hair. He was standing awkwardly in that plaintive stance young children adopt when they know they've done something wrong, but his pale blue eyes were bright and steady, and his timid smile brought an answering smile to Jordan's lips. The boy was dressed in very conservative, somewhat old-fashioned clothes, but they looked neat enough. *Hand-me-downs,* thought Jordan sympathetically. *We all go through it.*

He crawled out from under the table, got to his feet, and dusted himself off. "What's your name?" he asked the boy kindly.

"Geordie," said the boy shyly. "Everyone calls me Wee Geordie, 'cause I'm small for my age. Mother says I'll grow taller later on, though. Both my brothers are tall."

"Well, Geordie," said Jordan, "I'm Viktor. Now what are you doing in my chambers at this time of night. You're not really supposed to be here, are you?"

Geordie bit his lower lip, and looked down at his feet. "I'm lost. I'm looking for my mother. We got separated, and I can't find her. Have you seen her?"

"I don't know, lad. Can you tell me her name?"

"Lady Mary of Fenbrook. She's ever so pretty."

"I'm sure she is," said Jordan. "But I don't think I've met her. I'll tell you what. I'll talk to the guards outside my door, and one of them will take you to the steward. She'll find someone to look after you, while they look for your mother to tell her where you are. Is that all right?"

Geordie smiled, and nodded. "I know Kate. She's nice."

I just hope she doesn't mind my dumping you on her, thought Jordan, *but I'm damned if I can think of anyone else.*

A small hand nestled trustingly into his, and Jordan gave it a reassuring squeeze. He led the boy over to the main door and opened it. The guards looked in surprise at Wee Geordie, and Jordan glared at them both impartially.

"This young scamp managed to sneak in here without either of you spotting him. If you think you can stay awake long enough, I want one of you to take him to the steward and stay with him until they find his mother. Think you can manage that? Good. Because if I find out later that you just left him there on his own, I'll have you both peeling potatoes in the kitchens until your fingers turn brown! Is that clear?"

Both the guards nodded emphatically, and one of

them held out his hand to the boy. Geordie looked
up at Jordan, and he nodded that it was all right. The
boy transferred his grip to the guard's hand, and the
two of them went off down the corridor. Jordan
looked hard at the remaining guard.

"See if you can remain alert from now on. Because
if I get any more uninvited guests this evening, I am
going to be distinctly peeved with you. Got it?"

The guard nodded quickly. Jordan went back into
his suite and slammed the door shut behind him. It
had been a long day, and so far it had shown no signs
of getting any shorter. He looked longingly at the door
to his bedchamber, and thought wistfully about the
deep soft mattress that awaited him. *The next person
who disturbs me,* he thought grimly, *had better have a
bloody good reason. And even then I might not listen.*

He'd only taken a few steps toward his bedroom
when the commotion began. Someone roaring threats
and curses was charging up and down the corridor,
apparently pausing now and then to hit the floor with
something heavy. *I am going to ignore this,* thought
Jordan determinedly. *It's none of my business, and I
am not going to get involved.* He waited hopefully for
a few moments to see if the uproar would quieten
down of its own accord. It didn't. Jordan tapped his
foot impatiently, and began to seethe quietly as it became clear he was going to have to deal with whoever
it was, if he hoped to get any sleep that night. He
strode over to the main door and jerked it open.

Something about two feet high and dressed all in
scarlet shot between his legs, scurried into his suite,
and disappeared. Jordan barely had time to react before he looked up to see Damon Cord charging
straight at him, brandishing the biggest solid steel mallet that Jordan had ever seen. He jumped back out of
the way just in time to avoid being bowled over, and
Cord roared into the suite in hot pursuit of whatever
the small scarlet streak had been.

"Shut the door!" snapped Cord. "Don't let it get
away!"

Jordan shut the door. When he looked around

again, Cord was standing very still in the middle of the room, his mallet poised and ready to strike.

"Cord . . ."

"Quiet, Your Highness, it's gone to ground."

"I don't care if it's gone abroad for its holidays; what is it?"

"A redcap. Nasty little buggers. They hide in the wainscotting, and come out at night to feed on human flesh. They're particularly fond of children's flesh."

Cord began a slow quartering of the room, checking each possible hiding place with the maximum of caution. Jordan was reminded irresistibly of his own search for the disappearing bloodhound, but had enough sense not to smile. He didn't think Cord was in the mood to appreciate the funny side.

"Why a mallet?" he said finally. "What's wrong with a good old-fashioned sword or ax?"

"Redcaps are notoriously hard to kill, Your Highness. Fire's the only thing that'll do it for sure. That's why I chased it in here. If worse comes to worst, you can always use your fire magic to fry the little bastard. Got you!"

The two-foot-tall creature shot out from under an armchair and threw itself at Cord's ankles. Jordan had a brief impression of an impossibly wide mouth crammed with needle teeth, and then Cord's mallet swung down in a silvery blur and hurled the redcap away. It flew squalling through the air and slammed into an ornamental table, overturning it. The collection of porcelain plates carefully stacked on top of the table cascaded to the floor and smashed into hundreds of pieces. The redcap picked itself up, entirely unharmed, and effortlessly tore one of the legs from the overturned table. It hefted the ironwood leg like a club, and grinned nastily at Cord. Jordan watched sickly as the creature's mouth stretched almost literally from ear to ear.

The redcap was disturbingly human in shape, but impossibly thin and slender. Its arms and legs were little more than pipe cleaners, but its magical nature gave it unnatural strength and vitality. Cord swung his huge mallet, and the redcap dodged it. The mallet swung on, unable to stop, and demolished a glass display case full of china miniatures. The noise was tremendous. Cord hauled his mallet free of the wreckage, destroying what was left of the glass case, and then had to jump back himself as the redcap wielded its ironwood club. The table leg missed Cord, and sank half its length into the wall, driven into the solid stone like a nail into wood. Cord swung his mallet again, and in order to dodge it, the redcap was forced to abandon its weapon. It skittered away across the floor with Cord in hot pursuit. A centuries-old writing table and an ornamental hat stand fell prey to Cord's mallet along the way. Still entirely unhurt, the redcap took refuge behind an overstuffed armchair and screamed defiance at him.

A part of Jordan's mind was busy totting up the damages, even as he drew his sword and moved forward to join Cord. His new access to Viktor's memories enabled him to remember exactly how much each piece of furniture had cost originally, and how difficult they would be to replace. He had a horrible suspicion Viktor and Roderik would decide this was all his fault, and deduct the cost from his fee.

Jordan decided he'd better do something to help Cord get the redcap, while there was still some furniture left. He chose his moment carefully, leapt forward, and ran the creature through with his sword. The blade punched clean through the redcap's chest and out its back. No blood ran from the wound. The redcap chuckled throatily, and grabbing the edges of the blade with its tiny hands, began to pull itself along the blade toward Jordan. Its great mouth chomped hungrily in anticipation. Jordan dropped his sword and stumbled back a step. The redcap pulled the blade out of its body and threw the sword to one side. Cord's mallet whistled through the air, and the redcap was off and running again.

Cord chased the thing around and around the room while Jordan got his breath back. The redcap scuttled under chairs and over tables, hiding in every possible

nook and cranny, trying always to make it to the door
or to the wainscotting, but somehow Cord was always
there first to drive it back. Once Jordan would have
sworn the creature actually ran up one of the walls
and headed for the ceiling before Cord intercepted it,
but by that time he was so confused from trying to
keep track of it that he couldn't be sure what he'd
seen. All he was sure of was the continuing rising cost
of damaged furnishings.

Fire, thought Jordan desperately, *Cord said the redcaps hated fire.* He palmed one of his flare pellets,
and was surprised at how few he had left. He'd have
to be careful how he used them until he had a chance
to make some more. He pushed the thought to the
back of his mind, waited for his chance, and then
nicked the wax coating of the pellet with his fingernail
and threw it at the redcap. The pellet broke open on
contact with the redcap's chest, and burst into flames.
The redcap howled with pain and fear, and tried to
beat out the flames with its bare hands. Cord's mallet
swung down and around while the creature was distracted, and sent the redcap flying backward into the
suite's main fireplace. The tiny creature slammed into
the blazing logs and coals and shrieked horribly. For
a moment it scrabbled helplessly among the flames,
and then it exploded into a dirty smoky gas that shot
up the chimney and disappeared. The last echo of its
screams died away, and the suite was suddenly quiet,
save for the crackling of the flames in the fireplace.
Cord reversed his mallet and leaned on it, grinning at
Jordan.

"Nicely done, Your Highness. I was wondering how
long it would take you to lose your temper and blast
the little swine with your fire magic. And now, if
you'll excuse me, I must go. The steward needs me."

And he was out the door and gone before Jordan
could think to mention the mess Cord had made of
the suite. He'd seen battlefields that were less messy.
Jordan sighed, and shook his head resignedly. At least
the bedroom door had been shut, so he still had somewhere intact left to sleep. He retrieved his sword and

sheathed it, thought about making a start about cleaning up the mess and thought better of it, and then spun around suddenly as he heard the door open behind him. It was only Cord, frowning slightly. Jordan took his hand away from his sword.

"Forgot to ask while I was here, sire; have there been any outbreaks of the Unreal in this part of the Castle? We've had sightings practically everywhere else."

"Nothing here," said Jordan. "Apart from the redcap."

"No unusual visitors in the past hour or so?"

Jordan decided not to mention the Monk. Things were complicated enough as they were. "There was a young boy who'd got separated from his mother, but that's all. One of my guards is looking after him."

"Oh yes?" said Cord. "That wouldn't have been Wee Geordie, by any chance?"

"That's right. Do you know him?"

"In a manner of speaking."

"Good. I sent him over to the steward. Maybe you can help her find the lad's mother."

"I already know where she is, sire. In the castle cemetery. She and Wee Geordie have both been dead these past two hundred years. You should feel honored, sire; Wee Geordie doesn't show himself to many people. He's one of the rarer ghosts in Castle Midnight. Quite well documented, though." Cord frowned, his scarred face set and grim. "He was nine years old when he died. Now he's spent two centuries wandering through the corridors, lost and alone, searching for his mother. Poor soul."

Jordan looked at Cord blankly. "But he was real, solid . . . he held my hand."

Cord raised an eyebrow. "This is Castle Midnight, Your Highness."

"Of course," said Jordan quickly. "I've been away from home too long, that's all. Everything's fine here now, Cord. You can go."

Cord bowed formally and left, closing the door quietly behind him. Jordan sat down heavily on the nearest intact chair, shaken at how close he'd come to giving himself away. Of course the real Viktor wouldn't have been surprised about the ghost; he'd probably grown up surrounded by the things. The Great Jordan, on the other hand, had never seen a ghost before in his life and would be just as happy if he never saw another one. And yet, Wee Geordie hadn't been exactly frightening . . . he'd just seemed shy, worried, and lost.

Jordan frowned. Maybe Geordie didn't know he was dead, and a ghost. How could a child that age ever really understand what had happened to him? All he would know for sure was that his mother had apparently gone off and left him on his own, surrounded by strangers. Jordan shuddered, strangely touched by the young ghost's fate. Two hundred years . . . no child should have to suffer such a thing. There must be something he could do to help. Maybe the steward could do something . . . Jordan's frown deepened. He couldn't afford to ask such a thing; it would be totally out of character for Viktor. The prince wouldn't have given a damn if he'd met Geordie. He'd probably have put the boy out of his room on the end of his boot, in fact. Jordan stared broodingly at the wall in front of him. No, he couldn't get involved. It was too dangerous. Word would get around. Questions would be asked.

But Geordie had trusted him. No one had trusted Jordan in a very long time.

He sighed unhappily. More and more, Jordan was coming to the conclusion that he didn't like Viktor at all. On the stage, he'd always played his aristocratic roles as honorable men, noble and heroic. In reality, he was finding them to be devious, treacherous, and even openly evil. Jordan scowled. He didn't like the way his thoughts were running. He was here to do a job, not make character judgments on his employers. He'd worked for scum before, in his time, and it had never bothered him as long as their money was good. At Castle Midnight he was acting a part, nothing more, and being bloody well paid for it. Jordan sighed heavily. He was tired, and his head hurt. He'd think about it again in the morning. Things might seem clearer in the light of day.

He heaved himself up out of his chair, but before he could take a single step toward his bedroom, the air tore open before him, and out of the shimmering gap stepped a man with no face. The gap disappeared with a grating roar. Any other time, Jordan might have been impressed. As it was, the faceless man was just another damned visitor who stood between him and his bed. Jordan sank back into his chair and glared at the faceless man.

"What the hell do you want?"

A thin flat wound opened at the base of the blank face to make a mouth. "I have a message for you, from Prince Dominic."

Jordan watched as the wound closed and disappeared. "Out of all the uninvited guests I've had this evening, you have got to be the most repulsive and the least welcome. I can't think of a single thing Dominic might have to say that couldn't wait till morning. Now beat it, or I'll have you exorcised."

"I'm not a ghost."

"Keep annoying me, and that could change suddenly." Jordan glared firmly at where he imagined the eyes should be in the blank face, but the newcomer showed no signs of being intimidated. Jordan sighed wearily. "All right, get on with it. But keep it short, or I'll heckle you."

"Prince Dominic sends his regards. He bids me tell you that you now have twelve hours in which to leave Castle Midnight. Stay here one minute longer, and you will be killed. You're playing in a dangerous game, actor. Whatever they're paying you, it isn't enough. Leave while you still can. This is the only warning you'll get."

The world split open and swallowed up the faceless man. The air in the suite shuddered as he vanished, as though at a minor roll of thunder. Jordan closed his eyes. Did everyone in Castle Midnight know he was an actor and an impostor? Certainly it seemed both Lewis and Dominic at least suspected the truth. Presumably they weren't sure yet, or they'd have exposed him at Court. Jordan scowled unhappily. If they did have any real proof against him, the sensible thing to do would be to get out while he still could. But if Lewis and Dominic were just guessing, his sudden departure would be all the proof they needed. They might even send a company of guards after him to drag him back to Castle Midnight to answer questions. Always assuming Viktor's people didn't try to kill him for running out on them. And either way, it would mean giving up all hope of his fifty thousand ducats. Jordan felt very strongly about those ducats. He felt he'd earned them.

No, he was going to have to stay put, at least for the time being. Dominic's threat had to be at least partly bluff. Jordan relaxed a little as he thought it through. Roderik had assured him he was perfectly safe in the suite, and when he had to leave it he'd have Gawaine and the others to protect him. On the other hand, all that protection hadn't done much to keep out the apparently endless stream of visitors he'd had all evening. Didn't anybody sleep in this castle?

There was a knock at his door.

Jordan jumped to his feet and stared at the main door, his head down like a cornered stag. His hand twitched beside his sword hilt. "I don't care who it is!" he yelled. "I don't care if you're my long-lost rich uncle from Hillsdown, a ghost looking for his missing head, or a phantom with piles, you can all go to hell! I am tired and I don't want to be disturbed! Now beat it or I'll fricassee you!"

The door swung open, and the Lady Gabrielle Howerd walked in. "Really, Viktor, is that any way to talk to your own sister?"

Jordan ignored her and glared at the lone guard standing outside his door. "You're not making any friends here, you know. This is not helping your career at all. If one more person comes through this door, I am going to do something extremely unpleas-

ant to you—probably involving boiling oil and a
funnel!"

He slammed the door on the heavily perspiring
guard and turned back to face the Lady Gabrielle.
"All right, you're here. I take it you've got a message
for me. Everyone else has. Take a seat. If you can
find one."

Gabrielle looked around at the shattered furniture,
and raised an elegant eyebrow. "Been throwing another of your parties, Viktor?" She picked up one of
the overturned chairs, tested the seat carefully, then
put the chair down facing Jordan and sat down on it.
She smiled brightly at him, and laced her fingers together in her lap. "I don't have any particular message
for you, my dear. I just thought you and I should have
a little chat. It's been four years since we last saw each
other, and a great many things have changed since
then."

"So they have," said Jordan. He sat down on his
chair and smiled politely at her. *You call her Gabby,*
said a quiet voice in his mind, a memory he'd acquired
from Viktor. *It's a pet name between you. You could
have been very close, if you hadn't both been so ambitious and competitive.* "I had a visit from your husband
earlier on, Gabby. He seems a solid enough sort.
Quite decent, in his way."

"He's an honest man," said Gabrielle. "Father
thought well of him."

Jordan grinned. "What did Dad have to say about
your marriage?"

"I don't use language like that," said Gabrielle
primly. " He came around, eventually. Which is more
than can be said for Lewis or Dominic."

"Stuff them," said Jordan. "From what I can tell,
William's made a good enough Regent. But he
shouldn't have proclaimed the Rite of Transference.
It'll cause more problems than it solves."

"Perhaps," said Gabrielle.

"I liked the way you took care of those Unreal birds
at Court," said Jordan. "It must have taken quite a

bit of nerve to just stand there and trust to your magic to see you through."

Gabrielle smiled gratefully. "Thanks for noticing. People tend to forget I've got air magic in my own right. They tend to think of me either as Malcolm's daughter, or William's wife."

Jordan looked at her thoughtfully. "As I recall, you were never much of a one for little chats, Gabby. Why don't you just say whatever it is straight out? I've had a long day and a longer evening, and I'm really not in the mood for subtlety."

"Your time in exile has sharpened your wits," said Gabrielle approvingly. "I'm glad some good came of it. You want it straight; fair enough. Our time is over, Viktor. The present royal line simply isn't worthy to sit on the throne of Redhart. Lewis is degenerate, Dominic is insane, and you . . . to be honest, Viktor, you've never really shown any interest in what being king means. It was always too much like hard work for you, and duty and honor were just words.

"The Unreal is stronger now than it's ever been, and it's fighting to break free from Castle Midnight. Redhart needs a strong king on the throne, to hold things together and put down the Unreal. The Rite of Transference could give us such a king. Providing you and our brothers don't interfere. I'm sure William had already told you that Lewis and Dominic have declared war on each other. Don't get involved, Viktor. Their troops and my husband's guards are more or less evenly balanced, but if you and your forces were to join the fighting, there's no telling what might happen. You would almost certainly be killed, along with all your people, but the damage would have been done. Stay out of it, Viktor. For all our sakes."

Jordan studied her thoughtfully. Gabrielle's face was flushed, and her eyes were burning with an almost disturbing intensity. Without knowing how or why, Jordan knew she was holding something back. Important as this obviously was to her, there was still something she wasn't telling him, something that burned beneath her calm and reasonable words with the red sullen glow of obsession.

"For all our sakes," he said finally. "Tell me, Gabby; would it really matter to you at all if I was killed?"

Gabrielle's mouth twitched in what might have been a smile. "Perhaps. Just a little. You used to be a fairly likable sort until that bitch Elizabeth got her claws into you. And you did keep quiet when William and I first got engaged. If Dad had found out we were cousins by Blood, he would have banned our marriage. I couldn't have stood that. William is everything to me, and always has been. You knew about our Blood, but you never said a word. We owe you one for that. But in the end, I have to be more concerned about the kingdom. A civil war is destructive enough at the best of times, but with the Unreal poised to break loose at the first opportunity, a civil war now would be madness. I need to know your answer, Viktor. Never mind what you told William, tell me the truth."

"It's yours," said Jordan. "And it's the same answer I gave your husband. I'll stay neutral if I can, but I doubt very much if Lewis and Dominic will let me. I'll have to fight sooner or later, to protect my life if not my claim to the throne."

"You could always leave."

"Dominic already suggested that. In fact, he said he'd kill me if I didn't."

"Are you going to leave?"

"No."

"So you learned stubbornness as well, in your exile." Gabrielle got to her feet. "I hope you'll reconsider your position, Viktor, but knowing you, I doubt it. I'll talk to you again tomorrow. Good night."

Jordan got quickly to his feet and escorted her to the door. She nodded a brief good-bye, and then left. Jordan shut the door firmly behind her. He then leaned wearily against the door and wondered if he had enough strength left to barricade it. He didn't think he could stand another visitor. He shook his head and started yet again toward his bedroom door. He'd almost made it when the globe of water appeared around his head, and suddenly he was drowning.

He clawed frantically at the globe, and his hands splashed freely through the water without affecting it. He staggered back and forth, mouth clamped shut to avoid breathing water, and the globe moved with him so that his head was always completely surrounded by water. It wasn't a very large globe, only just big enough to enclose his head completely, but that was enough to kill him. Already his lungs were aching for air, and his head was growing muzzy. Soon his mouth would open despite him, and once he started trying to breathe water, he was lost. He looked desperately around him, the world rendered vague and distorted by the water before his eyes.

His gaze fell on the rack of clay pipes Viktor had set out for his guests, and an idea came to him. He lurched over to the rack, still somehow miraculously intact despite all the damage around it, and grabbed one of the long slender pipes. He broke off the bowl, leaving a long hollow tube in his hand. He slipped one end in his mouth, and the pipe was just long enough that the other end stuck out of the water. He sucked in air through the tube, and the ache in his lungs slowly lessened. His head cleared, and some of his panic began to die away. If nothing else, he'd bought himself some thinking time.

He didn't have long to come up with an answer. This was water magic, and that meant Dominic. He must be watching somehow, despite the wards, and as soon as he realized why his water spell wasn't working, all he had to do was increase the size of the globe of water, and the Great Jordan would have given his last performance. He had to get rid of the globe. But how? He didn't have any magic. He forced himself to think calmly and logically. This was an attack by elemental magic. Certain elements canceled each other out, like fire and water . . . Fire. That was the answer.

He palmed one of his flare pellets and crushed it in

his hand. Flames roared up around his fingers, and he thrust his hand into the water surrounding his head. There was a great burst of steam, and then both fire and water were gone. Jordan spat out the clay tube and slumped to his knees, gulping in air. His breathing finally slowed, and he shook his head disgustedly. He should have stuck to the theater—the worst you had to worry about there was the critics.

Jordan leaned back against an overturned table, and enjoyed the simple luxury of breathing. It would appear Dominic had decided not to give him twelve hours, after all. And yet . . . if Dominic had really wanted him dead, there were any number of other ways that he could have done it, most of them much more efficient. Filled his lungs with water, for example, or drained all the water from his body. Dominic might be crazy, but he wasn't stupid.

Dominic's messenger, the faceless man, had known he was an actor. Or at least suspected it. Perhaps they weren't sure one way or the other, and the water attack had been a test, to see if he had fire magic. If they were watching, they should be thoroughly confused by now. Jordan got slowly to his feet. He supposed he should be feeling scared or angry or both, but he was just too tired. All that mattered to him now was getting some sleep. Anything else could wait till the morning. He entered his bedroom and flopped down on the bed fully clothed, too worn out to even make an attempt at undressing. He stared up at the ceiling for a moment, and then his eyes slowly drifted shut.

Fifty thousand ducats . . . fifty thousand ducats . . . Stuff the bloody ducats.

CHAPTER 5

Sanctuaries
and Damnations

Prince Dominic sat alone in his private quarters, slumped elegantly in an ivory throne carved from the skull of a sea creature long since extinct. The room was dark and gloomy, lit only by a dull blue glow from the wall of water before him. Dominic stared into the endless depths with brooding, unseeing eyes. His water attack had failed, and Dominic wasn't used to failing. It had only been a simple spell, but it should have been more than enough to take care of some overambitious actor pretending to be a prince.

Dominic had watched intently as the man staggered back and forth, slowly drowning . . . and then Viktor had destroyed the spell with his fire magic. From now on Viktor would be constantly on his guard, and his death would be that much harder to arrange. Moreover, Dominic had been made to look a fool. He frowned, and gestured sharply with his left hand. The air stretched and split open, and the man with no face appeared before him. He sank down onto one knee before the ivory throne, and bowed his blank head.

"You told me the man in my brother's apartment was an impostor," said Dominic. "You told me you had arranged an opening in the protective wards, and that this actor had no magic of his own. But my water spell failed, dispersed by fire magic. Why did you lie to me?"

The faceless man jerked silently as long hairline cracks appeared in the skin of his blank face. Blood ran sluggishly from the cracks, and dripped from his

chin. He raised his hands to Prince Dominic in suppli-
cation, and more blood ran from hairline cracks in his
palms and fingers. "I didn't lie, sire. I swear, I didn't
lie to you. The impostor is a conjurer, and very quick
of mind."

"Why didn't you tell me this before?"

"It didn't seem important, sire." Blood ran down
his face in a steady stream, and his unfinished features
twisted in agony.

"From now on," said Dominic, "tell me everything.
I'll decide what's important and what isn't. How long
before you can arrange another opening in the wards?"

"A few hours, sire. Maybe more." The wounds on
his face slowly began to close. The last of the blood
began to dry on the blank face. He remained kneeling
before Dominic, head bowed.

"Viktor's death isn't really important," said Dominic finally. "He's no threat to my position, as long as
I have you to tell me his plans. And the poison will
kill him soon anyway. But this actor annoys me. He
has intruded into a situation where he doesn't belong,
and he seeks to meddle with my life, my destiny. And
the low-born scum actually has the nerve to play at
being a prince. His presence in my home offends me.
I could kill him easily, but that's not enough. I want
him broken and publicly humiliated first."

"There is a way," said the faceless man. "There's
a Testing scheduled for tomorrow, before the Stone.
A young man from one of the minor lines is laying
claim to Blood. Traditionally, the royal line always
attends such ceremonies. Even after everything that's
happened, a Testing is too important to be ignored,
so both you and your brothers will be expected to be
there. You can use the occasion to call out the actor
as an impostor. He won't dare spill his blood on the
Stone; he'll have been told that would kill him. So,
when he refuses, everyone will know him for what he
is. The use of such a double will also serve to discredit
Viktor, and isolate him from any support in the Court,
during whatever time he has left."

"Yes," said Dominic. "I like that. We'll do it. Make

the arrangements. You've done well, my slave. You can go now."

The faceless man didn't move. "Your Highness, you know I can't leave yet."

"Really? There's nothing more we need to discuss, is there?" Dominic's voice was calm and easy, but his eyes were mocking.

"I need you to renew the spell before I leave," said the man with no face. "The spell that keeps me alive."

"Of course," said Dominic. "How remiss of me. How could I have forgotten that?" He gestured lazily with his left hand, and a great bloody wound appeared on the faceless man's chest. It was an old wound, and the edges were crusted with dried blood, but at the base of the deep cut the heart muscle could clearly be seen, pumping wetly. "A very nasty wound, my friend," said Dominic. "I think I judged the blow rather well. Deep enough to cause a mortal hurt, but not so deep as to kill you outright. Without my magic, you'd bleed to death within moments, but as it is, you may live forever. Or at least, for as long as I need you."

He spoke a Word of Power, and a blinding light crackled fiercely around the faceless man. He screamed in agony, twisting and writhing in the grip of flames that did not consume him. And then the light was suddenly gone, and he fell forward onto his blank face, twitching and moaning. Dominic prodded him with the toe of his boot. "Get up and be quiet." The faceless man rose shakily to his feet. The wound on his chest had disappeared again. Dominic smiled. "I've given you another day of life, slave. Perhaps tomorrow I'll give you another day. If you please me. Now get out of here."

He gestured impatiently, and the air split open and swallowed up the faceless man. Dominic leaned back in his throne, and ran one hand caressingly over the smooth ridge of bone that formed his arm rest. Soon the real throne would be his, and all of Redhart. And then the land would see some changes. All the kingdom would bow down to him, to his wishes and his whims. Everyone and everything would be his, to do with as he pleased. He wasn't quite sure yet what he wanted to do with them, but no doubt he'd think of something. And if nothing else, at least then he wouldn't be so horribly bored all the time.

He scowled at his wall of water. He usually found the subtle changes of light soothing, but today nothing seemed able to comfort him. For as long as Dominic could remember, he'd always been bored. As a prince, he'd soon discovered that nothing was really barred to him. Every action, every sensation could be explored and experienced. But when things come without cost or effort, they quickly lose their flavor.

Dominic had tried everything in his time, to keep his frenziedly active brain occupied. He'd tried sex and politics and magic, and all of them had failed him. His mind worked frantically on, never quiet, never letting him rest, until he felt like screaming. Boredom gnawed at him like a cancer, or a hunger that could never be satisfied. To feed that hunger, to stave off the boredom that tormented him night and day to the edge of hysteria, he would sacrifice anything and anyone. All that was left to him now, his only hope, was the Stone and the power it promised him. Power over the Unreal . . . the endless change and novelty of the Unreal.

His bedroom door suddenly swung open, and Dominic looked around to see Elizabeth standing in the doorway. She was wearing a clinging silky nightdress and a fur wrap that between them revealed as much as they hid. Dominic nodded politely to her, and looked back at the wall of water. Elizabeth chuckled softly.

"You've been brooding again, haven't you, my love? Staring into the water and getting all depressed. Come to bed, my dear, and I'll make the darkness go away for a while."

Dominic smiled sadly, and got up from the huge skull throne. "Do you love me, Elizabeth? Really love me?"

"Of course, Dominic."

"That's nice."

There had been a time when he'd thought she might be enough to keep away the darkness. Certainly he'd never wanted anything before as much as he'd wanted her. But in the end, even she began to pall on him, and the never-ending horror of boredom crept back over him. He kept her with him anyway, because he had a use for her, and it wasn't the use she thought. He went to her smiling, and she only thought she knew what he was smiling about.

Catriona Taggert ran down the corridor at full pelt, struggling to keep up with the guard leading the way. This was going to be a bad one, she could tell. She hadn't been able to get much sense out of the guard when he'd come to summon her, but from his pale face and stuttering voice she knew it had to be something really nasty. It took a lot to upset a Castle Midnight guard. Taggert fought for breath as she ran, and wondered, not for the first time, why she hadn't resigned long ago. She'd never planned on being steward. Her father had been the previous steward, and he'd spent years training an apprentice. Then the Dark Horse had broken loose in the North Passage. Her father had been lamed, and the apprentice died. Catriona had started out helping her father just as an excuse to keep an eye on him while his injuries healed, but somehow she became his apprentice in spite of herself. Being steward of Castle Midnight was a hard job, even at the most peaceful of times. It killed her father when he was still in his early fifties. There was a bitter irony in that. All the terrors and creatures he faced, and he finally died at the dinner table, of a heart attack. That was seven years ago, and Taggert was only now beginning to realize that her father's early death had left her dangerously unprepared. She just wasn't experienced enough to handle this level of emergency. But with her father gone, there was no one left for her to turn to. She had to be good enough, because there wasn't anyone else.

Cord tried to help, bless his heart, but he wasn't

what you'd call bright. If you couldn't hit it or stab it, he was mostly lost for an alternative. Taggert almost smiled, but then she realized the guard was leading her into the South Wing. Up until now, the worst outbreaks of the Unreal had all been in the north. If it had established a foothold in the south as well, that could mean the beginning of the end. She couldn't fight on two fronts at once. Taggert silently cursed King Malcolm's murderer yet again, for having dropped her in this mess. She'd been kept so busy since the king's death that she hadn't even been able to help hunt down the murderer. Strictly speaking, that was security's province rather than hers, but she'd never trusted Brion DeGrange, geas or no geas. And with the king's death, she was cut off from the Stone, which meant she had to rely on her own High Magic. Which meant she had no time for anything but the job she'd grown to hate. She ran on after the guard, her sword slapping painfully against her leg. Her breathing was growing harsh and ragged, but she was damned if she'd slow down before the guard did. She had an image to maintain. Besides, sometimes a few minutes' difference in getting to the scene was all that stood between saving someone from the Unreal, and standing helplessly by as they died horribly.

One of these days, we're going to have to organize a better system, thought Taggert determinedly. *There's got to be an easier way. Or at least one that doesn't involve so much running. I must have lost ten pounds in the last few days . . .*

She finally rounded a corner and stumbled to a halt as her guide leaned against the corridor wall and gasped for breath. He gestured weakly at the group of guards ahead, and Taggert started toward them. She felt a little better as she saw the captain in charge was Matthew Doyle. She'd worked with him before. He knew his job, he didn't panic easily, and his men trusted him implicitly. He didn't bathe often enough, but you couldn't have everything. Doyle left his squad of worried-looking guards and stepped forward to greet her. He was a tall, wiry man in his late thirties, with a shock of dark curly hair and a perpetually thoughtful expression. His uniform was scruffy, he'd been on report for insubordination more times than any other guard in the castle, and he was resigned to never rising any higher in rank than captain. If he gave a damn about it, Taggert had never seen it. Doyle grinned at her as she walked breathlessly toward him.

"Getting out of shape, Kate. Too much good living among the swells."

"Stick it in your ear, Doyle," said Taggert, managing a smile of her own as her breathing slowly returned to normal. "I'll run you into the ground any day. It's good to see you, Matt. What's been happening here?"

Doyle nodded at a closed door halfway down the corridor. His guards were keeping it under close observation while being very careful not to get too close to it. "That's the problem. We've been trying to open that door with everything from crowbars to curses, and the damn thing won't budge an inch. From the smell of it, something very nasty's going on behind that door."

Taggert nodded, and walked over to inspect the door. Doyle stayed close beside her. She stood before the door, and sniffed the air cautiously. There was a sharp, acidic smell, like game meat that had been left to spoil too long. She looked closely at the door, being careful not to touch it, and then frowned as she saw that the door's edges had grown into its surroundings. The wood flowed seamlessly into the stonework as though they had always been one piece. She glanced at Doyle.

"All right, it's tricky enough, I'll grant you, but a good ax'll open it fast enough. What's the emergency? What's so special about this door that I had to be called in?"

"This is Count Penhalligan's new chambers," said Doyle. "He and his entire family were at home when the doorway became sealed. We haven't been able to get an answer out of any of them since."

Oh great, thought Taggert disgustedly. *Just what I needed. The king's cousin, and next in line to be Regent if anything happens to Count William.*

She glared at the closed door, and fought down an urge to kick it. "I take it you've sent for a sanctuary, Matt?"

"Sure, but most of them are busy. Laughing Boy is dealing with the sewers, Sweet Jenny is guarding the kitchens, and Mother Donna's still stuck in the Musician's Gallery."

"Right," said Taggert. She closed her eyes for a moment. She couldn't remember when she'd last felt this tired. When she opened her eyes again, the door was still sealed. "I think we can forget about Mother Donna. You can't hurry a mass exorcism. How about Grey Davey?"

Doyle shrugged. "I sent word, but you know what he's like."

"He's good at his job."

"When we can find him."

"Quite. All right, Matt, it looks like we'll have to do this the hard way. Have your men draw their swords and then fall back in a semicircle facing the door. If anything gets past me, kill it. I don't care what it looks like; if it gets a chance it'll kill you, so make sure you get it first. And Matt, if that smell is what I think it is, we can forget about the Penhalligans. If they're lucky, they died quickly. Now let's get on with it. Stay alert, and we might manage to contain this yet."

She scowled unhappily at the unresponsive door as Doyle muttered quiet commands to his men, and they shifted quickly into position. More and more, she didn't like the look of the sealed doorway. It looked too *planned* for her liking. In the past, the Unreal had always seemed random and undisciplined, but of late, the outbreaks had seemed to be following a pattern, almost as though the Unreal was somehow alive and aware . . .

Taggert took a deep breath and focused her will, calling on the High Magic she'd mastered under her father's patient teaching. She reached for the light within her, the roaring blinding light that was her mind and her soul and so much more, and brought a little of it out into the world. The vivid white balefire crackled around her right hand, spitting and flaring, and slowly formed itself into a glowing sword. Taggert gripped the hilt firmly, feeling the familiar cold pulse of life beat against her palm and fingers. She was vaguely aware of Doyle and his men watching her silently. She didn't need to see their faces to know that some of them were afraid of her. She didn't blame them. Some of the things she could do frightened her, too. She swung her sword of light against the closed door.

The balefire bit deep into the thick wood, cutting clean through and out again. A vile, choking smell poured from the jagged rent in the wood, and Taggert fell back a step, coughing harshly. The guards screwed up their faces as the smell hit them, and one or two stirred unhappily, but they all stood their ground. Taggert scowled at the door and struck again with her sword, widening the opening until she had a hole big enough to look through. She dismissed her sword, but kept the unfocused balefire crackling around her hand as she waited to see if anything was going to come flying or oozing out of the opening she'd made. Nothing did. The silence dragged on, broken only by the unsteady breathing of the guards, and the spitting of the balefire. Not a whisper of sound came from the room beyond the door. There was only the smell, thick and corrupt and nauseating.

Taggert conjured up a small ball of light, and sent it gliding through the jagged opening and into the room beyond. She dismissed her balefire, and stepped cautiously forward to peer through the hole in the door. She was still careful not to touch the door, and did her best to breathe only through her mouth. The room was dark, lit only by the glowing ball. The walls were a glistening wet pink, and so was the low-domed ceiling. Slender purple veins traced disturbing patterns in the pink. The room was half full of a dark, viscous liquid that lapped sluggishly against the rosy walls. Bones floated on the surface. They might have been human once, but already they were losing shape and definition as the liquid dissolved them. Taggert sighed tiredly, and stepped back from the door. The ball of light winked out, and darkness returned to the room.

"They're dead," she said flatly. "They're all dead."

She'd known it from the first moment she'd recognized the smell, but somehow she'd still hoped she might be wrong. She always hoped. It was all she had left to keep her sane.

"What happened in there?" said Doyle quietly. "And what the hell is that stench?"

"The room ate them," said Taggert. "And I don't suppose the inside of your stomach smells any better. We're going to need a sanctuary. Putting this right would take all the High Magic I have. Let the sanctuary take care of it."

"Of course, my dear," said Grey Davey. "That's what sanctuaries are for."

Grey Davey was a man of average height, but more than a little on the scrawny side. He always looked as though he could do with a good meal to put some meat on his bones. His face was drawn and gaunt, and seemed to fall naturally into apologetic lines, as though he felt he should be apologizing for his very existence. His clothes were well cut, but old and faded. Taggert always had the feeling on meeting Davey that he was covered in cobwebs. He was supposed to be in his early forties, but he looked old beyond his years, as though drained by having to struggle against a consistently unfriendly world. And yet he was still a sanctuary, and a power burned steadily beneath his gray exterior. Taggert felt better just for seeing him, and one by one Doyle and his guards sighed and relaxed a little as a feeling of peace swept over them. The lights seemed to burn a little more brightly, and the shadows were just shadows again. Even the smell didn't seem as bad. In Castle Midnight, there were always a few places and a few people that remained unaffected by the Unreal. Places of ease and comfort, people of good cheer and better company. Sanctuaries against the darkness of the world, where reality remained safe and constant.

Grey Davey was a sanctuary.

Taggert bowed respectfully to him. "Got a nasty one here, Davey. Four dead that we know of, maybe more. See if you can put the room right, at least."

Davey nodded. "I don't know what the world's coming to, Kate. I'd swear the whole damned castle's coming apart at the seams. And now four more dead. How many is that now?"

"Too many. And it'll get worse before it gets better."

"Wouldn't surprise me. If I had any sense, I'd have left here years ago. I've always said this place was unstable, but who ever listens to us? We're just the poor sods who have to clean up the mess afterward. Still, I'm here now. Let's see what I can do. Get those guards out of the way, Kate, there's a dear. They're distracting me."

Doyle glanced at Taggert, who nodded. He started moving his guards away while Davey studied the sealed door. No one took any offense at Davey's attitude: it was just the way he was. They could tell he didn't really mean it. Mostly. Davey placed his hands flat against the door, and pushed. The wood gave reluctantly under the pressure, stretching unnaturally, like taffy, and then the door tore itself free from the surrounding wall with a rending of splintering wood. It hung inward from one hinge, and the stench was suddenly worse. Davey didn't even seem to notice it. He glanced into the dark room, and muttered to himself under his breath. Taggert conjured up her ball of light again, and sent it over to hover above him, casting its glow into the room. Grey Davey grunted a terse acknowledgment as the silvery light showed him the bones floating on the dark liquid. As he watched, the liquid heaved and swelled, lapping against the glistening walls, but some invisible barrier held the liquid back from spilling out into the corridor. The smooth

white bones spun slowly on the surface as they
dissolved.

Grey Davey walked slowly forward into the room.
The dark liquid surged back from him, its unreality
repelled by his presence. The pink walls stirred uneasily. Davey's scowl deepened and his walk slowed, as
though he was contending against some unseen presence. He hunched his shoulders, tucked his chin in,
and pressed forward. The room changed. The purple
veins faded away as the walls and ceiling became solid
and sensible stone again, and the dark liquid vanished.
Scattered across an ordinary, everyday room were
some smoothly rounded shapes that had once been
furniture, and various odd bits of metal too tough to
dissolve. Only a few bones were left, none in any
condition to be identified. The vile smell lingered on
the overly warm air, like a fleeting memory of a bad
dream.

Grey Davey looked around the room once, and
then turned and walked back into the corridor. His
face was pale, but he carried himself as though this
was just another day's work. Taggert smiled at him
fondly. Davey was an irritating bastard, when all was
said and done, but you couldn't help liking him. He
reminded Taggert of her father, but then Grey Davey
reminded everyone of their father. He kept the darkness at bay, and always seemed to know what to do
for the best. His company was like a cool breeze on
a hot summer's day—bracing but comforting.

"That's it," said Grey Davey to Taggert. "End of
problem. For the time being. If I were you, though,
I'd nail that door shut, barricade it, and declare this
whole corridor out of bounds until things get back to
normal. Once I'm gone and out of range, I wouldn't
put it past that room to revert back again. The Unreal's
getting sneaky these days. Not to mention stronger
and more determined. The sooner we've a king on the
throne and you can get to the Stone again, the better
I'll like it. I don't like the way things feel around
here . . ." He glanced briefly at the broken door,
hanging from its single hinge. "Pity about the Penhal-

ligans. I never liked him, but she was a pleasant sort. Always a smile and a cheery word. I suppose there's no chance the children weren't there when it happened? No . . . I thought not. Ah well, can't stop and chat, I've got work to do."

He turned abruptly on his heel and stalked off down the corridor. Taggert and the guards watched him go in a respectful silence. The corridor seemed colder and darker without him.

"Sometimes I wonder about him," said Doyle.

"You're not alone," said Taggert.

Doyle glanced uneasily at the broken door. "Was he right about the room? Could it revert?"

"I don't know," said Taggert, "but I think we'll seal it up anyway. Just in case. Take care of it, Matt. And you'd better send word to the Regent that Count Penhalligan and his family are dead."

"Of course."

Taggert looked up and down the long corridor and chewed on the insides of her cheeks. Davey had wanted the whole corridor closed, but that would mean uprooting a great many important people, just on the off chance that something nasty might happen in the future. The courtiers would not take kindly to that. In theory, as steward she outranked everyone not actually of royal Blood, but she had enough sense not to push that too hard in practice. Of course, things were different now . . .

"Start evacuating this corridor, Matt. I want everyone moved out of here, as fast as possible. No exemptions, no excuses. Then set guards at each end of the corridor to stand watch. No one is allowed in or out, unless accompanied by a sanctuary."

Doyle raised an eyebrow. "The people here aren't going to like that."

"Yeah," said Taggert. "Isn't it a pity, all those wealthy courtiers and nobles having to put up with a little inconvenience, like us common folk."

She grinned at Doyle, and then walked away and left him to get on with it. The grin stayed on her lips for some time. Every now and again, she got a little back for every time a noble had sneered at her or her father for not having any Blood. All in the line of duty, of course . . .

The old dining hall in the East Wing hadn't been used for a major gathering in more than thirty years, and it looked it. A small army of servants were still scrubbing the floor, laying rush mats and lighting wall torches as the main courses of the meal were being served. The Regent said nothing, and did his best not to notice the scurrying servants. He'd intended to use the dining hall in the North Wing, but at the last moment Prince Lewis's men had occupied it, and he hadn't felt like fighting a war to get it back. So here he was, presiding over a banquet in one of the dingiest parts of the East Wing. God knows what they'd been using the place for previously, but from the smell that still lingered on the air, he should have ordered the hall fumigated first.

Count William Howerd leaned back in his chair and looked out over the crowd of nobles and courtiers and traders who sat packed shoulder to shoulder at the freshly scrubbed tables, filling the air with their chatter. There was more than enough wine for everyone, and the food was surprisingly good, under the circumstances, but William only picked at his. He had too much on his mind to allow for an honest appetite. He didn't really want to be there at all, but his presence was necessary to prop up the weaker elements, who needed to see him being calm and strong. As long as he didn't look scared or worried, they could convince themselves they weren't either.

The Regent looked out over his supporters, and fought to keep a weary frown off his face. They weren't the kind he'd have chosen for his friends, but he needed these people if he was to establish his own power base. Whoever eventually ended up on the throne of Redhart, they were going to need help to govern the kingdom, and the Regent intended there should be only one person able to give that help. Him. Let the princes have their troops and their magicians.

He would control trade, prices, and politics. And at the end of the day, he could control the king, too.

In a way, although he regretted King Malcolm's death, in the long run it was for the best. The royal line had grown weak and corrupt, distorted by their own power. Malcolm hadn't been a bad sort, all told. He'd just listened to too many stupid ballads about the honor and glory of the warrior's life. William had found a great deal of pleasure in Malcolm's company, when they weren't arguing politics, but their separate positions had meant they could never be the close friends they might otherwise have been. Still, William was determined to catch Malcolm's murderer, and see him hang. He could do that much at least for his friend.

Even if it turned out to be one of Malcolm's sons. William stirred uneasily in his chair. They had to be the most obvious suspects, if only because they had the most to gain, but as yet no real evidence had turned up to incriminate any of them. Strange, that. You'd have thought something would have surfaced by now. Instead, they were busy gathering their forces and preparing for civil war, and he was trapped in this gloomy old hall, surrounded by chattering fools. Sometimes, William wondered if Malcolm hadn't been right after all about the joys of battle.

Down below, at the end of one of the tables, some minor noble lurched to his feet and proposed yet another toast. William lifted his glass to his mouth and wet his lips with the wine. Everyone cheered and went back to what they were doing before. William was getting fed up with toasts. There had been too many of them, and they were beginning to sound increasingly hollow. Someone else got to their feet, cup in hand. William grabbed the nearest wine goblet and threw it at the unsuspecting courtier before he could open his mouth. The solid steel goblet hit him square between the eyes, and he toppled over backward. The gathering roared with laughter, and cheered William again. Perhaps it was only in his mind that the laugh-

ter sounded strained and forced. Gabrielle leaned in
close beside him.

"My dear, that was a very nice throw, but I
wouldn't do it again. One outburst they'll explain
away as high spirits, but more than one would be
taken as a sign of tension."

"I hate jesters," growled William.

"That wasn't a jester."

"Better safe than sorry."

Gabrielle smiled despite herself. William made a
placating gesture with his hand.

"I know, dear, it was a stupid thing to do, but I'm
going crazy just sitting here doing nothing. How much
longer before I can diplomatically leave?"

"No more than an hour or so, my love. Now eat
your dinner. It's delicious."

"I'm not hungry."

"Eat it anyway. There are too many rumors of poison going around the Court at the moment, and we
can't afford to look timid in front of our guests."

William looked unenthusiastically at the platter of
roast beef before him. "Where's the mustard? Can't
eat beef without mustard."

"Right in front of you, dear."

A messenger hurried in through a side door, spotted
the Regent at the high table, and hurried over to him.
William smiled graciously at him, but his pulse quick-
ened. He'd left instructions he wasn't to be disturbed
unless it was vitally important. The messenger bowed
briefly to him, and then leaned forward to murmur in
his ear.

"A Captain Doyle to see you, my lord. He says it's
urgent."

"Doyle?"

"One of the steward's men, my lord."

"Bring him in. I'll talk to him."

The messenger hurried away, and William settled
back in his chair, frowning in spite of himself. He
knew he wasn't supposed to look worried in front of
his guests, but of late the steward seemed only to have
bad news for him. It wasn't her fault, of course, but

more and more he had to fight down an urge to shout and rant at her for letting things get so out of hand . . . William rubbed tiredly at his aching eyes. Had the Unreal broken through again? And if so, what did Taggert expect him to do about it? He'd already given her carte blanche to do whatever she thought necessary to protect the castle. The messenger returned with the guard captain, and William looked him over dubiously. Doyle had to be the scruffiest guard he'd ever seen. The man was a disgrace to his uniform. Doyle came to a halt beside the Regent, and gestured with his head for the messenger to leave. The messenger looked at William, who nodded. Doyle waited till the messenger was out of earshot before speaking, and William felt his tension build.

"Sorry to be the bearer of bad tidings, my lord," said Doyle quietly, "but Count Penhalligan and his family are dead."

"Dead?" William looked at the guard blankly. Richard Penhalligan had always been one of his closest friends and his staunchest supporter. "You're sure?"

"I'm afraid so, my lord."

"And his family? Even the children?"

"Yes, my lord. The Unreal broke through in their chambers. It was very sudden. There was nothing anyone could have done. We used a sanctuary to put the room back to rights, but the Penhalligans were long dead by the time we got to them."

"I see," said William. "Thank you for keeping me informed. Perhaps you could start arrangements for their burial."

"I'm afraid not, my lord." Doyle's voice was rough, as always, but there was an honest compassion there as well. "There isn't enough left of them to bury. We did everything we could . . ."

"I'm sure you did." William looked away from the guard. He suddenly felt very tired. His family were all dead and gone, and he'd lost most of his real friends in Malcolm's bloody campaigns. Richard Penhalligan had been the last; a brave knight and a cunning politician. He played the dulcimer badly, and always knew the latest jokes. And now he was gone, like all the others. William looked back at the waiting guard.

"Where is the steward now?"

"Up on the roof, my lord, dealing with the gargoyles."

"Tell her I'd like to see her, when she has a spare moment. It's not important, but I would like to see her."

"Yes, my lord."

Captain Doyle sketched him a quick bow, and scurried away. William watched him go. Not all that long ago, it had been the custom for rulers to execute those who brought them bad news. William could understand why. There was a sick, hollow anger churning within him, and he wanted to lash out at someone, anyone, but he knew he couldn't. He had to appear calm and controlled at all times, even when he was falling apart inside. His followers expected it of him. Damn them. He leaned back in his chair, and wished that he could leave. He was tired; he was always tired, these days. He was so tense he couldn't ever relax, and what little sleep he got didn't refresh him. Gabrielle did her best to help and support him, but there wasn't really anything she could do. He looked across at her, and saw she was looking at him concernedly. He managed a small smile for her.

"Don't worry, my love. I'm all right. Just thinking."

"About Richard? I am sorry, William."

"I know. I'll miss him, more than I can say. But no, I wasn't just thinking about him. More and more I keep wondering if I'm doing the right thing. The Rite of Transference is a hell of a gamble, and it could all so easily go wrong. We could end up with a real villain for a king. And the alternatives may not be as bad as we thought. My little talk with Viktor went a lot better than I had anticipated. Exile's changed him a lot, and all for the better. Maybe I was wrong to meddle in the succession after all."

"Now, stop that," said Gabrielle quickly. "You and I spent months weighing up the pros and cons of what we might have to do when father died. This is the only way to save Redhart, and you know it. They're my family, William, and I know them far better than you ever could. None of my brothers are fit to be king, least of all Viktor. Ah, he's mellowed a lot, I'll grant you that, but if anything he's weaker and more indecisive now than he ever was. They're my father's sons, all three of them—worthless to the bone."

"Now, Gabrielle, that's not true. Your father and I had our disagreements, but there was still much in the man that I admired."

"He was a fool," said Gabrielle flatly. "He wasted his life on endless battles for a few extra miles of land. All he ever really cared for was bloodshed and slaughter. Never had any time for his family. My mother worshiped him, and she was lucky if she saw him one day in ten. And his children hardly saw him at all. If he'd spent more time with his sons, they might not have turned out the way they did."

"He can't have been all bad," said William, smiling. "He managed to produce you, didn't he?"

"Don't change the subject. Redhart needs a strong king, a king it can rely on, and the simple truth is that none of Malcolm's sons are fit to rule. Were any of them to become king, Redhart would face utter devastation. You can change that. History will remember you as the man who put an end to the nightmare. I know it's been hard for you, my love, but it's nearly over now. Just hang on a little longer. I know how close you and Richard were, how much he meant to you, but you're not alone. You still have me."

"Yes," said William, smiling gently. "I still have you."

Grey Davey glared down the wide corridor that led into the West Wing. Oil lamps and flaring torches burned at regular intervals along the walls, but halfway down the corridor the light faded away into an impenetrable darkness. The tense air was hot and moist, like a midsummer night before a thunderstorm. It smelt vaguely of urine and burning cloth. There was something unsettling about the darkness that filled the corridor. The longer Davey looked at it, the more he began to feel dizzy and light-headed. It felt almost like vertigo, as though he was looking down from the top of a tall tower. He deliberately looked away for a moment, and the feeling began to fade. Davey glanced at the guard captain beside him, who nodded understandingly.

Captain Timothy Blood was an average height man in his early forties, with short dark hair and unremarkable features. Put him in a crowd, and you could walk right past him without noticing. Which was why he'd spent most of his early career as a spy. He'd been very good at it. He worked mostly in Hillsdown and the Forest Kingdom, and they never even knew he'd been there, until they discovered something secret had gone missing. And by then he was always long gone. But eventually the life began to pall on him, as his need for thrills and excitement gave way to a deeper need to be able to trust someone. Anyone. His years in service had earned him a captain's rank in the guards, and he took it with never a single regretful thought. It wasn't a bad life in the guards, all told. Or at least it hadn't been, until King Malcolm's death. Now he was kept busy from dawn to dusk trying to keep the princes' troops from each other's throats, and the Unreal seemed to be breaking through everywhere at once.

Blood stirred uneasily. None of the hard lessons he'd learned playing the ancient game of danger and deceit were any use when it came to facing the Unreal. He tapped the flat of his sword against his leg, and wished he'd brought along something heavier as well, like a mace or a morning star. He smiled slightly. Why not wish for a suit of armor while he was at it? The Unreal might be somewhat disturbing, but it was just a part of his job, and he'd deal with it in the same way he dealt with all the other problems his job produced—by hard work, perseverance, and if need be, cheating. He flexed his shoulders, trying to keep the muscles relaxed and easy. Having Grey Davey nearby helped. The sanctuary's presence was both calming and invigorating. Problems seemed simpler and easier to deal with, and fears and insecurities faded away into the background. Unfortunately, sanctuaries were immune to their own power.

Grey Davey glared down the corridor, his glare deepening into an angry scowl. "This shouldn't be happening," he said finally. "I mean, this is the West Wing, damn it. Nothing ever goes wrong in the West Wing."

"Great," said Blood. "That means the darkness ahead is nothing more than a mass hallucination, and we can all go back to our beds. Only it isn't a hallucination. Is it? Tell me what to do, Davey. You're the expert."

Davey sniffed sourly. "When it comes to the Unreal, there aren't any experts. Just people who've stayed alive longer than others. Fill me in on what's been happening here, Tim. Maybe we can still nip this in the bud before it has a chance to establish itself."

"Things started to feel wrong about an hour ago," said Blood, glancing briefly at the darkness down the corridor, to make sure it wasn't getting any closer. "One of our regular patrols in this area hadn't reported back. I sent in another patrol to see what was keeping them. They didn't report back either. And then I started to hear some disturbing rumors. On a normal day, people pass in and out of this wing all the time, just going about their daily business. Only now people were still going in, but they didn't seem to be coming back out again. And people who went to look for them just vanished without a trace. So I sent for a sanctuary. Just before you got here, this darkness appeared in all the corridors that led into the West Wing. Whatever's in there knows you're here."

"That's what I like about you, Tim," said Davey. "You're always such an optimist."

"Would you rather I lied to you about our chances?"

"It couldn't hurt."

They stood together awhile, looking down the corridor. The darkness seemed to shift and stir, as though it was watching them. Behind them, Blood's company of guards murmured uncertainly among themselves, and waited for orders. Blood glanced back at them, and knew he'd better get them moving soon. Once they were doing something, they'd be too busy to be scared. He wished for a moment that he'd brought more than just the one squad. A dozen guards weren't much to set against the Unreal. On the other hand, when it came to the Unreal he could have a hundred guards at his back and he still wouldn't feel secure. He looked at Grey Davey, and decided he'd better start the ball rolling. Left to himself, Davey tended to forget the urgency of the situation, and just stand around thinking. But Blood couldn't give the order to go in himself: that had to come from Davey. The sanctuary outranked him.

"Any advice for my men, before we go in?" said Blood, tactfully.

"Yeah. Try not to get killed." Grey Davey scowled suddenly, and glanced sideways at Blood. "Sorry, Tim. This business has got me all upset. The West Wing has always been the most stable part of the castle: the one area you could depend on. If that's been breached by the Unreal, then nowhere's safe anymore. Get your men ready, Tim. We're going in."

Timothy Blood nodded to his men, and there was a brief whisper of steel on leather as they drew their swords. Blood moved unhurriedly among them, checking their weapons and equipment, and murmuring the odd word of encouragement where needed. He forced himself not to be overanxious. The Unreal was always dangerous, but these were good men. Professionals. He could trust them to do their job. Blood detailed three of them to carry torches. He wasn't sure how much use they'd be in the Unreal darkness, but he wanted the option. He racked his brain for anything he might have forgotten, but quickly realized he was just putting off the moment when he'd have to lead the way into the darkness. It was at times like this that he really missed being a spy. He nodded brusquely to Grey Davey, and the two of them set off down the corridor toward the darkness, the company of guards close behind them.

The darkness seemed to swirl hypnotically as they drew nearer. The temperature dropped sharply, and Blood clenched his teeth to stop them chattering. He shivered once, and hoped no one would mistake it for nerves. The Unreal night loomed up before them, and Blood and Davey hesitated only a moment before stepping into it. It was horribly silent inside the darkness, as though they'd suddenly been transported miles underground. The light from the guards' torches produced a pool of light just big enough to move in. Beyond the pale golden glow there was nothing but the night. The small sounds the party made as they moved along seemed strangely distinct and magnified, but there were no echoes. Blood had no way of telling where he was, or what if anything might lie outside the pool of light. He hefted his sword nervously, and then lifted his hand suddenly to call a halt. Something was moving out there in the darkness. The guards stirred nervously as they heard it too: soft scuffing sounds, not far away, and something that might have been the stealthy pattering of clawed feet. The sounds circled the group slowly, never once entering the pool of light. And then, from out of the darkness, there came the sound of something giggling. Blood's hackles rose. There was nothing human about the shrill laughter.

"Can't you do something about this?" he whispered to Grey Davey.

The sanctuary shrugged unhappily. "Maybe. I don't know. If I use my power to dispel this darkness, it might not leave me much to face whatever's out there. The Unreal is very strong here, Tim. I can feel it pressing against the light."

"Get rid of the darkness, Davey," said Blood flatly. "We're too vulnerable like this."

"All right. But I've got a bad feeling about this."

"You're always having bad feelings."

"And they're usually right."

Grey Davey pulled his power about him like a

cloak, and the darkness faded away, unable to withstand the sanctuary's presence. Blood stared about him. The corridor seemed to stretch away forever in both directions, without beginning or end. The walls had sagged inward, bulging out into the corridor, as though the solid stone and plaster had somehow melted and run and then reformed. The floor was covered with thousands of crawling insects. Some of the guards cried out in disgust as the scurrying creatures swarmed over their boots. Black tar dripped from the low ceiling, hot and smoking.

"How much of this is Real?" Blood asked Davey.

"I'm not sure," said the sanctuary. "When the Unreal is strong, some of its changes can't be undone. The changed state becomes Real. Stay close by me. Nothing can harm you as long as I'm here, but . . . something's wrong here, Tim. Something's horribly wrong."

He looked around him, his hands clenching into fists. Blood felt it, too: a deep unsettling feeling of being watched.

"Something's coming our way," said Davey quietly. "Something awful."

Blood nodded tightly. His men had picked up on the tense atmosphere, and were hefting their weapons and glaring about them. Blood knew he'd better find them a target soon, or they'd start coming apart.

"So what do we do, Davey? Stand our ground, turn and run, try to press on? What do we do?"

"I don't know! I've never seen anything like this!" Stray magic sparked and sputtered around the sanctuary's clenched fists. "I think we'd better go back, Tim. I'm not up to this. We need the steward and her High Magic."

"All right," said Blood quietly, "everyone start backing away down the corridor. Keep your eyes open and your swords ready. Take your time, there's no need to hurry."

He kept his voice carefully calm and even, but already some of his men were starting to panic. Blood didn't blame them. So far, his example had kept them from breaking into a run, but he didn't know how long that would last. Grey Davey wasn't helping. His face was ashen white, and his eyes were fixed on something in the distance only he could see. Blood glared at the corridor that stretched away behind them. He couldn't tell if they were any closer to the West Wing's boundary or not. He didn't even know if what he was seeing was Real or only an illusion. He would have sworn they hadn't walked very far into the West Wing . . .

And then the roaring began. The air pressure began to build, and the rising wind tugged at the guards' clothing. They turned and ran, charging down the corridor. Blood grabbed Davey by the arm and hurried after them. Something big was coming down the corridor after them: something huge and unstoppable. Blood glanced back over his shoulder and swallowed sickly as he saw what it was. A change wind was sweeping down the corridor, transmuting the world from gold into dross, from Reality into nightmare. The walls erupted as the wind passed over them. Gaping mouths opened in what had been stone and plaster, and howling voices shrieked in agony. The floor began to melt and run away, revealing jagged-edged holes full of bloodred flowers. The ceiling caught fire. And the change wind roared on, leaving damnation in its wake.

Timothy Blood looked for the end of the corridor ahead, and couldn't see it. It didn't make much difference anyway. The change wind would catch him in a matter of moments, and whatever was left of him after that wouldn't care about anything anymore. He looked around for the sanctuary, and then skidded to a halt as he saw that Grey Davey had stopped and turned to face the change wind. The guards kept on running.

"Move it!" Blood screamed to the sanctuary. "We've got to get out of here!"

"You go," said Grey Davey, raising his voice to be heard over the roar of the approaching wind. "I'm needed here. My power will buy you and your men

the time you need to escape. You've got to tell Taggert about this. Warn the castle. Tell them nowhere's
safe anymore."

He stood his ground, and pulled his power about
him. Blood looked over his shoulder at his disappearing guards, and then looked back at the
sanctuary.

"Ah hell," he said finally. "Someone's got to watch
your back, Davey."

He stepped forward to stand beside Grey Davey,
sword in hand, and the two of them stood together as
the change wind came howling toward them.

Prince Lewis strode angrily back and forth in his
private quarters, gulping at a glass of wine without
really tasting it. Apart from a few bruises and a nasty
gash on one hand, he'd come out of Dominic's ambush pretty much unscathed, but he was still fuming
mad. A third of his men were dead or wounded. Almost another third had deserted his ranks and left the
castle. He had the satisfaction of knowing that the
Monk and Ironheart had done some considerable
damage to Dominic's troops, but the attack itself still
rankled. He'd gone to negotiate in good faith, and
they'd laughed at him. Lewis kicked at the thick grass
covering his floor. All right; he'd made a mistake. He
wouldn't make the same mistake again.

He threw himself into his favorite chair and stared
sulkily at his feet. Nothing seemed to be going right
lately. The Monk had failed to destroy Viktor and his
people at Barrowmeer, the alliance with Dominic was
over before it had even begun, and now his oak tree
was dying. He glared at the great tree in its corner.
The leaves had fallen from its branches, and the bark
was mottled with some kind of fungus. Lewis had almost exhausted his earth magic trying to keep the tree
alive, but something in the tree resisted him. Either
the Unreal had got past his wards and undermined his
magic, or Dominic had somehow managed to poison
it. Lewis frowned sulkily. He was fond of that tree.
And if all that wasn't bad enough, now Ironheart was

getting mulish. He scowled at the tall suit of armor standing motionless in its corner. The battered armor was clean and gleaming, with only a few flecks of dried blood around the gauntlets' knuckles to show that Ironheart had recently been in a battle.

"You promised me my freedom," said Ironheart, his voice as always distant, echoing, and slightly slurred. "You gave me your word, Prince Lewis."

"So I did," said Lewis. "When I become king, you shall be free of all obligations to me."

"That wasn't the deal."

"The deal has changed! My dear Ironheart, you must see that I need your protection now more than ever. I really can't do without you until I am safely on the throne, and the Stone is mine to draw on."

"You may never be king," said Ironheart. "I see and hear many things denied to your limited senses. Castle Midnight is under seige. The Unreal is finally breaking free of the chains that have bound it for so long, and creatures of the night wait impatiently in the dark places for the last few barriers to fall. It may already be too late to stop them."

"Do you know that for sure?" said Lewis.

"No. But I suspect it."

"Your suspicions don't matter. Nothing matters to you and I but the bond between us. You're mine, Ironheart, body and soul, and your only hope for freedom is to obey me in all things."

"Yes, Lewis. I'm yours. For now."

"You're mine until I decide otherwise." Lewis emptied his glass, and dropped it carelessly onto the grassy floor. He was tired, and his injured hand ached. He wanted to go to bed and forget the day's troubles in sleep, but he had to wait for the Monk's report, and as usual the Monk was late. Lewis scowled. He had to know what was happening in Viktor's camp. There was a polite knock at the door, and Lewis growled for whoever it was to enter. The door swung open and a young serving maid came in, bearing a cold meal on a tray. Lewis remembered ordering the meal earlier, but he wasn't hungry anymore. He started to wave the maid and meal away, and then stopped and took a second look at the maid as a different hunger awoke in him.

"Come here, girl. Let me look at you."

She moved reluctantly forward, holding the tray out before her as though it could protect her from him. Lewis gestured for her to put the tray down on a nearby table. She did so, her hands trembling visibly, and turned slowly back to face him. She was good-looking in a simple, healthy way, with wavy shoulder-length hair and a firm supple figure. She looked to be in her midtwenties, but her pale face and wide eyes made her seem much younger. Lewis smiled at her easily, but she didn't return the smile.

"They've been telling stories about me again, haven't they?" said Lewis. "You don't want to believe everything you hear, my dear. My enemies tell lies about me, and try to make me out a monster, and I tell the same kind of lies about them. It's all part of the game we play. It's called politics. Now stop shivering and shaking, and relax. Do I look like a monster to you?"

The maid blushed slightly, and shook her head. Lewis nodded surreptitiously to Ironheart, and his mailed hands shot out and grasped the maid's arms above the elbows. She shrieked, and tried to break free, but couldn't. Lewis rose slowly out of his chair, and walked over to stand before her. He reached out a hand to caress her face, and she shrank away from him. Lewis smiled slightly.

"The one thing you should know by now about Castle Midnight," he said softly, "is that nothing is necessarily what it seems."

His hands tore at her clothing. Shortly afterward, she started to scream. She screamed for a long time, but nobody heard her.

An hour or so later, the air rippled in Lewis's quarters as the Monk appeared. His empty cowl turned slightly to observe the still, bloody form lying limply on the floor. Her wide staring eyes saw nothing at all, and her face wasn't pretty anymore.

"Get rid of that," said Lewis, gesturing vaguely in the body's direction.

The Monk bowed, and the body disappeared. Air rushed in to fill the gap where it had been. "The body will not be found, sire."

"You're late!" snapped Lewis.

"My apologies," said the Monk. "There is much of interest happening in the castle at present, and I like to keep you well-informed. For example, I was right in my suspicions about your brother Viktor. He's using a double for his public appearances. The man you saw in Court this evening was merely an actor under a glamour."

Lewis frowned. "I would have sworn it was Viktor. It looked like him, it was his voice . . . damn it, he had fire magic! I saw it!"

"A conjuring trick, Your Highness—sleight of hand. Nothing more."

"Dominic already knew about this," said Lewis suddenly. "That's what he was hinting at earlier on."

"Exactly," said the Monk. "It appears he's known about this for some time. He's already set in motion a plan to discredit the impostor. There is to be a Testing before the Stone tomorrow morning. Dominic will challenge the double to spill his blood on the Stone, and when he can't, thus proving himself an impostor, Dominic will demand to know what has happened to the real Viktor. His people will then be forced to reveal how ill and helpless your brother really is."

"Not a bad idea," said Lewis, "and one we can take advantage of. My friends, we are going to attend this Testing. Once the impostor has been revealed, I'll raise a clamor about who else is pretending to be what they're not. In the confusion, my men will attack Dominic's, and you, Monk, will kill my brother. I'd prefer to do it myself, but you're the only one of us strong enough to stand up against his sorcery. Afterward, we'll claim he was an Unreal double that had managed to replace the real Dominic, and there'll be no one left who can prove otherwise. Yes. I like that. Make the arrangements, Monk."

He turned away, chuckling happily, and disappeared into his bedchamber. Ironheart and the Monk watched in silence as the door slammed shut behind him. There was a faint rasp of metal on metal as Ironheart's steel gauntlets closed into fists.

"I want to kill him," said Ironheart quietly. "I want it more than I've ever wanted anything before."

"In good time," said the Monk. "For the moment at least, we need him. As long as the castle believes we serve Lewis, we're protected from too close a scrutiny. The steward suspects our nature, but Lewis's position keeps her from doing anything about it. Put aside your anger, my friend. Lewis is useful to us."

"He won't always be."

"That's right. And then you and I will teach him the true meaning of fear and suffering."

Ironheart stirred, his metal joints creaking softly. "It won't be enough. No matter how much he suffers, it won't be enough. I need him to burn and writhe as I have all these long years."

He reached up with his mailed gauntlets and lifted off his helmet. The room's soft lamplight shone palely on the dead white face. The flesh was slack and utterly colorless, even where the left eye had recently been cut in two by a sword thrust. No blood had flowed from the jagged edges of the wound, nor ever would.

"I've been dead almost twelve years now," said Ironheart slowly. His words were faintly slurred, as he fought to make the dead flesh of his lips and tongue do what they used to do so easily. "Twelve years since I took my life, and damned myself by magic to this unliving hell. I did this to myself, Monk, and all for revenge on a man whose face I can't even remember now. I always was a fool where a woman was concerned. Now my organs rot and decay within me, and my bones grow brittle, and still the preservation spell won't let me die the true death. I can feel the rot and corruption within me, and the pain burns endlessly every hour of the day and night. I can't rest, I can't sleep, and I'm always so damned tired! Sometimes I think the tiredness is worse than the pain. Can't you help me at all, Monk? You have power. Can't you at least let me sleep, just for a while?"

"I'd help you if I could, my friend," said the Monk, "but the curse on you is beyond my undoing."

"I can't stand this much longer," said Ironheart. "I can't. I'll go mad. I move and talk and fight and pretend I'm still alive, but every day it gets harder to hold onto my memories of who I was. I'm losing them, bit by bit, to the endless pain and rage and frustration. Lewis swore he had a counterspell that would free me from this curse and let me die at last. But sometimes I think I'm too useful to him, and he'll never let me go. I'm losing hope, Monk, and hope is all I've got left."

"You must be strong, my friend," said the Monk. "It won't be long now, I promise you. Just hang on a little longer, and all your suffering will be at an end. I give you my word on it."

Ironheart looked at the Monk, and his dead mouth tried to smile. "You're the only friend I have, Monk, and I'm not even sure you're Real. It doesn't matter anyway. I don't care. You've been a good friend to me. At least when I'm with you, I can almost forget the pain for a while."

"I can't stay with you long, Ironheart. But I'll stay as long as I can."

"I get so scared sometimes. Scared that when I finally get my chance to die, I won't have the guts to take it. This is worse than any hell I ever dreamed of, but even so sometimes the thought of dying scares me even more. I wasn't a bad man, in my day, but since I died, I've done . . . questionable things, just to cling to this horrid existence. I'm afraid all the time now, Monk: scared to die, but just as scared of going on like this."

"Don't be scared," said the Monk. "I'm here with you."

They talked together for a while, their quiet distant voices so soft they raised no echo in the huge room. Finally the Monk could stay no longer, and he disappeared in a ripple of disturbed air. Ironheart replaced his featureless helm over his dead face, and stood motionless in his corner. After a while, a distant voice began to sing very quietly a song that had been popular some ten years ago, of the tragic love of a fair knight for a wicked lady.

Up on the roof, the guards were chasing gargoyles. The ugly gray creatures ran nimbly back and forth across the uneven slates, dodging the chasing guards with contemptuous ease. The guards ran doggedly on in pursuit, brandishing their nets. The full moon shed its light across the hills and valleys of the massive roof as though it was having trouble believing what it was seeing. The quiet night was full of the curses and harsh breathing of the running guards, and the mocking laughter of the fleeing gargoyles. Damon Cord stood perched on a bulky chimney stack, calling orders that were mostly redundant even before he finished giving them. Those gargoyles were *fast*.

Catriona Taggert pulled herself up through the open trapdoor and out onto the roof. She shivered once at the cold wind, glared disgustedly around her, and then shook her head. As if she didn't have enough problems, she now had orders to capture each and every of the gargoyles intact. If the orders hadn't come from the Regent himself, she'd have told him where to stick them. And even then, it had been close. Apparently, the current belief at Court was that when the Unreal outbreaks had passed, the gargoyles would go back to being statues again. As and when that happened, the Regent wanted them intact. On the grounds that replacing them with new stone carvings would cost a small fortune. The Regent was well-known for being very careful with a ducat. All of which meant that Taggert couldn't kill the gargoyles, or even do anything that might risk damaging them. Which was why so many of her best men were currently running around the roof like idiots, waving bloody big butterfly nets.

We'd better catch something soon, thought Taggert dryly, *Or I'm going to have a mutiny on my hands . . .*

She clambered unsteadily across the uneven roof, heading for Damon Cord. At any other time, she might have stopped to admire the view. Castle Midnight's roof was an architect's nightmare of tiles, slates, and chimneys, rising here and there into peaks and gables for no apparent reason, and peppered with pipes and protrusions and anything else the castle's designers had felt might be a good idea at the time. Under a full moon, it all looked very picturesque. It was also a hell of a roof to have to chase anything over. Particularly gargoyles. The nasty creatures were short and stocky, with lots of teeth and claws, and a set of stubby bat wings that luckily weren't strong enough to let the gargoyles do more than glide a few feet at a time. They were definitely dangerous, and vicious by temperament, but as yet hadn't managed to inflict any real injuries on the chasing guards. Probably because the damned things were laughing too hard. They'd never had such a good time.

Taggert watched, wincing, as a guard slowly closed the gap between him and a fleeing gargoyle. The creature was whooping happily, carefully keeping his speed down to the point where the guard still thought he had a chance of catching the thing. Of course, the moment the guard got too close, the gargoyle just put on a burst of speed and vanished into the shadows. The guard skidded to a halt, looked frantically around him, and then threw down his butterfly net and jumped up and down on it. Watching gargoyles rolled around on the slates, giggling hysterically. Two guards tried to jump a running gargoyle from different sides. The creature stopped dead in its tracks at just the right moment, and the two guards slammed into each other. They ended up in a dazed, cursing pile. Watching gargoyles leaned helplessly on each other, shaking with laughter. The gargoyle who'd caused the collision howled with glee, and Damon Cord leaned out from his chimney stack and clipped the creature neatly above the left ear with his mallet. The gargoyle looked very surprised, blinked once, and fell over. The fallen

guards finished untangling themselves from their nets
and set about tangling up the snoring gargoyle.

Taggert made her way over to join Cord. He
grinned down at her and started to brandish his mallet
triumphantly. His smile quickly faded away as he took
in her grim face. He sighed heavily, and climbed down
from the chimney stack.

"All right, what have I done wrong this time? I
didn't kill it, just rattled its brains a little."

"That's not the point," said Taggert carefully. You
had to explain things very clearly to Cord, or he
sulked. "The point is, you've been up here for over
two hours, and all you've got to show for it is one
gargoyle. The other forty-nine are still charging
around the roof and crapping in the guttering. And I
hate to think what they've been doing down the chimneys, but the smell in the kitchens is appalling. How
many men have you got up here, Damon?"

Cord's eyes unfocused as he counted silently, trying
not to move his lips. "Thirty-two," he said finally.

"Thirty-two men, and it's taken you two hours to
catch one gargoyle." Taggert sighed, deeply. "I should
have come up here with you. Whose bright idea was
the butterfly nets?"

"Mine," said Cord proudly. "We tried roping them
at first, but that didn't work out too well."

"I just know I'm going to regret asking this, but
why?"

"Well, every time a guard lassoed one, the gargoyle
just kept on running and dragged the guard after him.
They're a lot heavier than they look, those gargoyles.
We lost eight men to injuries that way."

"Damon . . ."

"Then we tried trip wires, but the gargoyles have
better night vision than we do, and in the excitement
of the chase, we kept forgetting where the wires were.
We lost ten men to injuries that way."

"All right! I get the picture!" Taggert glared at
Cord, who shrugged unhappily. She felt like sighing
deeply again, but knew it would be wasted on Cord.
"All right, Damon. Call the men in. I've got an idea."

Cord raised his voice in a carrying shout, and the guards came back to join him in ones and twos. All of them were breathing hard, and some of them were limping. The gargoyles gathered together in little groups, and waited eagerly to see what new game the guards were going to come up with. Speaking calmly and quietly, Taggert got her men cooled down and explained her plan to them. The guards brightened up, and went back to work with cautious enthusiasm. They split into groups and chose two chimneys set close together. They then stretched their nets across the gap and secured them lightly. The gargoyles watched frowningly, and muttered uneasily among themselves.

Taggert gave Cord his instructions, and he brightened up as he discovered it involved using his precious mallet. He looked happily about him, and then set off at a run toward the nearest gargoyles, who scattered hastily before him. Cord might be heavy on his feet, but he could build up quite a bit of speed when he put his mind to it. If only through sheer momentum. The gargoyles took off in different directions, but Cord chose one and kept stubbornly after it. For a while, everyone else just stopped where they were and watched as Cord grimly pursued the gargoyle across the uneven roof, with his mallet poised and ready to strike. The gargoyle kept just a few feet ahead of him, ducking, dodging, and plunging back and forth, and generally having too good a time tormenting Cord to realize it was being gradually herded toward the hidden nets. It ran full pelt between two chimneys and crashed to the slates as the nets wrapped themselves around it. The watching gargoyles screamed with rage at such an underhanded trick. Taggert ignored them. The creatures weren't what you'd call bright, and had very short memories. It would take a fair bit of running, but the gargoyles were as good as caught. Luckily, she wouldn't have to do the running. That's what guards were for.

Two of the guards dragged the trapped gargoyle away, and the others set about making more traps with the remaining nets. Cord leaned against a chimney stack and had a quiet wheeze. Taggert nodded, satisfied. Maybe now she could get back to some real work. She frowned suddenly, and turned to Cord.

"I thought Mother Donna was supposed to be up here with you. What happened to her?"

Cord thought hard, trying to remember. "She was called away. Some sort of emergency in the West Wing."

Taggert raised an eyebrow. The last she'd heard, the West Wing was perfectly quiet. As always. There was a sudden clattering behind her as Captain Doyle pulled himself up through the trapdoor and out onto the roof. He hurried over to her, and barely paused to salute before speaking.

"You'd better come back down, Kate. All hell's broken loose in the West Wing."

"What is it?" said Taggert. "A manifestation? A poltergeist? What?"

Doyle swallowed hard. All his usual swagger and bravado were gone, and his face was deathly pale. "You're going to have to see this for yourself, Kate. It's bad. Very bad."

Taggert and Cord hurried after Doyle as he led them down the gloomy corridor that led to the West Wing boundary. The air was close and muggy, weighed down by a stench of burning flesh. Water ran slowly down the corridor walls, as though they were sweating from the heat. The floor shook and trembled beneath their feet, as though something heavy was tramping back and forth in the distance. As they approached the boundary, Taggert tensed as she began to hear sounds coming from deep in the West Wing: screams and curses and animal howls. Doyle began to slow to a walk, and Taggert and Cord slowed with him.

"How long has this been going on?" asked Taggert breathlessly.

"About three hours, we think," said Doyle. "It caught us all by surprise. I mean, nothing ever happens in the West Wing. Then two of our patrols went into the wing and didn't come out again. Captain Blood took a sanctuary and some men and went in after them. They should have been safe enough; Grey Davey is one of the strongest sanctuaries we've ever had."

"What happened?" said Taggert.

"The Unreal is loose in the West Wing. It found them, and rolled right over them. They never stood a chance. Only five of them came back, all of them horribly injured. The sanctuary's dying."

The three of them slowed their pace as they came to a makeshift barricade that blocked off the corridor. Tables and chairs had been dragged out of adjoining rooms, stacked roughly together and tied in place. A dozen or so guards manned the barricade. They nodded grimly to Captain Doyle as he approached, and a few of them even managed some kind of salute for the steward. She gave them her best calm and reassuring smile, but inwardly she was shocked by the guards' faces. They were white and drawn and very frightened. The guards all had drawn swords, but their hands were trembling. The men looked to be on the edge of exhaustion, as though they'd just been through a major battle.

"Report," said Captain Doyle. "Has the situation changed while I've been gone?"

The guards looked at one another, and finally one of them stepped forward. When he spoke, his voice was little more than a whisper.

"It's getting closer, sir. We can feel it. About half an hour ago something came flying toward us out of the darkness. It was bone white and ugly, and it screamed like a hungry child. We cut it to pieces, and it still didn't die. In the end, we had to burn it before it'd stop moving. We're still holding the line, sir. But I don't know how much longer we can hold it, without reinforcements."

Doyle nodded grimly. "How's Captain Blood?"

"'Asking for you, sir. I think you'd better see him."

Doyle gripped the man's shoulder for a moment, in

silent recognition of what he'd been through, and then he led Taggert and Cord into a nearby room. Five men lay on the floor on makeshift stretchers. Two of them had blankets pulled up over their faces. Another was asleep. He twitched and moaned constantly. Both his arms were covered in bloodstained bandages. Captain Timothy Blood was sitting on his stretcher with his back to the wall, and his sword across his lap. His right arm ended too soon in a wad of bloodstained wrappings. His face was wet with sweat, and his eyes were haunted. Grey Davey lay beside him, hunched and twisted under a thick blanket. Blood nodded to Doyle, and then to the steward. He started to get up, but Taggert quickly waved him back.

"Tell me what happened," she said quietly.

"For a while it didn't look too bad," said Blood. His voice was unnaturally calm. Probably shock. "Scary, but nothing Davey couldn't handle. Then the Unreal came roaring out of nowhere and swept over us like a wave. Davey tried to buy us some time to get out, but he couldn't hold it back. Most of my men died in the first few seconds. The rest of us got out by staying close to Davey. He took the worst of it on himself, deliberately."

"What happened to him?" said Taggert.

"See for yourself."

Cord stepped forward and knelt beside the sanctuary. He pulled back the blanket as gently as he could, and then had to look away. Taggert wanted to, but wouldn't let herself be weak. This was her job. Grey Davey's body was twisted and misshapen. His ribs had swollen and burst out through the flesh. His legs had fused into a single boneless tail. His hands had scales and claws. His eyes were gone.

"He didn't live long," said Blood, "fortunately. We left a lot of good men behind us in the West Wing, you know. Good men. They never stood a chance. We got back here, the four of us, dragging Davey between us. Started the barricade, and found Doyle and his men. And that's it. That's the story. And God have mercy on all our souls."

Cord covered Grey Davey with the blanket again. Taggert blinked away the beginning of tears. She couldn't be weak now. The others needed her to be strong.

"You did well," she said finally. "Now take a rest. I'll have you and the others escorted out of here as soon as possible. And don't worry, we'll put the West Wing right again, I promise you."

She turned and left, and Cord and Doyle followed her out. In the corridor, Taggert wiped sweat from her face with a shaking hand, and looked at Doyle.

"Anything else I need to know, Matt?"

"I've sent for another sanctuary. Mother Donna's on her way. She's supposed to be the best, but Davey wasn't exactly a beginner and he couldn't even slow it down."

"We're going to have to stop it here," said Taggert, "while it's still limited to one area."

"Sure," growled Cord. "But how are we going to stop it? You can't fight this kind of Unreal with swords and axes. Can you?"

"I don't know," said Taggert. "I think we're going to have to go in there and see for ourselves."

"I had a horrible suspicion you were going to say that," said Doyle. "And I would like to point out before we go any further that I am not volunteering to go back in there with you."

"This breakthrough must have a heart," said Taggert, ignoring him, "some gateway to act as its entry point into reality. If we can find that and destroy it, maybe we can still stem the tide. Assuming we survive long enough to reach it, of course."

"Of course," said Doyle. "I'm still not volunteering."

"Good man," said Taggert. "I knew I could depend on you. As soon as Mother Donna gets here, we can make a start."

"Then what are we waiting for?" said Mother Donna. "Let's do it."

Everyone looked around, startled. It never ceased to amaze Taggert how silently the Reverend Mother could move when she chose to. Taggert started to say something polite in welcome, but stopped as she took in the sanctuary's face. There were harsh, tired lines around her eyes that hadn't been there a few days ago. Taggert put a gentle hand on Mother Donna's arm.

"I'm sorry about Davey. From what I hear, he died bravely, doing his duty."

"He always did have more guts than sense," said Donna. "He thought being a sanctuary was enough to protect him from anything. Stubborn as a mule, and half as bright. But he always had time to listen to a hard luck story, and he was the softest touch for a loan I ever knew. I'm going to miss him. God grant he rest easy. Well then, Kate, looks like it's left to us to push back the darkness. Are you ready?"

Taggert nodded, smiling. Like all sanctuaries, Mother Donna carried with her an aura of peace and calm, but Donna also had more genuine love and caring in her than any three other people. She was a medium-height, broad-based woman, who gave an immediate impression of strength and determination. There was something of the bulldog about her, though only the cruel ever applied that insight to her face. She was plain, as she'd be the first to admit, but her wise eyes and ready smile kept her from being ugly. She was in her early fifties, and looked it. She spent her early years as a priest, before coming to Castle Midnight to train as a sanctuary. She'd never said why she made the change. She wore plain, sack-like robes, and hacked her gray hair carelessly off at shoulder length. All in all, she looked more like a retired mercenary than an ex-priest. Mother Donna was perhaps the most powerful sanctuary Castle Midnight had ever known. She was loved and admired by practically everyone. Even though most of them thought she was crazy. If only because she'd given over her entire life to fighting evil, and had a tendency to walk right through anyone who got in her way.

"I'm ready," said Taggert. She could feel her fears and worries easing away in the sanctuary's presence.

It was clear the guards were feeling it, too. "Damon, you'll have to guard us from any physical manifestations. I've got a feeling I'm going to need as much power as I can raise to deal with the Unreal heart. As and when we find it. Mother Donna should be able to hold the worst off until we get there. Doyle, I know this will break your heart, but you can't come with us. I need you here, in charge of the barricade. If we don't come back, send word to Court of what's happened, and get the hell out of here. After that . . . I think the best bet would be for the Regent to order a complete evacuation of the castle, and look for help outside Redhart. Though, where you might find it is beyond me. Maybe the High Warlock, if he's still alive."

Doyle bit his lip. "You can't go in there without an armed backup, Kate. Cord's good, we've all seen him work, but he's just one man. I think I'll tag along, with a few good men. Just in case."

Taggert smiled warmly at him. "Thanks, Matt, but no. Like Damon said, this isn't the kind of Unreal you can fight with swords and axes. You and your men wouldn't last ten minutes once the going got rough. But it was a nice thought. Now do as you're told and don't argue."

Doyle nodded glumly. Taggert turned and looked at the ramshackle barricade. It wouldn't be much use against what she feared was coming, but its solid presence was still somehow comforting. Beyond it lay the unknown, and all the horrors of the Unreal. Taggert turned to Cord.

"Don't just stand there, Damon, give me a leg up."

Her apprentice grinned, and leaned forward to make a stirrup with his hands. Taggert put her foot into it, and Cord boosted her effortlessly up the side of the barricade. She quickly pulled herself over the top and clambered down the other side. Mother Donna followed, a little more slowly, and Cord brought up the rear, the barricade groaning loudly under his weight. The three of them stood together a moment at the base of the barricade, staring into the

West Wing. The sounds from up ahead were growing
gradually louder and more disturbing. There were
roars and howls and squeals, and something low and
unnerving that thrummed on the air like a racing
heartbeat. Taggert took a deep breath, and started
forward. The sword of light formed in her hand,
crackling and spitting, and the glowing shield appeared on her arm. The scintillating light of the balefire reflected brightly from the polished wood-paneled
walls. Cord still had his mallet. He carried it loosely
in one hand, as though the huge steel weapon was
virtually weightless. Mother Donna strode quietly
along between them, her hands empty, her face calm
and determined. Cord looked at her thoughtfully from
time to time, when he thought she wasn't looking.

They passed through a series of deserted corridors,
and strange undercurrents hummed on the still air.
They knew they were being watched, and that not too
far ahead, something awful was waiting impatiently
for them to come to it. The light seemed to vary from
corridor to corridor, though the number of wall
torches was always the same. The shadows were too
dark, and subtly misshapen. Finally, Taggert rounded
a corner and crossed the boundary into unreality.

She stopped dead in her tracks, and the other two
stopped with her. The corridor was lit by a lurid crimson glow that came from everywhere and nowhere. A
man was crawling along the wall. He was naked, and
covered with patchy black fur. Thorned vines hung
down from his eye sockets, and maggots burrowed in
his legs. Something long and flat with too many legs
scuttled back and forth across the floor in frantic little
dashes. The flagstones on the floor formed into distorted faces with mad eyes and wide-stretched mouths
that roared, grunted, and howled. And then they disappeared, and where the floor had been, there was
only a darkness that seemed to fall away forever. Fox
heads on the walls barked, howled, and slavered hungrily. Birds flew up by the vein-covered ceiling, and
turned into moths that dripped blood. Snow fell
through the air, and disappeared before it hit the

floor, which had reappeared as crude wooden slats. Smoky flames flickered up between the slats. A man was weaving a web in a corner. His head was twisted so that he looked permanently backward. Beside him, a woman with too many eyes sat propped against the wall and stared in horror as the flesh on her legs decayed and fell away from the bones. Something like a distorted hog's head emerged suddenly from the wall beside her, and bit off her face.

"Dear Lord, protect us now and in the hour of our need," whispered Mother Donna. "And deliver us from the powers of darkness."

Cord took the opportunity of her distraction to silently indicate to Taggert that he wanted to talk to her. They fell back a few paces, out of earshot. Cord looked worriedly at Taggert.

"How are we going to handle this? It's all I can do to stay here, with her so close. And she's not even really using her power yet. When she does, I'll be banished, along with everything else that's Unreal. And once I'm gone, I don't think I can come back again."

"I'm sorry," said Taggert. "I hadn't thought . . . Look, her range as a sanctuary is limited. As long as you stay at least ten feet away, you should be safe enough." She smiled at him fondly. "Why have you stayed with me so long, Damon? You know that as soon as there's a king on the throne, I'll have to use the Stone to banish the Unreal from the castle. You'll be gone. It'll be as though you never existed."

"I won't, really," said Cord. "I'm not Real. I'm just an idea, a whim made flesh and blood by the strength of unreality. I came to you because you needed me so badly. But I'm also your friend, and that's why I've stayed. Just because I'm not Real, it doesn't mean I don't have feelings."

They shared a smile. And if it was a sad smile, they both pretended not to notice.

"You look after Mother Donna," said Cord. "I'll cover your back. From a distance."

Taggert nodded, and walked forward to rejoin

Mother Donna. The Unreal had moved no closer during her absence, held back by the sanctuary's presence. Taggert even felt a little of her own unease fall away as she fell under Donna's calming influence again.

"The focus for all this is a gateway not far from here," said Mother Donna. "We have to shut it down, while we still can. It's growing stronger all the time. Follow me, and stay close. It's going to be a bumpy ride."

She walked unflinchingly forward into the madness, and Catriona Taggert walked at her side, silver balefire glowing in her hand and on her arm. Cord watched them go, and waited a while before bringing up the rear. He threw his mallet away into nothingness, and took instead out of thin air a huge mace. The shaft was four feet long, and the great steel head was studded with barbed spikes. And so a man who wasn't Real went forward to battle the unreality that birthed him.

The air heaved and sparkled around Mother Donna as she walked deeper into the West Wing. Distorted, melting creatures fell back before her, hissing and spitting, their flesh crawling and bubbling like hot wax over a flame. But the floor beneath her feet was just a floor, and the air directly around her was fresh, clear, and pure, and nothing that was not Real could tarry in her presence. A few of the more stable creatures tried to block her way. Taggert cut them down with her balefire sword. Some way behind the two of them, Cord cut a bloody path through a growing crowd of horrors to keep up with them. His mace rose and fell with inhuman regularity, and the creatures from the dark places couldn't stand against him.

And still Mother Donna strode on, more slowly now as the strain began to tell. Nightmares scuttled around her, changing and reforming even as she looked. The limits of her power grew steadily smaller as the pressure of unreality weighed down upon her. Taggert swung her sword until her arm ached and sweat ran down her heaving sides, but for every creature that fell, there were always more to take its place. She called upon her High Magic, and spoke a Word of Power. A blinding light flared up around her and the sanctuary, consuming everything Unreal it touched. The creatures fell back and disappeared, and for a while they walked through an empty corridor. But the magic took its toll in pain and energy, and all too soon the light was flickering unsteadily. Taggert fought to maintain it, but it had been a long day and she'd done too much already. The light faded away, and one by one the creatures returned. Taggert still had her sword and shield, but for the first time, she began to wonder if they were going to be enough.

Mother Donna suddenly came to a halt, and Taggert stopped beside her. The gateway was somewhere up ahead, but the pressure of the Unreal was now so strong it was all Donna could do to hold her ground. Sweat ran down her straining face as creatures that could not have existed in the Real world pressed close about her and the steward. She'd gone as far as she could, as far as her power and her courage could take her, and it hadn't been far enough. The first faint stirrings of panic tugged at her calm, and she wondered suddenly if this was what Grey Davey had felt, before the Unreal took him.

Taggert swung her sword with desperate strength. The sanctuary stood motionless at her side, her eyes clenched shut, despair written openly on her face. Taggert looked back for Cord, but he had disappeared beneath a horde of swarming creatures, back down the corridor. The steward fought on, her arms and back screaming for rest, but the creatures before her wouldn't stay dead. They were Unreal, and they were strong in their own world.

Taggert wondered what it would be like to die in the Unreal world. And if she would stay dead, or if something with her face would return to wage war against Castle Midnight in the cause of unreality.

CHAPTER 6

Wolves
At The Gate

Sir Gawaine Hellstrom, once of Tower Rouge, lay stiffly in his bed, staring up at the ceiling, unable to sleep. He'd blown out his night-light a good hour ago, but despite heavy eyelids and the weary ache in his bones, sleep still eluded him. Hazy shafts of light spilled into the darkened room from the corridor outside, and his night vision showed him the familiar shapes and shadows of his bedroom. Emma had insisted their furniture be transported from Kahalimar to the castle. Gawaine didn't care; Viktor was the one who'd end up footing the bill. It wasn't as if he'd chosen any of it himself. He'd never had the time or the inclination to develop domestic instincts. He'd spent most of his life as a soldier, and most of that on the move. His time at Kahalimar had been the longest he'd ever spent in one place. Four interminable years . . . He'd waited so long for them to be over, only to discover that what came next was worse.

He shifted himself into yet another position, trying to get comfortable. Emma stirred at his side and he lay still, not wanting to wake her. The years in exile had been hard on Emma. She lived for the gossip, friendships, and factions of High Society, and there was little of that in Redhart outside Castle Midnight. She'd been just the same at the Forest Castle . . . Gawaine frowned in the darkness, and for a moment an old bitterness threatened to surface, but he pushed it back. He was Sir Gawaine of Redhart now, for better or worse, and the past should stay in the past.

Gawaine lay very still beside his wife, not touching her at all, for no matter where they were there was always something between them.

"What's the matter, Gawaine?" said Emma quietly.

"I'm sorry. I didn't mean to wake you."

"You didn't. You're not the only one who's had trouble sleeping lately."

Gawaine smiled indulgently into the darkness. "According to you, you never sleep."

"Well, I don't. I never have. Any night I get more than a few hours sleep is a good night for me. But I'm used to that; you're not. What's the matter?"

"Nothing in particular. Just . . . things. Go to sleep, love. Busy day tomorrow."

They lay in silence for a while. Far away, they could hear the Night Watch being changed. Gawaine smiled and relaxed slightly. There was something very comforting, even cozy, about lying in a warm soft bed and listening to the sound of marching men whose job it was to see you slept safe and undisturbed. Gawaine in particular appreciated it. He'd done his fair share of marching back and forth in the cold on Watch duty in his time.

"Remember the bed we had back at Forest Castle?" said Emma dreamily. "I used to love that bed."

Gawaine grunted. "Damned ugly monstrosity. Far too big, and it creaked every time you moved."

"But it was comfortable . . . you could just sink into that mattress. And the furniture we had then: this stuff is all very well, but it's not a patch on what we used to have. But then, that's true of everything here."

"Well you'll just have to make the most of it," said Gawaine irritatedly. "We won't ever be going back to the Forest."

"We might," said Emma. "Someday."

"No we won't! We can't go back!" Gawaine started to sit up in bed, and then made himself lie down again. They'd had this argument before, and shouting only made things worse. "Emma, after what happened we can never return to Forest Castle. They'd hang both of us."

"I only wanted to help," said Emma. "It just got out of hand."

All the long years of bottled up anger suddenly came together in Gawaine, and he finally asked the question he'd promised himself he'd never ask again. "Why did you kill him, Emma? Why did you have to kill him?"

"He was your rival, Gawaine. He stood in your way. If you were ever to get on at Court, he had to die."

"But suspicion was bound to fall on . . . us. And I never gave a damn for his position, or *getting on*. I was happy as I was."

"You never were ambitious enough, Gawaine. So I had to be ambitious enough for both of us. Looking back, yes, it was a mistake to kill him. But it was such a clever plan, and it would have worked if we hadn't been betrayed." Her hand drifted across under the bedclothes and fastened onto his. Their fingers intertwined. "And you took the blame for me, Gawaine. I've never forgotten that. You gave up your position and your honor to save me. What other woman was ever loved more than I?"

"What else could I do," said Gawaine, and if there was the faintest tinge of weariness in his voice, Emma didn't hear it. Gawaine gave her hand a comforting squeeze. "Go to sleep, love."

She snuggled up against him, her hand resting on his shoulder, and her slow breathing gradually deepened as sleep took her. Gawaine lay still, staring into the darkness. King John had trusted him, knighted him, loved him as a son. He had been honored and content as a knight of the Forest Kingdom. And then everything had gone wrong, and in the space of a few months, he'd had to give up everything he'd ever cared for, to save his wife. Perhaps the saddest truth of all was that deep down where it mattered, he was no longer sure he loved his wife. He kept it from her, as best he could. If only because he felt guilty for not loving her as much as she loved him.

I did it for you, Gawaine.

I know, Emma. I know.

Jordan woke slowly and reluctantly from his slumber, but the persistent voice and the tugging at his arm wouldn't let him rest. He sat up on the bed and looked blearily about him. The candles were still burning in their holders, but were little more than stubs. He'd had almost three or four hours sleep, and it felt like a hell of a lot less. His head was muzzy, and his mouth tasted as though something had died in it. He yawned, stretched, and scratched at his ribs. He hated sleeping in his clothes.

"All right," he said roughly, "I'm awake. What's the emergency?"

He glared around to see who'd disturbed his rest, and then snapped wide-awake as he found himself face-to-face with the ghost child, Wee Geordie. The young boy's face was screwed up with fear and worry, and he was tugging urgently at Jordan's right arm with both hands. Jordan's first thought was that he ought to be frightened at being woken in the early hours of the morning by a ghost, but the open dismay on the boy's face wouldn't let him be scared. Geordie was already frightened enough for both of them.

"What is it, Geordie?" he said more gently. "What are you doing back here?"

"You've got to help her! She's going to die if someone doesn't help her!"

"Who is? Who's going to die? Slow down, lad—I'll help you, I promise. Now who is it that's going to die?"

"Kate Taggert, the steward lady." Geordie's voice choked up for a moment as though he was going to burst into tears, but he got control of himself again and carried on. "She went into the West Wing with Damon Cord and Mother Donna, and it's awful in there. The Unreal's broken loose. It's out of control,

and they're all going to die if you don't do
something!"

Jordan swung down off the bed, buckled his sword
belt about him, and headed for the bedroom door. He
wasn't sure what Geordie was on about, but he knew
genuine terror when he saw it. He'd been very impressed
by the steward's style in the Great Hall earlier on,
and if she was in trouble, he wanted to help. He
strode quickly through the suite and pulled open the
main door. He was glad to see both the guards were
back on duty. He had a use for them.

"I want Count Roderik and Sir Gawaine, as fast as
you can get them here. Now move it!"

The two guards looked at each other, and the one
on the left cleared his throat. "With respect, Your
Highness, I really don't think the count would take
kindly to being disturbed at this hour. And we were
given strict orders not to leave you unattended, for
any reason."

Jordan stepped forward, thrust his scowling face at
the guard's, and gave him his best intimidating glare.
"Get moving right now, soldier, or so help me I'll
deep-fry you on the spot." He raised one hand in a
vaguely mystical gesture, and the guard turned and
ran. Jordan turned to glare at the other guard, but he
was already off and running.

There are advantages to being a prince, thought Jordan grimly. *Particularly if they're half convinced you're
crazy as well.* He looked down at Wee Geordie, who
was hovering at his side. "Why did you come to me
for help, lad? I don't even know the steward very
well."

"You were nice to me," said the ghost in a small
voice. "You spoke to me. Most people are stupid.
They won't talk to me at all. Kate always does, but
she's different. She's been my friend for a long time.
But most people don't want to know me. I do try to
be friendly, but they just yell or scream or run away.
Do you know why they won't be friends with me?"

Jordan looked down into the young boy's trusting
eyes, and fought hard to keep the pity out of his face.

The poor lad didn't even know he was dead, and that the mother he was looking for had been in the cold ground for centuries. And Jordan knew that even if he could explain it to the boy, Geordie probably couldn't understand it. How could a boy that age ever really understand what had happened to him? He was groping for something to say in answer to the boy's question when luckily he was interrupted by the sound of approaching feet. He looked up, and saw one of the guards returning with Sir Gawaine. The knight looked as though he'd dressed in a hurry, but he was carrying his ax at the ready. Some of the worry left his face when he saw Jordan standing there apparently unharmed, and the concern was replaced by a heavy scowl.

"This had better be a real emergency," he growled, slowing to a halt before Jordan. "You're lucky I was already getting up when your guard arrived. There's a General Alarm in the castle, although so far I haven't been able to find anyone who can tell me why."

"I can," said Jordan. "The Unreal's broken through in the West Wing, and everything's gone to hell in a handcart. The steward's in there with it, and she's in trouble. If we don't do something fast, she's dead. You got any ideas?"

"Yes," said Gawaine. "We go in there after her and get her out."

"I was afraid you were going to say something like that."

Gawaine looked at him narrowly. "How is it you know so much about what's going on?"

Jordan indicated the boy at his side. "Wee Geordie told me."

The knight looked at the young ghost, who smiled shyly up at him, and moved a step closer to Jordan so he could hold his hand and half hide behind him. Gawaine nodded slowly.

"You do have a gift for making friends, Your Highness," he said dryly. "If Geordie told you, I've no doubt it's true. We'd better get moving."

"No one's going anywhere!" snapped Count Roderik, hurrying down the corridor toward them. He was wearing a sheer silk dressing gown tastefully decorated with gold and silver piping and mother-of-pearl buttons. The last time Jordan had seen a gown like that, the owner had been running a Hub City brothel. A smile tugged at the corner of his mouth, but quickly disappeared as Roderik came to a halt directly before him. "That's far enough, *Your Highness*. You know you're not supposed to be out at this hour. The night air's bad for you. Now get back into your room, and stay there."

"The Unreal's broken loose . . ." Jordan began, but Roderik cut him short.

"That's none of your business. There are people here in the castle whose job it is to deal with that. You'd just get in the way, Viktor. I thought I'd make it quite clear that you were not to leave your rooms before morning for any reason, unless I was with you. Gawaine, escort His Highness back to bed, and tuck him in."

Jordan looked at Sir Gawaine, and raised an eyebrow. Gawaine bowed to him. "Awaiting your orders, sire."

"Then let's go."

"That's enough!" Roderik stepped forward so that his face was only inches away from Jordan's. "You forget yourself," said Roderik softly, pitching his voice low so that the two guards wouldn't hear. "Now do as you're told. I have more than enough magic to knock you cold if I have to, or I could simply order the guards to put you back in your rooms. So, Your Highness, do you want to walk back in or would you rather be dragged?"

Jordan smiled slowly. "I don't think you understand the situation, Roderik. Guards, escort the Count back to his rooms and tuck him into bed."

The two guards stepped forward, took one of Roderik's arms each, and then dragged him backward down the corridor. Roderik disappeared quickly into the distance, speechlessly mouthing threats and curses.

Jordan and Gawaine shared a smile. Something poked Jordan in the back of the knee. He looked down, and found that the bloodhound had chosen that moment to make his reappearance.

"Isn't he lovely!" said Geordie excitedly. "Is he yours, Viktor?" He knelt down and hugged the dog's neck. The bloodhound wagged his tail briskly and licked the young ghost's face.

Gawaine looked at Jordan. "Where did you get that from?"

"Came with the room," said Jordan.

Geordie reluctantly stopped petting the dog and looked appealingly at Jordan. "Please, we've got to go now, or it'll be too late and the steward'll die! Please!"

"Lead the way, lad," said Sir Gawaine, and Wee Geordie set off down the corridor at a run, the bloodhound bounding along beside him. Jordan and Gawaine followed on behind. The West Wing turned out to be a great deal closer than Jordan had realized, and in a matter of minutes he'd drawn close enough to hear the insane babble of sounds that warned of the approaching madness. He and Gawaine slowed to a halt as they drew near the barricade at the West Wing's boundary. Wee Geordie and the bloodhound were already there waiting for them. There was blood on the floor by the barricade. Some of it was still drying. A guard captain came out of a side room and stared at Jordan for a long moment before raising his hand in a salute. He looked tired and drawn, and there was blood on his uniform that didn't look to be his.

"Captain Doyle, at your service, sire. You shouldn't be here. It's too dangerous."

"We know about the Unreal," said Jordan. "I hear the steward's in there with it."

"That's right," said Doyle slowly. "She just went in, a few minutes ago."

Jordan looked thoughtfully at Wee Geordie. At least half an hour had passed since Geordie had told him the steward was in danger . . . Perhaps time moved differently when you were a ghost. He looked back at Doyle, and smiled reassuringly.

"We're here to help, Captain. How many guards do you command?"

"Four guards, two walking wounded. I've been promised reinforcements, but God knows when they'll get here."

Jordan scowled, and looked at Sir Gawaine. "We can't wait. According to Geordie, Taggert needs us now."

"You can't be thinking of going in there, sire," said Doyle quickly. "There's nothing you could do. Even your brother Dominic would be hard-pressed to stand against this much unreality."

"The steward's in trouble! She needs us!"

"Your concern does you credit, Your Highness, but we've already lost a sanctuary and a dozen good men. It's death to go in there now."

Jordan looked at Gawaine. "He does have a point, you know."

"But you promised!" Wee Geordie looked accusingly at Jordan, and he sighed heavily.

"Yes," he said. "I promised. Let's go, Gawaine."

He climbed up and over the barricade, with Gawaine close behind him. It gave uneasily under their weight, and Jordan couldn't help wondering how long it would hold if something nasty decided to leave the West Wing. On descending the other side, he was somewhat surprised to find Wee Geordie and the bloodhound already waiting for him. Jordan decided he wasn't going to ask. It seemed there were definite advantages to being a ghost. A thought struck him, and he turned to Sir Gawaine as he climbed down from the barricade.

"Can Geordie be hurt by anything in the West Wing?" he said quietly.

"I don't see how," said Gawaine, just as quietly. "I mean, he is dead, after all."

Jordan led the way down the corridor, frowning to himself as he realized for the first time that he wasn't at all sure what he was going to do when he caught up with the steward. After what he'd seen her do in the Great Hall, his sword and conjurer's tricks weren't going to be much help. He shrugged mentally. He'd just have to improvise.

And then they came to the boundary of the Unreal, and they stopped dead in their tracks.

The corridor had given way to a night-dark forest, lit by dancing emerald fires that burned unsupported on the air. The boles of the trees were twisted and gnarled, the whorls of bark forming horrid faces that looked at Jordan with knowing eyes. Bugs and insects the size of Jordan's hand scuttled across the ground in the thousands, forming a heaving living carpet. A guard wearing torn chain mail came running through the forest, screaming and howling wordlessly. A great wind came roaring after him and tore the flesh from his bones as he ran. The man was dead before Jordan could even begin to look away.

"And this is just the edge," said Gawaine quietly. "It'll get worse the farther we go in. Stay close beside me."

He hefted the ax the High Warlock had given him so long ago, and started forward. The runes on the heavy axhead began to glow. Insects crunched loudly under Gawaine's boots, and some ran up his legs, their antennae waving furiously. Gawaine ignored them, and kicked a path through the ones swarming on the ground. Jordan drew his sword and hurried after the knight, his lips curling in disgust. He'd never liked bugs. He tried to step gingerly around the worst concentrations, but there were just too many of them. Wee Geordie and the bloodhound brought up the rear. Jordan didn't notice it, but the insects drew back rather than approach the young ghost and the dog.

Gawaine swung his ax at a tree that blocked his way. The bark oozed blood, and the branches thrashed angrily. Gawaine cut it down anyway. Branches from the surrounding trees reached for him with crackling fingers of sharpened twigs. Gawaine met them unflinchingly with his ax. He and his brother Vivian had held Tower Rouge against an army, and there was little left in the world that could scare him anymore. Jordan moved in beside him with his sword. The two of them pressed on, and the forest couldn't stop them. And then, in the space between one step and the next, the forest was suddenly gone and madness took its place.

They were deep in the West Wing now, and the Unreal had thrown away its masks. They were back in the corridor again, but the walls were studded with inhuman faces that disappeared when you looked at them directly, but smiled and snarled endlessly at the corner of your eyes. There were holes in the floor that fell away forever. The ceiling seemed to be miles overhead, its features blurred by distance. And in that corridor, creatures from a fever's nightmare swarmed about Damon Cord and fought to pull him down. His clothes were torn, and soaked with his own blood and others'. He swung his mace with frenzied strength, but in the end there were just too many creatures, and they brought him down.

Sir Gawaine howled a Forest warcry, and charged into the midst of the creatures. His ax was a shimmering blur as it sheared through a distorted shape that screeched in agony and despair and then vanished. Something with jagged teeth launched itself at Gawaine, and he spun quickly around to bury his ax in its breastbone. He staggered back a step under the creature's weight, and then it too was gone, and air rushed in to fill the gap where it had been. Gawaine grinned wolfishly. It seemed the ax's property of destroying inimical magic was working to his advantage. He gripped the haft firmly and swung again. The runes on the steel head burned with a bright silver fire.

Jordan did his best to guard Gawaine's back, but it was all he could do to clear a space in the press of inhuman bodies. Damon Cord reared up from under a crowd of monsters, and struck about him with his mace. Blood ran from a long scalp wound, making his face an ugly crimson mask. A crawling thing with too many legs and an insane woman's face ran down the wall to strike at Wee Geordie. Jordan saw the thing coming, but knew he couldn't hope to reach the boy in time. And then Geordie turned and looked at the monstrosity. He frowned, and it fell dying to the floor.

Good thing I decided to help him, thought Jordan.

The Unreal creatures suddenly gave up on their prey, and fled down the corridor, their shapes changing as they ran. Jordan and Gawaine stood together in the empty corridor, panting for breath. Damon Cord reversed his long-handled mace and leaned on it wearily.

"Thanks for the help. I couldn't have lasted much longer." He looked approvingly at Gawaine's blood-soaked ax. "That's some ax you've got there." He glanced at the bloodhound, and raised an eyebrow. "Though this is a hell of a time to be taking your dog for a walk."

Jordan looked at Cord's bloodstained clothing, and frowned worriedly. "Are you all right? Do you need a surgeon?"

Cord shook his head. "I'll live. Look, Your Highness, I'm grateful for your help, but we can't stay here. The steward and Mother Donna are up ahead, and they're in trouble. You've got to help them. I can't. The best I can do is guard your backs."

Sir Gawaine nodded briskly, and set off down the corridor. Blood dripped steadily from his ax. Wee Geordie hurried after him, the bloodhound padding close at his side. Jordan had to wait a moment to get his breath back before continuing, and that was how he saw what happened to the dog. It was trotting along quite happily when a long warty tentacle snapped out of the corridor wall and grabbed at the dog. Jordan opened his mouth to shout a warning, and then stopped as the tentacle passed clean through the bloodhound's body as though it wasn't there. The tentacle tried again, but to no effect. The bloodhound padded on, unconcerned, and the tentacle whipped back into the wall. Jordan's mouth closed with a snap.

It's a ghost. It's another damned ghost. No wonder it kept appearing and disappearing . . .

Jordan shot a glance at Cord, but he didn't seem to

have seen anything untoward. Jordan shook his head, and started after the others. He'd always heard Castle Midnight was lousy with ghosts, and it looked as though the stories were true. He soon caught up with Sir Gawaine, and they walked side by side deeper into the heart of the Unreal. Cord brought up the rear, silent and scowling. The corridor continued to fluctuate around them, but although strange shapes came and went like the threads of a drifting nightmare, none of them drew near the small party. Word of Sir Gawaine's ax had spread among the Unreal.

Jordan kept a careful watch about him, nonetheless. There was something horribly unsettling about the West Wing now, apart from the insane shifting and stirrings in the passageways. The very nature of the world seemed somehow different, as though all the old relationships like cause and effect were no longer valid, or at least no longer constant. You couldn't rely on left and right or up and down to mean the same things anymore. The simple everyday certainties upon which the Real world is based had become confused and contradictory. Time itself appeared to become slow and sluggish, and then speeded up again. Jordan had never felt so scared in his life. It was as though he'd woken from the worst nightmare he'd ever had, only to find he was trapped in the dream and unable to break free. He could turn and run, of course. No one was stopping him. He could run back the way he'd come and escape all this madness. No one would blame him. It was the sensible thing to do. But in the end, he only considered the thought seriously for a moment or two, and then discarded it. He wasn't going to turn back. He had his pride and his dignity . . . and his honor. He'd promised Wee Geordie his help. And Catriona Taggert needed him.

The world suddenly changed again. The corridor spun dizzily around him, and then settled. Jordan blinked dazedly as he discovered he and his party were now standing in a small circle of normality, together with the steward and Mother Donna. The sanctuary's face was gray and drawn from strain and exhaustion.

Taggert was sitting with her back to the wall, nursing a torn arm. Her glowing shield was gone, but her balefire sword still crackled quietly in her right hand. She and Mother Donna nodded tiredly to their rescuers, too exhausted even to be surprised.

"We've come to help you," said Jordan lamely.

"A bit late," said Taggert, "but none the less welcome for that."

"There's a gateway somewhere ahead," said Mother Donna. "I'm sure of it. If we're to stop the Unreal, it must be destroyed. The steward and I have done all we can. It's up to you now. There's a power in your ax, Gawaine—I can feel it. With that, and God's blessing, you might just live long enough to reach the gateway."

"Looks like I've been volunteered again," said Sir Gawaine.

"And me," said Jordan. Gawaine looked at him, and Jordan glared right back at him. "You're going to need someone to guard your back."

"You don't have to do this."

"Yes, I do. I gave Geordie my word."

Sir Gawaine nodded approvingly. Jordan felt proud, and just a little sick. Playing a hero onstage was one thing, being one was quite another. He swallowed hard, and turned to Wee Geordie and the bloodhound.

"I want you two to stay here and look after Mother Donna and the steward. Do you think you can do that?"

Geordie's lower lip thrust out. "I want to stay with you."

"I need someone to look after the ladies," said Jordan. "Someone I can trust."

Geordie thought about it, and then nodded. "I'll protect them, Viktor. I promise."

Jordan ruffled the boy's hair affectionately, and leaned down to pet the dog. It fixed him with its sad eyes, and wagged its tail furiously. Jordan turned back to Sir Gawaine, and nodded jerkily to show he was ready. The knight took a firm grip on his ax, then stepped out of the sanctuary's circle of normality and back into nightmare. Jordan followed him, sword in hand.

Beyond the circle, things were different again. The light was an unhealthy purple glow that flickered up from jagged holes in the pitch-black floor. Sir Gawaine started slowly forward, and Jordan followed him. He kept well clear of the holes. They looked a lot like mouths to him. The walls were covered with running sores, and the ceiling was so low he had to bend his head to avoid banging it. Somewhere up ahead, something was grunting like a gigantic hog at its trough. It sounded hungry, and horribly eager.

"It knows we're coming," said Gawaine softly.

"What the hell are we looking for, anyway?" said Jordan, just as quietly. He felt uneasy about raising his voice. He didn't know who might be listening.

"Beats me," said Sir Gawaine. "We'll know it when we find it. If we get that far. It could be a place or a person, or even an object. It's a gateway; a part of reality through which the Unreal can enter from outside. Rather like a sanctuary in reverse. It could be anything, anywhere. We just keep looking until we find it. And then we do something about it."

"Like what?" said Jordan.

"I haven't worked that out yet," said Sir Gawaine.

"Great," said Jordan. "Just great."

Gawaine grinned at him suddenly. "Sorry you came?"

"Damned right!" said Jordan, smiling in return. "What do you think I am—crazy?"

They continued down the corridor, trying to look in every direction at once. Jordan gripped his sword tightly, until his fingers ached. The passage was ominously quiet. The light blazed up through the holes in the floor. It waxed and waned and flickered unsteadily, as the color changed from a sickly purple to a dark crimson that reminded Jordan inescapably of blood. The harsh, garish light made Gawaine look like a walking corpse. The comparison disturbed Jordan, and he looked away. He paused briefly to look down into one of the holes, careful to keep a safe distance between him and the edge. Far below, something dark and indistinct swam listlessly in a sea of blazing magma. It was too far away to tell how big the thing was, but the slow ponderousness of its movements suggested something unthinkably huge. Jordan looked quickly away, and hurried to catch up with Sir Gawaine.

"The gateway can't be too far away," muttered the knight, as much to himself as to Jordan. "The Unreal hasn't had time to spread far."

"How does a gateway come about anyway?" said Jordan. "I got the impression they were pretty rare."

"They are," said Sir Gawaine. "I did some research on the history of the Unreal when I first came to Castle Midnight. I like to know what I might be up against. As far as I can tell, there have only ever been four major gateways, and they were all the result of High Magic gone bad."

"High Magic . . ." Jordan scowled unhappily. "There aren't many people in the castle with that kind of power. There's the steward, of course, but I think we can count her out. There's Roderik, but I don't see what he could hope to gain by it. And there's Count William, but I think we can count him out for the same reason. No, Gawaine, there's only one person in this castle with High Magic who's crazy enough to do something like this, and that's Dominic."

"I was wondering how long it would take you to work that out," said Sir Gawaine. "That's why we're going in this direction. Prince Dominic has a set of spare apartments down this way. I'm betting that's where we'll find him and his gateway."

A low rumbling began in the gloom at the end of the long corridor. It was quiet at first, like a roll of faraway thunder, but it grew steadily louder as it drew nearer. Jordan and Gawaine stopped where they were, and listened. The noise changed from thunder to something that might have been the growling of a huge beast, and Jordan stirred uneasily. But the sound rumbled on, always gaining in volume, roaring, churning, and splashing. Jordan gradually realized what he was hearing. He looked at Gawaine in horror, and saw his own shocked understanding in the knight's face. They looked back at the corridor, and the great wave of water came boiling down the passage toward them. Dominic had used his water magic to call up a tsunami: a gigantic tidal wave.

"Run!" screamed Jordan, but Gawaine grabbed him by the arm.

"There isn't time!" he yelled, over the roar of the approaching water. "Get behind me!"

He planted his feet firmly and held his ax out before him, using both hands to hold it steady. The runes on the blade glowed brighter than the sun. Jordan crouched behind Gawaine, and wondered how long it took to die by drowning. He'd only seen the ocean a few times in his life, and he'd never bothered to learn to swim. He clung forlornly to his sword, and wished he could have made a better showing as Viktor. Now he'd never know what kind of prince he'd have made. The great wall of frothing water came surging down the corridor and slammed against Sir Gawaine, only to break apart as it hit his glowing ax and split into two lesser waves that roared by on either side of him. Enough spray and rough water broke free to drench Gawaine and Jordan to the skin, but they were still able to snatch gulps of air and hold their ground. The water thundered on and on; breaking around them and beating against the corridor walls. And then, finally, the level of the water fell away, and the tsunami was past, its fury spent. Gawaine lowered his ax, and let out a slow sigh of relief.

"That was close. That was as close as it's ever been, and then some. Are you all right, Your Highness?"

"Fine. I've always wanted to play the part of a drowned rat." Jordan tried to squeeze some of the water out of his clothes, and then gave it up as a bad job. "That's some ax the High Warlock gave you."

"I've always thought so. We'd better get moving. Calling up that much water must have weakened your brother considerably, but it won't take him long to recover. His apartments should be just down here."

Gawaine splashed through the inches-deep water and headed for a closed door up on the right. Jordan followed him, wondering absently if the water was draining away through the holes in the floor, and if so, what would happen when all those gallons of water met the blazing magma down below. He decided that he'd rather not be around when it happened, and increased his pace to draw level with the knight. Gawaine finally stopped before a door that looked no different from any of the others. He tried the doorknob, and it turned easily in his grasp. Gawaine eased the door open an inch, and let go the handle. He looked inquiringly at Jordan, who nodded firmly. Sir Gawaine kicked the door open, and the two of them charged into Dominic's apartment.

The Lady Elizabeth was hanging on the far wall. Crude iron nails had been driven through her arms and legs, pinning her to the brickwork. She'd been gutted, her body split open from neck to crotch. And yet somehow, horribly, she was still alive. Her mouth worked silently, but there was no sanity left in the bulging eyes. In the center of what had been Elizabeth's abdomen, strange lights and colors moved sickeningly.

A gateway can be anything.

"Impressive, isn't it?" said Dominic.

Jordan and Sir Gawaine looked around sharply. Prince Dominic was seated elegantly in a comfortably padded chair, one hand cradling a brandy glass. Beside him stood a small table, bearing a silver tray with a dozen or so dainty little snacks. He looked like he'd been there for some time. As always, Dominic wore no sword or armor, but still he looked totally at ease, and in full command of the situation.

"You bastard," said Jordan. "How could you do that to her? She was your wife!"

"You're even more sentimental than the man you pretend to be," said Dominic, amusedly. "Ours was never a love match, actor. Elizabeth thought she was using me as a means to power. In fact, it turned out to be the other way around. Poor Elizabeth." He gestured languidly with his free hand, and all the water soaking Jordan and Gawaine's clothes suddenly disappeared. "There. That's better. I don't know why you're looking so shocked, Gawaine. You know perfectly well that you despised Elizabeth, and she you. Or perhaps you're merely worried about the castle. Fear not. The Unreal isn't nearly strong enough yet to break through without my gateway. As soon as it's caused enough chaos to suit my purpose, I'll destroy the gate, and the Unreal will be back under control again. Simple, but elegant, don't you think—like all the best plans."

"What do you hope to achieve by all this?" said Jordan slowly. A dizzying anger had begun to burn within him, but for the moment he kept it firmly under control. "What's so important that hundreds of people in the West Wing had to die because of it?"

"Just a little general chaos," said Dominic, "which my people, carefully forewarned, will take advantage of to gain the best positions in the castle, and destroy Lewis's troops. William's men will be too busy coping with the Unreal to interfere, until it's too late. By the time I finally close the gateway, my people will control Castle Midnight, and my rule will begin."

"You take care of Dominic," said Gawaine to Jordan. He turned to stare at the gateway. "I'll take care of this abomination."

"I'm afraid I really can't allow that," said Dominic. He rose to his feet in a single languid movement, pivoted on one foot, and kicked the ax out of Gawaine's hand. "Now, old man, let's see how good you are without a magic ax to protect you."

Gawaine cursed angrily, and reached for Dominic with his bare hands. The prince smiled, and gestured lightly with his left hand. Gawaine groaned once, and slumped to his knees. Fat beads of sweat formed on his face, and ran away in steady streams.

"Have you ever considered," said Dominic conversationally to Jordan, "how much of the human body is water? Water I can control, by my magic? In fact, have you ever considered what a man would look like, after every drop of water in him had been drained away?"

Jordan palmed a flare pellet from his sleeve, nicked the wax coating with his thumbnail, and threw the pellet at Dominic's face. The prince fell back a step, taken by surprise, but the pellet still cracked against his forehead and broke open. Flames roared up around his face, and his hair caught alight. He screamed, and beat at the flames with his hands.

Jordan ran over to the gateway, sword in hand. He stood before Elizabeth and then stopped, as he realized he had no idea what to do next. Compassion, outrage, and not wanting to look a coward had brought him this far, but the gateway was more horrible than anything in the corridors. Elizabeth should have been dead, but somehow the gateway was keeping her alive. The power that implied was far beyond anything Jordan could hope to defeat. He'd never felt so scared in his life. He couldn't seem to get his breath, his legs were shuddering, and his stomach churned with tension. He was no hero or soldier—he didn't belong here. Jordan swallowed hard, and shook his head doggedly. He remembered the tsunami, and his regret at never having had a chance to act as a prince should. Now he'd been given the chance. Whether he lived or died no longer seemed as important as it once had. All that mattered now was destroying the gateway before the Unreal broke free of its restraints, and killed everyone in the castle. Jordan raised his sword, and tried to figure out where to strike for the best. He was still just as scared. He just didn't care anymore.

The churning lights shining deep in the gutted body pulled at his eyes, mesmerizing him, and he jerked his gaze away with an effort. He could hear Dominic groaning and cursing, and stumbling back and forth behind him. And then Jordan looked up, and his gaze met the mad eyes in Elizabeth's face, and he knew what he had to do. He took a firm grip on his sword, and cut at the Lady Elizabeth's neck. His sword bit deeply, and blood spurted out in a thick jet. He cut again, and severed the head completely. It fell past him, and bounced once on the floor before rolling away. The eyes still moved, and the mouth worked silently. And then blood welled from the gateway in a steady stream, and in the blink of an eye the gateway fell in on itself, and was gone. The body hanging on the wall was just a body, and Elizabeth's head lay still and silent on the floor. Jordan turned away.

Sir Gawaine was sitting on his haunches, pale and drawn but now clinging grimly onto his ax. There was a scuffing sound to Jordan's right, and he looked quickly around to see Dominic leaning against the wall by the door. He'd put out the flames by conjuring up water, but not before the fire had done its worst. Half his hair was gone, and his face was horribly disfigured. There was a drifting smell of burned meat in the air. Dominic peered at Jordan with his one good eye, and raised a shaking hand in a mystical gesture, only to stop as Gawaine lurched to his feet again, ax at the ready. Dominic smiled at Jordan, his teeth horribly white against the scorched and blackened flesh of his face.

"I'll watch you die by inches for this, actor."

A split in the air opened before Dominic and swallowed him up. The air sparked with static, and then was still. Jordan and Sir Gawaine looked at each other.

"Always has to have the last word, your brother," said Gawaine.

They put away their weapons, and Gawaine glanced briefly at what was left of the Lady Elizabeth.

"Poor lass," he said quietly. "I never liked her, but no one should have to die like that."

"Let's get out of here," said Jordan. "I'm so tired, I'm asleep on my feet."

Gawaine smiled wearily. "I'd forgotten just how hectic life can be at Castle Midnight. You'd better grab some sleep while you can, Your Highness. We've closed the gateway, but it's only a matter of time before the Unreal grows strong enough to break through on its own. And we still don't know how much damage Dominic's troops have done under cover of the chaos."

"Doesn't this place ever quiet down?" said Jordan disgustedly. "I've appeared in murder mysteries that were less complicated than this."

"The only way this castle will ever know peace is when there's a king on the throne. That's the truth you always have to remember here. Castle Midnight needs a king. Any king." He stretched slowly, and shook his head. His chain mail rustled softly, as though protesting. "Let's go. And Jordan . . . I wouldn't mention Elizabeth's death to Viktor. Not just yet. It had better be our secret, for the time being."

Jordan nodded, and he and Sir Gawaine left the room and made their way back down the corridor. The Unreal was gone, and the West Wing was nothing more than cold stone and warm lamplight. There was a peaceful stillness to the air, like the calm after a thunderstorm has passed. Jordan felt a slow wave of tiredness moving through his body as tense muscles gradually unwound, but even so he wasn't fooled by appearances. Behind the air of normality, the Unreal was still there, waiting.

Jordan and Sir Gawaine found the rest of their party waiting for them back at the barricade. Captain Doyle and his men were looking after the exhausted steward and Mother Donna, while Cord stood guard a little distance away. Taggert had one arm heavily bandaged, but was well enough to be arguing firecely with Doyle as to whether or not she was fit enough to return to duty. The two of them broke off and looked around as the guards raised a cheer on seeing Jordan and Gawaine. Many willing hands helped to pull the barricade apart and make an opening for the returning heroes. Wee Geordie and the ghost dog were jumping up and down excitedly, and apparently vying with each other to see who could make the most noise. Gawaine took it all rather brusquely, but Jordan was in his element. It had been awhile since he'd known adulation like this, and he intended to enjoy it while it lasted. He clapped Doyle on the shoulder, and smiled magnanimously at the guards.

"The gateway's been destroyed," he said loudly, and grinned at Taggert. "You should have a slightly easier time of it for a while, Steward."

Taggert grinned back at him, and moved forward to stand before him. "You saved my life, Your Highness. Hell, you saved all our lives. I don't know what happened while you were in exile, but I thank God for it. You've come back a fine and honorable man, Viktor, and I'm proud to serve under you."

She drew her sword and raised it in the ancient warrior's oath of fealty. There was a clash of steel as the guards raised their swords, too, and then one by one they knelt and bowed their heads to Jordan. Captain Doyle and Captain Blood knelt with their men, their faces proud and glowing and just a little awed. Taggert, Damon Cord, and Mother Donna sank to one knee, and bowed their heads. Jordan had strong feeling that things were starting to get out of hand. He looked to Sir Gawaine for advice, and found the knight was kneeling, too. Jordan looked away, and found Wee Geordie and the bloodhound looking at him worshipfully. He swallowed hard and waved weakly at them all with his hands.

"Thank you, my friends. I only did my duty. Now get up. Please."

They got to their feet, adulation and respect still shining from their faces. Jordan felt decidedly nervous. Without quite knowing how, he'd raised a spirit here that wouldn't easily be dispelled, and he had no business doing so. He wasn't a prince, just a paid actor doing his job. He looked almost wildly about him for a distraction, and his gaze fell on Geordie and the bloodhound. An idea that had been simmering at the back of his mind for some time finally settled into shape, and he walked over to the two ghosts.

"Geordie, I think I know how we can find your mother for you. Do you know what kind of a dog this is? He's a bloodhound, bred and trained specially to

track people by their scent. If we can just find something that used to belong to your mother, I think this
clever dog might be able to lead us right to her."

The young boy's face lit up, and he ran forward
and threw his arms around Jordan's waist. He hugged
Geordie tightly in return, feeling tears forming in his
eyes. No child should have to endure what Wee Geordie had gone through for so many years. Sir Gawaine
stepped forward, and cleared his throat politely.

"I beg pardon for intruding, Your Highness, but
might I have a word with you?"

"Of course, Gawaine." Jordan eased himself free
from the young ghost's embrace. "I won't be a moment, Geordie, and then we'll make a start."

He moved over to Sir Gawaine, who carefully lowered his voice.

"Are you sure you know what you're doing? The
Lady Mary of Fenbrook has been dead and buried for
centuries. How is a bloodhound going to reunite her
with her ghostly son?"

"Because the dog's dead as well," said Jordan.
"He's a ghost bloodhound."

Sir Gawaine looked at the dog, and then at Jordan.
"One of these days I'm going to learn to stop asking
you questions. You always come up with such disturbing answers. Very well, sire. If you're serious
about this, you'll find a gold locket on a chain that
once belonged to the Lady Mary in the Old Museum.
It's here in the West Wing, just four corridors along
and clearly marked. You can't miss it."

Jordan nodded his thanks, made his good-byes, and
gathered up Wee Geordie and the dog. They set off
down the corridor together, the two ghosts barely able
to restrain themselves to Jordan's pace. He was glad
Gawaine hadn't volunteered to go with him. In some
strange way, he felt this was a personal business between him and the two ghosts. They had helped him
when he needed it; now he would help them. Perhaps
because he needed to believe he was worthy of the
trust Wee Geordie had placed in him. He glanced
unobtrusively at the young boy and the bloodhound

as they padded at his side. The boy had scruffy hair and dust marks on his face, and the dog was molting. It was hard to accept that they were both really dead, and that what walked so casually at his side were really nothing more than memories made flesh and bone. Jordan's gaze settled on Wee Geordie. All those years, spent searching for a mother who died centuries before. All the long years, wandering endlessly through bleak stone corridors, looking for someone, anyone, who would simply sit and talk with him instead of running away. Jordan's throat tightened, and he swore silently to himself that come what may, he'd do whatever it took to reunite Wee Geordie with his mother. He glanced at the boy and the dog one last time, and then stared resolutely straight ahead.

I wonder how they died . . .

They soon reached the Old Museum, and Jordan frowned. The brass plaque on the door looked like it hadn't been polished in years. The door squealed loudly as he pushed it open, and the room beyond was dark and gloomy. Jordan took a torch from the nearest wall holder, and led the way in. The museum was a large, spacious, dusty room. All four walls were covered with tightly packed bookshelves. The carpet was dry and hard underfoot, and the smeared windows looked as though they hadn't been opened in years, never mind cleaned. Jordan didn't know what the New Museum might be like, but it was clear no one had visited the Old Museum in a long time. Presumably the ever-present ghosts more than filled the castle population's interest in the past.

A large plain table stood alone in the middle of the room, bearing a number of exhibits in flyspecked glass cases. Jordan moved over to study them. Wee Geordie and the bloodhound trailed along after him. The boy was staring around him with wide eyes, but didn't seem interested in anything in particular. The bloodhound sneezed at the dust. Jordan found the idea of a sneezing ghost strangely unsettling. He concentrated on the exhibits before him, and carefully wiped some of the dust from the glass cases with his sleeve. The first case held a severed human hand, carefully stuffed and mounted. Spidery handwriting on a card at the base of the display case said simply *Rocca's Bane*. Jordan shrugged. The name didn't ring any bells. The next case held an ornate silver goblet, crusted with semiprecious stones. Just looking at it made Jordan's fingers twitch hungrily. He forced the thought aside, and concentrated on the display card. *Sebastian's Chalice*. Jordan shook his head, none the wiser. The next case held a slender silver knife, the hilt covered in tiny etched runes and glyphs, too small to be read with the unaided eye. The card said simply *The Starlight Duke's Dagger*.

Jordan's breath caught in his throat. He might not recognize any of the other exhibits, but this . . . the legendary Starlight Duke had founded Hillsdown some six hundred years ago. Children learned his life story at school, and the rulers of Hillsdown were still called duke rather than king, in honor of the great and famous man. And here was his dagger. *His* dagger. It had to be worth a fortune . . . Jordan shook his head slightly, and moved on. He didn't dare take anything but the locket. Too many people had known he was coming here. Unfortunately. The next case held a simple gold locket on a rolled-gold chain. Jordan studied it for a long time before looking at the card. It said simply *Lady Mary's Locket*.

Jordan slipped his torch into a nearby holder, and carefully lifted up the glass cover. It clung stubbornly to its base for a long moment, and then came free with a quiet sucking sound. Jordan put the glass carefully to one side, and then picked up the locket and chain. He felt more than saw Wee Geordie crowding in beside him, but he didn't look away from the locket. It was very light in his hand, and the oval locket opened easily once he found the clasp. Inside were two perfect miniature portraits. The one of the left showed a young boy with thin, pinched features and straw-colored hair. The right-hand portrait showed a beautiful young woman. She had long blond hair that fell in curls and ringlets to her bare shoulders. Her high cheekbones and pale blue eyes gave her a cold, almost harsh look, but her smile was warm and loving. Lady Mary of Fenbrook: dead and buried these past two hundred years. Jordan took a deep breath, and turned and crouched down beside Wee Geordie. He held the open locket so that the boy could see both portraits.

"That's me," said Geordie, looking at the left-hand portrait. Awe and wonder filled his face.

"Do you recognize the woman?" said Jordan.

"That's my mother," said Geordie. "I told you she was beautiful." He reached out a hesitant hand to touch the portrait, then lowered his hand again, and just looked at the calm, serene face. "Mother," he said quietly, "I've been looking for you for such a long time."

Tears stung Jordan's eyes again, and he fought them back. It wouldn't do for the boy to see him so upset. He sniffed quickly a couple of times, and then looked around for the dog. He started slightly on finding that the animal had moved silently up on his other side without him noticing. He straightened up, and held the locket before the dog's nose. The bloodhound sniffed the cold metal thoroughly. Jordan looked hard at the dog, and the animal stared back at him with old, wise eyes.

"We need you to find Wee Geordie's mother," said Jordan slowly, not knowing how much, if any, of what he was saying the dog understood. But there was something about the ghost dog that suggested he understood a great deal, in his way. He looked unblinkingly at Jordan, then at Wee Geordie, and then he lifted his great head and sniffed the air. He wagged his tail twice, and headed purposefully for the open door. Geordie hurried after him. Jordan tossed the locket back onto its stand and hurried after the two ghosts.

The bloodhound made his way unhesitatingly down the corridor, looking neither to the left nor to the right. He held his head high, and there was a calm certainty in his sad eyes and untiring gait. Wee Geordie walked close beside him, his gaze fixed hopefully on the dog. The animal turned into a side corridor, padded down the narrow passageway for a while, and then chose another turning. Its calm decisiveness was an eerie spectacle in itself, and Jordan's hackles stirred uneasily on the back of his neck. The bloodhound led them on, and they followed it through corridors and passageways, up stairs and down, along rotundas, and in and out of countless doors. And still the dog didn't hesitate in its stride, only stopping when it needed Jordan to open a door for it. The bloodhound headed down one gloomy passage after another, following a trail only he could detect.

The trail came to a sudden end at a blank wall that sealed off a deserted passageway. The bloodhound sniffed at the bare gray plaster and pawed at it a few times before turning to stare silently at Jordan. He looked down at the ghost of Wee Geordie, and searched for something comforting to say. To have come all this way, and all for nothing . . . The dog had lost the trail. If it had ever really found it in the first place. Jordan sighed, and stared helplessly at the blank wall. It had been a hell of a long shot anyway, when all was said and done, and it was really no surprise that it hadn't paid off. But he'd had such hopes . . . And what was he going to tell the boy? What could he tell him? That he'd picked the wrong person to trust? Jordan frowned suddenly as he caught a glimpse of something that didn't seem quite right. He moved closer, and studied the grimy plaster from only a few inches away. Under the plaster, just barely visible in the uncertain light, there was the outline of a door.

Jordan drew the knife from his boot, reversed it, and struck the plaster smartly with the hilt of his knife. The brittle stuff cracked and fell away in flakes, revealing the outline of a sealed-over door. Jordan swore silently. The door handle was long gone, and the door itself was undoubtedly locked, not to mention probably stuck fast in its frame. Getting the damned thing open wasn't going to be easy. He'd need half a dozen men with axes and crowbars, to start with

. . . He turned to Wee Geordie, standing patiently beside him.

"I'm afraid the way's blocked, Geordie. This door must have been sealed off a long time ago, and forgotten. I can't open it. We'll have to come back another time, when we're better prepared."

"No," said Geordie softly. "I don't think so." He looked steadily at the hidden door. "It's been a long time since I last came this way. A long time . . . I'd forgotten all about this door. But I remember it now."

The plaster cracked and splintered all across the wall, and the outlines of the door were suddenly starkly revealed. Wee Geordie continued to stare at the door, and it slowly stirred and groaned in its warped frame. The wood trembled violently, and then there was a shrill shearing of metal as the old lock burst apart. The door swung open on squealing hinges. An old, musty smell issued from the dark hallway beyond. The bloodhound padded confidently forward, and Wee Geordie followed him into the gloom. Jordan put away his knife, grabbed a wall torch from a nearby holder, and went after them.

The hallway had clearly been deserted for some time, but there was something about the dark, echoing hall that suggested it had been not so much forgotten as abandoned. All the furniture and trappings were still in place, though covered by a thick layer of grime and dust. Tapestries and portraits hung on the walls, while lamps and torches stood unlit in their holders. Jordan was tempted to light some of them with his torch, but didn't. He felt as though he was walking through the past, and he didn't want to disturb anything. Wee Geordie and the bloodhound pressed on, and Jordan had to hurry to catch up with them. The only sound in the hallway was the quiet crackling of the torch's flame, and Jordan's echoing footsteps. A sudden chill went through him as he realized neither the boy nor the dog made any sound at all.

"I remember this place," said Geordie suddenly, looking about him. "I used to come here with my mother. It was a short cut. But it didn't look like this.

Everything's so *old,* and dusty. How long is it since I was last here? I can't remember . . . there's so much I don't remember anymore."

He didn't look to Jordan for an answer to his question. Jordan couldn't have answered him anyway; his throat was closed by a pity so intense it was almost pain. A long time ago, something terrible must have happened: something that ended in the deaths of Lady Mary and her son Geordie. Perhaps they were both murdered, here in this hallway. The odds were he'd never know the whole story. All he knew for certain was an impotent rage at the injustice of a young child condemned to wander lost and alone for centuries, knowing only that somehow he had become separated from his mother . . .

The bloodhound stopped suddenly. Jordan's heart sank, and he looked ahead of him for another obstacle, but as far as he could see, the way ahead was clear. He held his torch high, and the hall stretched away silent and empty for as far as the light carried. And then Jordan's hackles rose as he suddenly realized he'd been walking down the hall for quite some time, and there was still no sign of it ending. He began to wonder just how far the hallway stretched, and where exactly it led to . . .

The dog suddenly barked happily, and wagged its tail furiously. It sat down and stared ahead into the gloom. Geordie stood beside the bloodhound, his face open and yearning. A light appeared in the distance, and slowly began to move toward them. Jordan felt very cold, and his hands began to tremble. He was near to something strange and magical, in a place where he should not be. Part of him wanted to turn and run, but he couldn't. He watched fascinated, as the light drew nearer, and wondered from what far boundaries that light had come. It grew steadily brighter, and began to take on a vague shape. Wee Geordie and the dog didn't move at all. The light slowly formed into the glowing figure of a young woman with long blond hair and pale blue eyes. She shone so brightly it hurt to look at her, but Jordan couldn't look away. She was awesome and terrible, and wonderful beyond words. She stopped a few yards away, and held out her hands to Geordie, and in her smiling face there was all the love in the world.

Geordie ran forward to join his mother at long last, and the bloodhound went with him. It looked back once for Jordan's approval, and he nodded quickly. The boy and the mother fell into each other's arms. The dog sat beside them, his head held proudly high. The silvery light faded away, and took the dead with it. Jordan raised a hand in farewell, ignoring the tears that trickled down his cheeks.

"Good-bye, Geordie," he said hoarsely. "Good-bye hound. Rest easy, my friends."

He turned and made his way back down the hall, heading back into the light, where he belonged.

When he emerged from the forgotten door, Gawaine and the steward were there waiting for him. He nodded silently to the question in their eyes, and they both bowed their heads for a moment. Jordan put the torch back in its wall holder, and used the move to take out a handkerchief and mop the drying tears from his face. He turned around quickly as he heard approaching footsteps, and stuffed the handkerchief back in his sleeve. Count Roderik appeared around the corner, accompanied by a dozen of his personal guards. They were all hard, professional fighting men, and Jordan knew without having to be told that their loyalty lay exclusively with Roderik, and not with Prince Viktor. Gawaine unobtrusively moved a step closer to Jordan, and let his hand rest casually on the ax at his side. Roderik stamped to a halt before them, glanced at the watching steward, and bowed curtly to Jordan.

"Pardon me for this intrusion, Your Highness, but it's imperative that you return to your quarters and consult with your advisers. A special meeting has been called at Court, and your presence there was specifically requested. We need to discuss this, sire. If you will excuse us, steward . . ."

Taggert bowed formally, and turned to the prince. It was clear something was up between him and Roderik, but their quarrels were none of her business. Besides . . . Viktor could take care of himself. She bowed respectfully to the prince. "I'll see you at Court, Your Highness. And . . . thanks again."

Roderik watched silently until she'd disappeared around the corner, and then whirled angrily on Jordan. "I don't know what you've been up to, *sire,* and right now I don't care. Either you return with me immediately, or so help me I'll slap a geas on you and compel you to follow me!"

"Temper, temper, Roderik," murmured Jordan, in the most infuriatingly polite voice he could manage. "Not in front of the children. If you're in trouble, of course I'll come back with you. Now what's this about my presence being required at Court?"

Roderik glared at him, and Jordan could tell the count had been hoping Jordan would give him an excuse to use the compulsion spell. Apparently being dragged backward down a corridor by Jordan's guards hadn't gone down too well with Roderik. Jordan carefully kept the grin off his face. Roderik finally stepped to one side, and indicated the way he'd come with an angry gesture. Jordan smiled languidly, and strolled off that way as though he'd been intending to do so all along. Roderik walked stiffly at Jordan's side. Sir Gawaine followed close behind, and Roderik's personal guards brought up the rear.

"A Testing is to take place at Court in an hour," said Roderik eventually. "A young noble has reached adult age, and by law and tradition he is required to prove his claim to Blood. He does this by spilling some of his blood on the Stone, in front of witnesses. If his claim is genuine, the Stone will awaken the elemental magic within him, and he will be admitted into High Society."

"What if something goes wrong, and it turns out he doesn't have Blood after all?" asked Jordan.

"The Stone will kill him," said Sir Gawaine.

Roderik nodded. "Our problem is that one, if not

both, of your brothers believe you to be an impostor. They plan to demand you prove your identity by undergoing the Test yourself. Failure to do so would of course be an admission that you are not really Prince Viktor."

"Tricky," said Jordan.

"We have just under an hour to come up with an answer," said Count Roderik. "For all our sakes."

They walked the rest of the way in silence, each busy with his own thoughts. Of them all, only Jordan wasn't thinking about the Testing. He'd already worked out a way around that. He was more worried about the worsening situation in Castle Midnight. As if the Unreal wasn't enough trouble, it now appeared Lewis and Dominic had declared war. Their troops were fighting running battles in the corridors, and Dominic had sacrificed his own wife in an attempt to gain more power. And despite the Regent's declaration of the Rite of Transference, there was still no sign of the damned crown and seal. Jordan sighed heavily. Trying to keep track of all the factions and their varying motivations made his head ache.

Back at Jordan's suite, the conspirators gathered together for yet another desperate gamble. Robert Argent sat stiffly in a chair by the fire, his dour face as unreadable as ever. Brion DeGrange, the head of castle security, stood with his back to the fire, his face set and grim. Prince Viktor sat in the most comfortable chair, opposite Argent. He still looked painfully gaunt and drawn, but some of the color had come back to his cheeks, and he looked a little stronger than before. His mouth was firm and his eyes were clear and sharp, but he had to clasp his hands together in his lap to keep them from shaking. The Lady Heather sat on the arm of his chair, one arm draped protectively across Viktor's shoulders.

Jordan stood with his back to the closed main door, and leaned against it. The more he dealt with his fellow conspirators, the more he appreciated the value of a nearby exit. He looked unobtrusively around for

Sir Gawaine, and was relieved to see the knight was standing at parade rest, not too far away. Jordan felt a little better knowing he had at least one ally in the room. There was an air of barely suppressed tension among the conspirators, and everyone was talking too much and too loudly while they waited for Count Roderik to bring the meeting to order. He, on the other hand, seemed more interested in trying to fire up the apathetic Argent, who looked even more tired and unhappy than usual. Jordan didn't blame him. If his entire livelihood depended on the success of this conspiracy, he'd be worried, too. It quickly occurred to Jordan that it did, and he was. He coughed loudly to get everyone's attention, and went on coughing till he got it.

"I think perhaps I can save us all some time," he said affably. "Yes, Roderik has told me about the Testing; and yes, I do have an answer. It's quite simple, really. I'll make a slight incision in Prince Viktor's arm, and collect some of the Blood in a small glass vial. I will then conceal the vial up my sleeve. At the Testing, I will pretend to cut my arm, but actually spill the prince's blood, from the vial. A simple enough illusion, but since they won't be expecting such a thing, it should fool them completely. You may now applaud, or throw money."

Roderik nodded slowly. "I can see a number of things that could go wrong, but given how pressed we are for time, I think we're going to have to go with the actor's plan. Unless anyone has a better idea . . ."

He looked around hopefully, but nobody said anything. Viktor stirred uneasily in his chair, and they all looked at him.

"I'm not sure I like the idea of being cut, like a pig being prepared for slaughter. It's not dangerous, is it?"

"Don't be such a baby, darling," said Heather. "It'll just be a little scratch, I promise."

"You're looking rather better, Your Highness," said Sir Gawaine slowly. "Would I be right in thinking there's been an improvement in your condition?"

"Damn right there has," said Viktor. "I'm feeling a lot stronger. And do you know why? Because I've stopped eating food from the kitchens!"

"Your Highness, there can be no question of your meals having been poisoned," said Robert Argent. "I've personally tasted everything you've eaten . . ."

"Then you must have a cast iron stomach," snapped Viktor. "Over the past few days I've eaten nothing but raw fruit and vegetables that Heather gathered and prepared herself. And this morning, I actually woke up feeling hungry for the first time in days. I've had all the kitchen staff hanged, of course."

Everyone looked at the prince speechlessly. Jordan was one of the first to recover, and took advantage of the moment to study the others' reactions. They all looked shocked, but it was the raw hatred in De-Grange's face that caught Jordan's attention. It was one thing to know DeGrange only served Roderik because of the geas on him; it was quite another to see the rage and hate that lay under the spell written openly on the man's face. The emotion was come and gone in a moment, but Jordan made a firm decision never to turn his back on DeGrange. Gawaine stepped forward to face Prince Viktor.

"You had them hanged, Viktor? All of them?"

"They supplied the food," said Viktor. "It was their responsibility to see it was fit to eat."

"There were twenty-five kitchen staff," said Gawaine tightly. "Ten were women, and seven were child apprentices in training. And you had them all hanged."

"Yes!" said Viktor. "It was my right! Now I don't want to talk about it any more! Is that clear?"

"Yes, sire," said Sir Gawaine. "Very clear."

Viktor settled grumpily back into his chair, and looked hard at Jordan. "For the time being you look more like me than I do, so you'd better go on pretending to be me until I've got my strength back. Now then, we haven't got long before you have to attend the Testing, so we'd better get on with this bloodletting nonsense. And be careful with the knife, actor. You leave a scar, and I'll have you flogged."

Jordan produced a slim glass vial from one of his hidden pockets. He usually used it as part of his Invisible Wine illusion, but it would serve here. Heather watched with interest.

"Just how much have you got hidden up those sleeves of yours, actor?"

"You'd be surprised," said Jordan.

He drew the knife from his boot and started toward Prince Viktor. And then Brion DeGrange stepped forward to block his way.

"You don't need to bother with that, actor."

His voice was flat, almost emotionless, but his smile and eyes were openly mocking. Everyone stared at him. The air felt suddenly charged, as though something important had happened without them noticing. DeGrange had changed subtly. There was a calm, dangerous look to his face and stance. Jordan clutched his knife tightly, and checked how far he was from the main door.

"I didn't give you permission to speak, DeGrange," said Viktor.

"I don't need your permission," said DeGrange. "I don't take orders from anyone, anymore. Those days are over."

"Be silent, Brion!" said Roderik quickly. "The geas binds you to my will, and I order you to be silent!"

DeGrange stepped forward and slapped Roderik contemptuously across the face. The harsh sound was very loud in the quiet. Roderik stepped back a pace, a thin trickle of blood seeping from his nose. DeGrange smiled at him.

"Shut up, Roderik."

He sauntered over to the main door and pulled it open. Ten men in assorted guards' livery spilled into the room, swords in hand. There was blood on their swords, and no sign of Roderik's personal guards.

"You should be proud of your guards, Roderik," said DeGrange easily. "They put up quite a good fight, while they lasted. But now there's no one left to stand between me and you. No one at all."

"You can't harm me," said Roderik. "The geas won't permit it."

"The geas no longer exists," said DeGrange. "Over the past few days, the Unreal has been growing steadily stronger throughout the castle. You people only ever notice the major outbreaks, but there's a continuing run of smaller changes going on in the background all the time. Things like milk going sour, calves born with two heads, illusions failing, and the occasional breaking of magical agreements and bindings. My geas disappeared seven hours ago. I've been very busy since then. I spent a lot of time in your service planning what I would do to you, Roderik, if I ever got the chance. You're going to pay for what you did to me—you and everyone else in this stinking castle. I've got my own army again: people like me who were held under a geas, or just servants with grudges. You'd be surprised how easy it was to build my army, Prince Viktor. You'd be surprised how many people hate your guts—you and all your damned family."

"I hear a lot about an army," said Viktor. "But all I see are ten men."

"There are others," said DeGrange. "And we're going to tear your castle apart, stone by stone."

"If you damage the castle, the Unreal will break free, without restraints," said Sir Gawaine. "Redhart would be devastated. There's no telling how many people would die."

DeGrange shrugged. "What did they ever do for me? Where were they when your king's magic turned me into something between a slave and a pet?" He turned to his men. "Kill them all."

The renegade guards moved forward, and for a moment the conspirators did nothing, still shaken by the sudden turn of events. And then Sir Gawaine drew his ax and swung it in a blindingly swift arc at the nearest guard. The heavy steel blade punched into the guard's ribs and out again, and he fell screaming to the floor in a welter of blood. Gawaine smiled coldly, and took up a stance between Prince Viktor and the rest of the guards. Roderik gestured sharply with his left hand, and a sudden wind roared through the suite, rocking everyone on their heels. Jordan palmed a smoke pellet from his sleeve and threw it into the midst of the guards. Choking black clouds enveloped them, and in a matter of moments the guards' confident advance had deteriorated into bewildered chaos. Robert Argent stepped forward and punched out the guard nearest him. The man's head snapped back, and the merchant snatched his victim's sword before the body hit the ground. He looked around for another opponent, his face as calm and unmoved as ever. Jordan drew his sword and cut down a guard still confused by the shifting wind and smoke. Gawaine killed one of the guards facing him, but another drove him back with a desperate display of expert swordsmanship. Another guard headed for Viktor, who was still struggling to get up out of his chair. Heather waited to the last moment, and then kicked the guard in the groin. He bent forward, groaning, and Viktor drew a knife from his sleeve and cut the guard's throat.

Jordan backed away as a guard came after him. He knew a few tricks with a sword, every actor did, but this man was a professional soldier, and Jordan knew his limitations. He glanced quickly about him for Gawaine, but the knight had problems of his own. Jordan reluctantly palmed one of his last few flare pellets and crushed it in his left hand. Flames roared up around his fist, and he thrust it in the guard's face. The guard automatically raised an arm to protect his face, and Jordan ran him through.

Roderik tried to raise his High Magic, but he'd been to the well too often in the past few days, and he just didn't have the strength. Even his air magic was beginning to fail.

Gawaine swung his ax double-handed, and beat his way past his opponent's defense by sheer strength. He buried his ax in the guard's thigh, and then pulled it free and looked impatiently around for another opponent.

DeGrange watched in shock as his men died, and then turned and ran for the door. Jordan went after him, his left hand still blazing hotly. DeGrange turned at bay in the corridor, his sword held out before him. Jordan skidded to a halt and realized too late he might have been just a bit foolish in going after DeGrange alone. DeGrange was by far the better swordsman, and both of them knew it. Jordan gestured mystically with his blazing hand, but the flames were already beginning to die down. DeGrange launched his first attack, and Jordan barely parried the blow in time. His sword arm jarred painfully at the impact. He backed away, and DeGrange came after him, intent on finishing him off before help arrived. Sweat ran down Jordan's face and blood pounded in his ears as he strove desperately to ward off DeGrange.

"Duck, Jordan!" roared a voice behind him.

Jordan threw himself to the ground without hesitating, and a gleaming blur shot through the air where Jordan had been standing and struck DeGrange squarely in the face. He staggered back a pace, still gripping his sword. Jordan looked up, and saw the haft of Gawaine's ax protruding from DeGrange's shattered face. The ex-outlaw slumped slowly to his knees, and then fell backward and lay still. Jordan lowered his face onto his arms, and tried to get his breathing back to normal. Gawaine walked past him. There was a pause, followed by an ugly sucking sound as the knight reclaimed his ax. Jordan started to get to his feet, and Gawaine was there to help him. Jordan looked shakily at Gawaine.

"You saved my life. Thanks."

"You saved all our lives when you destroyed the gateway, sire."

"I knew there had to be a good reason why I did that," said Jordan. He looked back at the suite's open door. "Everything all right in there?"

"DeGrange's men are dead, and none of us are badly wounded. A few scrapes and cuts, nothing more. Prince Viktor is safe."

"Good. Good." Jordan looked sharply at Sir Gawaine. "You know, we were lucky this time. We should have expected more treachery from within, and been better prepared to deal with it. The way things are at the moment, we can't afford to trust anyone."

"I take your point," said Gawaine. "But unfortunately, we don't have any choice. We all need each other to make this deception work. And anyway, by taking part in this conspiracy, we're all legally guilty of treason. If you're proved an impostor, we'll all hang beside you on the gallows."

Jordan shook his head slowly. "If I'd known things were going to get this complicated, I'd have asked for a raise."

"You did," said Gawaine.

"Let's get the blood sample from Viktor," said Jordan. "We've still got to get to Court yet."

The Great Hall was packed with nobles and courtiers, far more than would be expected to witness the Testing of one minor noble. He stood nervously before the throne, between the two seconds who would speak for him. He was unarmed, and naked to the waist, as tradition demanded. He was trembling slightly, possibly from the cold. There was a bitter chill to the air in the hall, despite all the several fireplaces could do. The hall was also decidedly gloomy. The overhead chandelier hadn't been replaced yet. Prince Lewis stood to one side, together with the Monk and Ironheart, surrounded by a good number of heavily armed guards. They stood grim, silent and aloof from the brightly chattering courtiers, and paid the young noble no attention at all. Count William and the Lady Gabrielle stood on either side of the empty throne. There was no sign of Prince Dominic anywhere.

"Just how badly did you burn him?" murmured Roderik to Jordan.

"Pretty badly," said Jordan quietly. "But with his High Magic he should have been able to heal himself."

"Magic is unreliable at the moment," said Sir Gawaine. "The Unreal is affecting everything. That's why so many of the people here are wearing swords. Swords always work."

The three of them stood closer together, inside a

defensive circle of their own armed guards. The assembled courtiers and nobles had muttered uneasily at the presence of so many armed men at Court, but nobody made any objection. They all understood the realities of the situation. Jordan looked sympathetically at the young noble waiting for his Testing. It must be bad enough having to prove your parentage and your social position in public, without having so many unpleasant undercurrents in the Court as well. His two seconds were trying to chat cheerfully with him, to ease the tension, but none of them were really in the mood. The young noble's mother and father stood by, prevented by law and custom from even approaching him. They both looked anxious, but composed.

A sudden stir ran through the Court as the hall's main doors flew open, and Prince Dominic made his entrance, surrounded by guards. Silence fell across the Great Hall. Dominic looked calmly about him, allowing the Court to study his ruined face, as though daring anyone to comment. When no one broke the silence, he moved unhurriedly forward to take up his usual position. He stopped as he drew level with Jordan, and the two men stared at each other past their guards. Half of Dominic's face had been burned away, leaving nubs of discolored bone showing through the dark, shriveled flesh. His right eye had been sealed shut, and his right ear was a shapeless lump of burned flesh. Flashes of teeth gleamed whitely through the torn cheek. The pain must have been appalling, but Dominic showed no sign of it. Jordan felt sickened at the sight of what he'd done. Guilt would have prompted him to speak, but the memory of what Dominic had done to his own wife kept Jordan silent. After a while Dominic walked on, and took up a position with his guards to the right of the throne's raised dais, opposite Lewis. The Regent stepped forward a pace, and everyone turned to look at him. His voice was calm and even.

"My lords and ladies, Your Majesties, we are gathered here in ancient tradition to witness a Testing, an oath of fealty to the Stone. Jonathon of Virbrook, son of Michael and Clarissa Trelawney of Virbrook, claims the power and prestige of Blood through his father's line. Let all here witness the truth or falsity of his claim."

The two seconds took it in turn to step forward and swear upon their Blood and upon their honor that the young noble was the man he claimed to be. There followed several more formal speeches and declarations, and Sir Gawaine took the opportunity to explain some of the background to Jordan.

"Like so many of the customs at Castle Midnight, the Testing came about as a result of the time of inbreeding. For a while, it became very important to establish true claims of parentage, so that the Bloodlines could be salvaged without further endangering them. Over the years, the power of the Stone has also helped to stabilize and magnify the various elemental magics. And, of course, the Test also serves to show up any Unreal impostor who might try to replace a Real noble. And finally, it's the main legal proof of parentage and inheritance."

He broke off as the speeches finally came to an end. The young noble stood alone before the throne, unaccompanied even by his seconds now. There was a tense, anticipatory silence in the Court. The Regent said something in a harsh guttural language that Jordan didn't recognize. There was a sudden grating sound, and the Stone slid jerkily out from under the throne. Jordan looked at it curiously. From where he was standing, it looked like just another piece of rough-hewn granite. Except granite doesn't come when you call it. Jordan tried to smile at his own joke, but couldn't. There was a definite feeling of age about the Stone, an ominous, disturbing sense of antiquity, of having watched impassively as time passed and history became legend.

What happens if he's wrong about his having Blood? The Stone will kill him.

Jordan looked away, and made himself think about something else. He pressed his arm lightly against his side, feeling the reassuring presence of the glass vial containing Viktor's blood. Getting it had proved just as difficult as he'd expected. After DeGrange's treachery, Viktor had become decidedly jumpy about letting sharp blades get anywhere near him. In the end, Heather had to hold his arm steady while Jordan made the necessary incision.

Lewis leaned close to the Monk's cowl, and spoke quietly to him while everyone's attention was fixed on the Stone. "Use your magic, Monk. If that's not really my brother over there, but only an actor, he must be under some kind of illusion spell. See if you can undo it."

The Monk's empty cowl turned briefly in Jordan's direction, and then back again. "There is no illusion spell there to undo, Your Highness."

Lewis glared at him, but still had enough sense to keep his voice low. "You swore to me that they were using a double in public!"

"They are."

"Then who the hell's that? If that's not an illusion, then he really does look like that . . ." Lewis's voice trailed away. "My God, could Dominic have been right after all? Could that be an Unreal double that's replaced Viktor?"

He fell silent as the Regent glared at him, and wrestled furiously with the possibilities. Count William gestured to the young noble, who knelt obediently before the Stone. The Court grew utterly silent to hear his words.

"I, Jonathon of Virbrook, son of Michael and Clarissa Trelawney, swear allegiance to the Stone of Redhart, and the king who rules by its grace."

One of his seconds handed him a slender knife. The young noble's hand shook slightly as he took it, and he stopped a moment to let his hand settle before continuing. He made a shallow cut on the inside of his left forearm, and blood ran down his arm and splashed onto the Stone. It looked very red and very bright against the cold gray Stone. The young noble swallowed once, and then placed his left palm firmly onto the bloodstained Stone. He made a soft, puzzled sound, and then the breath went out of him and he fell limply backward. His head made a flat, final sound as it hit the floor. His two seconds knelt beside him and searched for a pulse, but they already knew they wouldn't find one. The boy's mother fainted. His father let her lie where she fell, his face slack and gray with grief. The Regent gestured urgently to his guards, and two of them went to carry out the body, while others saw to the father and the mother. The Court buzzed with shocked whispers as soon as the great doors closed behind them.

"What happened?" said Jordan quietly.

"It seems the boy had no Blood after all," said Roderik. "Whoever his real father was, it wasn't Trelawney. His mother must have been . . . indiscreet."

Jordan said nothing. Without turning around, he could tell the Court was turning to look at him. Word of Lewis and Dominic's intentions had obviously got around. *Well,* thought Jordan, *when in doubt, grab the bull by the horns. And if that fails, try a swift kick at his nuts as he runs past.* He turned to face the Court, stepped forward a single pace to draw everyone's attention, and raised his trained actor's voice in a carrying declaration.

"My friends, it seems there are those among us who have become confused by the Real and the Unreal, and are no longer sure who is who and what is what. Some have even declared themselves uncertain as to who I am. I would have thought myself easy enough to recognize, even if I have been . . . away . . . for a while. But, to set the fainthearted at rest, I shall prove to you all here and now that I at least am who I say I am. With your permission, Regent?"

Count William bowed formally, and a path opened up in the courtiers as Jordan strode toward the throne. He held his head high and hoped he looked a damn sight more confident than he felt. Sir Gawaine moved quietly forward at his side, as they'd arranged; ostensibly as an honor guard, but actually to make sure no one got too close and saw something they shouldn't.

Jordan stopped before the bloodstained Stone, took a deep breath, and let it out slowly. *Just another show, Jordan. Say your lines, make your moves, and don't trip over the furniture.* He could sense Lewis and Dominic watching him closely, confused by the unexpected turn of events but not sure what to do about it. Knowing him to be an impostor, they'd been sure he'd try to bluff or bluster his way out of the Test. His volunteering had shaken them. What was supposed to be their finest moment looked like it was becoming Viktor's. Jordan smiled slightly and got down on one knee before the Stone. Better get on with it while everyone was still off balance. Give them time to think, and they might remember why candidates were supposed to be naked to the waist . . . He pulled back his left sleeve till it was rolled up just below the hidden glass vial, and then drew his knife from his boot. The Court stood still and silent.

"I, Prince Viktor of Redhart, swear allegiance to the Stone of Redhart."

Jordan mimed making a cut with his knife, and opened the hidden vial by pulling gently at the slender string tied to its stopper. Viktor's blood ran down his arm, and dripped steadily onto the Stone. Jordan licked his dry lips, and then placed his palm firmly on the Stone. Nothing happened. After a long moment, Jordan let out his breath in a quiet sigh, along with most of the Court. Jordan put away his knife and stood up, holding his left arm tightly as though to stop the bleeding. An old trick, simple but elegant. So simple it went right over their heads.

Lewis and Dominic were looking at him uncertainly. Jordan grinned at them both, and dropped them a wink. Lewis flushed angrily and started forward. His guards stirred around him, hands reaching for weapons. The courtiers between Lewis and Jordan backed hastily out of the way. Jordan glanced at his own guards, and saw they were a lot farther away than he'd thought. The Monk and Ironheart pressed in close beside Lewis, apparently arguing with him, but his face was mottled with rage and he wasn't listening.

Jordan wondered if the wink had perhaps been a mistake. Even though it had been good theater. Beside him, Sir Gawaine had drawn his ax. Jordan's guards finally arrived, and formed a defensive shield around him. He glanced quickly across at Dominic. It was hard to read expressions in the ruined face, but he seemed to be content just to watch, for the moment. Jordan let his right hand drop to his sword, and watched Lewis's approach with the best cold sneer he could manage. It would have to be the sword or a smoke pellet. He couldn't get to his flare pellets while his left sleeve was still rolled up.

"That's enough!" roared the Regent. "Stand where you are, or I'll have my men open fire!"

Everyone looked at the Regent, and then followed his pointing finger up to the spectators' gallery that overlooked the Court. The gallery was lined with dozens of archers, each with an arrow ready to fire. The Court grew very still.

"You wouldn't dare," said Lewis flatly. "Attacking a prince of the Blood is treason. The nobles would have your head."

"My position protects me from any such charge," said William evenly. "While I am Regent, my word is law. Believe me, Lewis, I'm quite ready to order one or all of you killed, if that's what it takes to prevent a civil war."

"I don't know about the rest of you," said Jordan, "but I believe him." He ostentatiously took his hand away from his sword, and gestured for his men to put away their weapons. After a pause they did so, Sir Gawaine last of all. Jordan bowed formally to the Regent. "My apologies for a creating a disturbance in this Court."

"You always were the gracious one, Viktor," said Count William, "Well, Lewis, Dominic?"

"It'll be a cold day in hell before I apologize to you," said Lewis. "I won't forget this, William." He turned and walked out of the Court. The Monk and Ironheart followed him, and his guards brought up the rear, still with their swords drawn. Jordan thought for

a moment that William would actually order his bow-
men to open fire, but he didn't. Instead he turned to
Dominic, who smiled with half his face and inclined
his head slightly to the Regent.

"Make the most of your position, William. While it
lasts."

He turned and left the Court, accompanied by his
guards. They didn't sheathe their swords either. Jordan noticed they were careful to leave in a different
direction from Lewis. Apparently Dominic didn't feel
ready for a direct conflict just yet. The Regent stood
by the empty throne, and for a moment looked very
tired and very old. Jordan sympathized with him.
Count William was in an impossible situation. No matter who finally claimed the throne, he wouldn't get
any thanks for his Regency. In fact, he'd be lucky to
come out of it alive. Apart from his own elemental
magic, his only power lay in the castle troops he commanded as Regent. He could of course protect himself
by making a deal with one of the princes, but William
wouldn't do that. He was, after all, an honest man.
That was why King Malcolm had made him Regent.

Count William raised his head, forcing the tiredness
out of his face and stance until he looked once again
at the calm, efficient Regent. It was a good performance, and Jordan appreciated it as such. The Lady
Gabrielle watched her husband silently, pride and support for him burning in her steady gaze. The Regent
formally dismissed the Court, his voice firm and
steady. The nobles and the courtiers began to drift
away in small clumps, quietly discussing the implica-
tions of what they'd witnessed. Jordan gathered his
people around him and made a grand exit, bowing
and smiling as he went. It was important to keep up
appearances, even if everything else was falling apart
around him.

Jordan hadn't said anything to anyone yet, but he
was beginning to feel somewhat depressed. For all his
time in the castle, he hadn't really accomplished anything. All right, he'd helped Geordie find his mother,
and he'd helped stop an outbreak of the Unreal, but

that wasn't what he was here for. He was supposed to be taking the pressure off Prince Viktor and his conspirators so that they could get on with searching for the missing crown and sword. Instead, all he'd done was attract unwelcome attention, while the crown and seal remained as elusive as ever. Jordan strode ahead of his people, his head bowed and his brow furrowed in thought. He was so distracted he didn't react at all when someone hailed him as Prince Viktor, and Sir Gawaine had to elbow him smartly in the ribs. Jordan jerked his head up, and smiled belatedly at Catriona Taggert, who stood before him waiting to be noticed.

"Sorry, Steward, I was miles away."

"I understand," said Taggert. "I'm sure you've got a lot on your mind at the moment. Look, I need to talk to you, Viktor. Right now, in private. It's very important, I promise you."

Jordan glanced at Sir Gawaine, who shrugged imperceptibly. Jordan knew what he meant. Of all the people he'd met at Castle Midnight, Taggert was the only one who'd struck him as being at all trustworthy, but he couldn't honestly say he knew her well enough to be sure of it. She could be bait for a trap set by Lewis or Dominic. They'd love to get him off on his own, away from his protectors. But after all the intrigues and mixed loyalties, Jordan felt an overwhelming need to trust someone, and it might as well be the steward.

"All right," he said crisply. "Where did you have in mind?"

Count Roderik coughed loudly, to get his attention. Jordan ignored him. Roderik coughed again, louder.

"Nasty cold you've got there, Roderik," said Jordan. "I'd take something for that, if I was you."

Gawaine stifled something that might have been a chuckle, and Taggert's mouth twitched.

"If I might remind Your Highness," said Roderik tightly, "there are urgent matters awaiting your attention. Whatever the steward has to say, I'm sure it can wait."

"No, it can't," said Taggert, her eyes locked on Jordan's. "There's a room just down the corridor where we can talk, Viktor."

"Very well," said Jordan. "Gawaine, you come with me. You can stand guard outside the door while the steward and I are talking. The rest of you stay here and block off both ends of this corridor. No one gets in or out until we're finished. Try and keep alert—Lewis or Dominic would quite happily kill all of you, just to get a chance at killing me."

The steward waited a moment to be sure he'd finished, and then set off briskly down the corridor. Jordan and Gawaine followed after her. Jordan could hear Roderik spluttering with what sounded like pure rage behind him, but he didn't dare look back to see. He didn't trust himself to keep a straight face if he did. Taggert led the way to an unobtrusive door tucked away in a shadowy corner. She opened the door with a heavy key on a chain, and gestured for Jordan to enter. He did so, and Taggert went in after him and shut the door behind her. Outside, Sir Gawaine drew his ax and took up his guard.

The room was small and bare, and the walls smelled strongly of fresh whitewash. The only light came from a single candlestub burning in a wall holder. Jordan let his hand drift casually closer to his sword. He trusted Taggart, but there was no point in being foolish. Taggert looked uncertainly at Jordan, as though wondering exactly where to start.

"Just say it right out," he said gently. "I don't think either of us have much patience with diplomatic language."

Taggert smiled suddenly. "You've changed a lot since you went into exile, Viktor. You weren't a bad sort before, for a prince, but after you met Elizabeth and she threw you over, you just fell apart at the seams. No offense." Jordan nodded to show he'd taken none, and she continued. "At the time, I thought you'd become as bad as your brothers. There's a well-established streak of instability in your family, you know. Comes from all that inbreeding for

Blood in the old days. King Malcolm used to think about that a lot. It worried him.

"We talked quite a bit, your father and me, after my father died. I suppose because my dad and I were the only people in the Court who didn't play politics. We never have. Our job is too important for that. Anyway, the point is your father trusted me. He told me where to look for his will if anything should . . . happen to him. So when he died, suddenly, I followed his directions: took the will, and kept it. I agreed with the Regent—you see, I thought neither you nor your brothers were fit to be king. And then I saw you, fighting beside me in the Court and again in the West Wing, and I knew I'd been wrong about you. I'm sorry, Viktor. Here's the will. It's yours."

She reached into her pocket and brought out a single polished ruby. It gleamed darkly on her palm like a single great drop of blood. Jordan looked at Taggert for a long moment, and then took the jewel from her. Their eyes met, and she shrugged and smiled, suddenly embarrassed.

"You stood up well in the West Wing, Viktor. Not everyone can cope with the Unreal—it takes more than ordinary courage. You were scared half out of your mind, but you didn't let it stop you. Watching you cut a path through the Unreal was like watching your father on a battlefield in his prime. Strong and brave and . . . royal. I was impressed. We all were. I've never listened to the will myself, but I suppose it contains instructions on where to find the crown and seal. If anyone's going to wear the crown, Viktor, I'd rather it was you. Now, if you'll excuse me . . ."

Jordan nodded dazedly, and she hurried out of the room. Sir Gawaine looked in, to make sure everything was all right with Jordan, and then went over to join him. Jordan speechlessly showed him the ruby, and Gawaine nodded slowly.

"Malcolm's will. You must have made quite an impression on the steward, Your Highness. I haven't known her to blush and go all tongue-tied since she was in pigtails. Now we'd better get back to the oth-

ers. I don't like us being off on our own, away from
the guards. And I think the sooner we've got that will
in a safe place, the better."

Jordan nodded, and slipped the ruby into one of
the hidden pockets in his sleeve. The jewel felt
strangely warm, its heat pulsing against his arm like a
living thing. He walked out into the corridor with Gawaine at his side, and only then realized he hadn't
even thanked the steward. He looked quickly up and
down the corridor, but Taggert was nowhere to be
seen. He shrugged unhappily and rejoined his party,
and Roderik cursed him in an icy monotone all the
way back to Jordan's suite. Not that Jordan listened
to any of it; he had too many other things on his
mind. The steward had placed a great deal of trust in
him by giving him the will, because she believed the
kingdom would be safe in his hands. But it wouldn't
be him on the throne—that fell to Viktor. And Prince
Viktor was rather different from the man who was
currently playing him. Admittedly, it was hard to tell
how different. The man had been deathly ill for some
time, and invalids were notorious for their bad temper. And yet . . .

There is a history of instability in your family.

Jordan began to wonder if he'd done the right thing
in letting Sir Gawaine know he had the will. Gawaine
was a good man, no doubt about that, but at bottom
the knight was still bound by his oath of loyalty to
Viktor. And Jordan was becoming increasingly unsure
as to whether Viktor was worthy of such loyalty.

Back in Jordan's suite, the conspirators watched in
silence as Jordan handed the ruby to Prince Viktor.
It glowed with a somber crimson light, until Viktor
closed his fist around it. He stood before the open
fireplace and grinned broadly about him. Heather
clung tightly to his arm, almost bursting with pride
and happiness. Roderik's mood had mellowed, and
Argent had actually been seen to smile briefly, once
or twice. Sir Gawaine stood guard by the door, and
though he watched the proceedings closely, his face

gave away nothing at all. He'd stopped off on the way back to check that his wife was safe, and Roderik hadn't wanted to spare the time. Gawaine had had to insist, and neither of them had been polite about it.

Viktor finally settled into his chair again, and Heather perched on the arm, as before. The others pulled up chairs around him, and Viktor spoke the Word of Power that would unlock the ruby's secrets.

The air before them shimmered and grew vague, and King Malcolm was suddenly standing in the room. Jordan studied the image closely. Unlike the others, this was his first look at King Malcolm of Redhart. The king was tall and muscular, and carried his regal robes well. His dark hair was shot with silver, but still thick and wavy. His eyes were a silvery gray, like Gabrielle, and he had the same harsh-boned face as Lewis and Dominic. His gaze was sharp and commanding, and his mouth was a firm, flat line. He looked like someone who expected others to listen when he spoke. His voice was calm and assured.

"If you're hearing this, then I am dead. I have no way of knowing how or when my death will occur, but I feel safe in assuming that the Court is currently in a state approaching panic. You will have discovered by now that my crown and seal are missing. I have ordered them hidden.

"I assume you are here, William, as Regent. I'm sorry for the trouble I've caused you, old friend, but I think you understand why it was necessary. According to custom, I should begin my will by declaring which of my sons is to inherit my position, my wealth, and my throne. I choose not to do so. It is my sad opinion that none of my sons are worthy to take my place as king of Redhart."

The dead king stood silently for a while, frowning unhappily. The conspirators looked at each other and at Viktor, but nobody said anything.

"Lewis has become degenerate. For a time I thought he might follow in my footsteps and continue the conquests I began, but more and more it seems to me that he considers nothing important save the satisfying of his various hungers. Dominic has always been unstable. I had hoped his marriage to the Lady Elizabeth might settle him, but if anything it seems her ambition has only fueled his madness. Of late, I fear Dominic has become dangerously insane. Were he not my youngest son, my last born, I would have had him killed years ago.

"After I lost faith in Lewis, I placed all my hopes in Viktor. He showed real promise—his only faults those of youth and inexperience. But unfortunately, he too encountered the Lady Elizabeth, and she taught him among other things the pleasures of ambition and intrigue. Perhaps his time in Kahalimar will calm his hot blood—but I doubt it. He has already tried to kill Dominic, and no man who would murder his own brother over a lover's quarrel can be trusted with the throne of Redhart.

"It is time for new Blood. I have therefore given instructions that in the event of my death, a trusted servant is to take my crown and seal and hide them where they will not easily be found. You, William, as Regent, will be forced to proclaim the Rite of Transference, and a new royal line will begin. This will inevitably mean a time of chaos, but that will pass, and Redhart will be the stronger for it. I have no regrets for what I have set in motion. More and more it seems to me that I have done more harm than good in the kingdom which was entrusted to my keeping. Weep no tears at my passing—I am old and tired. I have seen my wife die, and watched my sons grow to be monsters.

"I have no way of knowing who is listening to me now. It doesn't really matter. All I have left to say is that if you would find my crown and seal, you must look among those who have gone before. There. A final clue to help you on your way, whoever you are. Wear the crown proudly, use its power wisely, and beware of the Unreal. I am King Malcolm of Redhart. Hear my words."

The image of the king flickered and disappeared. For a long time nobody said anything. Viktor sat staring at the ruby in his hand. Finally Roderik stirred, and his chair creaked loudly as his weight shifted. Everyone turned to look at him.

"It's a good thing the steward did take the will and hide it. If this had been shown in open Court, civil war would have broken out on the spot."

"He called me a monster," said Viktor. "I came all the way back here to avenge his murder, and what do I find? He'd rather some stranger wore the crown than me. I fought in his wars, bled in his battles, even accepted internal exile rather than risk a civil war, and all for what?"

"Viktor . . ." said Heather.

"Monsters," said Viktor. He threw the ruby away from him. It hit the far wall, and fell back onto the carpet. It rolled a short distance, and everyone watched it till it lay still. No one made a move to pick it up.

"King Malcolm has at least given us a clue," said Roderik. "He said the crown and the seal lie among *those who have gone before*. Does that mean anything to you, Viktor?"

"I don't want to talk about that now," said Viktor.

"But darling," said Heather, "you must see that . . ."

"I said I don't want to talk about it!" Viktor's voice rose to a shout, and he glared about him. No one met his eyes. "Leave me, all of you. I don't want you around me for a while. No, wait, you can stay with me, actor. The rest of you, get out. I'll see you again in an hour."

Jordan looked at Gawaine for some clue as to what to do, but the knight just shook his head slightly. Heather made as though she wanted to say something to him, but a glance at Viktor's scowling face dissuaded her. One by one the conspirators left the suite, and Jordan was left alone with Prince Viktor.

Viktor sat in silence for some time, staring into the fire. Jordan waited for an invitation to sit down, and when it didn't come, he sat down hesitantly in the chair opposite Viktor. The quiet, crackling fire spread a pleasant warmth through the room, and despite everything, Jordan began to relax a little. What with one thing and another, this was pretty much the first chance he'd had to just sit down and take it easy since he entered Castle Midnight. Whatever else you could say about the place, it wasn't dull. Jordan stretched out his legs, and surreptitiously studied the prince sitting opposite him.

Viktor looked a little better than he had, but his face was still pale and gaunt. The strain of his long illness showed in his sunken eyes and the tired boneless slump of his body in his chair. Jordan sensed a basic confusion within the man, as though he was desperately searching for answers he wasn't sure were even there. Jordan tried to work out how he felt about Viktor, and wasn't surprised to discover he was feeling pretty confused himself. On the one hand, people seemed to agree that Viktor had been the most promising of the three brothers before he'd met Elizabeth, but given the competition that wasn't saying much. Sir Gawaine had stood by him through thick and thin, but how much of that was down to personal loyalty and how much to the oath he'd sworn to King Malcolm? The Lady Heather seemed genuinely fond of Viktor, but there was no doubting she was very ambitious. And ruthless . . . not unlike the Lady Elizabeth, in fact. Viktor didn't seem to be having much luck in his choice of women. He had tried to kill Dominic, which was a point in his favor, but in a stupid and amateurish way, which wasn't. Jordan sighed silently. He kept working around the main issue, reluctant to face it head on. Catriona Taggert had given him King Malcolm's will because she believed his version of Prince Viktor was worthy to be king. But was the real Viktor worthy? And if not, what was he going to do about it?

Victor looked up from the fire and looked soberly at Jordan. "It's strange to see another man with my face," he said slowly. "We have a legend, here in Redhart, of the doppelgänger—a supernatural double who appears to us only at the time of our imminent death. Are you a bad omen for me, actor?"

"I hope not, Your Highness," said Jordan carefully. "I'm here to help gain you the throne."

Viktor smiled slightly. "Yes. I will be king. I never really thought I would, when I was younger. Lewis was the eldest, after all, and Dad's favorite, so I always assumed he'd wear the crown. Not that he deserved it. He's been chasing everything that breathes since his voice dropped. And those he couldn't intimidate with his position, he took by force. You'd have thought he'd have more pride. I never liked Lewis. No one did really, but all the time I was here, Dad wouldn't hear a word said against him. Old fool. He didn't want to know about Dominic either, though we all told him often enough. Even Lewis couldn't stand Dominic. I think he was born crazy. One time, when we were all still kids, he took a puppy from the castle kennels and cut it open, to see how it worked. None of us were surprised when Dominic took up sorcery. I'm going to enjoy ordering his death."

Jordan looked at him, startled, and Viktor smiled.

"Oh yes, actor, Dominic is going to die. I should have taken my time and done the job properly when he first took my Elizabeth. That was when things started to go wrong . . ." His voice trailed away, and his eyes became distant, fixed on yesterday. "I loved her, actor. I loved her more than I ever loved anyone else . . . I used to walk around all day with a stupid grin on my face, just so happy that she loved me. I didn't believe it at first, when they told me about her and Dominic. I threatened one man with a duel, for spreading such vile rumors. I was so young . . . In the end, I had to believe it. I confronted Elizabeth with the truth, and she laughed at me. I should have taken more time, and done the job properly. I should have killed them both when I had the chance.

"I've learned patience since then, rotting in exile with only that stupid relic Gawaine for company. All he knows is duty and honor and taking orders. Those things are for the lesser people—not princes and kings. Kings don't answer to anyone but themselves. They don't have to. No, actor, I had a lot of time in exile to think of all the things I'd do if they were ever foolish enough to allow me back. On my first morning as king, I'll see Lewis and Dominic and Elizabeth die. Their heads shall sit on spikes outside my castle gates, and the ravens will eat their eyes."

Viktor heaved himself up out of his chair and stood with his back to the fire. His face was flushed, and his eyes were unnaturally bright. "Everyone who ever stood against me will die! All of them! Once I am king, the power of the Stone will be mine, and I will take vengeance for all those long years of insult and neglect. I will command the Unreal, and Redhart will become great again, through me."

Jordan looked uneasily at the prince, disturbed by the direction his thoughts were taking him. "From what I've seen of the Unreal, Your Highness, it's not something to trifle with. It's too dangerous . . ."

"Don't lecture me!" Viktor glared at Jordan. His voice was high and strained. "What do you know about the Unreal? I was born and raised in this castle, and I know more about the Unreal than you ever will. Now be quiet, actor. You're here to listen, not to talk. I'm sick of people advising me, telling me what to do. I don't have to put up with that anymore, and I'm not going to. There's a power in the Stone and in the Unreal, actor—a power beyond your comprehension. My father was afraid of it, but I'm not."

"Yes, Your Highness," said Jordan. "But what are you going to do with that power?"

"Whatever I choose," said Viktor, his eyes still far away.

"The harvests have been bad this year," said Jordan. "It's been a long hot summer, with little rain. I've traveled through your kingdom, town by town, seen the hardships and the suffering. Food's scarce, and market prices are high. Your people are hungry. By winter, many of them will be starving."

"Let them," said Viktor. "What did they ever do for me? Where were they when I was sent into exile? Damned peasants breed like rabbits anyway. As long as they pay their taxes on time, I'll leave them alone, and if they're sensible, they'll be thankful for that. They'll praise my name soon enough when I've made Redhart strong again. What do a few bad harvests matter? If we need food, we can always take it from Hillsdown, or the Forest Kingdom. After the battering they took in the Demon Wars, they're in no shape to stand against us."

"They're not that weak," said Jordan. "They'd fight back. There would be war."

"Does the word frighten you, actor?" said Viktor. "I thought you made your living from tales of the glory of war, of the heroes and their battles. Or perhaps the raw meat of war is too strong for your stomach? War is the true test of kings, where they can reveal their true strength and destiny. I've had a long time to think about all this, actor. All those years in exile, while another man had my woman as his wife. All those years in a backwater of boredom and idleness. But I didn't waste my time, actor. I made plans, forged partnerships, found willing allies for a man who would be king . . . I have many enemies, I know, but they won't stop me. They've stolen my woman, banished me from Court, left me to rot, tried to poison me . . . but I'm back now, and I'll make them pay. I'll make them all pay! No matter how many I have to kill, they'll pay for what they did to me!"

His voice had risen to a shout, but Jordan no longer listened to him. Viktor was as mad as his brothers: his years in exile had driven him over the edge. In his search for people to punish for his own pain, he would bathe the Castle corridors in blood and plunge his country into a war it couldn't win. Thousands of innocents would die. And he, the Great Jordan, would have made it all possible. Because of him, a madman would be king, and all the lands would be swept with blood and fire.

Jordan closed his eyes for a moment, and visions of death and destruction filled his sight. He couldn't allow that to happen. He rose slowly to his feet and stood behind Viktor. The prince didn't even know he was there. He never saw Jordan draw the knife from his boot and drive it into his back.

Prince Viktor died quickly, and Jordan knelt beside him as the breath and the life went out of him.

CHAPTER 7

Wolves
in the Fold

Jordan looked at the bloodstained knife in his hand, and automatically reached for a cloth to clean the blade. His senses suddenly cleared, and he scrambled to his feet. His fellow conspirators could be back at any minute, and if he was found standing over the dead prince with the bloody dagger still in his hand, the best he could hope for would be a quick death. Jordan swallowed hard and tried to think clearly. The first thing to do was hide the body. He slid the knife back into his boot and crouched down beside Viktor.

The prince's head lolled suddenly to one side as Jordan struggled to pick him up. The glazed eyes seemed to stare at him accusingly. Jordan gripped Viktor by the arms and got him half off the floor, but had to drop him again almost immediately. The deadweight was too heavy and too awkward to lift. Jordan stooped down, swearing under his breath at the time this was taking, and grabbed Viktor under the arms. He took a firm hold and then dragged the body over to the bedroom. He kicked the door open and hauled Viktor in. He got him as far as the wardrobe, and then let him drop.

Jordan sat down on the edge of the bed to get his breath back. He felt a little easier now that the body was no longer in open view. His gaze fell upon the wardrobe before him, tall, wide, and conveniently bulky. Jordan got to his feet and opened the wardrobe door. It was packed with clothes, but there was still a lot of spare room . . . Clothes. A thought struck Jordan, and he looked quickly down at his shirt front. Incriminating crimson blotches stared back at him. He must have got them while dragging Viktor's body. Jordan took off his cloak and vest, and pulled off the offending shirt. He couldn't stand the thought of being touched by Viktor's blood. The empty glass vial fell out of his sleeve, and Jordan froze as he saw the dried Blood that still marked his arm from the Testing. He screwed his shirt into a ball, and used it to scrub at his arm. It didn't help much. He threw the shirt onto the bed and turned his back on it. He grabbed a shirt at random from the wardrobe and pulled it on, his fingers fumbling clumsily over the buttons.

Easy, Jordan, easy. Take your time and get it right. You can't afford to look flustered.

He pulled on his vest and cloak, looked at himself in the full-length mirror, and decided unhappily that it would have to do. In his own eyes he looked guilty as hell, but at least now the evidence wasn't so clear cut. He threw the bloodstained shirt into the back of the wardrobe, and then bent down and manhandled Viktor's body in after it. He knew he should have hidden the body first and then got changed, but he wasn't thinking too clearly at the moment. He straightened up, and began to breath a little more easily. It was only then that he noticed Viktor's eyes were still open. They seemed to Jordan to be following him. He wanted to reach down and close them, but some last-minute squeamishness made him reluctant to touch the body any more than he absolutely had to. He stepped back and slammed the wardrobe door shut on Viktor's staring eyes.

He stood still and rubbed at his aching temples as a sudden wave of dizzyness passed over him. Strain, that was all it was—just strain and tension. Everything had happened so quickly . . . He'd never planned on killing Viktor. The thought had never even crossed his mind. But sitting there, listening to Viktor rant and rave, Jordan had slowly discovered that he couldn't bear to think of all the good people he'd met dying bloody deaths at this madman's whim. Those people had trusted him as Viktor, and he couldn't see them betrayed in that trust.

There were twenty-seven kitchen staff. Ten were women, and seven were child apprentices.

I had them all hanged, of course.

All right, Viktor was dead. What was he going to do now? Run for it? He wouldn't even get out of the castle. Jordan frowned. There was only one thing he could do: take Viktor's place for real. Be Prince Viktor. Give Castle Midnight the kind of prince and ruler it deserved. He'd always wanted to play the part as it should be played, and this was his chance. Of course, if his fellow conspirators ever found out what had happened . . . He decided he wasn't going to think about that. He'd just have to do such a good job that the others would never have cause to doubt that he was who he claimed to be. And he'd better come up with a damned good cover story to explain his, the actor's, sudden disappearance. They might believe he'd got scared and run off, but not that he'd leave without trying to collect his money first. They knew him too well for that. Jordan sighed. Right now, he wanted more than anything to just sit there and feel sorry for himself, but he couldn't spare the time. There was too much to be done. Somebody knocked at the main door, and Jordan's heart jumped madly. There wasn't time to come up with a cover story, or even to practice his new double role. The conspirators were back, and he was on.

He hurried out of the bedroom and back into the main room. He spotted the ruby will lying on the floor, and pocketed it quickly. If things went wrong, and he had to leave in a hurry, at least he'd have something to show for his trouble. A quick look around, to check that everything was as it should be, and then he took up a commanding posture by the fireplace, and called for whoever it was to enter. The door swung open, and Count Roderik and Robert Argent came in, followed by Sir Gawaine and the Lady Heather. Jordan nodded brusquely to them. Gawaine closed the door and stood guard beside it, one hand resting comfortably on the head of his ax. Heather started to smile at Jordan, and then stopped, suddenly unsure as to exactly who she was smiling at. The others glanced around the empty room, and stirred uneasily as they realized Jordan was on his own. He smiled coldly.

"If you're looking for the actor, he's in the jakes. No doubt he'll be back in a minute."

Roderik bowed formally. "Forgive me, sire. Now that you're recovering from your illness, you're looking so much better, it's hard to tell the two of you apart."

Jordan snorted. "I wasn't ill, I was being poisoned. And the day you can't tell the difference between a prince of the Blood and a strolling player will be the day I find myself some new advisers. I never thought he sounded much like me anyway."

"Now, darling," said Heather soothingly, "don't be so touchy. Come and sit down here, with me."

Jordan nodded grudgingly, and allowed Heather to sit him down in the most comfortable chair and fuss over him. As before, she ended up sitting on the arm of his chair, and Jordan slipped his arm around her waist, as he'd seen Viktor do. "Well then," he said finally, "let us discuss Dad's will. Oh do sit down, all of you. You make the place look untidy, standing around like that. If I'd wanted statues in my room, I'd have bought some."

Roderik, Argent, and Gawaine pulled up chairs facing him, and sat down. Jordan noted approvingly that Gawaine was the only one who'd placed his chair so that he wasn't sitting with his back to the door. Roderik frowned unhappily, and leaned forward.

"There isn't really much in your father's will that can be called favorable," he said slowly. "Favorable to us, that is. Malcolm mentioned his fear of a *sudden* death, which suggests he believed someone might be planning to murder him, but there's nothing in the will to suggest he knew who the murderer would be. Assuming, of course, that Malcolm was murdered. We have no direct evidence."

"It was murder," said Jordan. "Dad's death was too sudden and too convenient to be anything else."

"As you say, sire." Roderik bowed slightly, before continuing. "The only clue as to the whereabouts of the crown and seal lies in the single phrase *with those who have gone before*. It seems likely he was referring to the previous kings of Redhart—those who preceded him on the throne."

Jordan chewed on the inside of his cheek as Viktor's background knowledge bubbled eerily at the back of his mind. He looked sharply at Roderik.

"Dad hasn't been buried yet, has he?"

"No, Your Highness," said Roderik. "He's still lying in state in the family crypt, according to law and custom."

"So right now he's lying among his ancestors—those who have gone before. That's what the clue means. The crown and seal are hidden somewhere in the family crypt!"

Sir Gawaine coughed apologetically. "Our people have already searched there, sire. They found nothing. And it's a safe bet your brothers would also have had the place searched. If the crown and seal were there, someone would have found them by now."

"Not necessarily," said Jordan. "Dad said they wouldn't be easily found." He rose abruptly to his feet, almost bowling over Heather. "Let's go. I want to take a look at the crypt myself."

"Very well, sire," said Roderik, getting to his feet more slowly. "I'll summon a company of guards to escort us."

"No," said Jordan. "I think the less who know about this, the better. I don't know about the rest of you, but it's looking more and more obvious to me that we have a traitor somewhere among our people. Think about it. You were attacked twice when bringing the actor back to the castle. Outside of us, who knew the exact route you'd be taking? Then again, somebody told my dear brothers that we were using the actor as a double in public. That's why you were pressured into attending the Testing. And finally, somebody has been feeding me poison for some time. That had to be the work of somebody close to us— someone we trust. I'm not ready to point any fingers yet, but I don't feel inclined to take any chances I don't have to. We go alone down into the crypt—just the five of us."

"Six, including the actor," said Sir Gawaine.

"I'm not waiting for him and his damned weak bladder," snapped Jordan. "We'll leave word with the guards at the door, and he can wait here till we return. We don't need him. Now let's go. I've spent far too much time sitting around of late."

He strode over to the main door, and was somewhat gratified to hear the others scrambling to catch up with him. He'd started to wonder if he was overdoing the arrogance, but from the sound of their haste, he'd got it just about right.

The royal family crypt turned out to be a huge stone chamber on the lowest floor of the castle. They had to go through two basements to get to it. The crypt was also a sanctuary: one of the oldest stable places in the castle. No magic would work there, for good or ill, and the dead slept undisturbed. King Malcolm's family had lain in the crypt for generations, and their resting places were decorated with life-size bas-relief carvings, in varying shades of marble. Some looked unsettlingly lifelike in the dancing torchlight, as though the pale motionless figures were only sleeping and might awaken at a sudden noise.

King Malcolm lay in state upon the tomb that was to be his. His body had already undergone the undertaker's arts to ensure preservation, but he wouldn't be finally interred until the last protective spells had been woven around him. There were too many unpleasant things that could happen to a dead body in Castle Midnight. Jordan moved slowly forward to stand beside the king. The morticians had done their job well. Malcolm's face still held a normal color, and he looked so peaceful he might almost have been sleeping.

Almost.

The others held back as Jordan studied the dead king. Up close, the illusion of peace wasn't nearly as convincing. The makeup that gave the face a seeming of life was glaringly obvious to Jordan's experienced eyes, and when he looked closely he could see the tiny black stitches that held the mouth and eyes closed. There was no odor of decay: just a faint whiff of formaldehyde. Jordan tried to read a character in the king's still features, but death and the mortician's skills had wiped all personality from the face. It might as well have been a garishly painted doll. Jordan closed his eyes and let his mind drift, hoping some of Viktor's memories might hold a clue as to where to look for the hidden crown and seal. Nothing came to him but the beginnings of another headache. Jordan opened his eyes again, and thought hard. The answer had to be here somewhere. And he didn't have long to find it. Argent was keeping watch outside the crypt, but they could be interrupted anytime.

Jordan looked around him, taking in the eerie carved figures that surrounded him. They'd all been sculpted with the usual enigmatic smiles, but to Jordan they all looked unbearably smug, as though they knew the answer but weren't going to tell him, because he was an outsider and an interloper. He frowned suddenly. Different as the many faces were, they all had certain things in common. They were portrayed in their best and finest robes, each fold of marble lovingly detailed, and the sculptors had even added stone crowns and rings. Jordan smiled slowly as an inspiration blossomed within him. If you want to hide a crown and a seal, where better than among a great many other crowns and seals? Jordan glanced quickly around him. If they were here, they couldn't be under an illusion spell; the sanctuary would cancel that out. But since he couldn't see them, they must be physically disguised. He ran from tomb to tomb, checking each carved figure. The others watched uncomprehendingly. And then Jordan's fingers stumbled over one of the stone crowns as it moved under his touch. He pulled it free and tapped it gently against the side

of the bier. Brittle flakes of plaster fell away, revealing
a bright golden gleam.

The others crowded in around Jordan as he carefully stripped away the plaster to reveal the true crown
of Redhart. It was heavier than he expected: a simple
unadorned circlet of solid gold. *It is not the crown,
but he who wears it. That is where true greatness lies.*
Lines from an old play echoed through Jordan's mind.
It seemed a long time now since he'd last stood on a
stage, playing a simple straightforward role before an
undemanding audience. He pushed the thought away,
and pulled at the rings on the stone fingers until one
of them came loose. Under the thin covering of plaster
lay a heavy gold ring bearing the royal seal of Redhart. Jordan held the crown and seal in his hands, and
then closed his eyes briefly as his tiredness caught up
with him. The Lady Heather moved in beside him.

"Are you all right, Viktor? You mustn't overtire
yourself. You've been ill, remember?"

Jordan opened his eyes quickly and smiled at her.
"I'll be fine, Heather. The worst of it's over now. The
crown and seal are mine at last."

"Until I take them away from you," said Dominic.

The conspirators spun around, reaching for their
weapons, only to stop and stand very still as Dominic's
guards spilled into the crypt. Jordan counted seventeen, and he could hear others moving outside. Even
with Gawaine's ax, the odds stank. He ostentatiously
took his hand away from his sword, and smiled win-
ningly at Dominic . The prince smiled at Jordan with
half his mouth, but the single eye in the ruined face
was cold and unamused.

"You always were the brightest of us, Viktor. I
knew you'd work it out first, if any of us did. All I
had to do was keep a close watch on you, and sooner
or later you'd lead me right to the crown and seal.
Not that it matters, but how did you know where to
look?"

"Dad made a will," said Jordan, carefully putting
the crown and seal down on Malcolm's bier. "He
thought none of us were worthy to be king, but he

did leave us a clue. It brought me here—the rest was just common sense."

"So, you followed the clue and I followed you," said Dominic. "Just as I've followed you all along. No matter where you went or what you did, I was right there with you. You know, you've done very well, Viktor. I had you fed enough poison to kill a normal man twice over, but still you clung stubbornly to life. What a strong constitution you do have."

"Then it was poison!" said Heather. "But how? I checked the food every way I could, and Argent tasted the food himself . . ."

She stopped, and looked past Dominic. The others did the same. Standing just outside the crypt doorway stood Robert Argent. He stared calmly back at them.

"My own dear traitor," said Dominic. "My very own personal spy in your ranks. He kept me informed of your every move, and poisoned your food. Rather a nice touch, that, I thought. Who would ever suspect the food taster of being the poisoner?"

"I don't believe you," said Heather stubbornly. "I watched him eat the food and swallow it. He couldn't have faked it!"

"He didn't," said Dominic. "Why should he? What harm can poison do to a dead man?"

He gestured languidly with his left hand, and a great bloody wound appeared on Argent's chest. The sides of the wound were raw and livid, but no blood ran. Argent's face never changed. He looked as he always did: calm, resigned, and very tired. Jordan looked at Argent, and his mouth went dry. There was no way Argent could have survived a wound like that. He was a lich, a walking dead man. All this time he'd been working with a dead man. Somewhere in the back of Jordan's mind, a crazy little voice wanted to scream and jabber, but he fought it down. He'd already faced ghosts and monsters and reality gone wild. He could cope with a lich. He had to. Even if it was a man he'd fought beside, and trusted.

Roderik looked at Argent, his face twisted with grief. "Robert . . . why didn't you tell me? I would

have helped you. I would have found . . . some way
to help you."

Argent said nothing. Dominic smiled. "I killed him
several months ago. It was quite easy, really. He
didn't suspect a thing until it was too late. My sorcery
holds him at the very point of death. As long as I
keep on renewing the spell, he'll stay alive. Of course,
if I should happen to forget . . . It's the perfect form
of blackmail, really. I have complete control over him.
It's a pity I can't use the technique more often, but
the sorcery involved is very draining."

"You miserable bastard," said Jordan.

Dominic raised a mocking eyebrow. "You're a fine
one to talk, Viktor. Before we came down here, I had
my people search your quarters thoroughly. Just on
the off chance we might turn up something interesting.
And just guess what we found in your wardrobe."

"What's he talking about, Viktor?" said Roderik.
Jordan said nothing.

"Oh go on," said Dominic. "Do tell us why you
decided to kill your actor double."

Gawaine looked at Jordan in horror. "What have
you done, Viktor? Damn you, what have you done?"

Jordan's heart warmed a little at the shock and
anger in Sir Gawaine's voice, but he didn't dare let
the knight see anything in his face. He shrugged
coldly. "He was plotting to take my place for real, so
I killed him. We didn't need him anymore, anyway."
He turned back to glare at Dominic. "Dad never
meant for you to be king. He knew you were crazy.
There's bad blood in all our family, but you're the
worst, and always have been. You're not fit to be
king."

"You're in no position to stop me," said Dominic.
"I, on the other hand, hold all your fates in my keeping. You live or die according to what I decide, here
and now. And isn't that, in essence, what a king's
power is?" He laughed suddenly. It was a flat, ugly
sound. "Except, of course, I could always have you
killed, and then bring you back again. If I really
wanted to. Perhaps you'd like to beg me to save you.

I'm quite prepared to listen. I'm a reasonable man. I can always use another slave."

Jordan's hands flexed impotently at his sides. Dominic was out of reach of his sword, and his few remaining flare pellets were in the sleeve of the shirt he'd left in Viktor's bedroom. His mind worked desperately, and he let his eyes wander around the crypt. A flaring torch crackled quietly on the wall to his left. Jordan's gaze fell on Dominic's ruined face, and an idea came to him. Without hesitating, he grabbed the torch and thrust it at Dominic's face. The prince screamed and fell back a step, and Jordan threw the torch at him. It hit his chest and fell away, but Dominic's robe had already caught fire. He screamed again, and beat at the flames with his bare hands. He fell back to the crypt's doorway, and his guards formed a protective wall between him and the conspirators.

"Kill them!" screamed Dominic shrilly. "Kill them all!"

The conspirators drew their weapons, and the guards started forward. Argent drew his sword and blocked the doorway. His face was utterly blank. Jordan moved to stand shoulder to shoulder with Sir Gawaine, who seemed to hesitate a moment before accepting his presence. Jordan looked at the advancing guards and knew his luck had just run out. He wasn't going to win, he wasn't going to be a prince, and he wasn't even going to get his money. All he could do now was take as many guards with him as he could. He just hoped he'd stay dead. It was a pity he hadn't had a little more time. He was just beginning to get a feel for the part . . . And then the air echoed to a roaring challenge as Damon Cord burst through the door, throwing aside Argent and plunging into the guards. His mace gleamed dully in the torchlight as it swept viciously through the air. A troop of guards followed him in, wearing the Regent's colors. And behind them came the steward, her balefire sword crackling and spitting in her hand.

"Lucky I set some of my people to watching you,

Viktor," she called cheerfully. "Damn traitors are coming out of the woodwork these days."

Jordan grinned back at her, and then the two of them had to turn their attention to the matter at hand as Dominic's guards fought back. The two sides were evenly matched, and the fight raged back and forth across the great stone chamber. The clash of steel on steel and the stamp of boots on stone echoed dully back from the low ceiling, and the cold faces of King Malcolm's ancestors watched indifferently from their biers. Jordan and Sir Gawaine fought back-to-back, and dead and dying guards lay piled about their feet. Jordan swung his sword with cold desperation, and none of the guards were good enough to get close to him. At his back, Gawaine's glowing ax spattered blood and brains on floor and ceiling alike. Jordan snatched a brief glance at Dominic, and was relieved to see that he was leaning weakly against the wall, too shocked by his fresh burns to think about getting involved.

Slow tides moved through the battle, carrying the combatants in sudden, unexpected directions. Roderik found himself in the crypt doorway, face-to-face with Argent, and his sword faltered. Argent's blade flashed forward, and Roderik gasped as a thin red line of blood appeared on his cheek. If he hadn't flinched back, the point would have taken out his eye.

Roderik's sword moved automatically through a defensive pattern, but he made no move to attack Argent. He wasn't sure he could. Whatever had happened to Argent, whatever he had said or done, Argent was still his lifelong friend. He couldn't raise his sword against him. They'd been through too much together. It would have been like killing himself. But Argent pressed his attack more and more fiercely, and Roderik was hard-pressed to keep him at arm's length. It slowly occurred to Roderik that he was getting tired, while Argent was as fresh and determined as when they'd started. Dead men don't get tired. Angry tears burned in Roderik's eyes as for the first time he began to press the attack. If he had to kill his friend, he swore to himself that come what may, he'd send Dominic down into the dark after him.

Heather crouched down behind a stone bier, and tried to make herself as inconspicuous as possible. Just in case that didn't work, she kept a dagger concealed in her hand. The battle raged back and forth before her, and she couldn't tell who, if anyone, was winning. She could see Viktor right there in the thick of things, and her heart went out to him. She knew how weak he still was, despite his marvelous recovery, but he was swinging his sword with a verve that brought an appreciative smile to her lips. Viktor would defeat Dominic. It was inevitable. Dominic wasn't fit to be king. It was a pity Viktor had killed the actor, but it wasn't important. Jordan was just a jumped-up little nobody who wouldn't be missed. There was no reason why anyone else should ever have to know about his death.

Damon Cord led the Regent's troops in a charge through Dominic's men, but he couldn't keep the impetus going long enough to reach the prince himself. The fighting became slow and fragmentary, and the battle swiftly degenerated into a confused melee. Cord swung his mace in great vicious arcs, trying to clear some space around him, but the press of bodies was too great, and he had to stop for fear of striking down his own men. Instead, he concentrated on working his way through the crush toward Dominic. The prince had opened the gateway in the West Wing. Hundreds had died, very nearly including his own Catriona Taggert. One way or another, he was going to have Dominic's head for that. He met Dominic's gaze for a moment, over the crush of bodies, and Cord grinned savagely as the prince had to look away. He struck out at the guard before him, and the man fell screaming to the floor with his face torn away by the mace's spikes.

The fight went this way and that as the two forces jostled for position. Blood soaked the ancient stone floor, and the living stumbled constantly over the broken bodies of the dead and the dying. Jordan wiped the sweat from his brow with a hurried sweep of the back of his hand, and glared about him for Dominic. His heart missed a beat when he couldn't find him, and then he spotted the Prince inching his way along the wall toward the door. Time seemed to slow and stop for Jordan. There was no way he could reach Dominic in time: there were too many people in the way. Nobody else could get there either. Dominic was going to get away. Jordan howled with rage, lifted his sword, and threw it at Dominic. The whole battle seemed to hesitate as the sword went tumbling gracefully end over end through the air. Dominic caught a glimpse of something coming toward him out of the corner of his eye, and started to turn. The sword slammed into his chest, just below the left shoulder, and pinned him to the wall. He screamed once—the horrified, agonized sound rising clearly over the sound of battle.

The fighting slowly stopped as everyone became aware of what had happened. Dominic looked disbelievingly at the blood spilling down his chest. He shook his head dazedly and tried to pull out the sword blade with his bare hands. Blood dripped from his lacerated fingers. For a moment it looked as though he might actually pull himself free from the wall, and then Cord stepped forward and crushed Dominic's skull with his mace.

For a while there was only silence, and then one by one Dominic's men dropped their weapons and raised their hands in surrender. The fight was over. Robert Argent gave a low moan, and fell to his knees. Blood spilled between his slack lips as he clutched at the horrid wound in his chest. He began to crawl toward Dominic's limp figure, and all around him the guards fell back, horrified by the aura of death that hung around him like a palpable presence. Even Roderik could hardly bear to watch him. He finally reached Dominic, still hanging limply from the sword that pinned him to the wall. Argent raised his head painfully and pulled at Dominic's leg.

"Do something, Dominic. I'm dying! I'm *dying*!"

The blood at his mouth suddenly stopped bubbling.

A faint look of surprise crossed Argent's face, and then he fell forward and lay still as his death finally caught up with him. Roderik looked away. The steward sighed quietly.

"What a mess. All right, some of you men, get Dominic's troops out of here. Escort those who can walk to the nearest cells, and drag the rest out and stack them somewhere. We'll worry about identifying the bodies later, when we've got time. Now move it!"

She made her way through the crowd toward Jordan. He was leaning on his sword and breathing hard, but he still managed a small smile for her.

"Can't seem to keep out of trouble, can you?" he said finally. "I'd have thought you had enough problems of your own, without getting involved with mine."

"Can I help it if I feel responsible for your being here?" said Taggert, smiling. "After all, I gave you the will. And besides, I'd been itching for an excuse to go after that bastard Dominic. Now if you could just find an excuse for me to go after Lewis as well, you'll have made a friend for life."

"Funny you should say that," said Jordan. He reached over to King Malcolm's bier and picked up the crown and seal. He slipped the ring on his finger, and lowered the gold circlet carefully onto his head. The room went suddenly still and quiet. Jordan looked around him, as one by one the guards got down on one knee and bowed their heads to him. Taggert and Cord knelt and bowed, and then Sir Gawaine, and finally Count Roderik.

"We have a King again," said Gawaine. "Redhart has a King! Long live the King!"

"Long live the King!" roared the guards, and there was a clash of steel as they drew their swords and raised them to him in the warrior's salute. "The King! The King!"

They cheered him again and again, until the crypt was full of echoes. Jordan looked at Sir Gawaine. The knight nodded simply, and bowed again. Jordan looked at Taggert, kneeling grinning before him, and made a sudden decision.

"All right," he said crisply. "Let's strike while the iron is still hot. I may have the crown and the seal, but I'm not King until I've made my oath to the Stone. Gawaine, take charge of these guards, and clear a path between here and the Great Hall. Offer pardons to any man who'll support me. Cord, you stick with the steward and me. No one is to get close to us unless you know and trust them personally. Roderik, you stay close as well, in case I need any political advice. Well, don't just stand there, people, get moving! We've a throne to win!"

The guards looked expectantly to Sir Gawaine for his orders. He sighed very quietly, and bowed to Jordan. In a matter of moments he'd taken charge of the guards quickly and efficiently, left one company as bodyguards, and led the rest out of the crypt. Cord and Taggert fell in on either side of Jordan, weapons drawn and at the ready. Roderik gave him a hard, measuring look.

"You've got your confidence back in a hurry, Your Highness, but the fact remains that without me you haven't a chance of holding onto the throne. You're out of touch after your years in exile. There's more to being king than wearing a crown and sitting over the Stone. You need to know who can trust and who you can't: who'll take a bribe and who'll stay bought. I know these things. You need me, Viktor."

"Never said I didn't," said Jordan. "As long as you remember which of us gives the orders, I see no reason why we shouldn't enjoy a long and profitable relationship. Right?"

Roderik thought about it for a moment, and then bowed reluctantly. "Yes, Your Highness."

"Then let's get the hell out of here," said Jordan. "Dominic might be out of the running at last, but there's still Lewis to worry about."

"Just a minute, Viktor," said a cold voice behind him. "What about me?"

Jordan looked around and found himself facing the

Lady Heather. Her gown was spattered with somebody else's blood, and gore dripped from the knife in her hand, but she was apparently unhurt herself. She glared fiercely at Jordan, then looked at Taggert and if anything glared even harder.

"I never knew you and the steward were such good friends, darling. So close, in fact, that you forget all about me the moment she turns up! Do tell me all about her, Viktor. Leave nothing out. I never realized you had a taste for slumming."

I don't need this, thought Jordan tiredly. *I really don't need this right now.*

"We'll talk about it later, Heather," he said finally.

"We'll talk about it right now! Send this overmuscled cow about her business—I want to talk to you, Viktor. It seems to me you've had your first taste of power, and it's gone straight to your head. You've forgotten who your real friends are!"

"Overmuscled cow?" said Taggert.

Uh oh, thought Jordan. He looked around him for some support, but everyone was ostentatiously studying the scenery. This was his problem, and no one else had any intention of getting caught in the firing line.

"Overmuscled cow?" said Taggert again.

"Heather," said Jordan, very calmly, "I don't have the time or the inclination to put up with this nonsense. Go back to your quarters and stay there. You'll be safe there. I'll come and see you as soon as I can, but right now I'm rather busy." *Besides which, I have a strong suspicion that if I don't get you out of here right now, the steward is quite probably going to carve you up into handy bite-size chunks.* "I can't stay any longer. People's lives are at stake, and I have to think of them first."

"Cut the nobility crap, Viktor. It doesn't suit you." Heather's sneer made her look suddenly ugly. "I know you, Viktor. You can't fool me."

"No," said Jordan, "You don't know me at all, Heather." He nodded to two nearby guards, and they snapped to attention. "See that the Lady Heather gets safely back to her quarters, and then stand guard at the door until I send someone to relieve you.''

The guards saluted crisply, and stepped forward to stand on either side of Heather. She looked at Jordan for a long moment, speechless with rage, and then turned and stamped away. The guards hurried after her. Jordan sighed silently. She didn't really deserve treatment like that, but he had to do it. She was quite right: she did know Viktor well. Too well. It wouldn't have taken her long to work out who he really was. He'd have had to break off with her anyway, and her making a scene had solved the problem nicely. He wouldn't have felt half as guilty if he hadn't enjoyed it so much . . .

"I'm sorry that happened," said Taggert, tentatively.

"I'm not," said Jordan. "We were never really suited. It was bound to happen, sooner or later. Now let's make a start for the hall, before something else happens to delay us."

Jordan hurried down the castle corridors with Cord and Taggert at his side. His company of guards moved before and behind him, making sure that everyone kept a respectful distance. Gawaine and his guards had done their best to open up a route for him, but there was chaos everywhere. Rumors were spreading like wildfire, half of them contradictory, and no one knew where they stood anymore. No one wanted to commit themselves to anything until they were sure which faction was going to come out on top, and, of course, there were always those ready to take advantage of the chaos for their own reasons. A good many people wanted to swear allegiance to Jordan when they saw the crown on his head, but he didn't have time to stop. He just smiled, waved, and kept on running. A growing crowd followed on behind his guards. Jordan tried to step up the pace, and found he couldn't. Air was burning in his lungs, and his breath rattled in his throat. A stitch ached in his side, but he didn't dare stop for a breather. He didn't think he'd be able to get started again if he did. And besides, Lewis could still get to the hall before he did . . .

For a long time, he was so preoccupied with his own thoughts that he didn't notice what was happening to the corridor around him. In the end, Taggert hit him fairly hard on the arm to get his attention. He looked at her in surprise, and she jerked her head at the corridor walls. Jordan looked closely, and his skin began to crawl. The wooden wall panels were slowly writhing and twisting, as though they were alive. As Jordan watched, part of the wall split open like a rotten fruit, and something dark and spindly with too many legs darted out into the corridor. The steward's balefire sword appeared in her hand, but Cord got there first. He bludgeoned the creature repeatedly with his mace, and it struggled fiercely as it died. Its saliva spilled onto the floor, and steamed like acid. Cord glared into the opening in the wall, but Jordan just kept on going, and after a moment Cord hurried after him.

"Someone else must have opened a gateway," panted Taggert. "The Unreal's broken through again."

"Great," said Jordan breathlessly. "That's all we need. Who's behind it this time? It can't be Dominic."

"I don't know. This new one can't have been open long, but each time a gateway is opened, it gets that much harder to close. Our best bet is to get you to the throne, so you can use the Stone to control the Unreal."

Jordan was too short of breath to answer, so he just nodded and kept on running. Strange lights appeared on the air. Booming voices spoke in the earth beneath the castle. A burning man stood to one side, and laughed unpleasantly as his flesh was consumed by the flames. Visions flickered at the corners of everyone's eyes, always just on the edge of becoming clear. Jordan stared straight ahead and ran on, refusing to stop for anything.

Finally they rounded a corner, and there were the huge double doors that led into the Great Hall. And standing before the doors were Prince Lewis, Iron-

heart, and a company of heavily armed guards. Jordan
and his party came to a sudden halt, and for a moment
the corridor was still and quiet, save for the gradually
slowing breathing of the new arrivals. Lewis waited
patiently for them to get their breath back before he
began speaking.

"You took your time getting here, Viktor," he said
calmly. "As soon as I discovered you had Dad's will,
I knew it wouldn't be long before you headed back
here with the crown and the seal. You're really very
predictable, you know. Especially since I introduced
a spy into your people."

"Oh hell, not another one," said Jordan. "Who is
it this time?"

"No one important," said Lewis. "But someone
with access to everything that was going on. After all,
no man keeps secrets from his wife, does he?" Lewis
snapped his fingers, and two guards hustled forward
the Lady Emma. Gawaine groaned softly.

"I had to do it," said Emma defiantly. "Lewis knew
so much already, and he had Ironheart and the
Monk—you couldn't hope to win. I had to go with
the winner. He promised me he'd protect you, Gawaine, if I agreed to keep him informed of your plans.
I did it for you, Gawaine."

"Trusting little soul, isn't she?" said Lewis. "Now
then, Viktor, you let me have the crown and the seal,
and I'll let you live."

"Do I look crazy?" said Jordan. "You want it, you
come and take it. Or aren't you as brave without your
tame sorcerer to back you up? Where is the Monk,
anyway? Run off and left you in the lurch, has he?"

"He's around," said Lewis. "Keeping busy. I'm
afraid you don't understand the realities of the situation, Viktor. Either you hand over the crown and the
seal right now, or I'll have my people kill the Lady
Emma. Slowly and painfully, right before your eyes.
You see, I've been studying you, Viktor. You got soft
in exile. Now, do as you're told. Or else."

Jordan glanced quickly at Gawaine, but the knight
was staring fixedly at Emma. Jordan scowled desper-

ately, torn so many ways he didn't know what to do
for the best. But, of course, there was only one thing
he could honorably do. He pulled the heavy gold ring
off his finger and hefted it sadly in his hand. "The
royal seal," he said quietly. "It's all yours, Lewis."

He snapped back his hand and threw the ring with
all his strength. It struck Lewis squarely in the left
eye, and he lurched backward, screaming. Jordan and
Taggert leapt forward almost as one and cut down
the two guards holding the Lady Emma. And then
Ironheart's steel fist lashed out with murderous speed,
and crushed the back of Emma's skull. She fell limply
to the ground and lay still. Taggert's balefire sword
swept crackling through the air and sliced clean
through Ironheart's gauntlet. The severed hand fell
limply to the floor. No blood spurted from the armor-
clad stump. Ironheart howled horribly, the sound
echoing eerily in his featureless helm.

Lewis threw himself at Jordan, and sparks flew as
their swords clashed and danced apart. Their guards
milled around them, more interested in killing their
enemies and settling old scores than in protecting their
leaders. Sir Gawaine knelt beside his dead wife and
held her hand, oblivious to anything else. Cord swung
his mace with awesome strength and speed, but it was
all he could do to dent Ironheart's armor. The knight
took even the most punishing blows with virtual indifference. But while Cord kept Ironheart busy, Taggert
went to work on him with her balefire sword. The
crackling white fire sliced into the dull steel, whittling
away at Ironheart like a dull knife on a stubborn block
of wood. Gaping rents appeared in the armor, but
Ironheart took no hurt from them, and no blood ran.
Taggert's hackles rose as she hacked away at the stubbornly advancing knight, and wondered crazily if he
could die. But finally one last cut severed Ironheart's
head from his body, and the suit of armor fell heavily
to the floor, and never moved again.

Lewis's guards lost their confidence as they saw
their champion brought down, and when Cord and
Taggert turned to join the fight against them, they

dropped their weapons and surrendered. Only Lewis fought on, raining blows on the grimly defending Jordan. He continued to back away, and wished he had his flare pellets with him. Even a smoke pellet would have helped. Lewis was strong, fresh, and very experienced with a sword. Jordan was none of those things. So far he was holding his own, bar a few minor scratches, but he was tiring quickly, and Lewis knew it. Jordan kept backing away, his mind working furiously. All he had to do was say the word, and Taggert or Cord or any of his guards would rescue him. But if he did that, they'd lose all respect for him. It's not enough for a future King to be brave and strong: he must be seen to be brave and strong. Unfortunately, right now Lewis was the stronger.

Jordan suddenly remembered an earlier fight, when Gawaine took on Dark John Sutton. Dark John had all the advantages, but Gawaine beat him anyway. *He was a duelist, sire, and I am a soldier.* Jordan grinned as he remembered Gawaine's winning trick. He moved in closer, and spat right into Lewis's face. Lewis's blade faltered and he drew back instinctively, and Jordan ran him through. His sword punched out of Lewis's back, and the prince was dead before he could draw in enough breath to scream. He fell to his knees, almost as though bowing to Jordan, and then he fell on his side and lay still. Jordan pulled his sword free, and spurned the body with his foot. There was an impressed murmur from the guards, and Jordan nodded to them tiredly. With a bit of luck, they'd all been too far away to see exactly how he beat Lewis. They probably assumed he'd beaten the prince by sheer strength of will, or something. He rooted among the bodies of the fallen guards till he found the royal seal, and slipped the ring back on his finger.

"Pardon me, Your Highness," said the Steward quietly, "but I think you ought to take a look at this."

Jordan moved over to where she was kneeling beside Ironheart's headless body. She showed him the head she'd found inside the featureless helm, and Jordan's stomach heaved. The head looked as though it had been dead for some time. Half the face was already eaten away by decay. Taggert dropped the thing with a grimace, and wiped her fingers thoroughly on her robes.

"I doubt we'll ever know the answer," she said neutrally. "Lewis might have told us, but he's dead."

"There's still the Monk," said Jordan, helping her to her feet.

"Yes," said Taggert. "There's always the Monk."

Jordan looked around him, and saw Gawaine was still kneeling beside the body of his dead wife. He walked over to the knight, and stood awkwardly beside him. "I'm sorry," he said finally. "I thought I could save her. I did try, Gawaine."

"It's my own fault," said Gawaine. "I shouldn't have left her alone for so long. She was always easily led." He got clumsily to his feet. "Let's go, Viktor. You have a throne waiting for you."

"Do you think I care about that now?"

"Yes!" said Gawaine. "You have to! Because if you don't, Emma and everyone else who's followed you will have died for nothing! Now go in there and take the throne, Viktor. It's waiting for you."

"Yes," said Jordan. "I suppose it is. There isn't anyone left to stand between me and it any longer."

From inside the hall came an explosion of light and sound, culminating in harsh, echoing laughter. Taggert looked at Jordan.

"The gateway, Viktor—we forgot about the bloody gateway."

She stepped forward and threw open the double doors. Jordan stepped in beside her, and his stomach lurched sickly as he saw the new gateway. Midway between the doors and the throne, the Monk hung unsupported on the air. His robe was flung open, revealing a surging mass of light and color. There was no trace of a body within the robe, or that there ever had been. The Monk had become a living gateway, through which the Unreal could enter the Real world. Creatures out of a nightmare dripped in a steady stream from inside the Monk's robe, like maggots from a rotting carcass. They fell to crawl, slide, and scuttle across the floor, and there were always more close behind. A gusting wind blew from the gateway, hot and prickly and rank with burning ammonia. And above it all, the Monk's laughter rang on and on without ever a pause for breath.

Jordan stared in horror at the Unreal that had already taken root in the Great Hall. Horrid creatures scuttled up and down the walls, and clung upside down to the ceiling, feeding delicately on tiny morsels of fresh meat. Blood dripped from the ceiling in a steady stream. The floor was cracked and broken, and jets of flame shot up into the hall. The throne sat intact upon its dais, untouched by all the madness, but a barrier of seething thorns had grown up around the dais, sealing it off. Jordan looked helplessly at Taggert.

"I can't do anything to stop this madness until I can get to the Stone, and I'd need an army at my back just to reach the damned throne. What am I going to do, Kate?"

"Only one thing we can do, Viktor," said the steward evenly. "We'll have to destroy the gateway. You did it once before."

"That was different," said Jordan. "This time the gateway's aware and intelligent. And Unreal. The Monk's got to be Unreal."

"Right. I always thought he was, but I wasn't even allowed to run tests on him as long as he was under Lewis's protection. We've got to stop him, Viktor. If the balance here shifts too far, Castle Midnight will become one huge gateway through which the Unreal can run loose in the world."

Jordan swallowed hard, and wished there was somewhere he could run to and still be safe. But as long as the gateway was open, nowhere would ever be really safe. He looked quickly around him. Roderik and the guards stood clustered at the main doors, their faces white with shock and horror; but Cord, Taggert, and Gawaine stood calm and ready to back him up.

Their confidence gave him strength, and he nodded abruptly.

"All right, everyone, we're going into the hall. You'll have to try and hold off the Unreal while I make a dash for the Stone. Stay close together, watch each other's backs, and if you get a chance at the Monk, take it. You might not get another." He took a deep breath, and let it go. Keeping his voice calm and steady was one of his greatest acting triumphs, even if no one else appreciated it. "All right, my friends. Let's do it."

He moved forward into the hall, and the Unreal surged toward him in a monstrous tide. Misshapen creatures that had no place in the waking world boiled across the floor, and Jordan's guards met them with flashing swords. The tide faltered and broke against the unflinching steel, and Jordan and his people pressed forward. Gawaine fought at Jordan's left, his ax glowing bright as the sun. Taggert fought at his right, her balefire sword spitting and crackling as it hewed through flesh and bone alike. Behind them, Cord threw away his mace, and it vanished in midair. He pulled out of nowhere a huge and terrible war hammer, and swung it double-handed. The solid steel head alone had to weigh at least twenty pounds, and it was set on the end of five feet of polished oak. An ordinary man couldn't even have hefted it, but Cord swung the hammer as though it was all but weightless. He was no more Real than the creatures he fought, but still his face twisted with loathing at the sight of what faced him. He might have been born of the darkness, but his heart and his loyalties lay with the light. And above them all, the Monk rotated slowly on the disturbed air, and madness surged through him into the world.

Things that looked horribly like men crawled up out of the cracks in the floor. Something huge and dark scuttled lightly down the wall and dropped onto a guard, crushing him to the floor. Gossamer strands of pink and purple drifted on the air and wrapped themselves around the fighters, tightening inexorably into glistening cocoons that devoured their contents. One whole wall became a vast inhuman face. A dozen men looked into its great golden eyes and went insane from what they saw there. And still Jordan and his people struggled ever closer to the throne.

Sir Gawaine fought tirelessly, his ax falling and rising with grim efficiency. He gave no thought to anything save the struggle, and blood ran down his face like tears. With Emma's death, all his emotions had run out of him, save for a simple cold need for revenge. Nothing else mattered. Nothing mattered but killing the monstrous things that were responsible for all the evil in Castle Midnight. His ax rose and fell, rose and fell, and the creatures of the Unreal fell back before him. Gawaine cut them down and moved on to the next, feeling nothing, nothing at all.

Taggert fought at Prince Viktor's side, and smiled savagely as her balefire sword sliced through every monstrosity that walked or crawled of flew within her reach. Nothing got past her to strike at Viktor, though many tried, and a slow steady pride burned within her. Even in the midst of blood and carnage, she still had time to find a small smile at how fast her feelings toward Viktor had changed. He'd not been a bad sort before his exile: just weak and easily led by the wrong people. She hadn't cared much about him then, one way or the other. But the man who'd emerged from the chaos of King Malcolm's death had been a much finer sort. A true prince of the Blood, worthy to be king. And a man Kate Taggert was growing increasingly fond of. She smiled again, and then put the thought firmly out of her mind. She'd think about that later. Assuming there was a later. She fought on, sweat running down her face, and soaking her chest and sides as a grinding fatigue grew slowly inside her. The balefire was a constant drain on her strength, but she didn't dare give it up for an ordinary sword. It was the only advantage she had. She just hoped her magic would last long enough for Viktor to reach the Stone. If it didn't, then perhaps everything they'd been through had been for nothing, after all. Taggert cut viciously about her with her shimmering sword. She wasn't unhappy. She was doing what she'd been trained to do, in a cause she believed in, for someone she cared for. There were worse ways to die.

Cord swung his war hammer with murderous ease, and the Unreal fought each other for the privilege of dragging him down. Cord stood his ground and let them come to him. He felt no anger toward them. They were his brothers, in a way, born like him of random chaos and unreality, without mother or father, sprung adult and fully formed into a world that was forever alien to them. Cord looked like a man and felt like a man, but he had never made the mistake of believing himself to be a man. He was a whim made flesh and blood, a possibility given form and motion, nothing more. He was Unreal. And a traitor to his own kind, perhaps. But still he fought on, guarding the back of a man he'd come to admire, and a woman he might have loved, if he'd been Real.

Roderik cut and thrust with his sword, and wondered how everything could have gone so horribly wrong. His plan had seemed so perfect in the beginning, so simple and straightforward. Everyone had said so. But first the little things had got out of control, and then the bigger things, until finally he had come to realize that he was only a part in someone else's plan. A bitter resignation was all that kept him going now: that, and a burning hatred for the vile creatures that swarmed around him. Whatever he might have been and done, the castle was his home, and always had been, and while he might not fight for a prince or a king, he'd fight to preserve his home from the foulness that threatened it.

Jordan swung his sword with an aching arm, stumbling and sliding on the blood-soaked floor. His blows were getting slower and weaker, and his lungs burned in his chest as he fought for air. He was an actor, not a soldier, and he knew he couldn't last much longer. His will and determination were as strong as ever, but there was a limit beyond which even they couldn't drive his failing body. He glanced about him as he fought, trying to see how the battle went, but the hall had become a confused mess of struggling bodies that defied any clear interpretation. There seemed no end to the Unreal, and no matter how many creatures fell, there were always more to take their place. His guards were fighting fiercely, but one by one they were falling beneath bloody fangs and claws, and not rising again. His colleagues around him were still fighting well, but he could see strain and fatigue stamped clearly on their faces. The throne on its dais stood safe and secure, and the throne barrier that surrounded it was only a few feet away, but it slowly occurred to Jordan that he might not have enough strength left to take him those last few feet. He worked his way over to Taggert, and they fought side by side.

"Kate, how much magic have you got left?"

"Not much, Viktor—I was trained as a steward, not a sorcerer."

"Think you've got enough left for one good blast? Enough to clear me a path through the thorns to the dais?"

Taggert looked briefly at the gap between them and the throne. "Maybe. But that would take everything I've got. It'd be a hell of a risk. You'd only get one chance at the throne, and then the creatures would be all over you. You sure you want to risk that?"

"If you've got a better idea, I'd love to hear it."

Taggert laughed shakily. "All right, you're on. But you'd better be right about this, Viktor. Because if I get killed here, I'll never forgive you."

They shared a quick smile, and then Taggert focused her awareness inward, calling up the light of life that burned within her. It was already seriously diminished from what it should be, but there was enough left to do the job. If she was lucky. She dismissed her shimmering sword and discharged all her power in one controlled blast. Balefire flared up all around her, seething and churning, and then roared away from her toward the throne. The creatures in its path were incinerated in a moment, as though they had never been, and the thorn barrier exploded in a mass of flames. When the light died away again, a pathway to the throne stood clear and open. Jordan ran toward the throne, with Sir Gawaine close at his side. Unseen behind them, Taggert stumbled and almost fell as the last of her strength went out of her. Cord was quickly there at her side, beating back the Unreal with a cold, unyielding ferocity. Roderik gathered the guards together for one last desperate stand.

Jordan sprinted down the narrow aisle Taggert had opened up in the barrier. He could hear the thorns stirring feebly, but kept his eyes fixed on the throne. He scrambled up onto the marble dais, and then a barbed tentacle shot out of nowhere and scored a jagged red line across his shoulders. He gasped at the sudden pain and almost dropped his sword, but Gawaine was close behind him, urging him on, and a moment later they were both crouching beside the empty throne. Unreal life boiled all around the dais, but none of it dared draw near the Stone that lay beneath the throne. Jordan waited a few moments to get some of his breath back, and then pulled at the throne's arm. It didn't budge in the least. He looked at Sir Gawaine.

"All right, Gawaine, how do we get to the Stone?"

"Just say the words, Your Highness. The old words, handed down by tradition. Then the throne gives up the Stone, which rolls forward . . ."

"I know all that, Gawaine, but what exactly are the damned words?"

Sir Gawaine looked at him blankly, and then shook his head in disgust. "I'm sorry, Viktor. Of course you don't know the words. The King would have told the Regent, but it was up to him to pass them on to whoever was designated as heir. Stand back, Viktor. I'll get you the Stone."

He thrust the head of his ax beneath one side of the throne and heaved upward, using the ax's haft as a lever. The throne groaned and shifted, but didn't lift an inch. Gawaine put his back into it. Muscles corded on his arms and back, and he grinned mirthlessly as his face grew taut and strained. The ax head

glowed brightly, its magic negating the spells that protected the throne. The Unreal began to press slowly
closer. And then the throne suddenly heaved up and
fell over on its side, revealing the ancient Stone. Sir
Gawaine stood panting beside it, his eyes half-closed
with exhaustion.

"Well-done, Gawaine," said Jordan. "Now what do
I do?"

"Spill your Blood on the Stone, and swear allegiance to it as king. Then the Stone will accept you,
and give you power over the Unreal."

Jordan looked at him blankly. "Oh my God," he
said softly.

"What is it?" said Gawaine. "What's the matter?"

"I thought I just had to say the right words, once I
had the crown and seal . . . I never thought . . ."

"What is it, Viktor? We don't have much time!"

"I can't do it, Gawaine!"

"What do you mean, you can't? You've got to!"

"I mean I *can't* do it! I don't have any Blood! I'm
Jordan, not Viktor."

Gawaine looked at him, and a slow horror crept
across his face. "You fool. You've damned us all."

Jordan looked back across the hall. Taggert had
fallen to the floor. Cord stood over her, and fought
to keep the Unreal at bay with his warm hammer.
Roderik had been backed up against a wall, and was
fighting a dogged but losing battle against a crowd of
howling, shrieking creatures. Of the fifty or so guards
who had followed Jordan into the hall, barely a dozen
remained, battling bravely in small clumps against
overwhelming odds. The Unreal was growing stronger.
More creatures crawled up out of the cracks in the
floor, or stepped through the walls or fell from the
ceiling. The light pulsing within the Monk's open robe
was blindingly bright, and the power of the Unreal
thundered on the air in a never-ending roar. Jordan
swayed unsteadily on his feet, and shook his head to
clear it. There had to be something he could do. There
had to be something . . .

Gawaine grabbed him by the arm, and hauled him

around to face him. "Why did you do it, Jordan? Why
did you kill him? Did you want to be king so badly,
you were ready to risk destroying us all?"

"It wasn't like that," said Jordan wretchedly. "I
never meant . . . He was mad, just like his brothers.
I thought I could save the Kingdom . . . He was crazy,
Gawaine! He was going to start a war that would have
destroyed Redhart!"

"He had the Blood," said Sir Gawaine. "And without that, we're all going to die anyway."

He turned away, his face a mask of despair. Jordan
felt sick. Was Gawaine right? Had he really killed
Viktor only because he wanted to be king himself?
It didn't matter. It was too late now for doubts and
recriminations. He'd given it his best shot, and it
hadn't been good enough. He'd failed his friends, and
failed the kingdom. He looked slowly around him. A
dozen creatures swarmed over Damon Cord and
pulled him down. He went down roaring and kicking,
still trying to swing his hammer. Two of the creatures
tore it out of his weakening grip, and threw it away,
out of reach. Somehow Cord surged to his feet again,
flailing about him with his fists. He was covered in
blood, much of it his own. The Unreal milled around
him, clawing and snapping, and still Cord fought on,
trying to get back to protect the steward.

Catriona Taggert was back on her feet again,
though she couldn't remember how. She cut desperately about her with a sword she'd snatched from a
dead guard's hand. The Unreal closed in around her,
and she swayed drunkenly on her feet as she struggled
to keep her sword arm steady. That final blast of balefire had taken too much out of her, and she knew it.
The Unreal knew it, too. She could see Cord fighting
to get back to her side, but there were too many creatures between them. She risked a quick glance at the
throne, and saw Viktor and Gawaine standing over
the Stone. She tried to smile bravely. Prince Viktor
had got to the Stone. At least she wouldn't have died
in vain. Blood ran down into her eyes, and she lifted
a shaking hand to wipe it away. A glistening black

creature with a barbed spine lashed out at her while
she was distracted, and knocked her to the floor. She
tried to get up again, and couldn't. Something with
bloodred eyes and needle teeth stooped over her. Taggert snarled up at it.

Jordan saw Taggert go down, and screamed her
name. He knew he couldn't get to her in time. All his
rage and guilt burned within him, and he stretched
out a desperate hand toward her. A jet of roaring
flame burst from his hand and shot through the air to
fry the creature bending over Taggert. It shrieked
once as the flames consumed it, and then fell back and
lay still. The Unreal scattered away from the burning
corpse. The din of battle went suddenly quiet, and for
a moment it seemed that everything in the hall had
paused, aware that something vital was happening.
Jordan looked disbelievingly at the flames licking
harmlessly around his hand. Viktor had the fire magic,
not him. He was just an actor who knew a few conjuring tricks. But that was no longer true. He could feel
the fire burning within him, waiting to be used. A
bright-burning flame, to sear the world clean of foulness and evil. He looked up at the Monk, floating
high above the violence below, and realized for the
first time that the Monk had stopped laughing. He
raised his hand, and smiled grimly at the gateway of
the Unreal.

"Burn in hell, Monk," he whispered.

A jet of boiling flame shot across the hall from his
hand, and struck the Monk's robe. The gray cloth
flared up in an instant and burned fiercely. The Monk
screamed once, a wild, awful sound, and the robe was
just a robe, and a swath of burning cloth fell down
onto the heads of the Unreal creatures below. The
gateway was closed. Jordan slowly realized that Gawaine was tugging at his arm.

"Jordan, the Stone! Swear your oath to the Stone
before another gateway opens!"

"What are you talking about, Gawaine? I told you,
I'm Jordan. I don't have any Blood."

"You have the fire magic."

"I don't know how I did that. I don't know where it came from."

"It comes from the glamour spell Roderik put on you. It must have. It made you a physical duplicate of Viktor. An *exact* physical duplicate. Since Viktor had Blood, so do you!"

Jordan gaped at Gawaine, and then spun around to face the Stone. The Unreal howled with fear and rage, and surged forward, trying to reach the dais before he could complete the ritual. The remaining guards fought desperately to hold back the creatures for just a few more moments. Jordan nicked the palm of his left hand with his sword edge, and a few spots of blood fell onto the top of the ancient Stone. He leant forward to place his palm on the Stone, and then hesitated.

The young noble placed his palm firmly onto the bloodstained Stone. He made a soft, puzzled sound, and then the breath went out of him and he fell limply backward. His head made a flat, final sound as it hit the floor.

Jordan swallowed hard and slapped his palm down onto the Stone. "I swear allegiance to the Stone, and to the kingdom of Redhart!"

Power surged through him, fell and potent, and for a timeless moment he could see everywhere in Castle Midnight. He could see the Unreal swarming through the rooms and corridors, appearing through hundreds of minor gateways. Everywhere in the castle guards and sorcerers, and men and women armed with whatever they could find, fought to hold back the endless tide of savagery. They fought well and bravely, but they were still losing. Jordan called upon his power, and in the blinking of an eye, the Unreal was banished in its entirety from Castle Midnight, and all the gateways closed.

Tall shimmering creatures that were chasing a weaponless guard down a corridor disappeared in midstep. Something gray and dusty, sitting giggling over a pile of bloody bones, vanished from the entrance hall. A vast face that had formed in the brickwork of a cellar wall became still and inanimate. Cracks in walls and floors flowed together and were gone, and shadows lay still and undisturbed. The Unreal disappeared, and the world became sane again.

In the Great Hall, the battling creatures vanished, and air rushed in to fill the spaces where they had been. The darkness overhead disappeared, and the ornate ceiling returned. The creatures of the Unreal were banished, and with them went Damon Cord, who had known all along that this would happen, and had fought with all his strength and courage to help bring it about.

A slow, peaceful silence settled over the hall, and the handful of survivors knelt and bowed to their new king. Gawaine took hold of the throne, and heaved it back into position over the Stone. Jordan sat down on it hesitantly, and Sir Gawaine of Tower Rouge knelt before him and bowed his head.

"Redhart has a king again!" he said loudly. "Long live King Viktor of Redhart!"

And only Jordan saw the wink that Gawaine dropped him.

CHAPTER 8

A Few Last Truths

Jordan sat slumped on his throne, and watched exhaustedly as the last of the courtiers filed out of the Great Hall. If he'd known being made king would involve all these bloody ceremonies, he'd have thought twice about it. Jordan usually enjoyed a good ceremony, if only for the theater of the occasion, but it felt rather different when you had to sit to attention all the way through it, for hours on end. *It's all very well them wishing good health to his majesty. They're not stuck on this bloody throne. I'll bet I end up with piles. What moron came up with the idea of a throne made of marble, anyway?*

He sighed, and knuckled at his bleary eyes. It had been a long day, and it showed few signs of getting any shorter. For all practical purposes, he'd been the rightful king from the moment he made his oath to the Stone, but both law and tradition had to be followed exactly if he wanted the support of his people. First, he'd had to summon the entire Court, so that the nobility could make their individual oaths of fealty to the new king. A few people had been conspicuous by their absence. Jordan had ordered them banished, and wasn't surprised to learn that they had anticipated this and were already well on their way. Apparently they had been close associates of either Lewis or Dominic, and didn't trust in Viktor's forgiving nature. Jordan didn't blame them. The ceremonies had dragged on and on, and in the end Jordan had stopped trying to follow them. Instead, he dozed with his eyes open, and smiled and nodded when he felt like it. Which wasn't often. If the three princes had had to put up with this all their lives, it was no wonder they'd gone crazy.

But finally the ceremonies had ground to an end. The hall was quiet, the courtiers were gone, and only the really important people remained. Jordan sat up a little straighter, and tried to settle his crown more comfortably on his head. The damn thing was heavier than it looked, and was giving him a headache. Sir Gawaine stood at his left, beside the throne. Jordan's first act as King had been to make Gawaine his Champion. The courtiers had taken one look at the murderous ax in Gawaine's hand, and had hurriedly agreed that this was an altogether excellent idea.

Count Roderik stood directly before the throne. He'd said no more than the bare minimum necessary all through the ceremonies, which hadn't surprised Jordan at all. What Roderik had to say, and no doubt there was a great deal of it, could only be said in private.

Beside Roderik stood Count William and his wife, the Lady Gabrielle. Jordan had been keeping a careful eye on the ex-Regent. If there was to be any real threat to his succession, that was where it was going to come from. William had established a nice little power base for himself as Regent, and it was just possible he might not want to hand it over. Particularly to a man he'd already declared to be unfit to rule. But so far he'd minded his manners and said all the right things in all the right places. Jordan smiled slightly. One of the first things he'd done had been to split up William's troops, and put them under the command of men loyal only to the king. Just in case.

And finally, standing at the right of his throne, was the steward, Catriona Taggert. She had one arm in a sling, and the bandage around her head made her look both raffish and endearingly vulnerable. She and Jordan had been sharing little secret smiles all through the ceremonies. Jordan sighed happily, and smiled again. One of the other things he'd done was to banish the Lady Heather from Court, and send her home to Kahalimar. Not only was she a ruthless little baggage, but she'd known Viktor far too well for Jordan's peace of mind. And with her gone, it was only natural that the new king would turn his attention elsewhere. He grinned at Taggert, and she grinned back.

I think I handled that rather well, he thought smugly.

"Now that the ceremonies are over," said Roderik pointedly, "I think you and I should have a little talk, Your Majesty. In private."

"Do you?" said Jordan. "I don't." He watched interestedly as Roderik's face went an entertaining shade of purple. "Whatever you have to say, Roderik, just go right ahead and say it. No need to be bashful. You're among friends here."

"Very well," said Roderik tightly. "We made an agreement, you and I, on what would happen once you were king. You gave me your word . . ."

"So I did," said Jordan. "I agreed that you should be my chief adviser, and so you shall, but it seems to me that the word *adviser* has a very specific meaning. I'll always welcome your advice, Roderik, but whether I follow it or not will be my decision, not yours. As long as your bear that in mind, I see no reason why we shouldn't have a long and mutually profitable relationship."

"There are things I could tell the Court that they don't know," said Roderik.

"I imagine you could," said Jordan. "But do you think it would be in your best interests to do so?"

Roderik stood very still for a moment, his gaze fixed on Jordan's. Gawaine stirred restlessly. In the end, Roderik bowed stiffly to the throne. "I shall do my best to provide you with good advice, Your Majesty. I think you're going to need it. Now if you'll excuse me, I have a great deal of work that must be attended to."

"Yes, of course," said Jordan. "They're burying Argent soon, aren't they?"

"Yes. Do you object to my attending the funeral, Your Majesty?"

"No," said Jordan. "He was your friend. And I

think perhaps he was more sinned against than sinning. Perhaps he'll be at peace now."

Roderik bowed again, and left the hall. No one said anything until the great double doors had closed behind him. William looked quizzically at Jordan.

"He'd make a dangerous enemy, sire. He has a great deal of influence in both political and economic circles."

"I know. That's why he'll make a good adviser, once I've got him settled in."

William raised an eyebrow. "Is that what you have in mind for me, sire?"

"Why not?" said Jordan easily. "My years in exile have left me out of touch when it comes to the day-to-day running of the kingdom. I can use your experience and support. My father trusted you. He said you were an honest man. Every King needs at least one adviser he can rely on to tell him the truth, whether he wants to hear it or not. What do you say?"

William bowed formally. "I would be honored, Your Majesty. There was a time I thought you unworthy to rule, like your brothers. I was wrong. I give you my word that I shall serve you faithfully in all things, for as long as you have need of me."

"Thank you," said Jordan. "Now, my friends, we have one last matter to discuss—the most important of all. Who killed my father?"

The question hung unanswered on the silence. William finally stirred slightly, and all eyes went to him.

"As Regent, I ordered a full investigation into King Malcolm's death, under the steward's direction. The body was carefully examined by the castle surgeons. There was no trace of poison in the body, nor any sign of foul play. There was no sign of any struggle in his chambers. As far as we can tell, he died peacefully, in his sleep. The suddenness of his death made it seem suspicious, but truth be told he was not a young man, Your Majesty, and death comes to us all, sooner or later."

"Yes," said Jordan. "That's what we were supposed to think. But his demise was too convenient for too many people for it to have been a natural event. So, I've been thinking about who stood to gain most by his death. Lewis and Dominic spring to mind, but Malcolm's end was too subtle for it to have been either of them. My brothers were many things, but subtle was not one of them. Then there was you, sir Regent. But everyone said you were honest, and you made no attempt to seize power for yourself when you could have. That leaves only one other person who wanted the king dead, and had the means and opportunity. You, Gabrielle."

They all looked at Jordan as though he was mad. Gabrielle held her head high, and stood a little closer to her husband.

"Of all the people I've spoken to," said Jordan evenly, "you were our family's most outspoken critic. You hated Lewis and Dominic, despised me as weak, and abhorred our father's preoccupation with war. Over and over again, I heard you say that our line was corrupt: that none of us were fit to hold the throne. It was an obsession with you, Gabby. You believed that Redhart needed an honest man as king if it was to survive. And who do we all know that everyone agrees is honest beyond question? Your husband, Count William. I don't think for a minute that he knew anything about this. If he'd even suspected you meant to murder your father, he'd have stopped you. So you didn't tell him. You waited until you and Dad were alone together, and then you killed him. With him gone, William would become Regent, and after you'd had time to work on him, eventually he would have taken the throne by popular acclaim. If the will hadn't gone missing, and with it the clue to the crown and seal, your plan might have worked. William would have been king, and you would have been queen. All for the best of reasons, of course."

"Tell him he's a liar, Gabrielle," said William. "Tell him."

"How could I have killed Dad?" Gabrielle asked Jordan calmly. "There wasn't a mark on him, or a trace of poison in his body."

"You used your magic," said Jordan. "Your air magic. You use it so rarely people tend to forget you have air magic by your Blood. You used it to suck the breath out of his lungs. Just like I saw you use it against the Unreal birds at Court."

"All right," said Gabrielle. "You worked it out. What are you going to do about it?"

William looked at her, and all the color went out of his face. "What are you saying, Gabrielle?"

"There's no need for you to be involved in this, dear. I killed Father. It was all my idea, and no one else's. Redhart needed a strong king."

"And you as queen," said Jordan.

"Of course," said Gabrielle. "But what are you going to do, Viktor? If you put me on trial, it would be a major scandal. It could even lead to civil war, and you can't afford that. Not when your own grasp on the throne is still so precarious."

"He was my friend," said William. "Malcolm was my friend. How could you do it, Gabrielle?"

"My father never had a friend in his life," said Gabrielle. "He was pleasant enough to you because he needed your counsel. But if he'd ever found out that you and I were cousins, he'd have annulled our marriage without a second thought."

"So that's why," said William softly.

"Well, Viktor," said Gabrielle, "what are you going to do?"

"I can't let you stand trial," said Jordan. "You're right about that. And I can't banish you, either. You wouldn't go without your husband, and I need him. I could have you killed, but William would never forgive me. So, you'll remain here in the Castle, in your quarters, under unofficial house arrest. William will be your guard. For the rest of your life you will never leave your quarters, or talk with anyone other than your husband. Break my rules, and I will have no choice but to have you killed."

"No need for threats, Viktor," said Gabrielle. "I accept your conditions. It's more than I expected. You might turn out to be a worthy king after all."

She turned away and headed unhurriedly for the doors. William looked at Jordan. He nodded, and William bowed quickly and went after his wife. They left the Court together.

Jordan let out his breath in a long sigh of relief. Then he yawned widely, and stretched till his arms ached. He slumped back in his throne again and stared around the empty hall. It seemed very large and echoing with everybody gone. He'd never really thought about what he was going to do once he got this far. He hadn't had a chance. Everything had happened so quickly. One day he was just another traveling player, wondering where his next meal was coming from, and then suddenly he was part of a conspiracy to impersonate a prince of the Realm. And not very long after that, he was playing the part for real.

He didn't regret killing Viktor. The alternative would have put too many lives at risk. But that was as far as his thinking had gone. He had no training in politics, or the art of ruling. His only experience of Courts had been acting before them. And what he knew about enforcing the laws of the land could probably be engraved on his left thumbnail without undue difficulty. But he could learn. He had time, and good advisers. He looked at Gawaine, and grinned at him.

"How does it feel to be a king's champion, Gawaine?"

"At my age, somewhat dangerous," said the knight dryly. "Not that I don't appreciate the honor, but I would have settled for a less risky position, like collecting taxes single-handed, or fighting a dragon with both my arms tied behind my back."

"Moan, moan, moan. I've got to have someone in this Court I can turn my back on without wincing, and you're it." Jordan's smile suddenly faded, and he looked seriously at his champion. "Gawaine, you once swore an oath to protect . . . a certain man. I killed him. Where does that leave us?"

"The man who died was not worthy of my oath. I still serve and protect the true Prince Viktor."

"Am I supposed to understand any of that?" said Taggert.

"No," said Jordan.

"I thought not."

"Thank you, Sir Gawaine," said Jordan. "Now, if you don't mind, I'd like a private word or two with my steward."

"Of course, sire." Gawaine's mouth twitched. "I'm so glad you agreed to return from exile, Your Majesty. You've been a new man since you returned to Court."

He bowed formally, and then turned and walked chuckling out of the Great Hall.

"What was all that about?" said Taggert, as the doors closed quietly behind the new champion.

"Nothing important," said Jordan. "I need to talk to you, Kate."

Taggert smiled, and stepped forward to sit on the arm of his throne. "You can always count on me, Viktor. My life is yours."

Jordan grinned back at her, and slipped an arm around her waist. "I was hoping you'd say something like that."

ROC ⊘ **SIGNET** (0451)

FLIGHTS OF FANTASY

☐ **MASTER OF WHITESTORM by Janny Wurts.** Only time would tell whether death would defeat Korendir before he found the only treasure that could truly bring him peace.... (451678—$4.99)

☐ **NIGHTSEER by Laurell K. Hamilton.** When treachery fells the magic keep, only one woman has the power to wreak vengeance. (451430—$4.99)

☐ **THE WHITE MISTS OF POWER by Kristine Katherine Rusch.** An epic fantasy of a bard's quest for his stolen heritage. (451201—$3.99)

☐ **SORCERER'S SON by Phyllis Eisenstein.** "Outstanding."—Andre Norton. As Cray Ormoru, son of enchantress Delivev, grows to be a man in magical Castle Spinweb, he yearns to find his father, who disappeared years ago on an heroic mission. (156838—$3.95)

☐ **THE CRYSTAL PALACE by Phyllis Eisenstein.** A magical tale of a mortal's quest to find and free the soul of his one true love.... (156781—$3.95)

☐ **THE FIRE QUEEN by Jack Holland.** A pagan warrior queen uses wiles and witchery to win freedom for her people. (452046—$5.50)

☐ **BAZIL BROKETAIL by Christopher Rowley.** It is up to Bazil to rescue the Princess from The Doom's fortress before she is corrupted by its powers. In a labyrinth of evil, he must work magic to save the Princess ... and Bazil must prove himself against a terror of unknown magnitude in order to save his world. (452062—$5.99)

☐ **IRON CAGE by Andre Norton.** A marvelous fantasy/adventure novel that deftly points out the foolish and often dangerous distinctions we draw between man and animal ... as the struggle for a future world brews a violent clash between these two realms. (451937—$4.50)

Prices slightly higher in Canada

Buy them at your local bookstore or use this convenient coupon for ordering.

NEW AMERICAN LIBRARY
P.O. Box 999 – Dept. #17109
Bergenfield, New Jersey 07621

Please send me the books I have checked above.
I am enclosing $_____ (please add $2.00 to cover postage and handling).
Send check or money order (no cash or C.O.D.'s) or charge by Mastercard or VISA (with a $15.00 minimum). Prices and numbers are subject to change without notice.

Card #_____ Exp. Date _____
Signature_____
Name_____
Address_____
City _____ State _____ Zip Code _____

For faster service when ordering by credit card call **1-800-253-6476**
Allow a minimum of 4-6 weeks for delivery. This offer is subject to change without notice.

If you and/or a friend would like to receive the *ROC Advance*, a bimonthly newsletter featuring all the newest and hottest ROC books and authors, on a complimentary basis, please fill out this form and return it to:

ROC Books/Penguin USA
375 Hudson Street
New York, NY 10014

Your Address

Name _____

Street _____ Apt. # _____

City _____ State _____ Zip _____

Friend's Address

Name _____

Street _____ Apt. # _____

City _____ State _____ Zip _____